ESCAPE ROUTES FOR BEGINNERS

'The characters jump from the page, fully formed and brightly coloured. The dramatic descriptive passages play through your mind like action sequences as you read. Someone should snap up the movie rights quick' *Heat*

'It's a mark of the unusual talent of this young British writer that three generations of dysfunction can make for such a darkly comic read' *Marie Claire*

'Quirky, sharp and darkly subversive, permeated with the deafening rattle of skeletons in the closet' *City Life*

'Three generations of rebellious women fuel this unexpectedly dark, disturbing and deft tale' *Daily Mirror*

'Brims with dark wit and alarming surrealism. One of the most promising new writers of the 21st century' *Big Issue*

'A fascinating tale' *Eve*

By the same author

The Naked Season

Born in Essex in 1977, Kira Cochrane studied American Literature at the Universities of Sussex and California before moving to London to work as a journalist. Now based in Brighton, she writes regularly for *The Sunday Times*.

Escape Routes for Beginners

Kira Cochrane

POCKET BOOKS

LONDON · NEW YORK · SYDNEY · TORONTO

First published in Great Britain by Simon & Schuster, 2004
This edition first published by Pocket Books, 2005
An imprint of Simon & Schuster UK
A Viacom company

1 3 5 7 9 10 8 6 4 2

Simon & Schuster UK Ltd
Africa House
64–78 Kingsway
London WC2B 6AH

www.simonsays.co.uk

Simon & Schuster Australia
Sydney

A CIP catalogue record for this book is available from
the British Library

ISBN 0 7434 7842 8
EAN 9780743478427

Typeset by SX Composing DTP, Rayleigh, Essex
Printed and bound in Great Britain by
Cox & Wyman Ltd, Reading, Berkshire

For Colin Midson
and in memory of Eileen Midson

Chapter One

Las Focas, 5 May 1959

'Come on. Just the roots. We're just going to bleach the roots.'

Clara Jones began pushing her only child from the living room to the kitchen. 'It won't take long,' she said, one hand clasped around Rita Mae's upper arm, the other scraping a stool across the floor and bringing it to rest beside the sink. 'You just sit here for five minutes,' she pushed her daughter roughly on to the stool, 'and it'll be done.' Tucking a towel around Rita Mae's shoulders, Clara began mixing the peroxide, clorax and ammonia, her arm oscillating like a lawnmower rotor.

Neck arced obediently, head lolling in the chipped enamel sink, Rita Mae pulled faces beneath her hair. She rolled her eyes up under their lids, wrinkled her nose until it ached and thrust her tongue painfully inside her bottom lip. It was Rita Mae's thirteenth birthday, a landmark date, and she had hoped that her mother might relent for once and let her miss a single bleaching.

The optimism had proved groundless.

The dyeing of the roots was a weekly ritual, observed rigidly since the very first dousing. This was despite the dozens of arguments that Rita Mae had formulated over the years, progressing from the 'it hurts, Mama, it hurts' of her three-year-old self to the more complex attacks and counter attacks of her current form. She had argued that it was costly ('it's cheap,' said Clara), that it damaged her hair ('it doesn't,' said Clara), and offended her aesthetic sensibilities ('don't throw syllables at me, young lady'). Every week would come the familiar seesaw rhythm of whining and cajoling, ending with Clara's hands clamping vice-like around her daughter's shoulders and propelling her to the kitchen.

Why did she have to have blonde hair, thought Rita Mae, her bottom lip still ballooning out. Why couldn't her hair be allowed to grow naturally? How could her untreated locks be worse than the dry neon fuzz that crept so shockingly about her face?

On the sixth day after every bleaching, Rita Mae would pluck a strand directly from her scalp and examine the quarter-inch of dark brown, almost black hair that emerged from beneath the dull blonde. She would stare at it for a few minutes, determined to put up a more zealous fight the next day. Each time, though, despite her resolve, her mother's will proved far, far stronger.

All the most glamorous people were brunettes, thought Rita Mae. All the actresses she admired – those who shot wisecracks like bullets and stood their ground against men – they all had brown hair. Rita Mae wanted to be like Joan Crawford in *Johnny Guitar*, that strange anti-cupid's bow of a mouth hardening into a thick, imperious line. Or Bette Davis in *All About Eve*, spitting out sarcasm like watermelon pips. Ava Gardner in *The Killers*, wrapping her body constrictor-tight around her victims.

Brunettes could handle themselves; they could scare a man witless. In comparison, blondes would always look pallid, washed out as baby milk, shouldering the suspicion that they'd had to dye their hair to get ahead. Blonde hair, particularly dyed blonde hair, was a sign of weakness, thought Rita Mae. It suggested cowardice and capitulation. There were just two women who could carry it off – Marlene Dietrich and Lauren Bacall. And that was only due to their unusually cruel tongues.

Still, there was little chance of convincing her mother to stop. Rita Mae's mouth flew open as Clara began to paint the mixture, which was sputtering gently now, directly on to her hair. The smell was familiar, stretching back far beyond speech and memory, but it had never stopped making her gag.

Clara Jones had been bleaching her daughter's hair from the moment that the first black fluff had appeared, when Rita Mae was just six weeks old. Having prayed (in a wholly secular fashion) for her daughter to inherit her husband's light colouring, Clara had been shocked by the discovery of those sudden dark curls, affronted by their shade, and had subsequently slopped almost a whole cup of the tincture over her newborn's head. With fingers crossed behind her back she had secretly hoped that the mixture might seep down into Rita Mae's pores and brighten the shadowy fur beneath.

As Rita Mae staged her first and loudest protest – letting rip with a great, garrulous scream – Clara Jones had walked, unmoved, into the next room. It was important that her daughter acclimatize herself to this ritual, she had thought amidst the howling, important that she steel herself to the pain. Five minutes later, when Clara came to rinse the dye off, Rita Mae still bellowing, she had realized that she'd actually burned her baby's first strands of hair right away. Rita Mae's scalp, so smooth, shiny and brown before, was now a bright, flaky pink. When Clara's husband, Larry, arrived home and asked about it, concerned, she had shrugged. 'She must have had a reaction to the detergent.'

It had been worth it, thought Clara, fetching Rita Mae's birthday present (a new party dress) from the living room. Justifiable cruelty. Although her daughter's platinum hair had always looked slightly at odds with her olive skin tone – as did Clara's own – the lurid shade still worked its charm, brightening up the complexion, pouring light over the subject. When Rita Mae was tiny and they had lived on the mainland in Santa Monica, Clara had been stopped regularly in the street as neighbours peered deep into the perambulator and asked about her daughter's fluorescent hair. Had Clara, they wondered aloud, been dyeing it? She denied it every time. 'Her father's also a blond,' she would say, fingering her own curls, 'and very fair-skinned,' both statements being entirely true. Whoever had asked would then nod firmly and smile, while silently noting that they had never seen baby hair so brittle.

'It's burning, Ma, it's burning.'

Clara smoothed the dress over her arm and strolled back into the kitchen. 'A minute more, Rita Mae. I'd like to leave it a minute more.'

'My parting will be pink if you do that. Honestly, Ma, it's,' Rita Mae gasped, 'it's really, really burning.'

Placing the dress carefully on one of the kitchen chairs, Clara folded her arms and sighed. 'Are you sure you can't take it any longer?'

Her eyes sprouting tears, Rita Mae choked an answer.

'Come on, Mama,' she pleaded, 'it's my birthday. Please wash it off.'

Clara sighed. 'All right then. The effect won't be so good you know, but,' she paused, 'all right.' Pouring a jug of cold water over Rita Mae's head she watched as her daughter relaxed, shoulders loosening. 'I've got your new dress out, so I want you to dry your hair and be careful putting it on. I don't want it to get creased, OK?'

Rita Mae nodded dutifully as she walked to the bathroom. Once inside, though, the hair-drier grinding to a roar, her expression changed. Closing her eyes she tried to imagine herself in that dress. The effect was shocking. She was going to look disgusting, she decided, hideous. Eyes screwed tighter, she corrected herself. Not just hideous. Revolting. Worse than Charles Laughton in *The Hunchback of Notre Dame*. His character had at least preserved some dignity. Worse than the nurse in *The Bumper Book of Tropical Disease* who had travelled deep into the Congo and emerged, months later, festooned with warts. Rita Mae would be case study C. A specimen so ugly that the only possible description was, 'The horror!'

She had been dreading that dress for five weeks now, ever since her mother had shown her the pattern, culled from some long-unused book. 'What do you think?' Clara had said, not expecting an answer. Rita Mae hadn't given one. Instead she had smiled weakly while gnawing at a persistent ulcer on her lip.

The dress was more a punishment than a present, thought Rita Mae, as the familiar smell of singed hair filled the bathroom. Especially since she was being forced to wear it today, her own birthday, to attend another girl's party. It was typical of her luck, she thought, that her birthday fell on the same date as that of the Warden's daughter, Jenna Wright, who was treated, each year, to the most lavish, candy-coated party money could buy. Rita Mae imagined how the other kids would react to her dress: the pointed whispers, the laughter, the shifty avoidance of eye contact. It was going to be worse than last year's party, when she'd had to fake a vomiting spell. This time she didn't have that luxury. She had wasted her excuses. She would have to sit it out.

Brushing lightly at her hair (it had a tendency to snap) Rita Mae ventured back into the kitchen. 'Arms up,' said Clara, unzipping the dress and easing it over Rita Mae's head. She smoothed it on carefully, more for the garment's benefit than her daughter's. Clara was pleased with the outfit, satisfied that it would make Rita Mae look obedient, chaste and decent. The fabric itself was pretty, a dark cream sprinkled with tiny rosebuds. The style, admittedly, wasn't hugely fashionable, but suggested a certain innocence, with long, tight sleeves and a skirt that swept softly beneath Rita Mae's feet. Creeping up from the collar was an inch of brown lace, which buttoned to form a particularly elegant noose. Fixing the lace tight, Clara stepped back, surveying her work. 'Perfect,' she said nervously, 'perfect.' Rita Mae turned and scowled. 'You look like a proper young lady.'

As Clara went to check her make-up, Rita Mae sat down heavily at the kitchen table. She had always dreaded Jenna's parties, but never quite as intensely as this, never with such a churning rage. Of all the girls on the island it was Jenna, with her large, snub nose and mealy lips that she hated the most. A year older than Rita Mae, Jenna had an air of arrogance that suggested she was the prettiest girl on Las Focas. This was a misconception. There was something vulgar about ugly people who were self-confident, thought Rita Mae. It suggested such a basic lack of judgment.

Her hatred for Jenna stretched right back to childhood, past the clumsy unhappiness of Rita Mae's ten-year-old self, her shy jumpiness, aged eight, and her crying fits, in bed at night, aged seven. Somewhere in the background of all those memories trudged Jenna's thick mammalian legs, capped by the tiny shoes that Rita Mae had often suspected of hiding cloven hooves. Every so often those impish feet would appear in Rita Mae's dreams, tramping endlessly back and forth, exactly level with her sightline. Waking up, Rita Mae could always sense that they stood for something ominous. However hard she tried, though, she could never quite remember what it was.

Still, if she had always hated Jenna, the situation had intensified since the events of the past winter. Now Rita Mae found Jenna Wright repellent. As fetid as the bleaching mixture, but nowhere near as useful.

Every Christmas on the island, the resident children were charged with performing a play. This was always musical, rarely enjoyable, and acted mainly as a chance for parents to applaud their child's talent – a brilliance somehow less visible to fellow onlookers. At the helm each year was the resident English teacher, who had the unenviable task of producing a play that might justify the title *Las Focas Extravaganza*.

Last year the task had fallen to Mr Curtis, an idealistic teacher of about twenty-five, who had arrived on Las Focas in mid-summer to replace Miss Aitken, an unhappy woman (forever surprised by the savagery of the island's kids), who had eaten herself stealthily into a coma. The post was Mr Curtis's first teaching job and he was slightly cowed by the responsibility, anxious to do his best, determined to change young lives. Despite these concerns he had a fresh, unlined face, his sunny features addled only by a pair of cheap, round eyeglasses and the shaving rash that bordered his mouth. He had been a keen actor at college, directing a clutch of plays, each of them credited by the varsity magazine as 'an unparalleled success'. He was excited at the prospect of devising a children's play – sure that he could produce the best show the island had ever seen – and so, one morning in November, he had wafted into the classroom and announced that the Christmas production was to be *The Wizard of Oz*.

Rita Mae had been ecstatic. She had first seen the film of Lyman Frank Baum's book a few years before and had wept from the opening frame to the last, with loud, angry sobs. She loved the story, and the way that it unfolded, but her tears weren't for the deftly crafted script. Despite, too, the fact that some of the songs were plaintive, even upsetting, her tears weren't for the score. They didn't spring from fear of the witch or the wizard or the dark.

Rita Mae wept because Judy Garland had stolen her starring role.

Watching Judy on screen, trussed up in gingham, fuelled by amphetamines, Rita Mae knew that she'd been robbed. It wasn't that Judy couldn't act – clearly she could. Her singing was soft and true, her manner suffused with longing. Still, although Judy had made a credible stab at the part, Rita Mae was convinced that it was only she who could play the definitive Dorothy. The winsome expression, the crack in the voice, the longing for a home far, far away. She had it all.

Given how perfectly she suited the role, Rita Mae had felt

hopeful that Mr Curtis would see sense and cast her in the lead. She knew, after all, that he liked her. He had been giving her high marks for her classwork, her papers recently pock-marked with ticks. There had been times, too, when she had noticed him staring at her, gazing like an explorer might gaze at an opened Egyptian tomb, with Rita Mae the mummified prize. Mr Curtis would give her the lead, she knew he would.

After a cursory round of auditions (a formality really) Mr Curtis had read out the cast list in class, finishing with the announcement that Rita Mae would play Dorothy. She was grateful, naturally, but not surprised. Her audition had been brilliant, each mannerism perfect. Singing the show's most famous tune she had even been inspired to lower her eyes before looking up and over a long-imagined rainbow.

They had started rehearsals immediately, Mr Curtis at the piano in his apartment, his head thrown back as Rita Mae sang, his eyes opening only for the occasional glimpse of her smocked bodice. 'We can do this,' he kept saying, Rita Mae nodding as he took her hand and squeezed, knuckles jostling tightly together. 'We can do this.'

And then, abruptly, it had ended. Ten days after announcing the cast, Mr Curtis had told Rita Mae to meet him after class in the main hall. When she arrived, expecting an extra rehearsal session, Mr Curtis had asked her to hand over her sheet music. 'I'm afraid you won't be needing that any more,' he had said, his face sad but stern, the optimism punched out of it. 'From now on, you're a munchkin.'

The day before, as the island congregation had left chapel, Warden Wright had ascended into the organ loft, where Mr Curtis was beetling happily through a Bach

Prelude. Stopping the man mid-note, Warden Wright had gestured for him to come downstairs, and then, leaning nonchalantly on the altar, had asked Mr Curtis to give Jenna a more prominent role. She had been cast as Flying Monkey Number 3, and had been complaining incessantly – breakfast, lunch, dinner – whining to her parents that the part was undignified and inconsequential.

'Could you find it in your heart,' enquired the Warden, 'to give her a pivotal role?'

Mr Curtis had pondered this for a moment. 'Flying Monkey Number 1?' he had said hopefully. Catching the Warden's raised eyebrows he had rushed to convince him. 'It's unquestionably pivotal, very significant. Lots of singing, lots of dancing.'

The Warden had placed a hand gently on his shoulder. 'Dorothy?'

'What?'

So, there it was. Jenna Wright, girl of the bountiful chins, was to play Dorothy. Rita Mae had returned to the Jones apartment after this announcement, slammed her bedroom door, and screamed with a gouging rage left unexpressed since the day her baby hair had been burned off. She had cried like that for hours, roaring at the injustice of it all, the abuse of trust. She had cried until her throat and nose bled and the thread veins in her eyes burst their tiny bounds. And then, finally, she had sat up in bed and laughed. The sound was hoarse, but happy. She laughed at how Jenna was going to look on stage, with her reed-thin voice and fat-ankled body, struggling to remember her lines. She laughed at how red Jenna's face would become as she puffed and pratfalled her way through the long song and dance numbers. It was, Rita Mae decided, potentially hilarious.

And so it came to pass, she thought, smiling now as Clara bustled back into the kitchen. Jenna Wright's performance as Dorothy had been woeful, her voice like a heel on concrete, face artlessly blank. Peering out from the stage, clad in the candy stripes of munchkinland, Rita Mae had counted the winces that accompanied Jenna's most jarring notes. She had reached double figures within minutes.

Nonetheless, when it came to the final curtain, Jenna had been applauded and showered with African violets. The winces softened into false smiles and generous shouts of encouragement. 'Wonderful!' 'Excellent!' 'Superlative!' Rita Mae had been a little upset to see her parents among the people strewing the stage with petals, but not surprised. As her mother often said, life was a transaction. To really succeed you had to charm the most powerful people into helping you. The Warden, in this case, was watching.

'Come on, Rita, time to go.' Clara pulled on a pair of white cotton gloves, standing by the door, suddenly impatient. 'Where's Jenna's gift? Where've you put it?'

'I don't see why . . .'

Clara snapped, 'Just because Jenna doesn't give you a gift doesn't mean that you can be rude and not give her something. It's traditional for the party guest to bring a gift.'

'Why don't I ever have a party then?'

'You know that wouldn't be practical.'

'But why?'

Her mother barked with frustration. 'I don't have time to go into that right now, Rita Mae. You know the reasons. Just get the gift.'

Rita Mae slumped into her bedroom to pick up the parcel, a box wrapped neatly by her mother containing a stiff brown bear from the island store (Jenna would receive three identical ones that day). Why wouldn't it be practical? she thought, pulling gently at the parcel's ribbon. Was it just because she and Jenna shared the same birthday? (She could see that this might be a problem. Not many of the kids were likely to give up Jenna's butter-iced chocolate cake and bulging party bags to come and celebrate Rita Mae's birthday.)

But it wasn't just the date, she mused, staring up at the ceiling. Even if her birthday had been on a day so mysteriously dull that it lay blank in every diary across the world, it would still have been impossible. No one in this building had ever had a party. It just wasn't a good venue. Thrown up as a temporary measure in 1947, the plywood apartment block shook like a rookie soldier in even the lightest breeze. Moving in ten years ago Clara Jones had tried to brighten the place up, but the inner walls, clad in brown vinyl, wouldn't hold paint or paper. Ever since, the surfaces she'd coated had been peeling, flaking off as drily as the deadest skin.

These same walls were so thin that you could carry on a conversation with someone in the next room without the slightest strain. Earlier that spring a young couple from Oakland, the O'Hares, had moved into the apartment upstairs, their bedroom directly above Rita Mae's. Each night, after a few quiet minutes, a heavy panting would start, along with a rhythmic bang that sent her lampshade swinging. It sounded like they were playing basketball.

Rita Mae shuffled back into the kitchen. 'Got it,' she said.

Descending the steps from their fifth-floor apartment, they began the half-mile trudge up the hill to the Warden's house. Above them loomed the cellblock, its shadowy form noiseless and still. Come early afternoon the prisoners entrusted with work duty emerged on to the slope behind the cell house, some heading for the laundry and maintenance sheds, others to till the acres of land. Right now, Rita Mae's father, Officer Laurence Jones, was up there on shift, supervising the inmates who worked on the farm, helping them plant their crops and tend the ragged herds of cattle. The island had been carefully designed to hide the inmates away, so the cell house was the only obvious testament to them all. A great, greying tombstone of a building.

As with most days, it was searing hot, the occasional treat of a thunderstorm far off in the distance. The island had changed almost entirely since it was discovered, but nothing could be done about the heat. That was as it had been in the 1800s when a Spanish crew had first docked here and spent a day wandering over the island's peak, plucking the oranges that grew so inexplicably and laughing at the seals playing on its shore. Come the evening they had recognized the limitations of the tiny land mass – rising from the waves just three miles square – and marked it firmly on the map before moving on. They christened the place they'd marked Las Focas, in honour of the seals, and left the island to prosper.

It hadn't been until 1920 that a particularly fastidious clerk, working for the US government in Washington, had noticed the cross on an aging map and suggested that they might claim the island. Five years later, with the prison population spreading like dysentery, another suit, sat in an office somewhere, had suggested that they turn the island into a penitentiary – a place to shift the worst convicts until a mainland space opened up. Having hatched this plan, colonization was quick. Within a year the first hundred inmates had been shipped out, shackled together for safe-keeping. Las Focas was set up to house the most recidivist, vicious and unhinged men alive – only five per cent of its inmates would ever be eligible for parole. There were bank robbers, kidnappers, child killers and rapists, all chained together on that first ever shipment, a couple of them dying along the way. The first job for the new officers had been to quell those who were shackled to a corpse.

Although there was scant chance of escape – the swim was impossible and boats rarely docked – most of the prisoners seemed to prefer Las Focas to the mainland institutions. Somehow, despite the frequent cell house murders, rapes and rioting, the place often had an air of calm and tranquillity, an almost monastic quality.

The reason that the island was so calm, thought Rita Mae, shuffling along beside her mother, was that the whole place was dying. She had seen another dead bird that morning, the third in a month, lying on the concrete field beside their apartment building. Its eyes and feathers had been pecked right out. The whole place is dying, she thought again, a smile playing on her lips. First it had been the one-legged owl population and then the Hawksbill Turtles. Both species driven to extinction. After that came the seals, just a few of them left now. Every so often one would hitch its cumber-some mass up on to the stretch of beach, only to be found dead a week later, after bathing near the bilge pump.

If she could just get back to the mainland, thought Rita Mae, it would all be fine. It was a decade since her family had moved from California to Las Focas (she was only three years old at the time), but she still felt the pull of the place. The citrus-scented essence of the state was kept fresh for her by Maria Caesar, her maternal grandmother, who lived in

Orange County and mailed out a stack of movie magazines for her each month, full of glamour ('How Marilyn keeps that figure peachy-keen'), gossip ('Who's been flying too high with Marijuana Airlines?') and advertisements ('What *you* need is a stronger He-man voice').

Rita Mae loved those magazines, with their broad vistas of possibility, a world where plain girls could become movie stars and even poor people lived in pastel-coloured homes. She loved the pictures of those little houses, each a different sweet-wrapper shade, scattered haphazardly across the horizon.

It was all out there, thought Rita Mae, staring up at the vast colonnaded front of the Warden's house. She pulled Jenna's present more tightly to her chest. Beside her, Clara Jones mirrored Rita Mae's stance, gazing too at the neo-colonial residence. She could never get over just how white it was. If Clara's life had gone according to plan (and she had planned each detail very carefully) it was the kind of house she had imagined for herself by now. Not on Las Focas of course, but on a shady avenue in Beverly Hills, lined with luscious fan palms. Her husband would be a successful businessman, her daughter a successful cheerleader. When Rita Mae had been born they had seemed on course for all that.

Still, thought Clara, blinking painfully now, there was still time. The possibilities had narrowed, but they hadn't vanished completely. If she was clever and timed her hand well, there might still be a chance. Reaching for Rita Mae's arm she inspected her again. Bringing a comb from her clutch bag she pulled at her daughter's curls, prompting sharp yelps of pain. 'Quiet,' she whispered anxiously, 'be quiet, Rita.' She put the comb away. 'Now remember what I told you about etiquette . . .'

'Don't speak until I'm spoken to.'

'Good posture.'

'A pretty smile.' Rita Mae grimaced.

'That's right,' her mother said firmly, 'and speak politely.'

Leaning forward, suddenly hesitant, Clara rapped softly on the door. A second later the huge wooden mouth of the place groaned open to show Mrs Wright silhouetted there, hands on hips. 'Oh,' she said, on seeing the two huddled figures. Her lips pursed as if sucking on a particularly tart damson. Silence. 'Oh,' said Mrs Wright again, her mouth breaking into a strange stunted sneer. 'How lovely to see you, Mrs Jones. And Miss Jones,' Rita Mae stepped forward with the parcel, 'how grown up you look in that dress. It's quite, quite,' she paused, 'unusual.'

Arms outstretched, Rita Mae watched as Mrs Wright plucked the parcel away and held it up to the light, turning it slowly, as if considering a famously large diamond. 'How wonderful,' she said dreamily, 'a present, just for me.' She glanced with sly delight at Clara, whose skin was burning red.

'No, no, no,' stuttered Rita Mae, the words bumping and crowding against her tongue. 'No, I'm sorry, no. It's for Jenna.'

'Oh,' said Mrs Wright, face pinching inwards before she smiled graciously. 'Of course it is.' Turning, she started to walk up the hallway towards the noise at the heart of the house. 'Why don't the two of you come in,' she called over her shoulder. Struck by the literal meaning of this, neither Clara nor Rita Mae could decide whether to follow.

Chapter Two

Johnny stared up at Rita Mae, his mouth a wordless hoop, as she stalked towards him, head bowed intensely over the page, body trembling with nervous energy. She had been performing soliloquies for an hour now, the grass verge of the parade ground as her stage. So far she had ignored Johnny, but now she rushed up to him, shouting and jousting at his head with her script. 'How in hell do you think all that sickness and dying was paid for?' she screamed, crouching before him. Then she paused meaningfully. 'Death is expensive, Miss Stella!'

A few lines later, panting slightly, Rita Mae gave a deep bow and collapsed. The speech was from *A Streetcar Named Desire*: Blanche DuBois explaining to her sister that their family home had been lost to the money men. Its prodigious run of exclamation points had exhausted Rita Mae, and she knew that it would be a few minutes before she could perform again. Turning to Johnny, she sighed softly. 'So,' she said, 'what do you think?'

Johnny nodded in the way she knew he would, a kind of soft, convulsive shaking. 'It was fantastic,' he said, his voice low and reverent, 'truly fantastic. I think,' he paused, 'you may be the best actress I've ever seen.'

Rita Mae gave a vague smile of thanks before closing her

eyes. Tennessee Williams was a good playwright, she thought, and his words were especially powerful when declaimed by a great actress. Maybe it would be worth learning some of his speeches as audition pieces. Not that she had any impending auditions, of course, but all serious actors were meant to have a few speeches committed to memory, weren't they?

Mr Curtis had given her the scripts just before Christmas, his head bowed in shame, offering them up as a small apology for her exile in munchkinland. At the time Rita Mae had accepted them gracelessly, snatching them up with a snapped 'Thanks', affronted at a gift so paltry in comparison with the offence. Didn't Mr Curtis understand what it was like to have your talent consigned to the chorus, a chorus of tiny trolls at that? Could he really think that some scripts – *Streetcar*, *The Glass Menagerie* and *Our Town* amongst them – would quell her righteous anger? Did he truly believe that an artistic personality recovered so quickly? Had she not been injured? Did she not bleed?

Over the last few months, though, she had come to appreciate the plays, especially those by Mr Williams. His work was so dramatic, she thought, his characters so plagued by nerves and neuroses. Rita Mae loved to play women afflicted with this dissipating emotional blight, characters like Miss DuBois and Laura Wingfield. She enjoyed the challenge of inner turmoil.

'Maybe one day,' said Johnny hesitantly, 'I could direct one of those plays you like, as a movie, and you could star in it. We'd be a team, a famous team, like Tracy and Hepburn.'

Rita Mae opened her left eye and stared at him quiz-zically. Closing it again, she sighed. No comment. The thought of Johnny (a particularly small twelve-year-old) as a director was almost ridiculous. At less than eighty pounds, he was certainly no Orson Welles. Rita Mae struggled to imagine him controlling a small dog, much less a cast of temperamental actors, with all the attendant tantrums and sexual dalliances.

'I could create huge productions for you,' Johnny was saying, shuddering slightly as he reached out to stroke Rita Mae's hair. Feeling his hand, she shook her head, as if ridding herself of a large, angry bee. Johnny jumped back, chastened. As Rita Mae lay there, still again, her eyes closed, he tilted his head to gaze at her beautiful, impassive face.

Johnny had been in love with Rita Mae for two years now, ever since they'd sat together in maths class and she had flirted in return for homework answers. Although she only seemed to tolerate him, Johnny was sure that they were destined to be together, married eventually, living in a large condo in the Hollywood Hills, with children and a maid and the requisite pet monkeys. He would often imagine the two of them as adults, enjoying successful, interlinked careers. If he couldn't be her director, he thought, then maybe he could be her manager or a script assistant. If nothing else, then perhaps she'd let him arrange her diary.

Sensing Johnny's gaze, Rita Mae allowed herself a faint smile. She couldn't help it if she was irresistible. It was perfectly natural for Johnny to be devoted to her but she just wished, sometimes, that he wasn't quite so tactile. She wasn't a demonstrative person herself and (aside from her father's touch when she was a small child) she had never been able to bear stray hands on her skin, creeping across her body, working their way through the strands of her hair. Rita Mae preferred to keep skin on skin contact to a minimum. Doctor's appointments: sure. Random touching: no. If Johnny chose to admire her, then she hoped he might learn to do so from a safe distance, as he would an artefact encased in glass.

She heard a noise, feet on concrete, and felt the weight of a hard rubber missile bounce heavily off her forehead. On the parade ground in front of her there was laughing and shouts of, 'Good shot,' and, 'That has to have hurt.' Levering herself on to her elbows, Rita Mae saw that a group of five kids, including Jenna Wright, had gathered to play basketball. On the grass beside her, Johnny had jumped to his feet, barking furiously circumcized sentences.

'You want a fucking fight?' The laughter was dying down as Jake Hardwick approached, the offending basketball now firmly beneath his arm.

Rita Mae grasped at Johnny's ankle, pulling his leg from under him. 'Sit down,' she hissed, as he plummeted to the ground. 'Just sit down.' At fourteen, Jake was at least a foot and a half taller than Johnny and double his weight. There were also rumours, amongst the eighty kids who lived on the island, that he carried a knife, 'in case one of those fucking homo convicts gets out'. Somehow Rita Mae sensed that a fight would be a foregone conclusion.

'He's not trying to start a fight,' she said, shouting down to Jake, 'he was just trying to defend me.'

'Defend you?' said Jake. 'Well he's in for a challenge, isn't he? Slut.' Turning to grin at his friends, he began dribbling the ball to the opposite end of the playground, before dunking it safely through the hoop.

Rita Mae watched for a second and then lay back down. She would have liked to leave now, but the parade ground had a tall wire fence and the only door was at the far end.

To exit she'd have to walk past the other kids, and she knew that they'd taunt her more, and worse this time, for admitting defeat. There was a chance that they'd go soon, though. Maybe they were just out for a short game.

Still seething, Johnny had started to regain the power of speech. 'I hate them,' he was saying. 'Treating you like that, thinking they can get away with it. They're so rude. They think they have a right?'

'It doesn't matter,' said Rita Mae quietly, 'just shut up.'

He carried on, body tensed, 'I hate them. I should have hit that guy back then, I should have knocked him out.' He turned to Rita Mae. 'I could have taken him you know. I have that book on karate.'

Rita Mae grabbed his wrist, twisting the skin. 'I said, shut up.'

The last thing she needed was Johnny's support. Unusually small, Johnny was a target for them anyway, a fact exacerbated by his father's job as assistant janitor, one of the lowest-ranking positions on the island. For years now, the kids had been saying that Johnny's father smelled of sewage, and that his youngest son stank too. Sometimes, at the start of class, the kids would begin sniffing quietly, the nasal din rising until it was impossible to ignore. 'It's Johnny,' they'd say, when Mr Curtis asked what the problem was. 'Johnny just stinks.' Turning to the blackboard their teacher would stifle a smile. 'I'm sure he smells tolerable,' he'd say, before writing on the board in large chalk letters. 'TOLERABLE. Can anyone tell me what that word means?'

Still, as much as the kids disliked Johnny, most saw him as harmless, an object of derision at most. It was Rita Mae they detested. She had never quite understood why, thinking at first that it was because she stood out, that they were jealous of her talent. Lately though she'd come to suspect that her father, too, held some of the blame.

Larry Jones was one of the most ostracized officers on the island and the other men would often talk about him at dinner time, criticizing his behaviour, pondering his employment and mimicking his voice. These family discussions rarely remained private, many aired in class the very next day. This usually involved Rita Mae's classmates crowding around her, with one of them coming right up tight, nose-to-nose with his prey. While this one led the insults, other voices chimed in regularly, offering their tones to the chorus.

'I heard your dad's a fucking yellow belly who's scared of all the prisoners and can't control them at all. I heard he shits his pants when any of them starts fighting.'

'My dad said your dad's an embarrassment to the prison service. He said that if your dad was unfit for service during the war then he sure as hell shouldn't be allowed to join up as a prison officer.'

'I heard your dad never washes the shit out of his hair when the convicts throw it at him. He just leaves it there all day.'

A weak 'right' was Rita Mae's usual response, along with her most bored expression. There was nothing else to say really. Having watched other kids being bullied, Rita Mae knew that any heated response would only send the taunts escalating until the victim was a jellied mess, lying on the ground, all semblance of dignity gone. Such a display just wasn't her style. It was best to keep quiet. Watchful.

And anyway, Rita Mae thought now, even if she had wanted to respond, there was no clear defence to hand. It was true, after all, that her father *was* unsuited to prison work, a thin-skinned, easily bruised type in comparison to his brutal, thick-necked colleagues. As a kid she had often heard her mother complain of Larry's ineptitude, standing at the kitchen sink, grumbling about his lost career.

The voices at the end of the parade ground, caught up until now in easy cries for the ball, suddenly grew into a rabble of shouting. Rita Mae and Johnny sat up in silent unison. The kids were yelling at a group of four black inmates, shackled together, who were being led from the cell house to the landing dock, where a small boat bobbed expectantly.

Their eviction was the result of some of the worst race rioting ever seen on Las Focas. In the dining hall that past Wednesday, as most of the men quietly munched their mashed vegetables, a white inmate called Vince Webber had left his table, apparently to collect a jug of water. The guards were watching him carefully, their interest pricked by the quavering green swastika that he had recently tattooed (backwards, in front of the mirror) on to his forehead. Still, despite their scrutiny and awareness of the death threats Webber had made against all black inmates, they were still somehow too slow to do anything when he leapt over to Jonty Birdsall, caught him in a headlock, pulled out a jagged shank and tore it roughly across his neck. As Birdsall stood up with a roar, throwing Webber clean off his back, missiles began flying across the hall. Two hours later, when each inmate had been returned to his cell, the dining hall walls dripped with creamed potato. Birdsall, Webber and three other men were long dead.

When her father arrived home that evening, Rita Mae had waited for him to wash before assailing him with questions. What had started the riot? she asked. Who was responsible? How could riots happen anyway, when they were told that the cellblock was secure? Surely if it was possible for the prisoners to riot it might also be possible for them to escape?

Larry had ruffled her hair absently and shrugged. In the case of a riot, he was assigned to guard the cell-house gate and so had no clear idea what had happened inside. 'I don't know, darling, I just don't know.'

It was Clara Jones who had stepped in to answer her daughter's questions. 'It's the Negroes,' she had said, hovering by the cooker. 'They're always starting trouble.' She paused to drain a pan of beans. 'It's not their fault really, I suppose,' she sounded doubtful, 'it's just their animal nature. You see, Rita Mae,' her voice suddenly took on an expert tone, 'the Negroes have a very low level of intelligence, which makes them almost impossible to civilize. It's terrible really.' Clara started ladling beans thoughtfully on to each plate. 'That's one of the things that you should appreciate about Las Focas, Rita Mae.'

'What is?'

'Well,' Clara paused, 'aside from the niggers in the cell house, we're completely free of them here. If you were on the mainland there might be Negroes living right up close to you.'

Rita Mae thought about that comment now, watching as the kids shouted abuse at the inmates. She'd never found her mother's arguments very convincing – they just didn't add up. Of course, when it came to black people she didn't have much to go on. She'd never met one socially, and had only ever seen black men from a distance, crossing the island for some chore during work detail. But her mother's argument suggested that all white people were innately civilized and intelligent and superior, and she knew for a fact that that wasn't true. If all the white murderers, rapists and kidnappers in the prison weren't evidence enough, then Rita Mae only had to look at the kids on the parade ground.

Jake Hardwick had run through the gate now and was spitting at the prisoners, his feet essaying a boxer's dance, pivoting fast towards them before lunging back out of reach. Behind him were Jenna and the others, enjoying the spectacle and shouting abuse while the officer accompanying the inmates looked on indulgently. Given the dull responses of the shackled prisoners it seemed likely that they'd been drugged for the journey, their eyes blank and staring. Jake obviously suspected this too, moving a little too close to the flank at one point and being shocked by a sharp, jabbing blow to his upper arm. The weight of the punch threw him to the ground, where he snarled once more and spat bitterly.

Rita Mae lay back, laughing slightly, satisfied that the show was over. If her mother thought that intelligence depended upon race, then where did that place Hawaiians and Red Indians? A lot of the Las Focas maintenance staff had come over from the Big Island and Maui, and they all seemed perfectly astute – they were certainly the only people who could fix the generators. Rita Mae smiled wryly and stood up. Turning to Johnny she lent him her hand. He scrambled to his feet, puffing. The other kids had gone now and the sky was turning pink. 'Coming?' said Rita Mae. Johnny nodded.

Chapter Three

'Maria, Maria.' Toribio Cesares pushed gently at his daughter, whose head, heavy with bone and sleep, rested hard on his shoulder. 'Wake up, Maria, wake up.'

The eight-year-old girl shifted in her seat, eyes closed, and said nothing. Her face was hidden beneath a torrent of black hair, falling in great woollen waves from her crown, punctuated by the occasional burr or twig, the tangles of a long journey and a marked lack of female attention. Toribio smiled and shrugged at the passengers sat opposite, three brightly dressed but blank-faced campesinos, squashed awkwardly into a double berth. Two of them, he now noticed, had wrapped their feet in muslin, blood and pus seeping slowly through the cloth, mixing and coagulating with whichever herbal remedy they had painted on their wounds. 'I don't know how she can sleep,' said Toribio, hands rising in the air, motioning towards Maria. The strangers nodded, polite but uninterested. 'It's not such a peaceful ride.'

As if to illustrate Toribio's point, the train – so full that limbs thrust helplessly through the windows – hurtled over a rocky mound. Maria's eyes flew whitely open for a second then, glinting in her hair like nesting insects, before blinking firmly back shut. Through the vagueness of sleep she decided that she was, and always would be, impervious to bumps.

Toribio and Maria had been in transit for seven days now, three of them spent cloistered together in this dusty carriage which promised (perhaps optimistically) to help spirit them from Jalisco, Central Mexico to Los Angeles. Maria had spent most of the train journey determinedly asleep, eyes clenched wrinkly tight. Her father, meanwhile, had been staring through the smeared window, recoiling as they creaked past the schoolboy corpses that hung along the telephone lines, a warning to petty thieves. Whenever the rails veered near to a road he would see the small groups of peons, the Mexican peasant workers, stumbling along with their bundled clothing, padding to the US by foot. Toribio never came quite close enough to see their faces, but the shared gait was enough. Their spines had curved into shells, stride declined to a shuffle. They were a people in retreat.

Up ahead, Toribio saw a station, burned out and petrified, its remains just a gangling metal skeleton, a clawed fist rising from the ground. The train didn't stop here, accelerating as it passed. They had sped blurrily through many of these stations, places that might once have been the hub of a town, surrounded by small homes, populated by rail workers. Since the revolution had started, though, six years before, the stations had been targets for the insurrectionists. Given the wave of arson that had swept the country, thought Toribio, it was incredible that any of them had survived.

As it was, it had taken him and his daughter four days on foot to reach the nearest functioning station, four days with

just goat's cheese and a few dry tortillas for food, supple-
mented finally with a lizard and some roots dug up at the
side of the road. Despite the size of the train they had
boarded – its hundred boxcars caterpillaring across the
countryside – there had never been any guarantee that
they'd land a place, a fact that had made Toribio distinctly
jittery. He had been careful to keep this detail hidden from
Maria as they set off from their village, wary as he was of
cursing their luck. Instead he had tried to keep his young
daughter entertained and oblivious as they passed through
a string of ghost villages, the wooden buildings burned
white, crops parched and shrinking back to the earth.

Successful for the first few days, Toribio's resolve had
suddenly run dry as they reached the halfway point of their
walk. Here they came across a large town, just recently
abandoned. Turning blithely on to its main street, they saw
a town square ahead of them, carpeted with bodies:
stomachs ripped open, entrails unravelling, skin inside out.
It had been the same scene on each street they came to
then, and Toribio had eventually told Maria that she must
look to the sky until he signalled otherwise. Unusually
obedient, Maria had reached for her father's hand and tilted
her head back. The view was surprisingly dark. Above them
pulsed a dense cloud of flies.

It had been a full thirty minutes before Toribio instructed
Maria to look ahead. He had known, of course, that the
country they'd pass through would be deadbeat, brutalized,
but he couldn't have guessed at this. Through the years of
revolution, Toribio and his family had stayed close to their
homestead, rarely straying from its immediate environs. For
more than half a decade now, there had been the almost
constant fear that some random group of terrorists – and that

was the word for them, thought Toribio, not patriots or soldiers – would spring upon the village, and violate everything. It might be government paramilitaries, revolutionaries or just a group of opportunist bandits. No matter, thought Toribio. Whatever their allegiance, they all seemed to behave in the same way. Some spoke of protecting the land (and perhaps they truly meant it) but they were all given to looting.

Despite regular sorties in the Jalisco region, the Cesares smallholding had remained untouched until last year. The family farm only stretched across fifteen acres, but had nonetheless been a profitable concern for centuries, comfortably housing the whole Cesares clan in a cluster of lean-tos that hemmed the land. During the past decade the farm had been particularly successful, the subject of some local envy, since Toribio and his brothers had set about developing a technique for breeding mules. All five of the men had been educated by their grandfather, who had himself attended a small institution in Mexico City. Between his teaching and what they could glean from a handful of biology books, they had set off through a long process of trial and error until they'd created a technique that produced a healthy mule almost every time. Had that venture continued it was likely that the farm could have doubled its profits by now, perhaps even tripled them.

As it was, though, a large gang of insurrectos had muscled into the village late one night, twelve months ago. The family had been preparing for this attack for some time, and so, at the first hollering of the bandits from the crest of a hill above, the women and children had pulled sheets around them, run from their beds and held their breath as they dug into the colossal pile of chicken shit, stacked behind the lean-tos, that served as their bunker.

With the gang drawing nearer, Toribio and the other men, whispering amongst themselves, had decided that they must try and barrack their land, spreading out across the farm with rifles and bats, shaking with anticipation as the cluster of torches blazed nearer.

As the revoltosos hurtled on to the land, though, surrender became inevitable. Where there had at first seemed forty, maybe fifty men, it was now clear that they numbered at least a hundred. The word swept around the Cesares clan that defence would be impossible, probably fatal. Toribio had disputed this, arguing that they might use an element of surprise, of shock, to startle their aggressors and frighten them away. They had had to defend their land before, he argued, the local hacendado regularly pressuring them to give up the area to allow it to be subsumed into his already enormous property, and each time they had rejected his claims, fought against them cleanly and successfully.

His brothers had stopped listening now, though, and instead they too were heading for the chicken manure, from where they watched the insurrectos gallop in, trampling their crops and shooting their livestock before reaching the main house and taking all the supplies they could find. Food, liquor, clothes, cheap jewellery. Having carried out this sortie the revolutionaries threw their torches casually to the ground. Then they fled, watching from a safe distance as the flames spat contemptuously across the land.

Toribio could still sometimes see the silhouette of his wife, Perita, in the final month of carrying their second child, standing silent and bereft as the fire flared up behind her, stomach bent out hard and perfect, that great optimistic swell. Perita was normally so gregarious – renowned in the region for her wild dancing and wit – but at times of trauma she had an incredible talent for retreat, withdrawing completely from the people around her, almost as if her mind had filtered away from her body. It was a characteristic that Maria shared, thought Toribio, glancing down at his daughter, asleep now for almost three days. It was a form of protection, he supposed, this switch from exuberance to blankness, an instant change, evinced in a snap.

It had been a long, silent week later that Perita had started to bleed, just a few spots at first, in the early morning hours. They had thought, hopefully, that it was a sign of the forthcoming birth, but as the day went on the flow had grown heavier until, come evening, it seemed unstoppable, towel after towel dyed a deep red, a shocking vermilion flood. Toribio had stayed up all night to tend his wife, only allowing Maria to join him. Watching his daughter, just seven years old, he had been struck by her composure as she dampened her mother's brow and sang tuneless lullabies. As Perita drifted from the muggy wilderness of fever it was Toribio who had started to cry. When her pulse had faded altogether it was Maria who had held her father, climbing on to his back and using her weight to stop the shaking.

Looking out over the plains, Toribio coughed a laugh. The campesinos stared back, suspicious. Right here on this train, thought Toribio, were hundreds of believers: people whose faith had grown as their land disappeared; who framed their starvation as a worthy punishment; who saw the hand of God in every affliction, even when it reached into their community, snatched up their shelter, consumed their bread and their wine. For these people, each setback was a sign or a trial, devised on high to test their character, ensuring they were worthy of a place in heaven. The random cruelties that rained down upon them were transmuted into uneasy gifts, hardships to be held fast and welcomed.

It was ridiculous, thought Toribio, that tragedy could make God seem bigger for some people, more real, at the very moment He proved Himself non-existent. Toribio pulled Maria tight to his side. God offered nothing now. The only way to live, he thought, was to deify the dollar. Since the insurrection, Toribio had been using the family's one remaining mule to provide a delivery service, transporting oranges back and forth to a nearby market. For sixteen hours of this, a day's work, he was paid twenty-five centavos. It was a slave wage, he realized, an insult.

Mexico was lawless now, thought Toribio, stripped of resources. For men like him, the United States was the only option. Two of Toribio's brothers had moved to Los Angeles recently, three uncles soon following, all off to work for the Pacific Electric Railroad, helping to construct the interurban trolley system which would criss-cross the whole city. Apparently the company was desperate to recruit Mexican men, willing to pay wages of up to $2 a day for obreros who could cope with the blazing heat and inevitable double shifts. It would be perfect, thought Toribio. He knew that his brothers and uncles planned to return to their village as soon as the revolution ended, but for Toribio the move was permanent. He could not return.

As far as he had been told, most of his family members were living in a single colonia in the centre of the city. While he was out working, he figured, Maria could be tended by her aunts; she could spend time playing with her cousins and attending the local school. He knew, too, that she would enjoy the landscape. From his brothers' description he gathered that the city was covered with trees and flowers. Orange and lemon groves sat beside undulating poppy fields, pepper trees lined the tracks, anemones, freesias and marigolds thrived beside the all-conquering cacti, and golden rod and mustard grass spread out beyond. And then, of course, there were the palm trees.

From the front of their boxcar came a loud staccato cry, soon joined by more voices and then applause, a ripple of excitement pealing through. Glancing out of the window, Toribio understood this frenzy. He shook his daughter more anxiously now, not wanting her to sleep through this moment, this vital jolt of significance. 'Maria, Maria, look where we are.'

Maria wriggled, drawing her legs beneath her, before looking up at Toribio, eyes curtained with sleep. 'What is it?'

Her father pointed through the window. 'We're coming up to the border. We're about to reach El Paso.'

Maria frowned. 'Oh,' she paused, 'still a long way to go isn't it, Papa? A long way from Los Angeles?'

Toribio laughed. 'Of course, of course. But, Maria, we're entering the USA. Los Estados Unidos. We're about to become Americans.'

'Oh.'

Maria looked surprisingly glum as Toribio lifted her on to his lap. 'It's exciting, mi hijita, an exciting time. Listen to the people.' The whooping and wailing was reaching revival tent delirium, despite the desolation of the land outside. 'This is an important moment, Maria. From now on our lives will be different, better.' There came no answer as Toribio struggled to think of some way to mark this change, some grand gesture that might make it significant. 'Maria, you know, in this new country we'll be different, each day will be blessed, each idea transformed. When you wake up tomorrow you'll be a new person.'

'Oh.' Maria looked understandably worried.

'I know what we'll do.' Toribio pulled his daughter tight against his chest and whispered now. 'We'll take a new name. What do you think of that?'

'I like my name,' said Maria, turning to face him, eyes wide.

'I know you do, mi hijita, I know you do. But what if we chose another name that was like ours, but more American? How about that?'

'What do you mean?' Her eyes started to narrow.

'Well,' Toribio paused, suddenly unsure. 'Well. What if we took the name Caesar? That wouldn't be too different, would it?' He considered this now, rolling the syllables of this new name silently across his tongue, enjoying their brevity, their tight concision. 'Maria Caesar. How does that sound?'

Maria shrugged, chin falling hard on her chest. Shaking her for an answer, keen for a reaction, Toribio found that his daughter's eyes were, once again, clamped doggedly shut.

Chapter Four

'Here you are.' Vera Ellis, proprietor of the Las Focas general store, bounced her hand along the row of pigeonholes until it came to rest on the one marked 'Jones'. 'Ah,' she said, 'a package,' whistling through her teeth in mock excitement. Pulling it from the shelf, 'It sure is a big one,' she spun to face Clara, her grin crude as sticky putty. 'Rita Mae's a hell of a lucky girl.'

Noting the postmark – Orange County – Clara flashed what might have been a smile, but was perhaps just a trapped nerve. 'Thank you, Mrs Ellis,' she said, placing the package gently into her shopping bag, careful to cushion the small tray of eggs below. 'I'll be seeing you soon, I'm sure. Thank you so much for your help.'

Vera Ellis nodded, saying nothing until Clara had left the store. Then, taking up the dust cloth that she used to polish the green glass counter, she started a low, terse grumbling. Her words – if they were, indeed, words – were barely audible. Just a dark clutter of consonants, punctuated by the occasional padded thump of her cloth.

Clara Jones slipped down the hill as quickly as possible, anxious to get home and prepare for her appointments. Her progress was impeded by the tight, tapered line of her skirt, which stuck sweatily to the top of her thighs. Every few paces she found that she would have to stop, the material having gathered around her hips, forming four or five horizontal pleats, the hemline edging up inches above her knees. Clara smiled blithely in case anyone was watching, veered to a halt, and tried to look natural as she tugged violently and then smoothed out the fabric.

The package was addressed in a spidery scrawl, with a large, capitalized note, 'HAPPY BIRTHDAY!' inscribed above. Clara knew that her mother had sent it (a month late, of course) and exactly what would be inside – more movie magazines and scandal sheets. Her tongue began to cluck almost involuntarily as she walked. The magazines were inappropriate for a young girl, she thought, entirely unsuitable. Clara couldn't understand why they interested Rita Mae anyway, with their references to torrid affairs, cosmetic surgery and 'lavender lovelies'. Couldn't she entertain herself with a good romance novel? And whatever had happened to young people reading the Bible? Clara wasn't religious, but she'd rather read about Job or Jacob, she mused, than that sneering Elvis Presley.

Maria Caesar (or Granmaria, as Rita Mae called her) had sent out another batch of these magazines earlier that year, and Clara had found herself flicking through them, disgusted by the content but unable to prise herself away in favour of a more useful task, like, say, peeling potatoes. Of all the magazines, the one that pained her most was the gossip rag, *Confidential*. In the past six months this publication had suffered a glut of high-profile libel cases (Liberace suing successfully after the appearance of some quite dreadful aspersions) and had been forced to mellow its content. In response to this verdict, though, shocked by the outcome, Granmaria had sent Rita Mae a large pile of back issues that she'd been saving up for years.

As she scanned the *Confidential* covers, Clara had found her eye bouncing from headline to headline like a child in a fairground. 'The Tarzan of the Boudoir', screamed one, above another that warned against abortion pills. There was talk of 'muscle men', 'convicts', and 'Why Rita Hayworth walked out on Dick'. It was all so tawdry, thought Clara, so – she searched for the right word – unclean.

Still, she had felt it her duty to look more carefully at the magazines' contents, concerned as she was for her daughter's moral welfare. It would be remiss, thought Clara, poring over the gossip columns and the celebrity diet tips (apparently Jayne Mansfield thrived on a diet of steak and lettuce), to just avoid the situation, let this subject matter go unexamined. Such close reading only made her more anxious, though. It seemed to Clara that, in the years since she'd left the mainland, the American public had slipped inexorably into a deep moral swamp.

It had, for instance, quite clearly become fashionable for people to indulge in interracial coupling, with each issue of *Confidential* bringing further evidence of this trend. One had a feature on Sammy Davis Jr ('that engaging little bronze guy') that exposed his relationship with a buxom blonde singer called Meg. Apparently the two had spent many balmy evenings together, mooning over ground beef patties in Hamburger Hamlet before returning to his hotel. The thought that such liaisons could be played out in public made Clara reach for her handkerchief.

Then there was Doris Duke, the fabulously wealthy heiress, who had been flaunting her relationship with a man *Confidential* termed her 'African Prince'. Clara found this pairing incomprehensible. In some ways, of course, she understood the attraction that Sammy Davis Jr's showgirl lover might feel for the small black man. He was a means, it was true, of furthering her career. But Doris Duke could surely have attracted any man she liked. Not with her looks, Clara thought sagely, nodding to herself. Duke was particularly thin-lipped, with eyes so narrow that she seemed permanently mid-blink. But that fat bank balance could have bought up the most beautiful of white men. There was simply no need for Duke to be pursuing Negroes, unless her aim was specifically to shock. It was terribly upsetting, thought Clara, not to mention immoral.

The heat had transformed Clara's hair into a clammy helmet, each strand stuck close to her skull. As one curl broke free, she licked her finger and tethered it back down. A couple of years earlier, in one of her increasingly rare letters to her mother, Clara had asked, very politely, if she might stop sending these packages to Rita Mae. She had laid out the argument clearly, explaining that Rita Mae was very grateful, but that the magazine content was just too risqué for such a young girl. 'In trying to raise my daughter as a lady,' she had written, 'I'm eager for her to read more moral material. I don't want her to have her head turned by glamour, which – as you know – brings its own dangers.'

She had sent off the missive, unsure whether her mother would make sense of the argument or incorporate it into one of her bizarre delusions. On this occasion, Maria had responded defiantly, sending through the biggest collection of magazines and movie annuals so far. The tone of the accompanying letter was playful but firm. 'You remember how much I loved movie magazines when you were a kid,' she wrote. '*Motion Picture*, *Photoplay*, *Movie Mirror*.' Clara had nodded ruefully, recalling the times she had stood watch as her mother swiped copies from a newsstand in their downtown neighbourhood. 'They always made me feel better, more hopeful and excited. I know that you never liked them, even back then, but if Rita Mae enjoys them, where's the harm, my Clara? Doesn't your daughter deserve a little fun now and then? Doesn't she deserve a few treats from Granmaria?'

Clara thought of how much she had hated that argument ('resented' it, she corrected herself, always keen to avoid extreme emotions). She resented the suggestion that she was depriving her child of fun and excitement simply by policing her reading habits. It was the argument that liberals always used, thought Clara, as she climbed the stairs to the apartment. This idea that fantasy and imagination were somehow more valid than sober, dutiful behaviour, simply because they were more fun. Clara hated ('disliked', she corrected herself) the word 'fun' more than nearly any other. Enjoyment and humour and contentedness were all fine words, she thought, but fun had a clipped ring that sounded almost like an expletive.

Opening the front door, she found the kettle squealing in protest on the hob. 'Can't anyone hear that,' she shouted, placing her bag gently on the table and going to turn off the heat. 'Isn't anyone listening?' Still unanswered, Clara smiled, tight-lipped, and started to pour the boiling water away.

As the final drop spun around the plughole, Larry sauntered in from the bedroom, tucking his shirt into his trousers. Seeing Clara, empty kettle in hand, he gave a staccato laugh. 'You haven't just . . .'

Clara nodded.

'Chrissakes, Clara, I was about to use that.'

'You can't expect me to leave a kettle whistling, Laurence. I assumed it was unwanted.' She looked him up and down, brushing imaginary dust from his shoulder. 'I wish you'd stop cursing so much in front of Rita Mae, too. I take it our darling daughter's in?'

Larry grabbed a chunk of bread from the counter and sat down. 'I guess so.'

Clara sighed. 'Well I sure hope she didn't hear you use that language.'

Larry laughed properly now. 'You don't think she's heard worse than that at school? Geez, using the Lord's name is the least of it, Clara. Some of those kids are worse than sailors. I should think she's heard just about every cuss going.' He smiled ruefully. 'And if not I can take her for a half-hour in the cellblock.' Larry rummaged in the shopping bag. 'I wouldn't be surprised if Reet had even used a few cusses herself once in a while.'

Pulling out the package he noticed the postmark and smiled. 'Ah, it's good of your ma to send Rita a birthday present. Can't be easy for her.' He shouted over his shoulder. 'Rita Mae.'

Clara stepped swiftly towards the table, snatching up the package.

'What is it?' Rita Mae hovered in the doorway, leaning her head awkwardly against the wall. 'What do you need me for?'

Clara clutched the package tightly behind her back as Larry looked on, bemused. 'Honey,' said Clara, her voice oddly warm. Rita Mae stared back suspiciously. 'Honey, it's nothing. Just go to your room and do whatever it was you were doing.'

'OK,' said Rita Mae, her brows laid low with distrust,

sightline slightly obscured. She shrugged.

'Wait,' said Clara, suddenly nervy. 'Just what is it you're doing?'

'Homework,' said Rita Mae.

'Good,' Clara sighed. 'That's very good.'

'So, that was interesting,' said Larry, watching as his daughter slumped listlessly back to her bedroom. He turned to Clara. 'Can you tell me what all that was about?'

Clara sat down at the table, shaky and relieved. 'I just don't trust my mother,' she said, starting to rip at the brown paper, her nails bending perilously as she struggled to untie the tightly knotted string. 'She's just crazy enough to have sent Rita Mae something really,' she paused, aware that Maria would never intentionally hurt her daughter, but wanting to prove her point, 'really sordid.'

Larry sighed, reaching out for one of the magazines as the package fell open. 'Here,' he started to riffle through the pages, 'nothing particularly sordid here.' Peppered through the magazine were hastily scrawled notes, messages from Maria to Rita Mae. He paused, reading aloud a few words scribbled beside a full-page portrait of Clark Gable. 'Mr Gable! Such a naughty man! I knew him very well back before your mother was born. He looks like he could use a good meal these days, and someone to keep him off the liquor. I'd be happy to help!'

Clara snatched up the page. 'Let me see.' Scanning the words, her lips pursed until they were heart-shaped and tinged purple.

'She's a funny old thing, isn't she?' said Larry. 'All these fantasies of hers.' He paused. 'I guess it must be nice sometimes, to just live in another world, right up there in your thoughts. Maybe your ma's really happy.'

Clara's eyes narrowed. She stood up and started unpacking the shopping, before fetching her sewing bag from the bedroom. 'If you'd ever met my mother,' she said, Larry still sitting at the kitchen table, 'if you'd ever met her, you'd realize how silly your last comment was. My mother is not,' she shot the word, 'happy.' She combed through the bag. Tape measure. Scissors. Pattern paper. 'My mother might have a very vivid imagination, but she is not having fun.

'Anyway,' Clara glanced at the clock, 'I have to get going – I have a fitting with Mrs Beaumont.'

'Good luck,' muttered Larry. 'You'll need quite a stockpile of material.'

Clara smiled. 'I know.' She shrugged. 'Rita Mae,' she called. No answer. 'Rita Mae,' Clara yelled it now, 'you'd better get in here please.'

Rita Mae walked into the doorway. 'What is it?' She looked at her father, dressed in his officer's garb. 'Are you both going out?'

'That's right,' said Clara. 'I should be back in a couple of hours. I'm just seeing to some fittings up on the hill.' She turned to Larry. 'You have a full shift, don't you?' He nodded, mouth full of bread. 'Anyway, Rita Mae, I just wanted to give you these.' Clara scooped up the magazines, which had been obscured by the brown paper. 'They're a birthday present from your grandmother.'

Brushing the crumbs from his lap, Larry watched as his daughter's back uncurled, Rita Mae standing straight for a second and grinning. It was a relief that she'd received at least one good birthday present, he thought, something that she liked. Larry had been worried about his daughter back on her birthday, a month ago now, when he had gone to pick her up from Jenna Wright's party. She had seemed so utterly lost.

The plan, that day, had been for Clara to stay at the party with Rita Mae right through to the end, when the two could return to the apartment together. A separate room was always laid on for mothers anyway, so Clara would be free to enjoy iced buns while Rita Mae mingled in the main hall. Their daughter had never liked walking alone after dark, spooked as she was by the bloodcurdling yowls and frequent alarms that emanated from the cell house.

Arriving home after his shift, though, Larry had found Clara in the kitchen, making fish pie. Asking why she had returned early – the party wasn't due to end for another three hours – he had received only muttered tutting and something vague about work and deadlines.

At 7.30 p.m., Larry had therefore started the trudge up the hill, keen to collect Rita Mae and get home for dinner. As it was, he had spent almost a half-hour searching the Wrights' house before he found her. No one had seen Rita Mae since Clara left and Larry had had to pick his way through every cove of the ten-bedroom abode before tracking her down to the tiny second bathroom, right in the roof of the building.

Rita Mae had been sat in there for two hours, reading her way down the pile of *Vogue* magazines that Mrs Wright kept beside the toilet. Hearing her father's voice, she stuck her head around the door, aware that he might have company, not wanting to see anyone else, before venturing tentatively on to the landing. Standing there, her back hunched, Larry had sensed immediately why Rita Mae had gone into hiding. Her party dress – the outfit that doubled as her birthday gift – was hideous. Repulsive. Even with his scant fashion sense, he could see that it had been designed with something other than style in mind, some dated sense of propriety, making her as conspicuous as a Mormon at a

Hell's Angel rally. It had upset him, that second, to see his daughter like that. She couldn't have been less comfortable if clad in a coat of crawling ants.

And in that moment, too, Larry had caught a glimpse of himself, at the same age, standing amongst a bunch of boys in a Beverly Hills backyard, feeling equally uneasy. It hadn't been the clothes in his case – his mother had always ensured that he and Grady were dressed in the most stylish designs – but something about the happy camaraderie between the other boys. They were laughing about a girl in their class, a pixie-like blonde who had taken to wearing tight sweaters, and, while Larry smiled along with them, there had been something about the conversation that he just couldn't fathom. It was as if they were talking a second language and he was struggling to keep up, translating each word a beat or two after it was said. He wasn't like them, he'd realized, in one of those clumsy teenage epiphanies. He would never fit in.

Not that it mattered now, thought Larry. He gulped down some water. It was true, perhaps, that he might not have found his niche, but that didn't mean he would always be unhappy. It couldn't. Larry ran through his plans for the afternoon – he was due to pick up some new tools before discussing certain aspects of animal care with his work duty team. He had attempted this talk last week (a few of the cows seemed distinctly peaky) but Denny Clemens, the longest-standing member of his team, had cracked dumb jokes throughout, before treating the group to an astonishingly accurate array of animal noises. It had been funny, Larry smiled, no denying that. But he had a suspicion it had distracted the men.

Rita Mae was smiling at Clara. 'Great. Thank you for

picking this up. Thanks.' She started back into her bedroom, then shouted to her parents, 'Can I have a bath?'

'Of course you can,' said Larry, 'just don't use too much water.'

A couple of seconds later Rita Mae heard the front door slam.

Walking into the bathroom, she turned the taps on full and stacked her new magazines and movie annual on the floor. Granmaria always came through, she thought, staring into the bathroom mirror, pulling her hair tight against her scalp and imagining what she'd look like bald. She started to undress slowly now, avoiding her reflection, chary of her new curves, thinking about the trip that she had taken to the mainland, aged six, to visit Granmaria. She had stayed in that one-bedroom Orange County apartment for two weeks, almost the entire vacation spent indoors, Granmaria telling stories about early movies, silent movies, only venturing out when they had denuded their supplies of marshmallows and orange soda. They'd been joined most days by Great-great-aunt Consuela, a quiet, wizened woman, who lived a few doors down and had looked on affectionately as the two of them chattered, laughing through the babble and unintended quips.

Rita Mae had been fascinated by Granmaria's apartment – so dirty, cluttered, warm and intriguing. Around their feet had lain the forgotten remnants of a hundred meals, rotting foodstuff just distinguishable: a chewed and naked chicken wing or an old enchilada, wrapped tight in its mouldering fur. The corners of each room housed five-inch piles of dust, stacked neatly against the wall, small but budding structures that grew around lost clumps of her grandmother's hair. Then there were the bugs that came out after dark, a deftly tipped candle illuminating the silverfish, lice and cock-roaches before they scurried to a darker enclave. The mess seemed to upset Consuela, but, after months, years, of trying to control it, she had apparently accepted the dis-solution, aware that she could always go home.

It was from amongst all this mess that Maria had dug out her movie memorabilia – film posters, ashtrays, ticket stubs, magazines, advertisements and autographs – strewn across the floor. Layer upon layer of unexpected finds.

At the bottom of the drunken stacks were endless photos of Granmaria, caught in her late-teens, before Clara had been born, striking a host of different poses. Here she was in a flimsy silk halterneck, impractically long cigarette holder in hand, draped over a chaise longue. Here again with Billy Haines, a huge star of the era, clutching at him and laugh-ing, Granmaria wearing a rather scandalous lace nightdress and pouting. Inscribed on that photo was a message from Haines and his autograph: 'To my desperate little hummingbird, always my love'. Here she was caught in a clinch with Gilbert Roland, the muscular young Mexican star, formerly a bullfighter, who had changed his name on arrival in Hollywood from the strictly unmanageable Luis Antonio Damaso de Alonso.

'Those were colourful days,' Granmaria had said, 'colourful times. Confusing, you know, and bittersweet. I heard that word the other day, and I thought it was perfect. Bittersweet.' Consuela had nodded gravely as Maria turned to Rita Mae, biting her lip. 'I was one of the most famous girls in Hollywood you know, Reet, one of the most requested, most popular girls. All the men wanted to star with me.'

Rita Mae had gazed, goggle-eyed, at her grandmother,

thrilled at this revelation. Granmaria had been a film star! A famous beauty! Arriving back on Las Focas she had asked her mother about this and Clara had laughed in that scornful way which suggested that no one was good and nothing was true. 'Your grandmother wasn't a film star, Rita Mae,' she had said, 'you mustn't believe her. Why do you think she lives in that tiny place?' Rita Mae had shrugged, throat clenching. Clara gave another laugh, before enunciating firmly, 'Because she was a dressmaker, Rita, a bottom-rung studio dressmaker. Not famous at all.'

Rita Mae knew now that this was at least partly true; she recognized that Maria Caesar had never been a film star. Still, she could never erase those photographs from her mind, those star-dusted stills, tinged with such authentic glamour. She realized that as a studio dressmaker Granmaria might have come into contact with actors occasionally, might even have posed for photographs with them, but she couldn't understand why the pictures would have been so professional. Where would Granmaria have found the money or the need for such expensive silks, such beautiful clothes?

Given these anomalies, Rita Mae bowed to both her mother and her grandmother. Before Clara she would concede that Maria Caesar had never been a star, had never been famous or important or fêted. And in her letters to Granmaria she would go along with the ruse, asking about the well-known men she had met and the beautiful women she had befriended. Somehow, she had found, her grandmother always had an answer to her questions, some detailed snip of information that revealed inside knowledge. There was something to her stories. Rita Mae just knew it.

The boiling water lapped playfully at the sides of the bath as Rita Mae stepped in. Glancing over at the magazines, anxious to savour them slowly, to hold off for a while, she saw her hand moving (as if under another authority), plucking one from the top of the pile. Oh well, she thought, surveying the cover closely and then turning to the first page. Some things were just too tempting.

The magazines that Maria Caesar sent were glamorous, exciting, sometimes a little sleazy, but nearly always inspiring. This month *Movieland* magazine was running a special 'modern homes' issue, showcasing everything from movie star mansions to bungalows in the California suburbs. There, on the first double-page spread, were Stewart Granger and his wife, Jean Simmons, staring out from their recently acquired New Mexico ranch. The caption mentioned that they'd just had a baby daughter – Tracy – but there was no sign of this familial addition, only a small Pekinese dog on Simmons's lap. The baby was probably too messy, thought Rita Mae. You wouldn't want vomit on that green shag rug.

The suburban show homes were no less enticing. It seemed that the trend now was for each room to have a theme – the Space Age, Wild West, Hawaiian classic – that could be carried through the interior design down to the very last detail. Rita Mae loved the rocket ship light fixtures of one dream home, the curved plastic armchairs and sheer glass walls. Flipping the page she came to another fantasy paradise of wood-slatted swing doors, large stuffed animals and wagon wheels propped decoratively against the fireplace. However much she turned the page back and forth, she just couldn't decide which style she liked best.

It was as if, she thought, the whole of California was a

film set. Even the suburban enclaves, places which had risen up recently from the dust, seemed infused with a sense of make believe. Disneyland might have set up shop in Anaheim, but Rita Mae could see Walt's mighty vision spreading throughout the state. The mayhem of his cartoon animals was cropping up in every sitting room, a riot of colour, optimism and freedom, gambolling across the walls.

A piercing note started screaming from the cell house, across the island and through the officers' quarters. Pitched perilously high (sharp enough to pop an eardrum), Rita Mae nonetheless ignored it.

Slightly breathless, she ducked beneath the water, the noise pulsating up through the base of the bath. She just wanted to be on the mainland, she thought, somewhere she could study acting, singing and dancing without the aid of a correspondence course, plucked from the small ads in *Confidential*. Splashing up out of the water, hair thoroughly wet, she reached for her *Film World Annual*, propping it in the corner of the bath and placing her hands over her ears. Scanning the star profiles she searched for clues on how to make it, ideas for breaking through.

It was an exercise in frustration. Almost all of the actresses that Rita Mae admired seemed to have been established by their mid-teens. Leslie Caron, for instance, had been dancing solo roles, major solo roles, for a Parisian ballet company at age fifteen. Sophia Loren had been crowned 'Princess of the Naples Sea' in a beauty contest, age fourteen. Brigitte Bardot had been dancing and modelling before she even hit those difficult adolescent years.

They were all so lucky, thought Rita Mae, as the noise grew louder and her hands pressed more painfully against her head. She had wanted to take ballet classes ever since she'd first seen *The Red Shoes*. Smacking a hand against the water, Rita Mae watched as drops sprayed messily across the smiling faces of Shelley Winters and her husband, Anthony Franciosa. They didn't have any proper dance classes on Las Focas, none at all. Just Mrs Spagnola, a sixty-year-old spinster who dressed in a brown leotard and ordered them to imitate flowers. Rita Mae had been mimicking a just-budding violet in music and movement classes for ten years now, and she found it difficult, at this stage, to muster much motivation. How would a violet feel? What would the arc of its day be like? How would it respond to sun or rain? These were the questions that needed to be answered if she was to give a good performance, but she found no answers forthcoming. She had repeated the exercise too often to dredge any real inspiration. Moira Shearer would never have put up with it.

Lying back in the bath, ears just beneath the water, she began playing out an interview in her head. It was the Oscar ceremony, 1960, and Rita Mae was posing on the red carpet, the hotly tipped Best Actress nominee.

'So how does it feel to be the most beautiful actress in Hollywood?' she asked herself, smiling slightly. 'Oh,' Rita Mae answered, modest to a fault and giggling, 'that's simply not true. There are a lot of gorgeous lady actresses out there who are also very talented, and anyway,' she wrapped a strand of hair winsomely around her finger, 'I've always hoped to be recognized for my intellect rather than my looks.'

The siren screeched louder, a hard, driving wail. 'But do you think that your performance in,' she paused to think of an appropriate title, '*Ring of Fire* will come to be seen as your defining role? Is there any way that you can top such an elegant, funny, exciting, virtuoso,' she paused to think of more ecstatic adjectives, 'intelligent, subtle, musically gifted and vibrant characterization?'

She would sigh at that point, thought Rita Mae, sigh and say, 'Of course. When I took the role of Miss Bernadette, she was merely a supporting character in the drama, part of the subplot about the stolen necklace.' The interviewer would nod knowingly. 'But after seeing me perform in the first morning's rushes Mr De Mille just couldn't avoid the rogue pull of fate.' Rita Mae rammed a finger in each ear. 'He simply had to make Miss Bernadette the lead, even if that meant changing the whole script from the first page to the last.' She paused again. 'Which, naturally, it did.'

As the siren ratcheted up to its highest level, the note reverberating through the ceiling, papery walls throbbing, Rita Mae finally stood up. Stepping out of the bath, not bothering with a towel, she dripped through to the kitchen. The island regulations stated that all residents must lock their doors and windows when the riot alarm sounded, before pulling their curtains closed.

Standing by the door, naked, tugging at the heavy deadbolt her father had installed, Rita Mae wondered what it would be like if a prisoner burst in. The thought wasn't entirely unappealing.

Chapter Five

Downtown Los Angeles, 1923

'Consuela, Consuela, I'm going out.' Maria Caesar, long-limbed and puppyish, clad in just her greying underwear, bounded into the fuggy darkness of her Aunt Consuela's room, which sat below the ramshackle apartment she shared with her father. Standing before her aunt, hands on hips, Maria flashed her widest smile, the one her family suspected could have changed the politics of the ugliest tyrant (even Porfirio Diaz, Mexico's erstwhile leader).

'Consuela darling,' Maria's voice rose a few octaves as she wrapped a strand of hair around her finger. Her aunt squinted back, suspicious and amused.

'What is it, darling Maria?'

'Well, Consuela.' She paused. 'Well, you know I'm a very good niece?' Her aunt stayed silent, reserving judgment. 'Well. I wondered whether I might borrow that skirt you made last week.' Maria flashed her grin again, this time even wider, lips wet, teeth glinting. 'The one that looks so good on me.'

Consuela's smile dropped. Frowning, she glanced at her lap. 'No, no. You know that it's not my skirt, Maria. I'm sorry.' She set to work again on the bilious green dress she was embroidering. 'That skirt's part of the order, part of the contract. It belongs to someone else. What happens if you get it dirty, or it tears? I'll have to make another. I have too much to do already. I can't deal with that.'

Maria laughed. 'Consuela, Consuela, my favourite woman in all the world.' She perched on the arm of her aunt's chair and reached down to stroke Consuela's soft belly. 'I'd be so careful. You know how careful I can be.' Her aunt gave a snort. 'I can be careful,' laughed Maria in mock affront. 'I can be as good and as clean as a cat.' She stood up again and began wheeling round the tiny room, its walls allowing little more than the opportunity to turn on the spot, a perfectly balanced spinning top. 'I'd treat that skirt so well, and if anything did happen – which it wouldn't – I'd make a new one for the order myself, and pay for the material too.'

Consuela sighed and laughed as she watched Maria twirl. Her niece had grown into the most expert, alluring flirt she'd ever known, her smile inviting everyone she met, male or female, to speak to her. It was almost a privilege to watch Maria as she drew people into her confidence with her artless enthusiasm and easy laughter, not to mention the dance steps that she would sometimes pad through, silent and focused, mid-conversation. There was nothing particularly calculated about her flirting, nothing vampish or affected, it was just a natural response, as simple as the throb of tears. Consuela placed her sewing on the floor and stood up. Reaching out for Maria she held her niece still.

'All right,' said Consuela. Maria's eyes were blank, her head obviously still spinning. 'All right. You can borrow the skirt.'

Maria shook her hair wildly, as if freeing herself from a

trance. 'Yes!' she said, wrapping her arms around Consuela. 'Thank you, Aunt, thank you.' She crossed to the corner of the room and began sifting through a pile of neatly folded clothes. 'You won't regret this, Consuela. I'll help you out so much with the order this next week, I promise.' She threw her arms rapturously into the air. 'It'll amaze you. I'll be like a whirlwind. A tornado! I'll see if I can change my hours at the farm and come home a little earlier so we can get more done in the daylight. It'll be over in no time.'

Finding the bright red skirt, she kissed her aunt, 'Thank you, Consuela, beautiful, beautiful,' and ran upstairs to her room. There, she sat on her sunken mattress and held the garment at arm's length. She felt the ache of a smile. It was going to look perfect, she decided. With a quick, puttering gasp of approval, Maria set about getting dressed.

Just as she was preparing to leave, staring into a small spotted square of glass and pinching zealously at her cheeks, Maria heard the scratch of the door downstairs, and a hushed conversation between her father and Consuela. She had been hoping to escape the house before Toribio arrived home from work, knowing that he would be in a leaden mood after a shift that had stretched right through from yesterday morning. It was no use trying to avoid him now, though. Unless she left the house in the next ten minutes she would miss the start of the show. Maria swept up her bag and headed for the stairs.

'Maria.' Toribio was on his way, feet heavy on the half-collapsed steps. 'Maria, get back to your room.' Looking up he could see her standing above him, poured into a red skirt, the muscular shadow of her legs just visible through the fabric. 'Back to your room,' he said more urgently now, hands flapping. 'I want to talk to you.'

'Papa, can we talk later?' Maria stood on one leg, rubbing her other foot comfortingly against her calf. 'If I don't get out I'll miss the showing. It starts at one.'

'I don't care about the movie,' growled Toribio. 'I don't want you going out.' Arriving at the top of the stairs he took Maria's arm and led her forcibly to the bedroom, pushing her on to the mattress. 'I don't want you going out like that, Maria, going uptown in those clothes. You'll attract all kinds of trouble. You're staying here this afternoon,' he said, 'and helping Consuela with the contract. You know she has too much work to do by herself. You know you're being selfish.'

'But, Papa,' her lashes were like hummingbird wings, 'I've been helping Consuela all week. You can ask her if you want. And I stayed home last weekend to help her too. I've done five or six skirts,' Maria paused, 'and a dress. Don't I deserve just one afternoon for myself? It's another ten days before I have time off from the farm.'

'I don't care.' Toribio was determined not to be swayed, won over by his estimable daughter. 'We all have to work hard, you know that. I'm ashamed of you – ignoring your aunt's needs like this. How do you think she feels?'

Maria shrugged, wide eyed. 'She seemed quite happy when I spoke to her. She didn't seem angry.'

'Well,' Toribio puffed, not sure what to say. Consuela wasn't angry, that was true, she was advancing quite well with the latest contract, but, since starting this argument, he was keen to defend his main strand of attack. 'She might not have seemed angry, but that's only because she's more polite than you, Maria Caesar.' He took a step backwards, his bulk filling the doorway. 'Consuela isn't the type of woman who would desert her family at a time of need –

she'd work on regardless. Maybe I should have given her more of a say in your upbringing.'

Maria grimaced and stood up. 'Consuela did raise me, Papa, if you remember, so I guess my nasty habits just come naturally.' Walking towards the door, she tried to squeeze past. 'I'm going to the movie now.'

Toribio grabbed at Maria's wrists. 'You'll do what I say.' He tried to throw her on to the bed again, but she wrenched away.

'I'm going out, Papa, and that's it.' Maria began running, ankles buckling on the uneven steps. 'You can't keep me in.'

Toribio considered heading after his daughter, seizing her around the waist and carrying her back. After a triple work shift spent grovelling on his knees, though, affixing a new train track (just a snatch of sleep in the darkest hours, then up again, eyes hovering an inch above the ground), the prospect was too exhausting. He kneeled down on her mattress and stretched out. It wasn't that he didn't want his daughter to have fun, he thought, and he certainly didn't relish these arguments. It was just that the prospect of Maria Caesar, his mane-haired, coltish daughter, set loose amidst all those American men scared him rigid. There was a danger there, he thought, a threat that she was too young to notice.

Arriving in the US seven years before, Toribio had been almost as guileless and open as his daughter was now, optimistic, his bitterness left at the border pass, ready to spar with any and all of the opportunities that might present themselves. He knew, of course, that he would have a lowly start, employed for a time as an unskilled labourer, but the thought hadn't seemed too worrying. It was all part of the process, the usual migratory pattern. As Toribio saw it, within five years he should (by dint of his education and experience) have risen to a management position somewhere, a career that involved at least some precision and literacy. Within a decade, he hoped, he might have started his own business. Perhaps another farm (LA County was stock-full of fields), perhaps something entirely new. Whatever the case, Toribio had felt hopeful.

Consumed by these plans, he had worked hard from the start, not just in his job as a trackman, but on the much more difficult task of becoming an American. Changing his name was the first gesture and he had followed this with a concerted effort to learn the language, to assimilate his new culture. Sitting in the public trolley car with Maria back in those first days, he would rap her lightly on the arm if she spoke in her native tongue and demand that she practise her English. 'This country has welcomed us,' he would whisper. 'It has given us shelter, and the least we can do is honour that.'

He could understand, though, why his daughter felt less than grateful towards her new home. They had lived in relative poverty during their last year in Mexico, of course, were used to hardship, but that had somehow been different. It had been an equal kind of poverty, he thought now, the boot-boiling straits shared alike. Here, he and his family seemed to exist in an isolated cesspool, their fellow citizens tiptoeing around the perimeter of their lives, careful not to come too close, scared by the desperation, worried it might afflict them.

Crossing into El Paso, Toribio's image of Los Angeles had been of a place verdant and fertile, populous of crops rather than people. It hadn't taken long after arriving in the barrio, though, for him to realize his mistake. The washing facilities were the first clue: close to thirty people sharing a pair of water hydrants and a toilet. Then there was the city authority's blind eye: no garbage collection, the roads just dust tracks, potholed and dangerous for all but the hardiest vehicles. Some days, returning from work, he had seen young neighbourhood children, clutching sticks or throwing a threadbare ball, playing within a steady stream of sewage. It was a sight that made him gag. He had aimed to escape the chicken shit.

And the situation was made worse, of course, by the proximity of dollars, the riches that were spreading so quickly through this jazz-hungry city, the communion of cash that seemed to shout its gospel from every rooftop and storefront. The Los Angeles he stared in upon was a boomtown, filling up with streams of immigrants, more accepted and appreciated than him, flivver emigrants they called them, the hoe and hair shirt mid-westerners who arrived in their Ford Model Ts and were immediately transformed into walking, talking advertisements for the city. He would hear them as he trawled the streets, passing small groups as they stood, jabbering together, heads bowed intently, extolling the virtues of this city, lauding its energy and colour, the bright, pulsating strength of its economy which had officially seen it marked as a 'white spot' on the national map, a place of burning, unprecedented growth.

These newcomers, with their tobacco-spit enthusiasm, were supported by those other street-corner preachers, the local realtors, who seemed to have purchased every lima bean field in the state, all ready for their eager customers to snap up for a suitably astonishing profit. There they stood, with pencil moustaches and white-as-a-die spats, hollering and preaching on each commercial street, handing out leaflets, encouraging the hordes to come visit their office, to inspect the proposed site of their 'fabulous new home', enjoy a prize ham lunch before a private meeting with the 'closer' (otherwise known as 'thumbscrewer-in-chief'). These dapper, almost delinquent men were always quick to retract their hand when they saw Toribio approach and, although he knew why, he couldn't resist picking a flyer up off the sidewalk one day to have his thoughts confirmed.

'DON'T pause another MOMENT,' the flyer said (the advertisers much given to random capitals). 'You and I BOTH KNOW that these lots – these pick of the bunch lots – will BE GONE SOON. Act now, don't BE a fool. Buy WHERE profits are guaranteed. All values up and UP. Each lot comes COMPLETE with oil and mineral RIGHTS.' And then, at the close, in a smaller typeface, not a hint of capitalization: 'These lots are restricted purely to purchasers of the white race.'

It had been in that second, standing motionless in the street, picking carefully over those words, the blur of the city passing on and around him, that the reality had hit Toribio. This place wasn't for him, he thought, it had nothing to do with him. While its other citizens strode at ease, embroiling themselves in the drama of this town, the sudden possibilities, the get-rich-quick schemes with their slew of coinage, money glittering and tumbling through the air, as they held up their hands, dancing, singing, their lives one great Ziegfield set piece to enjoy and enjoy and enjoy, he and his compañeros were just their captive audience. That was their role.

Striding towards the Red Car stop that would transport her to Hollywood, Maria was also thinking about their living conditions, the constraints and cruelties of the barrio.

Although she loved living with her rabble of cousins, loved the powdery calm of her Aunt Consuela, Maria had never grown used to the claustrophobia of the place and the smell, the stench of too many people packed into a space, of too few washing facilities, of too much time spent working, scrubbing, picking around for a living. Adding to the stink were the animals that bred through those loose-defined streets – the chickens, goats, occasional sheep. Barely a space for them, they were sometimes tethered to a fence post for days, mess piling up, untended. Most were mangy, their coats moulting whether it was the season or not, and they would mew through the night for food. Sometimes, when their keening kept her awake, Maria would imagine creeping out and untying each and every one of them. She would overturn the chickens' cage, push the goats out on their way.

It infuriated Maria that her father would try to trap her in the barrio, tether her there too, amongst the smells, the laden clotheslines and weather-beaten buildings. It wasn't as though she was spending his money when she went out. She was fifteen now, and had been working long hours as a fruit picker ever since leaving school two years ago. The farmer who employed her had never taken on a woman before, protesting that they had neither the strength nor the sense to cope (born ugly, he was a committed misogynist), but Maria had convinced him that she would toil twice as hard as the other obreros, and she had kept her word. It was bone- and mind-rotting work, and the only way that she could bear the boredom of it all, the twinge of existential misery as the next ripened blueberry hove into view, was to focus on her plans for the coming day off.

This usually involved a trip to Hollywood and a visit to

one of the iridescent, often turreted, picture palaces that had shot up. Maria couldn't understand why these excursions bothered her father (they seemed so blameless) but there was no ignoring his response. If she even made mention of a movie the blood would begin stealing up his neck, rising like a water level in flood season, until his whole face was engorged. It was a sight that suggested he might one day simply burst, popping from his skin just as satisfyingly as one of those berries.

In truth, it wasn't the movies that bothered Toribio – although he couldn't grasp their appeal himself – but the people who frequented them. Maria tended to visit the picture palaces alone, and Toribio knew enough about his daughter's unsuspecting effect on men to imagine the stares and attention she must receive. During the years that they had spent in the US, Toribio had become more and more suspicious of American men, paranoid of their proclivities. He had seen these folk looking at Maria, their eyes crawling grubbily over her body as she sashayed along the street, and he could sense their desire curdling with contempt. To these men, Toribio felt sure, Mexican women, particularly young Mexican women, were essentially whores. He had overheard their comments, seen their type. He just wanted his daughter to be safe. He just wanted to free himself from the live ache of tension that welled whenever she stepped out.

As far as Maria was concerned, though, her father was just flexing his muscles, aping the other men in the barrio with their batter of machismo, their delusion that they were still in Mexico, that they could fall back on the old ways and keep their women wed to the home. Her father hadn't always been so uptight and old-fashioned – she could remember the days as a kid when, despite the chaos around him, Toribio would bounce her on his knee and tell stories about the monsters of the Sierra Madre. Since then, it was as if a layer of bone-hard cynicism had calcified around him. Intransigent but growing, there seemed no way to break through.

Arriving on Hollywood Boulevard, with its lights and bustle, all thoughts of her father were pushed aside. The whole city was awash with building permits at the moment, crews swarming suddenly to a site, throwing up a structure and moving on. Nowhere, though, was this insouciant building work more obvious than Hollywood Bull. Maria came out here at least once a month, and each time there seemed to be a new crop of restaurants, gaming and dance halls, bars and hotels, punctuated by the occasional shocking spire of a church.

Up ahead loomed the newest picture palace, so brilliant and gargantuan that Maria reared back. The discovery of Tutankhamen's tomb had lent an Egyptian theme, and the designer had decided that the building should reflect every sign and symbol of that country that he could muster. Around the courtyard stood massive columns, four foot wide, while hieroglyphs were etched frantically, indecipherably over the walls. Each detail spoke of life and grandeur and surplus: tropical plants so large that they seemed ready to burst complete from their pots and go running, wild-limbed, down the boulevard; a fountain that sprang disarmingly alive, soaking unwitting guests. Guarding the entrance were two twenty-foot sphinxes, their dog-like faces utterly unforgiving. Staring at their blank, stone-cast eyes, trying to think who they resembled, Maria thought seriously about heading to another theatre nearby which sported a simple front.

She had agreed to meet a friend here, though, so stood her ground. Venezia lived a few doors up in the barrio and had been working at the theatre since it opened, auditioning successfully for a job as an 'authentic Egyptian serving girl', taking customers' tickets and putting on a short dance show with her fellow employees just before the main feature. The proprietor had apparently been very impressed with her 'Egyptian' looks, despite her birthplace in the Yucatan valley. She had shown Maria her costume a few nights before – a small blue sheet that she swathed loosely around her shoulders and hips, paired with a glistening headdress – and urged her to come and see the theatre. 'It's like a palace,' she'd breathed, 'all gold inside. The ticket people can sometimes be nasty about letting Mexican kids in, but I should be able to smuggle you past. Just meet me outside, and I'll make sure there's no trouble.'

Edging towards the entrance now, Maria caught sight of Venezia swaying up to a male customer, bowing slightly and gesturing at the lobby. The man followed the curve of her arm appreciatively. Waiting for him to move on, Maria skipped over to her friend, who was facing the entrance. 'Venezia,' she said, her voice low. 'Venezia.'

'Maria!' Turning, her friend beamed back at her. She spoke more quietly. 'I'm so glad you came. I was thinking you might be too nervous. You sounded kinda nervous.'

'No, no. I'm fine.'

Venezia grabbed Maria's hand and led her into the cavernous, velvet-lined lobby. It really was like a tomb, thought Maria. 'I can't really talk now,' said Venezia, 'but I got you a ticket.'

'I have some money.'

'Don't worry about it.' She slipped Maria the piece of

card. 'I didn't want you to get stopped at the counter. They sometimes make people leave.'

Maria looked down.

'But it's gonna be great. You'll have a great time. I love the movie. Anyway,' Venezia caught sight of an Anglo couple, the woman dripping diamonds, the man clearly confused, 'I have to go and help over there. If you go up to that door,' she pointed to another girl, 'Luz'll help. I've told her to expect you.'

With a nod, Maria walked up the stairs and passed into the theatre. Standing there, before her seat, she was amazed to find that the place fit even Venezia's hyperbolic description. It was more like a temple than a movie house, she thought now, sinking down slowly, taking in the bursts of gold-plating, the dazzling patterns that sprang out around the screen, or rather, bowed down to it, all of this sheen, this lustre, stooping in reverence to the movie itself.

The next few hours passed in a snap: a short dance number by the Egyptian girls followed by the main feature. The first movie to be shown at this theatre was almost as overblown as the building – certainly one of the longest Maria had seen. Cecil B De Mille's *The Ten Commandments* had garnered a glowing review in *Motion Picture Weekly*, and now she could see why. Maria gulped audibly as the Red Sea parted (the woman beside her offered a kerchief) and was engrossed by the rapacious behaviour of Nita Naldi. At five-minute intervals she found herself blinking wildly, almost unable to cope with the reflective glare of her surroundings.

With the close of the movie, Maria stumbled back into the courtyard, her legs nearly crumpling beneath her. She often felt a little disorientated on emerging from a theatre, a reaction to the sudden brightness and heat she supposed, but she had never experienced this before. Leaning on one of the columns, she waited as the crowd fanned around her. It would take a few minutes for her to catch her breath, she thought, and it seemed prudent to stay here until then, just in case her legs failed.

As the moviegoers dispersed, though, Maria still slightly breathless, she felt a hand close firmly around her wrist. Scared to look up for a second, she figured that it must be Toribio, still angry, still unreasonable, come out to Hollywood to track her down and, quite literally, drag her home. Head remaining bowed, she realized that this didn't make sense – she hadn't told her father where she was going and the thought of him here, now, was just too incongruous. In his overalls and work boots he would stand out so much amidst this crowd of smartly dressed white folk that she felt sure she would have noticed him approaching. And besides: he had much hairier hands.

More frightened, she glanced up to see a man in his late-twenties, hair brilliantined to his skull. Hoping that Venezia might come out, remembering she'd gone home, Maria struggled to pull her hand away, skin twisting and bruising beneath the man's grip. When it became clear that he wasn't going to let go, she kicked him lightly.

'Get off.'

The man smiled, released her and dropped to his knees to brush the dust from his trousers. 'Hey,' he said, 'not so violent, OK?' His eyes wrinkled with amusement as he stared up at Maria. 'I just thought you could use some support. You looked like you were about to collapse there for a second, lady. I was worried.'

He stood up and stuck out a hand. Maria shook it gingerly. The man leaned towards her. 'There, that's better, isn't it? We're friends now. I didn't mean to scare you.' He paused. 'What's your name?'

'Why do you want to know?'

'Geez, you're defensive, aren't you? I just thought, since we're talking, it might be worth knowing each other's name.'

Maria stared at him. Could he be an undercover cop, she thought, come to bust any Mexican audacious enough to visit this theatre? Staring at his hair, she thought it unlikely. 'I'm Maria,' she said, 'Maria Caesar.'

The man nodded, obviously satisfied. 'Maria Caesar, eh? What a great name. You sound like a movie star already.' He put an arm around her shoulder and began leading her away from the theatre. 'My name's Max, Max Edelson.'

Maria pulled away. 'What do you want, Mr Edelson?'

He laughed. 'Oh, Maria, look, don't worry. It's nothing bad.' Sighing, he reached for some papers in his pocket, each of them headed with the crest of Pantheon Pictures, one of the biggest studios in Hollywood. 'I work for Pantheon, see. I'm a talent scout. They sent me here this afternoon to stake out the theatre, so to speak. I've been sitting in the Montmartre for an hour now, waiting for the film to end.' He smiled benignly and Maria could sense he was trying to win her over. 'They could have told me it was an epic, eh?'

She blushed, thoughts racing, and smiled back. 'That is a long time to wait.'

The man clapped his hands together. 'It sure is. I was thinking of packing up and leaving, but then the film ended and I saw you, see. And all that waiting was worth it. Maria,' he paused significantly, in what was clearly a staple of his routine, 'have you ever wanted to work in the movies?'

'Oh.' Maria's head went blank. Then she laughed just a little too loudly, slightly nauseous. 'You're joking of course, Mr Edelson. You shouldn't do this to a girl.'

Stopping on the sidewalk, he pulled Maria around to face him. 'I can let you take another look at the papers, Miss Caesar, any proof that you need of my work at Pantheon.' He paused, throwing her his softest smile. 'I know how odd this must seem to you, Maria, to be approached like this, but I promise it's real. You have a very lovely face.'

He started moving again, leading her towards a gleaming eggshell-blue car, a Stutz Bearcat. 'This is me,' he said, crossing to the driver's side. 'I don't know what you want to do, Maria, I mean, I suppose that I could take your address and visit you sometime at home.'

The thought of this man – in his perfect pinstripe suit, symmetrical creases pressed tight along each leg – entering the barrio, passing the pigs, the goats and the toilet blocks, was almost enough to make Maria smile. Instead, she shook her head firmly and stuttered, 'That might not be best.'

Max Edelson raised an eyebrow and smirked. 'Really?' He sighed. 'Well, I don't know what to do then, Miss Caesar. If I can't contact you then it's going to be difficult to set up an appointment, isn't it? I'd love you to meet the studio chief, James Crawfish. I think that would be a necessity.' He walked around the car to where she was standing and took her hand. 'Of course, if you had a few hours, I could always take you for a tour of the studios now. That wouldn't be a problem. We've got a dash or so more of daylight, and there'll certainly be a lot still happening on set. What do you think?'

Maria recalled what awaited her at home – the inevitable argument with Toribio, the shouted threats, a possible beating – and nodded shyly. With the money she'd saved on the movie there'd be no problem getting back. 'That sounds good,' she said.

'Excellent,' beamed Edelson. He reached over and opened the car door for her. 'Why don't you hop in?'

Setting off, Maria wedged her hands hard beneath her legs to still them. This couldn't be happening, she thought, it couldn't be this easy. She had read of stars being discovered at drugstores and nightclubs and tram stops, but still it seemed incredible. Too much. The studios were in Culver City, and, as he drove, Max Edelson chattered away about the recent success of Pantheon Pictures, its swift rise up the movie firmament, where it jostled for position with Metro and Famous Players-Lasky. 'I love working in movies,' he said, as Maria nodded politely, 'it's just so exciting. I think maybe you and I'll be kindred spirits in that respect, Miss Caesar. I think you'll love your work if you do choose to take our offer. Personally I think you'd be a fool to say no.'

They arrived then at the main studio building, modelled on a Grecian temple, a dazzling hotchpotch of marble and mouldings rising imposingly into the sky. 'This is where the boss works,' whispered Edelson. 'Crawfish has the biggest office I've ever seen – if you stand at one end you can barely make out the far wall.'

Maria didn't answer, sure that any comment would be rendered incomprehensible by the shaking in her jaw. Helping her out of the car, Edelson began to lead her past the office building to the studio lot behind.

'This is where it all happens,' he said, hand sweeping across the horizon. 'We have more than fifty acres here, Maria, more than fifty, and at any one time we're probably making,' he paused and looked up, his fingers tensing in turn, 'at least seven or eight pictures, sometimes more.' He pointed to his right where, in the middle distance, there stood the open box of a set, housing a huge imitation pirate ship. 'That's for the swashbuckler we're making at the moment, they're starting work next week I think.' He leaned down to Maria. 'You like swashbucklers, Miss Caesar?' She nodded. Edelson laughed. 'Well, that's good, 'cause so do we. This one that we're making at the moment, *King of the Pirates*, is about a rich American kid who runs off to join a pirate crew and ends up becoming their leader. It's going to be amazing, you'll see. We're using all the best technology, the fight scenes should be fantastic.'

He veered off to the left, leading Maria towards another set, this time what looked to be a romance movie, an actress surrounded by huge swathes of voluminous gauze. She was lying on a bed, sobbing artfully, holding her balled-up hands to her eyes every now and then, and tilting her wrists. As they drew near, the director hollered 'Cut!' and the actress (a woman Maria recognized as one of the biggest stars in Hollywood) immediately sat up and smiled, before leaning back on her elbow. Although she tried not to show it, Maria was shocked by the actress's appearance: ghoulish, almost repulsive. Rather than wearing normal make-up – in pinks and reds and whites – her skin was caked with a bright yellow foundation and her lips coloured brown. A circle of kohl a half-inch thick had been built up around her eyes so that they appeared punched and bruised.

Catching the expression on his charge's face, Edelson laughed. 'They don't look like that on screen, eh, Maria?' She shook her head. 'It's always a bit gruesome for people when they see that for the first time, I think. Their make-up's just done like that for the lights, though. It wouldn't look natural if they did it any other way, which is hard to believe, huh?'

It seemed that they were heading for a far corner of the lot, though Maria couldn't be sure. She wanted to ask Edelson, but she suspected that in the tight-throated excitement of it all he might have explained their destination already. She didn't want to look stupid. They carried on past a man-made swamp that was being used in a Southern epic, and a recently burned village set that had been filmed for the same picture. 'No expense spared,' said Edelson, 'no expense spared.'

As the sets thinned out and they neared the edge of it all Maria saw a house up ahead which she assumed to be another façade. It was quite an old-looking building, clad in dark slatted wood, faintly intimidating, perhaps the set for a horror picture. Coming within fifty metres of the house, though, Maria realized that it wasn't an artificially aged set. It looked well-populated.

'Is this another office building?' she said, her voice hushed with awe. 'Are you taking me to see someone?'

Max Edelson put his arm jovially around her shoulder and pulled her close, almost as if they were sweethearts. 'Not an office building, no, certainly not, but there is someone I'd like you to meet here.' Glancing down, he saw how frightened she was, and felt sorry for a second. 'Don't worry, darling, it'll be absolutely fine.'

Reaching the door he rapped sharply against the wood and looked at his watch. 'There should be someone in now,' he said, 'I think this is one of their busiest times.'

As he put his hand up to knock again, the door flew open, revealing a blousy-looking woman in her early thirties, hair the colour of cornfields. Breathless, she looked anxiously at Edelson and then at a clock on the wall behind her. 'Max, please tell me we don't have an appointment now. I'm sure it's not in the book.'

Edelson smiled. 'No, no, don't worry, Dora, I don't have anything arranged.' He pushed Maria forward a little as Dora looked her up and down. 'It's just that I've brought you a new girl.'

Chapter Six

The Pantheon Pictures brothel, Culver City, Los Angeles, 1927

'Pull the cord, pull the cord.'
    'We're ready, baby, come on.'
'What's hiding back there, Dora? You know we want skin.'

Clad in just a tailcoat, thick moustache and pink silk knickers, Dora peered out through the baying throng, gauging whether the fervour was growing or had peaked. It was the night of the brothel's monthly cross-dressing party, and this one was proving particularly popular, with three hundred dragged-up men having arrived already (set designers, lighting mechanics, assistant directors, bit-part actors). Right now they were crushed into the main hall, teeth bared, as Dora stood on the steps of a small stage constructed for just this occasion. As their voices rose, yapping and barking, she clung loosely to the curtain cord, determined to wait. As Mistress of Ceremonies, she thought, timing was all.

There was a surge towards the stage then, more men pushing into the room, and Dora saw bodies start to contort, gin and bourbon spilling, limbs seeming to bend in places where there sat no natural joints. With it finally impossible for anyone to stand square-shouldered in the crowd, she decided that it was time for the revelation, before a snap of bone spelled chaos. Raising her hand, Dora demanded hush. Decisive and imperious, she tugged at the cord.

There followed a collective gulp. Behind the curtain, completely naked, was Maria Caesar, sibylline and supine on a red chaise longue. Her back to the crowd, head turned to face them, she was – as just a few of the men noticed – completely expressionless.

It wasn't quite what had been expected (they had been hoping fervently, as always, for an orgy scene), but a smatter of applause and shouting signalled their approval.

Over the past few years it had become traditional for Dora (who, in a universe of luck and equality, might actually have been a film director) to style a tableau for her guests. She was always anxious to impress, keen to air her more high-flown sentiments, to raise both herself and her girls into the realms of art. Usually she would gather a large group to imitate a painting, often tending towards religious scenes culled from her Catholic youth. It was a preference that had led, in the past, to some ironic casting. Submarine Daisy, for instance (renowned for the way she went down), as Mary, mother of God.

To Dora's chagrin, however, the girls' taste for the tableau seemed firmly on the wane. She had bribed, cajoled and belittled them in an attempt to pose a group scene this month, but they had all refused. It was dull, they said, old-fashioned, protesting that they would rather dance for the guests or tell fortunes or learn a variety of astonishing magic tricks. The Indian fakir and entertainer Rajesh Shah was a regular at their parties, and some of the girls had silent, unrequited hopes of becoming his assistant, prancing about in a scanty costume on stage and allowing red hot pokers to be pushed through their flesh, pokers which would then emerge bloodless. Despite ideas of this ilk, though, Dora had been adamant – the tableau vivant was a tradition now, and, in the fickle world they inhabited (a world where girls were dishcloth-grey and discarded at twenty-five), she had always seen tradition as important, a muted antidote to the fleetingness of it all. And besides, dammit, it was fun.

Just as she had begun to despair, faced with the girls' sniping and scrapping, Dora realized that she had failed to ask her most talented artist, the girl who most closely followed the lines of an Old Master. On being approached, Maria had agreed at once, and, after some contemplation, Dora had suggested that perhaps – with her long, sinuous back and peerless skin – she might like to imitate Ingres's *The Grand Odalisque*. She didn't have the skin tone or hair colour for it, of course, thought Dora, but that was a mere detail. Unacquainted with the work, Maria had nonetheless smiled graciously. It sounded wonderful, she told Dora; she was sure that it would be a success.

The truth was that Maria didn't much care about the subject matter of the tableau – it made no difference if she was representing Mary Magdalene, Joan of Arc or one of Breughel's trolls. What she enjoyed was the shelter of the stage. Up there, cut off from the partygoers, completely immobile, Maria could escape the incursions of brothel life: the prodding and poking, wetness and stink. On stage she was visible but off-limits, her boundaries distinct as the chalked white outline of a murder victim.

It helped, of course, that Maria had such a talent for

stillness. The girls who objected most viciously to the tableau were those who couldn't stop moving, the junkies whose bodies pulsed with activity, hands shaking, hearts springing punchily through sunken chests. Maria, though, she could pose for hours. Faced with a crowd of men like this, her eyes, unblinking, would start to glaze over, growing cold, dusty and hard. Next, she had found, her hearing would fold, peripheral noises fading first, before all sounds were eventually obliterated. Finally, then, her muscles would freeze, until she could feel almost nothing.

It was at this point, when it had all slipped silently away, her faculties shut down and forgotten, that the displacement occurred. During the last year Maria had realized that after a period of silence and stillness – five minutes, perhaps ten – she was able to break free from her body and go flying above the crowd, passing over their heads like an avenging angel, spitting in their drinks, eavesdropping their conversations, kicking devilishly at their fat old faces, while they failed to see or hear a thing.

She could feel this process starting up now, the loss of each sense in turn, her view of the crowd quickly fading, until her eyes fell on blackness. It was going, she thought – her body, her flesh – she was leaving it all behind. Daze falling deeper, she could feel that perfect moment approaching, the severance padding nearer, steadily, surely. There was no noise, she realized dreamily, the crowing and boasting and bellowing had drifted off, toppling into a distant abyss. It would all be gone, she thought, all of it. And her limbs were numbing, she had no sense of them, where they were, what they were doing. All gone. Everything, she felt, was slipping away, sliding. And then. It was coming. She knew it, knew it. And then. There it was.

The detachment was especially strong this time and Maria wondered happily whether she would ever return to her body. Floating up to the ceiling, untrammelled, free, she saw the ragtag throng that had gathered that evening. As usual the men had raided the Pantheon warehouse, emerging, in these pre-Production Code days, with pieces from films noted more for their nudity than costumes. She could see chest hair sprout above plunging necklines, towering wigs beginning to list. There were men clad in body stockings, transparent save a few coloured sequins, genitals straining uninvitingly at the mesh, while others wore eye masks, aping von Stroheim's starlets. One man flaunted false eyelashes, expertly crafted from human hair, attached to a string that made them flutter. 'Max,' he kept saying, 'Max made them for me.'

Maria assumed he meant Mr Factor.

There were fat men in drop-waist dresses, their bellies straining against the ribbon trim. Thin men in corsetry, ribs poking above their outfits, vying for attention with the whalebone.

And amidst all these were the girls, some of them her friends, dressed in suit jackets and monocles, faces stained white. Directly below her stood Missy, the prettiest of them all when she had first arrived, wrapping a length of rubber hose around her arm, a man with collapsed cheeks on hand to assist. All of the girls were laughing, mouths tonsil-wide, but their happiness had a strange timbre. It was tinny, she thought. That was it.

Maria hovered there, taking in the scene, wondering how long she could sustain this separation. Looking back at her body, frozen and empty on stage, she was surprised by how pretty it looked, how muscled and perfect. In her years at the brothel, Maria had come to hate the touch of skin, had come to view all bodies, including her own, as lumpen tracts, undistinguished and amorphous, a voluble part of the great human orgy, where bodies melted together, limitless and undefined, a slurry soup of compound flesh from which nothing could ever be saved or enjoyed, from which nothing good could come. She had lost her body to that, she thought, had gone under within months, subsumed by the corporeality of it all. There had seemed no escape then. The world had collapsed. Just flesh and holes and fluids.

Maybe this was it, she thought, maybe she could stay up here for ever, out of it all, up and away. Floating around the room, she swooped to poke one of her clients in the belly, as he chattered on, oblivious. Perhaps there would be a bruise, she thought happily. Drifting out of the window, Maria began sailing across the back lot, passing the fire department and the props room, ebbing towards the costume shed. If someone had left a window open, she thought, then she could squeeze right in there and peek through the racks, see what outfits they were tailoring, whether the costumes for that latest romance were really as ornate as rumoured.

Just then though, suddenly as it had started, Maria found herself back inside her body, the two halves snapping definitively together. She was disappointed, of course, but accepting. The dislocation was a new thing, she thought, a gifted experience, and its boundaries were to be respected. It could only be held for a short while so far, but over time, given concentration, maybe it would develop.

Arriving at the brothel four years earlier, Maria could never have foreseen this desire, strange as it was, to float out and away from her body. Back then, the worst excesses of brothel life, the feral men and their scatological demands, had been kept well hidden and she had been sold this work as something quite different: a passport to the screen, to the Vaseline haze of the lens. She had wanted to be like the starlets she saw posing on the back lot, girls who had attained the intangible sheen of celebrity, their skin seeming bathed, whether on set or off, in the golden pool of the spotlight. She would watch these girls sometimes, being fussed over by costumiers, and wonder what penalty pertained to stealing their discarded clothes, their own outfits, and wearing them for a time. While the starlets were in character before the cameras, thought Maria, their own personas were left oddly vacant and unwanted on the side of the stage. If only she could take on that role for a few hours, it might be enough to sate her.

The brothel managers knew of this yearning, typical as it was of all the girls they lured here. They knew, too, that each of the girls had to be eased into brothel life, treated to handsome clients in their first month, convinced that this world offered prospects. To this end new girls were always treated to exquisite clothes – chantilly dresses and chiffon knickers – and spirited away to some empty set, where they would pose for a series of glamorous photos. It was only after that that they would face their first trick, usually an actor. Exposure to celebrity, it was assumed, would be enough to keep them there awhile, a couple of years at least, until cynicism set in, lining their face and making them immediately redundant.

In Maria's case, her first string of dates had been with the musical star Dancer Billy, who, as his name suggested, was perhaps the most elegant hoofer in Hollywood. These dates had been set up under the orders of James Crawfish, the studio head, who was keen for Dancer Billy to be seen around LA with a succession of beautiful women. Pantheon's biggest male star, it seemed, was a former rent boy and voracious homosexual, who was loath to give up the libidinal antics of his youth. The only difference now was that he did it for free.

Crawfish didn't much care about his stars' proclivities, so long as they were discreet. When word reached him that Billy had propositioned a well-known screenwriter, quite openly, in the restroom of the Ambassador Hotel, Crawfish had been incandescent. Calling Dancer Billy into his office, he had sat him down and given him an ultimatum: sex or the movies. Sitting on his hands, fingers crossed, Billy had apparently plumped for his career.

Hence those nights out with Maria. Each date being charged to the studio, Dancer Billy had squired his innocent young companion gleefully around town, exclaiming merrily at her dresses and making a great show of pecking her on the cheek. He liked the girl, he really did – she was cut-glass pretty, with a naivety and charm that only made her more interesting. They had partied until dawn at the Coconut Grove, sipping Martinis between ramshackle tangos (Maria had never danced formally before. Unfortunately, it showed). They had sucked up noodles noisily at the Chinese Garden, a private members' club and restaurant, Billy pointing out Hollywood dignitaries, as Maria nodded, her eyes bulging froggily.

And then, after three weeks (in which Maria hadn't once been asked for sex), the dates had abruptly stopped. Keeping a close eye on his male lead, Crawfish had told Dancer Billy to move on to another escort, dictating that he would prove his virility by sporting a new girl each month. Maria still saw him on the lot occasionally, and he was always friendly, often stopping the routine he was preparing and bounding over, kissing her on both cheeks and heading back. Had he been her main client she would have been thrilled.

It was after the departure of Dancer Billy, though, that reality had set in. Like the other girls, most of them teenagers, Maria was still utterly entranced by the glamour of the movies, still sometimes dreamed that a Pantheon star – one of those magical, gilded creatures – would drop by the brothel and sweep her away, insisting she move to his Malibu mansion (a red-tiled villa, Mediterranean-style, with cypress trees shooting up across the lawn) before showering her with expensive trinkets. The truth, however, was that the vast majority of her tricks were crew members. Over the years Maria had been forced to bed a series of sweaty cameramen, obese cinematographers, buck-toothed lighting specialists and unkempt construction workers. Men with weeping sores and hairy backs, clawed feet and fungal infections. Pitched into sharp relief by the movie stars she'd met, these men seemed especially repulsive. They were, she had noticed, all clammy to the touch.

'Hey.'

Maria heard the voice, reedy and breaking, and ignored it. There was every possibility that it was addressing someone else and she knew that if she reacted it would signal the end of the tableau and encourage other men, no doubt pasty men with potty breath, to approach her. Maria resolved not to move.

'Hey, lady.' Maria felt a tap on the sole of her foot, but didn't flinch. If you ignored men they were sometimes sensitive enough to recognize your feelings and retreat. This had never actually happened to her, mused Maria, but she was sure it was possible.

'I'm talking to you, sweetheart.' The voice was more aggressive now. 'I wanna talk to you.'

Lowering her head just a quarter of an inch, Maria won a perfect view of the speaker, a short, ratty man with skin so translucent that she would have sworn, for a second, that she could see the progress of blood through his veins. It was as if the top layers of his skin had been peeled right away, scythed off in some horrific (but technically very precise) industrial accident. Raising her head, Maria said nothing.

'Look, lady, I got an important friend who wants to meet you and I don't need none of your silent treatment.' His voice, coarse and slightly accented, made him sound like an Eastern European who had learnt English from the Chicago mafia (which, indeed, he was). 'I don't have time for this.' She felt his fingers clamp roughly around her thigh.

Dora came pushing through the crowd then, slightly breathless. 'You can't touch Maria, I'm afraid, she's supposed to stay still.' She paused. 'What is it that you want, sir? I have some very pretty girls upstairs. They're all ready for you.'

The man's lips buckled. 'I was just talking to her, see, and she wasn't saying nothing. My friend wants to meet her.'

'Oh,' Dora smiled. 'Well, she'll be free later on, she can't stay here for ever, you might be able to catch up with her then. Who's your friend?'

The man looked smug as he motioned towards the entrance of the main hall. The crowd had thinned out a little now, men crawling through the house, peopling its boudoirs and antechambers, searching for their favourite girls. As Dora followed the man's signal she gasped before trilling a laugh and Maria knew then that the friend in question was either unusually ugly or unusually famous. Dora was used to dealing with hordes of men each day, many of them actors, and it was rare for her to have any reaction, let alone an intake of breath. Only the other week Charlie Chaplin had visited the house, brought in by one of the Pantheon directors, and he had warranted just a smile and demand for cash up front.

Considering this, Maria couldn't resist a peek. Head turning slowly, she suddenly understood Dora's response, and it took all the will she could muster not to gasp herself. A few feet away, towering above the crowd, was a man with the highest of foreheads and an aquiline nose, currently the most popular star in the world. He was a Russian, this man, and the only person in the room who had decided against dragging up, unless you counted Maria Caesar, of course, who, blithely naked, was arguably the least ambiguous of them all. He stood still now, gazing back at her, sweating lightly in his trademark overcoat and Cossack hat. Given the LA heat it was a bewildering choice, but undoubtedly striking.

'Sweetie.' Dora rushed up to the stage now. Bending down, she rooted beneath the chaise longue, pulling out the silk robe that Maria had been wearing before she posed. 'Sweetie, I think you'd better get down from here, quick, have you seen who's over there?' Maria nodded, speechless. 'I can't fucking believe it,' said Dora, a nervous laugh running through her voice. 'He's asked for you,' she whispered. 'He wants to see you. It's so exciting.'

Dora held the robe open as Maria stood up. Fastening it tight around her then, Maria glided over to the Russian man as slowly as she could. She wanted to make a good impression, she thought, she wanted him to like her. He was more beautiful in the flesh, she decided, than he could ever have been on that screen, where his features were so subtly distorted. Sidling up she held out her hand. With a small smile he raised it to his lips.

'Ya see?' The tiny translucent man (who reminded her of a baby mouse she'd once found dead beneath a tree) was standing at her elbow. 'He likes you. I said to him that I'd get you down and I have.'

'I'm sorry,' she looked down at the man, 'I don't mean to be rude, but who are you?'

The man sneered. 'I'm his translator, see?' He pointed a gnarled finger at the Russian. 'He might look good, lady, but he don't speak a fuckin' word of English, not a fuckin' word. Ya might say he's mute.'

'He doesn't speak at all?'

'Yeah, he speaks Russian, course.'

'So he's not mute?'

'However you wanna put it, lady. I don't care.' The man stabbed at the air. 'He shares everything with me, see, I don't have to worry about nothin'. We're like brothers. I'm kinda behind his success, you know. I guess I'm the key.'

Peering more closely at the short man, reflecting on his precise lack of charm, Maria doubted this. She turned to the Russian, pushed back her shoulders and smiled up at him. 'Would you like to come upstairs with me, sir? I'd really love to take you.'

There came no answer until the short man prodded her. 'Did you hear what I said back then, lady?'

'What?'

'He don't fuckin' talk. That's just what he don't do. He smoulders,' the short man pulled his lips into a gammy pout, 'and he can cry when I tell him to. He's best in the business when it comes to cryin', I tell ya. But he don't do no talkin'.'

'Oh.' Staring again at the Russian, Maria realized that this was probably true. He was still smiling at her, eyebrows raised expectantly, but had stayed resolutely dumb. Gazing at him, not wanting to be rude, but completely transfixed, she noticed that his face changed faintly each second, his expression passing from simple yearning to worried hope to a brief, almost imperceptible, flicker of happiness. She realized in that soundless moment that he was, perhaps, the ideal client.

But, of course, there was his friend to contend with first.

'We wanna go to another party.'

'Oh,' Maria smiled, 'you don't want to stay here? We've got a lot of gin in tonight – more than you'll find in town – and there are other girls to take care of you.' She pointed at Missy, slumped in the corner, eyes rolling back into her head. 'Missy might not look so much at the moment, but she's a great girl, I'm sure she'd look after you.'

The short man grimaced. 'No, no. We wanna go to this party in Hollywood – it's gonna be wild, crazy. I've gotta car waiting outside, so we're all ready to go.' He poked a finger at the Silent Russian. 'He wants you to come.'

'Oh. I should put some clothes on.'

'Naw,' the man shrugged, 'you're wearing a robe and it's gonna be a pretty wild party. We don't wanna miss it, we wanna go now.' He looked her slowly up and down before leering, 'You'll be fine like that.'

'I don't think so, sir, I don't think so.'

'You'll be fine.' The short man took Maria's elbow and started marching her through the main hall to the door. He was brisk, a little rough, and, as they stood by the brothel's entrance, the Silent Russian, loping behind them until now, pushed the short man's shoulders and started babbling furiously. Maria stepped back as the two of them argued, their bodies pitching angrily forward, hands carving the air, as if engaged in a life or death game of charades. After a frantic five minutes, the Russian fell silent again, anger sufficiently quelled, and the transparent man took Maria's hand.

'I'm sorry,' he said, voice brusque. 'Sorry. My friend here says I treated you badly, he doesn't like to see girls treated that way. So,' he paused, 'I'm sorry.' He held his hands up in surrender. 'Sometimes I don't think of people like you as real, you know.'

Maria could think of no response. Waiting in the yard was a white limousine, a chauffeur at the wheel, smoking. As he saw them he stubbed out his cigarette and jumped from the car, opening doors. Maria was surprised to see the Silent Russian and his friend squeeze into the front seat, while the rumble seat in back was saved for her.

It was dark as they drove out to Hollywood, and, as the angular, consonant-heavy sounds of foreign speech filled the car, she sank down into the buttery leather and closed her eyes. It had been a few months now since Maria had been away from the brothel and although she was excited, shaking slightly as the enormity of this date set in, she also felt anxious. Her family still lived downtown and the thought of seeing one of them, out for the evening in Hollywood, was, frankly, terrifying.

Not that they didn't know about her work. When Maria had first started living at the brothel she had tried to hide the details, writing a long letter to Toribio that stated she had been employed as a maid at Pantheon and would, thereafter, be living on site. Toribio had been angry and suspicious, penning a screed on the dangers of the American male: his immorality, malice and sexual designs. Despite his obvious anger, though, he had ended the letter on a positive note, stating that he would see Maria soon, and that he was quite sure her Aunt Consuela had imbued her with the keen moral sense to respond to any danger. The letter had been signed 'with love'.

Maria had felt guilty about this lie, but in those early days it had seemed worth it, the brothel somehow offering better things, a standard of living far above the barrio. There were the constant parties, the free-flowing absinthe, the exquisitely designed clothes passed on after use in a film. And there was Dancer Billy to escort her around, with the prospect of more movie stars to come. It had been an easily seductive life back then, before the seamy trail of grotesques that had lately conquered her bedroom.

It was just a few months after her father's letter that one of Maria's sprawling network of cousins had scored a contract at Pantheon, toiling on one of the many maintenance and construction teams. The studio heads had realized, by now, that location filming was almost always more expensive than building their own sets, and so these groups of mainly Mexican men arrived on the lot daily, endlessly constructing and painting facades. One day, early in his tenure, this cousin of Maria's had asked after her, giving his fellow builders her address and explaining that she worked as a maid. He had been bemused by their response – heady laughter and smiles – as they led him across the studio lot to a dark wooden house that loomed on the edge. As the door was opened, though, by a young girl posing in a flimsy negligée, he had begun to understand. Realizing the extent of Maria's disobedience he had lost no time in telling Toribio.

This revelation had prompted a second missive from her father, this time very short, informing Maria that she should no longer use the Caesar name. The letter had sent Maria into a month-long depression – she barely spoke, didn't eat – which only lifted slightly on receipt of a note from her Aunt Consuela. 'Your father is upset,' Consuela had written, 'and we can all see why, but he will come out of this, mi hijita, in time, perhaps. We all wish that you'd stayed at home and we miss you very much, but we will find a way to welcome you if you do return.'

Maria knew that her aunt was sincere, but she couldn't see how this welcome might be effected unless Toribio was lobotomized or left the country. She was dead to him now, she thought. Absorbed inside this fleshly grave.

The volume of the Russian voices increased as they pulled into a parking space. Lifting her head to peer out, Maria recognized their destination as a modish hotel that she'd visited once before. A collection of small bungalows and rooms, it was owned by a garrulous Armenian who had been a huge star until recently, when the trend for sex symbols had switched from well-padded women in their thirties to impish teenagers. The hotel buildings were all painted pink and they surrounded a huge courtyard occupied by sun loungers, palm trees and a heart-shaped swimming pool.

The last time Maria had been at the hotel was to visit an up and coming young American actor, under contract to Pantheon, who had been housed by the studio in one of the biggest bungalows. Maria had been impressed by the man, excited – he was handsome, uncomplicated and clean – but less enamoured of his companion. While Pola Negri kept a panther and Natacha Rambova a pet lion cub, the young American had decided to follow the vogue by adopting a chimpanzee. When they had retired to bed, the animal had insisted on watching the action, sitting on a side table, eyes level with their bodies, peering in contemplatively as he shelled a bag of peanuts.

Helping her gently out of the car, the Silent Russian walked Maria through the courtyard, where a group of about fifty people had gathered; some sat on the edge of the swimming pool, sipping blue cocktails, legs dangling in the water, others perched on sun loungers, smoking and talking. Dwarves were circulating with trays of food – saltine crackers with anchovy paste, gobstopper-sized olives, slabs of chocolate brownie that induced crazed giggling.

The young American actor was sat on a large straw throne at the far end of the pool, the chimp at his feet, starlet in his lap. Besides him, Maria also recognized some of the girls – a few had worked at Pantheon and been poached by other brothels. She had attended parties like this before and recognized the scene: the forced loucheness, hacking laughter, the cigarette holders so long that they were a threat to all but the most attentive eyes.

As people noticed the Silent Russian, his arm draped around Maria's shoulders, most of the chattering stopped, the noise winding down. This was broken only by a squawking to their left, an English voice babbling furiously. As the Silent Russian walked over to the bar, gathering drinks, Maria headed for a just-vacated sun lounger. She was always slightly intimidated at these parties until at least her third cocktail. Closing her eyes, she pictured the Silent Russian's face. It was incredible, she thought, how becoming a movie star seemed to change people's features, rectifying ungainly bumps, softening facial quirks. She had been following the Russian's career for a few years, and had watched as his face (which once sported a broken nose and forcep scars) had subtly changed. He was beautiful now, she thought. Beside him, everyone else was just a bulbous mass.

The obnoxious English voice continued, and, looking over, Maria saw the source: a large middle-aged woman with a black bird's nest of hair rising above her puffy face. Encircling the woman were five or six girls of about Maria's age, all in states of undress, their mouths arranged in weak expressions of interest. Closing her eyes again, Maria regretted that her sun lounger was so close.

'Super, darling, super.' In spite of her looks, the woman was evidently one of the self-professed 'Beautiful People', the international set who spoke almost exclusively in superlatives and epithets. 'I simply love the feel of this hotel, the divine decadence. It's brilliant, don't you think?'

Whoever she was talking to answered quietly or not at all. Opening one eye and looking over at the English woman, Maria immediately sensed her mistake. Staring straight back at her, the woman rose shakily to her feet and sat heavily on the side of Maria's lounger.

'My goodness, darlings, who's this?'

'Maria,' she smiled faintly.

'Maria?' The woman paused, considering this. 'How wonderful!' Leaning over, she pushed Maria's hair back from her face. 'Why, but you have the most beautiful features, don't you? You're trying to get into the movies? Have I seen you in anything?'

Maria paused. 'I work at Pantheon,' she said, motioning to the Silent Russian. 'I'm here with him.'

The English woman gasped. 'With him? Oh, you lucky girl. So you like him, do you?' She pushed at Maria, creating just enough space for them both to lie down. 'I've heard that he's not much of a lover, darling, not particularly interesting.' She turned and winked. 'There's less to him than meets the eye, if you understand.'

Maria didn't reply, staring vacantly into her lap. She was aware, at that moment, of the English woman's companions sitting in a perfect line on the edge of the adjacent sun lounger, listening intently to what was said. It was odd, she thought, how similar they all looked. Some had light hair, some dark, but each had had it rollered into undulating, chin-length curls, and they were wearing identical dresses, knee length and button front, with a rash of beads around the collar.

'You should come to my bungalow,' the English woman was whispering as she snaked an arm between Maria and the seat. 'These are all my girls, they're very devoted, and we have a marvellous time together. Wonderful, wonderful fun.'

Maria laughed politely. Since starting at the brothel she had developed a few extra senses, one of which was an instant recognition of malicious types. The English woman seemed supremely volatile. 'I don't think I should really, though it's a lovely offer.' She pointed at the Silent Russian. 'I don't think he'd like that.'

The woman's voice was scoffing. 'You don't have to worry about him. You could just say that you were off to the powder room and I could meet you at the bungalow in secret. There wouldn't be any trouble.'

Maria stood up now. 'I don't think so.'

Across the pool she could see the Silent Russian, holding

a couple of cocktails and talking intensely to his country-woman, Veruschka Czechikova. Maria didn't want to disturb their conversation. She had been at parties with Czechikova, an aging actress, before, and had seen her humiliate other young working girls, talking loudly and publicly about their rates and background. A couple of yards from the Silent Russian stood the short, translucent man, his skin even more gossamer beneath the glare of an oil lamp. He was talking to a man she recognized as a popular escort, their hands travelling over each other, almost clinical, as if feeling for disease.

Maria started striding towards the courtyard entrance. At least she could wait there, she thought, and watch until the Silent Russian was free. As she walked, though, she heard the English woman behind her, footsteps keeping pace.

'Where are you going, darling?' There was a snarl in her voice, an unmissable threat. 'I just wanted to speak to you some more.'

Head turning briefly, Maria saw the woman, hair unravelling on to her shoulders, the army of girls backing her up.

'I just want us to be friends, darling, best of friends.'

As her pace quickened, Maria felt her ankle turn. She wouldn't look again, she thought, to look was dangerous. Hobbling now, she felt a hand on her arm, the English woman pulling her round.

'Why won't you talk to me?' The woman's face, bright red as it was, seemed to be inflating. 'I won't have people ignoring me, especially silly little girls like you.' She stopped to look Maria slowly up and down. 'Everyone knows you're a whore,' she said, 'dressed like that, hardly anything on.' Her voice rose. 'You've no right to ignore me, fucking whore.'

Everyone seemed to have stopped now, all conversations left hanging. Across the pool, Maria could see the Silent Russian pause, mid-sentence. The English woman kept right on shouting, up against Maria, words crashing out like beads on wood, rolling into each and every crevice of the courtyard.

Just then, without warning, the woman lunged forward, jerking violently at Maria's arm. As she toppled wordlessly into the murky swimming pool, Maria could hear the laughter swell up around her. Sinking quickly to the bottom, robe rising like wings, she determined never to resurface.

Chapter Seven

He had done away with the chauffeur's services, leaving him at the party, chatting to a starlet, as he padded wetly to the long white limousine (his clothes still dripping) and purred away. Driving fast now, through the massed lights of Hollywood, the flicker of nightspots whose colour was their only purpose, the Silent Russian felt suddenly calm. The translator, the chauffeur, the bodyguards, the dressers, the hair stylist, the eyebrow specialist (each addition to his household just that smidge less useful than the last) were all important to his myth, he realized, they all bore witness, but, in truth, he had tired of their attentions. Wherever he was these days (public restaurant, private bathroom, packed nightclub, empty boudoir) it seemed there was always someone at his shoulder, poised to take the shine from his nose or flick the hair behind his ears. There were so many hands, he thought, flying at his face, swooping and fluttering, often so abrupt that he had no time to identify them: rubbing, primping and perfecting him, whether he welcomed the results or not. It was like being the subject of an ongoing experiment. A different kind of elephant man, but no less freakish.

Hitting a long, straight stretch of road, he turned to glance at Maria Caesar, splayed on the back seat. Her robe, tinged slightly green with swimming pool moss, clung damply to her body, while his trench coat perched on her shoulders. With her eyes closed, hands balled protectively to her chest, she had the tranquillity of complete absorption. Despite her profession, he realized, she was, somehow, untouchable.

As he accelerated, anxious to reach the brothel now, Maria mulled over the events of the night, pulling the coat close around her. Lurking down there, at the bottom of that pool (amongst the slime symptomatic of dreadful maintenance), she had genuinely had no intention of moving. This was it, she had thought (a sullen and sullied mermaid), one of those vaguely scandalous deaths that implicate the Hollywood in-crowd, peppering the gossip columns for a month or two, before being forgotten altogether.

He had dived in, though, hadn't he (stripping off his trench coat first), and pulled her to the surface, no hesitation. Other stars, she thought, would have sent a member of their entourage to save her, pointing haughtily at the pool and indicating something was amiss. But he had done it himself. He had proved himself the man he played in the movies. All sand-blasted skin and old-fashioned bravery.

As the Silent Russian sped his charge to the shadowy grounds of Pantheon Pictures, Toribio Caesar took to the stage in one of downtown's few speakeasies. He had been careful not to drink too many whiskies, and now, as he teetered on the edge of the wooden platform, he was pleased to find that the faces of his fellow rail workers, packed into this joint, were only slightly blurred. Holding up his glass, he shouted, 'Here's to us!' wanting to spawn a positive start. A cheer echoed around the room, the proprietor, Enrique, suddenly startled, waving his arms maniacally, imploring everyone to hush, aware of the police presence in these parts. With his efforts finally successful, Toribio nodded his thanks and began.

'Compadres, we know why we're here tonight, and I'd like to thank you all for coming. It's a good start, a fine start,' he set down his drink and pounded a fist into his palm, 'and it might just get us somewhere. Now, you've all heard about the plans, some of you will have read my outline, and I hope you agree that what we need, compañeros, is action. I've thought this through from all sides and I honestly think that a union is our best hope. I think it could really swing things for us. If we band together to make demands, they'll—'

'They'll fire us,' came a voice in the crowd. 'They'll kick out any cholo who does that, and you know it, Toribio. It's a dumb plan. We'll be desocupados. They've been signing us to yellow dogs for months now. It ain't worth it.'

The crowd grew voices then, a few shouting down the heckler, many agreeing.

'But, if you think about it, compadres, we're already on strike,' said Toribio, determined to stay calm. 'We're already supporting the Anglo strike, it's just that, whether they win or not, we see no benefits. They're striking for their workers, not ours, and yet they expect us to support them. How weak does that make us look? We're prepared to go out for them, but we ain't making any demands ourselves. It's crazy. They're laughing at us, compañeros, laughing. They must think we're stupid, that they can do whatever the fuck they want to us.' Toribio paused, aware that his next comment was dangerous. 'We look like we have no cojones, com-pañeros, no fuckin' cojones.'

'Fuck you, Toribio.' It was another voice. 'You talk about tanates, cojones. We're thinkin' about our wives and families. I can't afford to lose this. What happens if I'm deported? You say all this like we ain't proper hombres, but who d'you think we are? We got cojones. We just know how things work.'

Toribio glanced at his feet. He had hoped to get through at least a few minutes of his speech before facing the criticisms. Why couldn't they see? he thought. How could he convince them?

'I hear all this.' He held a hand to his brow and peered through the crowd. 'It's Juan Carlos, isn't it?' The man nodded. 'We worked together in Maravilla, didn't we? I understand, Juan Carlos, you want to keep your job, you're worried about the outcome, but hear this, all of you – it's Mexicanos like us who make up three-quarters of the company workers. Three-quarters! We stand by and watch the gringos get pay rises and better hours and better contracts, and what are we left with? The shit. They send us out to shitty camps, expecting us to pay prices in their canteens for food you and me wouldn't feed our pigs. The company bosses know how hard we work, that we'll put up with the sun for hours, but they ignore any calls for more money. It's gotta stop. It can end here. If those demands were made by all of us, standing together, there'd be nothing they could do but agree.'

'But what about deportations?'

'They can't deport us all! I know they got agencies in the homeland, bringing obreros across, but there's no way they could lose all of us at once. The company would collapse. I figure,' he paused, 'if we struck sometime soon, just after the gringo strike has finished, they'd cave in to our demands in days. We could get higher wages, work less, make sure they give us better camps. We could do this!'

Quiet now, unsure how this had played with the crowd, Toribio took a gulp of whiskey, looked out at the workers and felt himself start to sway. If this failed, he thought, he would be a pariah, the butt of every joke back on the tracks, the firebrand who failed to light, the leader with a limp dick.

He had known before he arrived this evening that there was the potential for wounded pride, but it was only now, as he felt the first hot flush of nerves, that he realized how crushing it could be. Somehow he had thought that prior knowledge would protect him from embarrassment, but standing up here, exposed, he realized that when it came to the visceral pull of failure, foresight, for the most part, was worthless. However much you thought you'd prepared yourself for the fall, told yourself that it might not work out and that that would be OK, it really would, the emotional pull was just too strong to override the best laid plans of the cerebellum. Humiliation, he thought, real humiliation, was enough to shatter a person. He had been so sure this would work, had built up so much support in the last few months, snaking through the work camps, handing out leaflets, that he hadn't really considered the alternative. He hadn't thought how impossible it would be to return to work a chastened man.

But there was noise in the crowd now, a slow applause that seemed to be gathering speed. Squinting slightly, trying to focus, Toribio saw that most of the men were smiling or nodding, mouths forming words of approval, all the signs of a triumph. They want to do it, he thought suddenly, realizing that he hadn't truly considered success either. If he could win over every man in this speakeasy tonight, and they won over their friends and relatives, they'd have done it. It would actually happen.

Raising his glass, he laughed. 'You want to do it?' There came a hollering in reply. 'You really fuckin' want to do it?'

As the noise began to rise, apparently unstoppable, Enrique ascended the stage, holding a bucket of water. 'Shut up, ya bastards,' he said, eyes narrowing. 'Shut up or I'll soak the fuckin' lot of ya.'

Walking through Pantheon's titanic grounds, the Silent Russian reached for Maria Caesar's hand. He had parked outside the studio's main office building, knowing that this meant a stroll through the murky back lot to the brothel. He had been on empty night-time sets before, and he enjoyed the sense of a world shut down, packed up suddenly and suspended until morning, that second, next day, when the lights would blare on again, the actors arrive and the props dance right back to life. There was something compelling, he thought, about a world that could be vanquished with a simple yell of 'Cut!'

Maria, too, enjoyed the dark spectacle of the back lot, much of it covered in dust sheets, like a giant house in the midst of refurbishment. It made her feel small and slightly frightened, both sensations she sometimes welcomed. As the Silent Russian pulled her close, stealing his arm beneath the trench coat and lightly round her waist, she imagined this as real. She imagined that she was an ordinary girl, working at a diner, who'd delivered the star his steak and potatoes, curtseying slightly as she lay the plate down, giggling at his artfully raised eyebrow, only to find that he liked her. She could be that girl, she thought, squired here by this man, led through the night on the first of their great adventures.

They were approaching one of the sets now, a huge structure, clad in white sheets, looming like the clumsy, avenging ghost of a B-movie. Lifting a corner of the fabric, poking his head underneath, the Silent Russian saw the interior of a mock-Tudor mansion, detailed down to the very last doorknob, built that week for the studio's upcoming epic. The set was balanced on a raised platform and so, putting his arms round Maria's waist, he lifted her up, hitching himself on to the stage then and leading her into the room. There was something about the silence, he thought. Something mesmeric.

Arranging herself on the waiting chaise longue, Maria found it less cushioned than she'd hoped, not cushioned at all in fact, just a showy replica. The Silent Russian was staring at her now, an expression she remembered from his hit film *The Duel*, pitched somewhere on that slow continuum of sadness and desire. Wriggling from her robe (she had never learnt to do these things sexily; to act seemed so demeaning) she saw the glimpse of a smile on his lips. Lying back, eyes closed, she pretended that this wasn't their first time. They were married, she thought, and this was just one of hundreds of times, each one closer than the last, more perfectly, humanly, transparent.

As he planted a kiss on her cheek, hand falling predictably to her breast, Maria imagined that she was with this man properly. Permanently. If they were together, she thought, they would be a team, protecting each other from the world, from the invasions and sallies of wild-eyed fans, from the stream of men who'd been forced upon her. They would have beautiful children, too, small, spooky-eyed, silent children, all quiet, pent-up intelligence and tidily furrowed brows. The first of them, she thought, as she felt him move on top of her, naked now, would be a girl. A perfect little girl, with brown bobbed hair, just like Clara Bow. The Brooklyn girl was a huge star, almost as famous as the Silent Russian, but she was still down-to-earth, had still chattered nervously to Maria when she'd bumped into her, literally, on the Pantheon lot, spilling Maria's drink. Clara was a good name, she thought, it had the right ring. The child they would conceive (she felt him between her legs) would be called Clara.

Weaving back to the barrio, Toribio tried to stop smiling. This feeling, he realized, was elation, something he hadn't experienced for years, not since that moment, in fact, when he'd passed into the USA with all that knotted anticipation that was both sickness and a gift. Since then, his natural optimism had waned, veering closer to ground level with every setback. He had been scared, recently, that he could fall no lower, that any further knocks would fell him completely, sprawl him carelessly across the ground, that final plunge.

Coming to Los Angeles more than a decade before, he had known it would be rough, but he'd had no idea that the obstacles were so ingrained, so trodden down into the earth that he imagined them now occurring deep beneath the surface, all those prejudices and fears as old as the dinosaur bones they'd begun disinterring from the tar pits of West Hollywood. Like all the other tired, dry-eyed dreamers who glanced up to the sky as they crossed that border, he had believed in the unimpeachable principles of the US constitution, the right of every man to pursue his patch of happiness, however modest. There had been no God for him, but he'd held to that.

Scuffing his feet along the ground, reaching the edge of the barrio, Toribio began to whistle. Passing a stray goat, he petted its head, noticing the startled look on the animal's face, which softened then to curiosity. The thing was probably covered in fleas, thought Toribio, drawing his hand away, like most of the animals on this land. If his plan worked out, it wouldn't be long before this turf was considerably more spruce. They could change it all, he decided, the thought arriving with sudden drunken conviction. They would not be ignored.

Arriving in his stretch of the barrio, he saw his neighbour, Agustin, sitting on an upturned orange crate, puffing at a pipe. 'Hello, Agustin,' he called, unable to contain his elation. 'Beautiful night, isn't it?'

Agustin seemed to twitch. 'Sure is, Toribio, sure is. You just take care now, won't you? You hear me?'

They were all so primed for disaster, thought Toribio, so ready for the cosh, that even their greetings held a note of doom. Veering towards Consuela's front door, he saw a couple of figures outside, gesturing violently. Probably some of the older kids, he thought.

Moving closer, he noticed one of them flinch and then straighten up.

'You Toribio Caesar?'

'Who's asking?'

The two figures moved into the half-light. 'Just tell us.'

'Who are you?'

Before they'd answered, he saw three more men coming

towards him and felt his arm being pulled up behind his back, until his palm was almost touching his neck.

'It ain't none of your business who we are. Let's just say we're officials. You, my friend, are about to take a trip home.'

Pulling the limousine into his driveway, the Silent Russian decided to walk the half-mile to his house, the grey, Gothic mansion standing overstuffed, replete, in the midst of this grand spread of bean fields. He felt like walking tonight, wanted to feel the air, the chilly touch that kidded you you could sense those microscopic hairs on your face. The evening had worked out perfectly, he thought, almost too perfectly: that girl, with her eerie sweetness, had almost changed his mind. As she'd lain on that couch, eyes closed, the bruises on her thighs from all the times before, he'd felt somehow – and he knew this was dumb – that this was new to her. They should get that girl into acting, he thought. A whore with a talent for romance.

To his left he heard a shuffling as his llama farm awoke, heads telescoping beadily into the air and peering out. He wondered briefly what would happen to those animals, but realized that he didn't much care – for all their uniqueness, they were oddly unlovable. He had bought them to prompt column inches, and, in that sense, they'd certainly been useful. He couldn't say they'd failed.

The large oak front door loomed ahead now, on which his interior designer had suspended a pair of antlers. Pulling on these, a series of bells rang throughout the house, a sound that usually brought the maids running. There was no one on duty tonight, though. He let himself in.

It wasn't a house to live in alone – too big for that – and, besides, the décor was so over-awing that the place always made him anxious, slightly vertiginous, as if he'd stumbled upon a murder scene, the killer potentially lurking around every corner. His publicist and designer had encouraged him to buy the most 'luxurious' version of each item, and so he had bar stools clad in the penis skin of sperm whales, walls covered in silk made by Nepalese midgets, the furs of four Bengal tigers curtaining a lounge. The hallway was reserved for his display of rare butterflies, each sample boxed individually within a small square of glass.

The designer had pressured him into some of these purchases, but, to be fair, he thought, it had, finally, been his decision. Coming out to Los Angeles, eighteen years old, he had resolved to become a myth that very day the studio had signed him up as a bit player. To be a star, he thought, you had to invent yourself, create a world compelling enough to intrigue your audience, prompt their wonder at your sensitivity and imagination. He had known what he was doing, had been determined to carve a myth strong enough to survive the hazards of time and taste. The silence of the movies had helped, he supposed. It made him and all the players just that touch more enigmatic. They existed in a world where they could mouth the words, certainly, but no one could ever really know what they were saying.

But now, of course, it was coming to an end. He had been bullish, he realized, when sound was first mooted, sure that audiences would reject the plan, would pledge their fidelity to the silent screen, with its piano music and pace. In these last months, though, he could see his mistake. The studio had been on to him recently, pestering him for a voice test, but he knew it was no use. The session had been scheduled, eventually, for next Monday, but he wouldn't be able to do it. A voice coach had been helping him with the script, but he still couldn't make it comprehensible. He had no ear for languages, he thought, that was the problem. The moment his fans heard him speak it would all be lost.

And if he couldn't make a talkie, then was there really any chance to bridge the gap in his finances? Despite the incredible box office receipts of his last three films, the Silent Russian was yet to see the money himself, had been promised a succession of cheques that had never materialized. He had bought the house on credit, of course, as well as everything inside, and now there was no way to pay. The myth might sell fan magazines, he thought, but it was an expensive ruse. Not for the lily livered.

Inventing yourself was a young man's game, he thought, walking to his study. Somehow, though only twenty-eight, he felt it was beyond him now. It would be so much more difficult a second time, especially with his reputation so recognized and ingrained. Sitting down at his desk, he pulled out a leaf of white linen paper and began printing the words across it, a message, in Russian, deliberately romantic, that would soon become immortal. 'Nothing has been so important to me as my audience,' he wrote, 'who have always been my guardian angels. I would have loved the chance to meet you all, but that time must come in the next realm. Thank you so much for your good wishes. My eternal love is with you.'

Inspecting the message, admiring his penmanship, the Silent Russian pinned it firmly to the wall above him. He didn't want it to get stained. Taking the revolver from his secret drawer (every desk must have a secret drawer) he stalked to the back of the room. Then, quite calmly, he did it.

Chapter Eight

Lying on the beach behind a ragtag collection of weeds (a shelter from both the sun and any kids who might stray down here) Rita Mae hitched herself on to her elbows. She had been meaning to send a letter of thanks to Granmaria for a few weeks now, and, sucking pensively on the end of her pencil, she stared down at the empty page.

'Dear Granmaria,' she finally inscribed, 'thank you so much! I really love all the magazines you sent for my birthday, and particularly the *Film World Annual*, which was just perfect! All those houses they had in *Movieland* magazine too – they were amazing. I did what you said and looked really hard at all the different styles those people had for their homes, and, when I come to live with you (I don't know when that will be yet) I thought maybe we could go for a Tiki look, with bamboo and tropical plants and those carved wooden heads that everyone seems to like so much right now. What do you think? I know it would be a lot of work, but I think we could make the apartment look just swell. That joint, "The Luau", had an indoor waterfall as well, which was great, but maybe that would be a bit much. I don't know. What do you think?'

Rita Mae reread this, before pushing the letter slightly aside and flicking through one of the magazines Granmaria had sent. A few pages in she found an article on Rock Hudson that had been specially bookmarked, accompanied by photographs of him barbecuing for friends, brandishing a spatula and smiling as he slapped huge bloody steaks on the grill. The article ('At home with Hollywood's biggest hunk') noted that Hudson was so large he'd had to have special 'man-size' furniture hand-crafted for him by a band of carpenters.

Alongside the pictures of Hudson, Granmaria's comments wove across the page in a heady scrawl. 'Rock Hudson is a nice man,' she wrote. 'It says here that he's fun and lots of good value. He likes spending time with his friends. He was divorced last year, Rita Mae, so he's ripe for the picking! I know he doesn't seem as interesting as someone like Marlon Brando (I know how you love Marlon!) but sometimes it's best to go for someone simple. When you get out here, Rita Mae, and start up your movie career, I think we should try and arrange a date with Rock. I think you should pursue him. It would be divine!'

Rita Mae closed the pages and started writing again. 'I see what you're saying about Mr Hudson, Granmaria, he is a good-looking man and very large (his fingers seem a lot like sausages) but I don't think he would be right for someone like me. Not that I wouldn't go to a few pictures with him, that would be fun, we could go to big premieres and I could wear fur, that would be peachy, but I don't think he'd be clever enough in the end. You know the kind of person that I'd really like, Granmaria, someone artsy as well as hunky. Maybe Marlon would be a little too,' she paused, trying to remember the word that Johnny had used recently, 'intense, but I don't know. Maybe intense would be nice. We might fall in love and spend all our time talking about clever things. Mr Hudson seems more interested in barbecues.'

She sighed and started on her next paragraph. 'I've been getting great marks for my classwork this week. Well, only in English actually. I'm not so good at math. Or science.' Rita Mae tilted her head. 'Or geography. But my English teacher, Mr Curtis, he says that I have an old soul. I don't know what that means. Better, though, he says that I'll make the best ever Cleopatra someday. He says I'd be brilliant in that part. He gave me that play the other day, the one by William Shakespeare, with Cleopatra in it, and I guess it's probably pretty good (I think it's meant to be) but I found it strange. He just doesn't write clearly at all. Not like Thornton Wilder. I think I shall have to ask Mr Curtis about it and see what he really thinks of Shakespeare. I bet he doesn't like it as much as he pretends.

'Anyway, I have to go now and find my friend Johnny. Thank you again for my present, Granmaria. It made me super-happy. I hope you're well and having fun in Orange County. Maybe I'll see you soon.' Rita Mae sighed. 'Lots of love,' she wrote, before carefully signing her name.

Chapter Nine

She was mad, thought Larry, slamming out of the apartment. Fucking insane. Running late for his shift, he pitched helter-skelter down the steps, tugging fruitlessly at his uniform, dishevelled as all hell. As far as he could see, he thought, feet falling finally to the ground, his wife was (Larry considered what he was about to think, trying to configure some eloquent way of putting it, some way that made sense, but his mind, all a-scurry, kept hurtling on forward) psychologically blind. That was it, 'psychologically blind'. Clara could see nothing beyond the glossy patina of manners and doctrine and status. Through all the time that they'd been married, what she had craved, thought Larry, was a life that fit some preconceived structure, in which the only movement was progress, each step leading, inexorably, towards social triumph. All she could see was the ladder. She had no idea of those spaces in between, through which most people's lives seemed to fall.

They had been arguing, of course, one of those arguments where any object or thought – any past slurs or slip-ups – could be used, indiscriminately, as a weapon. Although they bickered constantly, it was quite rare for Larry and Clara to have such a major row. These screaming imbroglios occurred, at most, twice a year and always grew from the same root: Larry's stalled career path. There was a certain pattern that usually preceded the arguments and, aware of this, Larry had been watching this one approach, waiting a few days now for it to hit.

The pattern went roughly like this. First would come talk in the cell house that one of the men above Larry – a lieutenant or captain – was leaving. Second, this information would filter through the island grapevine, circulating amongst the wives, until it arrived, smugly enunciated, in Clara's ear. Third, Clara would accost Larry in the kitchen and ask him why in God's own name he hadn't discussed the vacancy with her, and – more importantly – why he hadn't sprinted straight to the Warden and begged for the job. And then, after that, chaos would ensue and any further pattern would become gradually obscured, like a world map brought closer and closer to your face until all you could see was Sicily.

This time it was Lieutenant Curzon who was leaving Las Focas, having deteriorated in his three years of service from a normal, avuncular family man to a violent cur whose psychosis brought his skin out in itchy scales. Given Curzon's emotional state (he had been caught sobbing in the staff toilets, scratching at the walls, convinced he was possessed) the officers had been taking bets for some months now on when he would decide to leave, and Larry knew that many of them had petitioned the Warden for the post, 'if, by any chance, it should suddenly become vacant'. He had suspected that Bernie Lowell, with his immaculately shined shoes and forehead, was front-runner, and this had proved correct. As Curzon boarded the prison launch – the *Warden Wright* – bound for California, Bernie had arranged an emergency appointment with Clara, a fitting for his new uniform.

'Why didn't *you* petition the Warden?' said Clara, arriving home from Lowell's new house, an attractive three-bed that came with the appointment. 'Why couldn't *you* just have *tried* a little? I don't understand how you can be so totally devoid of ambition. You're like a sloth, aren't you, a sloth.'

Larry had sighed. 'I am not like a sloth.' He paused, anxious to stay in control. 'You know that they wouldn't have given me that job, Clara, even if I *had* begged the Warden. You know that, which is why I fucking—'

'What!'

Larry took a deep breath. 'Which is why I fucking wish you would leave me alone. We have to do this every time, don't we? Every fucking time,' his voice was escalating now, 'and I'm sick of it. You're driving me mad.'

The argument had ricocheted out from that point, becoming less and less coherent, Clara's voice lurching about, never quite settling on an octave. Rushing up the hill, Larry ran through it all again, marvelling, with each line, at his wife's insensitivity. She was well aware, she must be, that approaching the Warden would be a mistake, but still she couldn't resist goading him, wouldn't accept his very valid arguments against the idea. It was as though she wanted to present the Warden with an opportunity to humiliate him, thought Larry, a perfect chance to sit him down and spell out his professional failings in slow and graphic detail. Given her knowledge of his career and its shortcomings, Larry couldn't help suspect that his wife's motives were malicious.

If there was one thing that he and Clara should have agreed upon, thought Larry, it was that he wasn't suited to the higher echelons of prison leadership. He could just about manage the position he'd been employed in, that of officer, but to rise further a man had to have certain qualities that he could never possess, would never even wish to possess.

To really succeed on Las Focas, a man needed endless supplies of confidence, a dictatorial tone and a penchant for easy violence. Larry's traits were more muted. He felt that he was a pretty good father, he had a way with plants, and, overall (despite his constant disputes with Clara), he thought of himself as a fairly placid man. He was trying to make the best of their situation, the best of a job that he needed in order to support his family, but that he would never have chosen. In a better world, thought Larry (or perhaps just a better marriage), his wife would have recognized the sacrifices he had made. She would have embraced his good points rather than harping on his faults. She would have supported him through the everyday difficulties he faced, the problems with his colleagues, the regular abuse from inmates.

Had Larry applied to Las Focas prior to the Second World War his lack of experience would have barred him from even the interview stage, let alone acceptance. In those years the prison managers assured staff competence by insisting on men who had had a long military training, rising through the ranks to some appreciable height. Prison officers of the era were a hard-bitten bunch, much afflicted by cauliflower ears and foreshortened fingers, who approached the cellblock as they would a war zone, as merciless as they were serious. If an inmate so much as looked at one of these officers he could be assured a brutal beating with a blackjack. Woe betide, too, any prisoner who tried to escape. They were welcome to go ahead, of course, but were wise to recognize the unofficial policy that they could be shot not just once or twice, but as many times as it took for their flesh to fall from the bone, disintegrating like buttery lamb.

Come 1945, though, with thousands of ideal personnel wasted in Europe, human resources on the island were at an all-time low. The Federal Bureau of Prisons had vacillated for a year or so then, debating whether to employ non-military staff, but eventually they'd had to accept the inevitable. Come the winter of 1946, with Las Focas staff levels at a record (and potentially fatal) low, Warden Wright had called a meeting to discuss the imminent arrival of untrained men. The serving officers had greeted this new policy with undisguised hatred, many calling for strikes and boycotts, fighting talk that came to nothing.

In the end, they decided to express their displeasure simply by snubbing the new staff. When he and his family had arrived on the island in 1949, Larry had immediately sensed animosity from the other men, and it hadn't been long before someone had alerted him, rather abruptly, to the fact that they thought him useless. An empathetic man, Larry had said nothing. He could, after all, see their point. Here was a young guy, stood before them, who had spent his entire working life (all three years of it so far) sat in an office, perfecting his paper airplane construction. And that wasn't the worst of it. Even given the relaxed employment standards it was unlikely that Larry would have been accepted at Las Focas had it not been for a quiet word from his brother, Grady Jones, a high flier in the Federal Bureau of Prisons. It was fair to note then that, as an unqualified rookie officer, he was barely prepared for the vicissitudes of America's most violent prison. Still, at that point Larry had been somewhat optimistic. He had felt confident that he might make a fist of this.

The fact that his outlook was, at best, misguided, became rather frighteningly clear in his very first month on the island, when Larry was assigned to a guard post inside the cellblock. For the first few weeks this had seemed fine, the inmates surprisingly polite, asking his name, offering him cigarettes, the atmosphere eerily calm. In these weeks Larry could often be heard whistling at work, relieved that this unlikely career turn seemed somehow bearable, much less terrifying than expected.

Come Larry's third week on the job, though, all that had changed. The reason for the inmates' docility had become abundantly clear then, when a group of them staged an audacious, and very nearly successful, escape attempt.

On seeing the men break out of their cells, Larry had dispensed with the guidelines handed down on his first day – escaping men must be confronted – and had, instead, wedged himself firmly behind a wide concrete pillar. The inmates had somehow managed to strip the armed staff of their guns and were marauding through the cell house, terrorizing both inmates and officers. As Larry crouched there, he had heard the cries of a colleague, screams snagging on each disc of the man's trachea, truly the most inhuman sound he had ever heard. Slowly these screams had faded to a whimper, which continued for hours, low and dirge-like, while Larry stayed hidden behind the pillar, knees paralyzed by cramp, hands clasped over his ears.

It had only been the next morning, when the inmates had finally been caught and consigned to solitary, that a fellow officer had sought Larry out, convinced that he would be found dead, possibly sodomized, another gruesome casualty of the escape bid. When he tracked Larry down, alive and unharmed, the officer's mild relief was clearly overridden by disgust. As he pulled Larry to his feet, he had spat lightly in his face.

Shortly afterwards the Warden had called Larry into his office and explained that, while he would be allowed to keep his job (they needed staff very badly and he was loath to upset Larry's brother), he could forget any notion of career progression. From now on, his role would be confined to supervising the inmate team that tended the island farm. Only the least volatile prisoners were ever chosen for work duty and it was rare for them to play up, so this was the easiest post available to a Las Focas officer.

Larry had felt both chastened and relieved. It had been a reasonable solution on the Warden's part, he thought now, a fair way of responding to the mess. As a work duty officer Larry had few front-line responsibilities, and he had proved almost talented when it came to managing the farm. Not that the standard of his work was appreciated by any of the other staff. From that first month on Las Focas, throughout his entire tenure on the island, Larry had been cast as a pariah, either ignored by his fellow officers or, worse still, openly derided. Had there been any other job options open to him he would, naturally, have left. Sadly, though, there were none. He had no choice but to stay.

If only Clara could accept the stasis in his career, the fact that, whatever her ambitions, their social and financial position was likely to remain much as it was now, distinctly modest. It was so tiring, thought Larry, to be constantly upbraided on his performance, criticized for a way of life that he hated as much as she did. Striding past the violets that lined the edge of the path, violets that he had planted, he thought, as so many times before, of divorce.

Larry had written to a lawyer on the mainland a few years previously, asking him to send over a list of the current grounds for divorce, the various get-out clauses. On receipt, Larry had carried this list around in his overalls for months, stealing away in quiet moments on the farm to read through it again and plot imaginative routes out of his marriage. As it stood, there were seven possible grounds for divorce, all of them fairly unforgiving: adultery, extreme cruelty, wilful desertion, wilful cruelty, habitual intemperance, conviction of a felony and incurable insanity.

The problem was, thought Larry, that in perpetuating any of these grounds, he was more than likely to lose his job, and, if that happened, he would be destitute: no home, no savings, no food or drink. In all the years that Larry had been on Las Focas, there had never been a divorce and this was, perhaps, the explanation. To cut yourself off from your spouse you had to commit an offence that the island authorities just couldn't tolerate.

For people resident on the mainland, people whose lives were less tied up with their work, the situation was that much easier. As a teenager Larry had heard stories, quite regularly, of both men and women who would pay strangers to pose in adulterous scenes with them while a friend took photos. These snaps would then be presented to a court to prove that the marriage had broken down irretrievably. It was a simple, almost faultless scam.

But not if you were employed on a prison island. Even if Larry had travelled to the mainland and found an anonymous woman to pose, taken the matter to court and cut himself off from Clara, it would have been impossible for him to return to Las Focas. The social code simply wouldn't have allowed it. Small communities thrived on unity and cohesion. The tiniest snag represented a very real threat that the whole structure might be rent asunder.

And even if he had tried his hardest, secured a job on the mainland and left this place, then there was still Rita Mae to think about. His daughter was a truly resilient child, thought Larry, had endured things that might have felled a lesser character, but still he imagined she'd have trouble coping alone with her mother. At least with him around, thought Larry, Clara's verbal (and occasionally physical) brutality was kept slightly in check. Without his presence, he imagined that his wife's more vicious impulses might run swiftly out of control. There was every possibility that Rita Mae's life would be made unbearable.

Arriving at the cell house Larry nodded at Tommy Irvine, the lieutenant in charge of the prison entrance, and waited patiently as the first of the three mechanized doors was levered open. Stepping through the last of them, he found himself standing nose to nose with Irvine, whose mouth was strangely warped.

'For Chrissakes, Jones, what the fuck d'you look like?' Irvine took a step back and swept his hand up and down, motioning at Larry's uniform. 'You're supposed to be a fuckin' officer. Get it together.'

'Right,' Larry sighed. 'I'm sorry, Lieutenant Irvine. I had kinda a family emergency, so I came out in a rush.' He smoothed down his jacket and smiled nervously. 'That better?'

Irvine shrugged. 'It'll have to do, won't it? You're late for your shift as well, I'll have to tell the office, guess they'll be docking your pay.'

Larry looked up at the clock in Irvine's office – three minutes late. 'Right, yep.' It didn't seem strictly fair.

Passing into the work duty room, he picked up his keys and started off through A-Block, where the more rational of the inmates were housed. There were five men on his farming team, most of whom had been doing the job for at least a few years, and Larry had gradually grown to like them. He might not get any respect from the other staff, but he had few problems with these men, they all rubbed along just fine together. There was Denny Clemens, a child murderer; Foxy McCoy, a small-time (but vicious) gangster; Ritchie Francis, a bank robber; Chuck Fletcher, who had killed his wife and child; and Domingo Rodriguez, a petty thief (as a Mexican, you could aim perilously low and still be classed a maximum security risk).

It was interesting, thought Larry, as he strolled along to Denny's cell, how there were certain acts so momentous that they overrode any other characteristics. Denny, for instance, was a fantastic mimic – could imitate just about anyone within five minutes of meeting them – but some-how, Larry guessed, no one in the outside world would ever remember him as 'Denny Clemens, that fabulous impres-sionist'. Once you'd strangled six neighbourhood children, cut up their bodies and fed them to wolves, any other deeds or traits suddenly became oddly irrelevant. You were 'Denny Clemens, evil murderer', however fine your Jimmy Stewart impersonation (complete with facial likeness and speech impediment) might be.

It was usually only fellow inmates who could see beyond a man's crimes, thought Larry, beyond those basic labels of 'rapist' or 'murderer'. He felt that he had achieved it too, though, which made him strangely proud. Each member of his team had been released from their cell now, and they trooped along quietly behind Larry, as he led the way to the exit. They had a fair bit of work to do today, and he was pleased to note that they all seemed quite subdued, ready to face the graft ahead.

Once outside, he handed them their tools and watched as they dispersed, everyone knowing exactly what they had to do. The opportunity of work duty was highly prized on Las Focas, offering, as it did, at least some reprise from the intense boredom and monotony of cell-house life. For those who weren't given work – because they were either irresponsible or incapable – the time spent in their three by seven cell could stretch to twenty-three hours at a time, almost a full day, without magazines, books or TV. It was a situation that could have sent the sanest man crazy, and, as Larry noted, the residents of Las Focas rarely started their visit in the best frame of mind. It was no wonder that they liked getting outside, even when the farm required some physically punishing work.

Chuck Fletcher, one of the most accomplished members of the team, had stayed back with Larry at the tool shed. Some months ago Fletcher had suggested that they plant an orange grove, an idea that Larry felt was ambitious but compelling. If they were going to do it, though, he wanted it done right. Today, finally, a collection of books on the subject had been delivered to the farm store, and so, while the other men ploughed ahead with their work, Larry had suggested they start drawing up some plans.

Sitting down at his desk (a small folding table) Larry took out his pencil, while Fletcher crouched beside him. After a few minutes' silence, poring over the books, Fletcher looked up.

'D'you think this can work, Officer Jones, d'you think orange trees will thrive here?'

Larry nodded sagely. 'I don't see why not, Fletcher. It should be just perfect. Actually, I meant to tell you, I was round at the Warden's house the other day, picking up my daughter, and I saw photographs of this place' – he tossed his head back towards the cell house – 'being built, and there were orange trees all over the island then. I guess they must have gotten in the way of some of the staff houses and been cut down, but they'd definitely been native a while. It was good thinking on your part to come up with planting an orange grove.' He smiled and glanced at the sky. 'Everyone likes oranges, don't they?'

Fletcher looked pleased. 'Yeah, that's right.' He closed his eyes. 'It's been years since I've tasted an orange.'

'Me too.' Larry paused, before tapping a finger on Fletcher's book. 'Anyway, get reading. We've got a lot to do.'

They were quiet again for a time, Larry drawing diagrams as he read. Then Fletcher closed his book.

'Do you have a pencil and paper I can use, Officer Jones? I'm getting a lot from this, but I need to make some notes.'

Larry nodded, 'Sure,' and ripped a page from his pad. He passed this and a pencil down to Fletcher. 'Here you go.'

As Larry watched, Fletcher began sketching out a map of the farm, marking the areas that – due to emptiness and soil quality – might be best for their orange grove. He worked quickly, with clean lines, carefully noting which crops were housed on each section of land.

'That's really very good,' said Larry, head cocked to take it all in. 'I had no idea that you were so good at sketching. I would have had you helping out with other plans if I'd known.'

Fletcher passed the map to him, and Larry studied it more closely. 'D'you do any other sketching in your spare time? This is really pretty good.'

'Yeah, I do pictures of people mostly – I've drawn some of the guys, but I work a lot from memory. I do a lot of pictures of women.'

'Oh, really.' Larry raised an eyebrow. 'You'll have to show me sometime.'

Fletcher nodded, thinking of the stack of pornographic sketches beneath his mattress, some of which he'd given to officers in exchange for cigars. Somehow, he had a feeling that Larry wouldn't like them. 'Sure,' he said. Then, smiling slyly, 'Do you have a lady friend?'

Larry laughed. 'We're supposed to be working on orange groves, Fletcher. What kind of question is that? Anyway,' he paused, 'you know I have a wife. And I've definitely mentioned Rita Mae. She's my daughter.'

'Oh yeah, you have a daughter. How old's she?'

Larry looked at Fletcher, and bit his lip. 'We're meant to be working, Fletcher, let's get back to the books.'

His companion seemed to have lost his concentration, though. 'I wasn't meaning to pry, Officer Jones, honest I wasn't, it's just that you can get so,' he paused, 'so low in that cellblock, and sometimes you just want to hear about families, normal life, you know.'

Larry laughed now. 'Normal life, huh? That's not how I'd describe it.'

Smiling, Fletcher tilted his head. 'What do you mean?'

'Ah, you know, women are difficult, aren't they? Not as reasonable as men, by any stretch of the imagination.'

'Oh, I don't know,' Fletcher shrugged and gave a leering grin, 'girls always seemed OK to me.'

Larry grimaced. 'I'm sure they did, Fletcher, but,' he laughed, 'sometimes, when you're married, things get a little out of hand. 'Specially living on an island like this, it's not easy you know. A lady can seem kinda OK one minute, you're getting along fine, she's happy with your work, and then, BAM!' he paused. 'She's crazy as hell the next. Crazy!' He shot a smile at Fletcher, which quickly faded. 'Anyway. I shouldn't really be talking about this.'

Fletcher stood up to stretch his legs. 'Why not?'

'You know exactly why not.'

Fletcher was wide-eyed. 'No I don't.'

Larry pushed his books to one side and looked up at his charge. 'I know what each of you men is in for, and, really, I don't think it's appropriate to be talking about ladies with someone who's, well, you know.'

'What?'

'Well. Someone who did what you did.'

Fletcher said nothing, sitting down on a grass verge in front of Larry. Finally he muttered, 'Oh.'

'Exactly.' Larry brushed down his pants and prepared to go and supervise the other men. Just as he was about to stand up, though, Fletcher spoke.

'I didn't do those things, you know, those things they convicted me of. It was all a mistake.'

Larry sighed and held out a hand. 'Look, Fletcher, I'm sorry, I've heard it before. I don't have time for this.'

'But I didn't.'

Larry crossed his arms. 'You're innocent, are you?' He smiled. 'Fletcher, I haven't seen your file, and I like you, I really do, but some of the officers told me what you did to your wife and son, and they had enough evidence for me. I don't need to run through it again.'

'But you don't understand.' Tears welled in Fletcher's eyes. 'It wasn't me.'

'Right, OK, who was it?'

'I don't know, if I knew I could have done something about it.'

Larry watched as tears started coursing down Fletcher's face, and felt oddly sorry. Standing up, uncomfortable, he began stacking the books they'd been using. 'Look,' he paused, 'it really would have been better not to talk about this, wouldn't it? We should probably get on with some other work.'

Fletcher was standing up now, though, and he came over to Larry. 'Officer Jones, please don't think that I'd be capable of that crime. I can't stand that you know about my wife and Tommy and you honestly think I could have killed them.'

Larry tried to look impassive. 'It's really not my business, Fletcher. My job is to supervise you.'

His charge stepped back, so that Larry might catch a better view of his face. He knew he had a chance here, an opening. 'I really didn't kill them, Officer Jones. Please believe me. I'd hate to think that we've been working together all this time and you think I'm capable of something like that. Every night I dream of them, strung up, the way I found them, and I can't stand it. You don't know what it's like to lose your whole family and then be accused of killing them. It's torture, torture.'

Holding a hand to his brow, Fletcher gave a huge sob. Staring through glazed eyes at Larry Jones, watching as the officer's face grew anxious lines, creasing with concern, he suspected that he might be making some progress here, might actually be convincing the man. Whimpering slightly, he decided to release another sob, even more harrowing than the last. His eyes closed then. Fletcher felt Officer Jones take a step towards him and put a comforting hand on his back.

'All right,' Larry said softly, 'maybe I do believe you. Maybe you aren't guilty.'

And, just for that moment, Chuck Fletcher almost believed he was innocent too.

Chapter Ten

The Pantheon Pictures studio lot, 1933

She had been told not to go out. If she remembered rightly (and, unfortunately, she did) that had been the only rule. Her mother had made it perfectly clear that morning before she left for the cemetery, wagging her finger and smiling down from beneath the veil, promising deathly horrors if Clara disobeyed, the black lace billowing in and out, in and out, snagging on the tides of her breath.

Her mother had been firm, but fair too she supposed, promising definite if undisclosed treats should Clara stay indoors. Despite the twin spectres of punishment and bribery, though (those bastions of the parenting trade), Clara Caesar found herself, three hours after her mother's disappearance, sitting cross-legged in the centre of the kitchen table, munching on a dry tortilla, sighing plaintively between every bite and surrendering to a still higher authority. Boredom, she realized now (though, as a five-year-old, she wasn't thinking in quite these terms), could be utterly (make that completely) devastating. Faced with the gaping white gulch of nothingness, an afternoon stretching out empty and dense ahead, a person could be forgiven for just diving head first into the canyon. Or, as in Clara's case, they might begin a mantra. 'Bored, bored, bored, bored, bored, bored, bored . . .'

She had been in this situation many times before, of course – left at home by her mother or forced to wait while she surfaced from a trance – and it had never gotten any easier. She just wanted someone to *play* with, thought Clara anxiously, picking at a hangnail, noticing it start to bleed. She just needed something to *do*. The boredom was grinding to such a nag that she began to feel nauseous. If only she had a toy, she thought, a puppet maybe, a telescope. Or one of those baby dolls she'd seen once for which you could spend whole afternoons fashioning diapers out of towels. That would be good. Knots were fun. There was nothing, though, nothing, she worried (fretful, bitten lipped), and she was feeling even sicker now. Dammit, fuckhole bastards, she thought, words picked up from Dora that she had yet to understand. She would go outside.

With a succession of energetic jumps, Clara grasped the iron door handle, hanging there patiently until the catch released. Walking through, door closing, she found herself in the midst of a hot, clammy day. Shuffling across the grass to the big house, she stared determinedly at her bare toes (too young yet to warrant proper shoes), avoiding eye contact with any adults from the studio, any cunty fuckface (Dora again) who might ask why she was alone.

She kept this up for at least ten paces, until a butterfly veered myopically towards her head. Seeing its black body and antennae rear close, Clara gasped angrily and ducked, curling into a ball until she was sure it had passed. Standing up, she dusted herself down. Lots of girls probably liked butterflies, she thought, but those girls were dumb. They should grow up. What they saw, Clara realized now, were just those wings, cast out prettily. They hadn't looked closely (as she had one day, dissecting a dead butterfly with her mother's hair grip) and noticed that the body was just about as ugly as that of any other bug. They hadn't clocked the whole package.

Now here she was at the back door to the big house, which stood, as always, wide open and welcoming, casting around for trade. At this time, midday, most of the girls were out, sunning themselves on the grass verge above the studio lot, posing in long earrings and short bathing suits, smoking those spindly cigarettes they were so fond of and observing the action through Dora's pince-nez. They enjoyed watching the filming of the romantic productions the most, the ones centred around idealistic lovebirds, bound together by eternal passion, a spiritual connection that made their characters swoon at a debilitating rate. The girls all lived in hope that one of the actresses would suddenly fall sick (malaria, heat stroke, a poisoned dart aimed perfectly, untraceably from a vantage point just above) and need a last-minute replacement. To this end they would often wave to the director and catcall, ensuring he knew of their presence. Just in case.

The brothel, then, was deserted. Clara's mother usually brought her here at a more social hour, about mid-morning, and so she was surprised to find the place quiet, devoid of the noisy, mottled girls who otherwise peopled the corridors, running past Clara, laughing and pushing, those strange lines of holes stitching wildly up their arms, teaching each other some blurry Charleston, or slugging from vaporous bottles of gin. Missing their younger siblings, they were all apt to fuss over Clara, tossing coins for who might dress the girl, wrapping her in stolen chiffon scarves and smudging her face with panstick. Clara, in turn, basked in the attention. The times when her mother had been laid out – stretched on the bathroom floor, breathing shallow, eyes like glass almonds – the girls were the finest antidote.

Starting down the first corridor, past the stairs, Clara felt suddenly cowed. The house was the kind that flung abrupt shadows, dark trunks falling hard across her path. She was uninvited here, she thought now, shaking and slightly nervous, and if one of the big girls found her creeping alone (one of the ones with the long nails and face like a cat) they might be angry. They might chase her out, she thought, might chase her with one of those strange wooden paddles that her mother had once retrieved from a bag of dirty panties.

Still, what had she to lose? On visiting the house before, the only room Clara had seen had been the large, steamy kitchen where Maria collected the week's dirty laundry and downed endless cups of coffee. Now, on exploring, she found that the house was actually full of coves: nooks and cupboards and antechambers all furnished with mattresses, whatever their size. Some of the bedrooms were more individual than others (decorated with tiny photographs or sprigs of lavender) but all shared the same heavy silk sheets and velvet curtains.

She had seen the silk sheets before, of course, on the piles of clean laundry that her mother stacked at their front door, ready to be returned to the big house. Once, when she was even smaller, Clara had stolen one for a while, stroking it back and forth against her cheek. Some day, she thought now, as she padded a step or two into a particularly pretty room (packed with plumped cushions, bunches of flowers, a swing suspended, oddly, right above the bed), she would sleep in nothing but silk sheets. She would live someplace fancy then, with one of those dark green velvet lampshades the girls all had, the fabric ruffled perfectly, bows fixed to the side. That was what she wanted. Dark silks and lampshades.

Moving further into the house, she heard strange noises, a procession of moans, as though someone had stubbed their toe and was experiencing the pain in reverse, not so pressing at first, but growing more torturous. Clara had stubbed her toe herself last week, smacking against the big house stove, and so she knew how painful it could be. Her toe was still a little swollen from the bump, and the bruise was visible too, despite its softening from black through blue to yellow, a process in which Clara had taken a great, almost scientific, interest. If someone had hurt themself as badly as she had, she thought, face serious now, then they would need a cold compress. Otherwise they'd be moaning like that for a long, long while. She, Clara Caesar, had cried and cried, and that hardly ever happened. It takes a lot to make me cry, thought Clara solemnly. She was a very measured girl.

Not wanting to disturb the person, but anxious to help, Clara pushed gently on the door to these noises. As she entered the room the moans grew on regardless, and edging closer, Clara realized, to her surprise, that the source of the problem almost certainly wasn't a stubbed toe.

Lying on the bed, eyes closed, clad in just his shirt and socks (his hairy legs incongruously bare) was a man she recognized from around the lot for his habit of chucking her beneath the chin like a puppy dog. Face closed with concentration, Clara tried to remember his name, ticking through the times they had met. Mr Edelson. That was it.

Mr Edelson's legs were splayed, and, crouching at their crux, Clara could just make out Dora, her mother's best friend, blonde hair piled messily about her face. Dora's head was bobbing rhythmically up and down, and, shuffling further into the room, Clara saw that she was sucking on a part of Mr Edelson's anatomy as though, for all the world, it was the most satisfying lollipop she'd ever tasted. It was in response to this, Clara realized, that Mr Edelson was groaning.

For all her smarts, Clara just couldn't work this out. It didn't make sense that Dora was sucking someone else's body, even if Mr Edelson had, perhaps, hurt that place between his legs. Clara lifted her thumb to her mouth and tried sucking on that. It felt vaguely comforting, she supposed, but nothing more. If someone had hurt themself, a cold compress (as she had already thought to suggest) would be of much more comfort than a ready mouth. Why, then, would anyone want to suck on another person's skin? Could it be that Mr Edelson was particularly tasty, that he had some tangy flavour? And, if she wasn't very much mistaken (she moved still closer, peering in, trying to focus properly, catching just a tense, twitching curve of rump) wasn't the part that Dora was sucking on the exact same place where men kept their pee hole? Ugh. Clara shuddered silently. Why would anyone want to go near a pee hole, let alone put their mouth to it? It seemed a little disgusting.

Clara stared at her feet again, considering her strategy. There were two options, she thought: she could either back out of this room quietly, hoping that no one noticed, or she could stay here, stock-still, until the noises finished. She knew that Dora would look after her, entertain her even, once she realized Clara was alone, so that was a factor. That said, what was going on in this bedroom seemed awful private, and Clara didn't want to cause trouble. She didn't want to be a nuisance.

With Clara considering her choices, Max Edelson opened his eyes a squint. He always liked to watch when someone was going down on him, even if the woman was Dora, who, to his reckoning, had recently trespassed from ripe fruit to rotten. Normally, he would have gone with someone else, but today Dora had been the only one in, and so there it was. He couldn't deny, he thought, watching that blonde hair spring up and down with the liveliness of a spaniel (he really was very fond of dogs), that the woman gave fantastic head. She was a true professional.

Leaning back, eyes closing again, Edelson caught sight of a movement in the corner. Eyes wide open and focusing now, he saw a little girl, all bobbed hair and worry, staring straight back.

'Hey!'

Edelson sat up, almost choking Dora. 'Hey, what in hell are you doing?'

The small girl bit her lip, eyes welling, as Max Edelson pulled his trousers off the floor, stepping and stumbling into them.

'Can't you keep some order in this house, Dora, can't you keep it a bit better than this? You're meant to be running a fucking business here. This is crazy.'

Dora had jumped off the bed, wiping her mouth with a handkerchief. A fucking business, she thought wryly. He wasn't wrong. Crouching beside Clara, she took the girl's hand. 'Are you all right?' she whispered. Clara nodded. Turning to Max, Dora threw up her hands.

'I'm sorry, Max. You know this has never happened

before. I can't imagine how Clara got in here. It's a mess.' She crossed the room, brisk and businesslike, handing him his tie. 'If you want to wait ten minutes I can take her home and we can finish off. That would be fine.'

'It's a bit late now.' Clara watched Max Edelson's saliva arc through the air, violently dispersing the dust motes. 'I've got meetings to go to, and I can't be late because of you. I'm fucking angry about this, Dora.' He came up close to her. 'It's so irresponsible.'

Dora shrugged. If Edelson was invoking Maria's responsibilities as a mother, then the man had a point. She suspected, though, that he was inferring some liability for his orgasm: in which case, he could fuck off. 'I'm sorry, Max,' she smiled widely, 'it won't happen again.' Taking Clara's hand she led the little girl out of the room. 'I'll see you soon.'

Edelson pushed through the doorway, knocking them both against the wall. 'Don't count on it, Dora.'

As he barrelled out, Dora laughed. 'Good timing,' she said, patting Clara on the back. 'I certainly won't miss that bastard.' Clara stared up at her, blinking. 'Right,' said Dora, regretting her crudeness. 'I'd better get you home.'

Walking through the brothel, Clara clasped Dora's hand. 'You shouldn't be on your own,' Dora was saying. 'Why did Maria let you out? What's been going on?'

Clara bit her lip. 'I was meant to stay in. Mama told me to stay in. She's been gone.'

'Right,' said Dora. She kneeled down next to Clara, smoothing the girl's hair. 'Was your mother wearing her black dress today?'

Clara nodded. 'She was wearing that veil she likes, too, the black one.'

'OK. And did she say how long she was going to be out?'

There was a pause. 'I don't think so,' said Clara. 'It seems like a long time.'

'All right.' They were approaching the bungalow now, the door swinging open. 'Did you leave the place like that?'

As Clara went to speak, the answer came flying through in a flurry of black. Maria's arms closed around her daughter.

'I just came back and I couldn't find you, Clara. I didn't know where you'd gone. I thought someone had taken you. I was so worried.' Maria was shaking as she looked up at Dora, whose mouth had arched into a sneer. 'Have you been looking after her, Dora darling, did she come and find you?' Maria stood up hurriedly, dusting herself down. She had been so worried, panicked really, thoughts haemorrhaging, black and colliding, but it was fine. She breathed. It was fine. Except, it seemed, that she had upset her friend. 'I thought that she could stay inside for a few hours. I left her with lots of things to do.' There was a pause, Dora still silent. 'I honestly didn't mean for her to bother you, Dora. I thought she'd stay in. You didn't have a client booked, did you, I haven't kept you away from work?'

Dora placed a hand gently on Clara's back. 'Why don't you go inside and,' she glanced down at the girl, 'I don't know, maybe you could brush your hair. It's a little tangled.' Clara seemed stricken by this. 'It'll only be for a few minutes, darling, and then your mama and I'll come in too and prepare us some lunch. Maybe we can eat outside. It's a nice day, eh? Picnic?'

This appeased Clara, and she trotted dutifully into the bungalow and through to the bedroom she shared with her mother. It had been a strange day all in all and she supposed the least she could do was brush her hair. In the face of upheaval, even chaos, she could at least foster a fine appearance.

Outside, Maria could tell that her friend was angry. There was the slightly raised voice, the lowered eyebrows, and now she noticed a thin stream of air escaping Dora's mouth. Hoping she might dilute the situation (she really couldn't face an argument) Maria put an arm around her friend's shoulder and kissed her full on the cheek. 'Thank you so much for watching Clara, darling. If I'd known for a second that she'd come and bother you I would never have gone out. But, naturally,' a nervous smile tore at her mouth, and she raised her eyebrows, 'I had no idea. Children today,' she laughed, 'they're so very, very naughty.'

Dora shrugged, dislodging Maria's hand. 'I don't want to hear this, not again, not this time. You can't keep leaving Clara alone. It's not right. She's a little girl, Maria. She can't be left. Not here.'

Maria sighed and sank to the grass. Here it was, the very same discussion. She could never explain it, she thought, this need, acute as it was, arriving without warning, to be alone, far away from Clara, no distractions at all. She reverted to her usual defence. 'You know it's not my fault, Dora. It's a tragedy, really, a tragedy. I'd take Clara to the cemetery if I could, but it's meant to be a place of silence, contemplation, and she's just not ready for that, is she?' Maria looked up at Dora, eyes set pleadingly wide. 'I've tried to limit the number of times I visit him, tried to keep it to just once a week.'

Dora could feel a headache start throbbing doggedly beneath her brow line. Not again. She was used to her girls having crushes on actors, of course, but she'd rarely seen one so obsessive or long-term as this, particularly when the man in question was dead, and therefore (it was fair to assume) unreachable and off-limits. Maria had been visiting the Silent Russian's graveside regularly, often daily, ever since his premature death, on the night he'd saved her from the murk of that hotel swimming pool. He'd been found in his mansion the next day, brains spilling on to the floor and the news had sent Maria into a frenzied depression; she moved into the darkest room of the brothel, only leaving it for the cemetery, smoking and drinking as though she had one wish (to follow him), servicing her clients in the most joyless, deadened haze.

At least, thought Dora (grasping for consolation), Maria had lately given up her claim that the Silent Russian was Clara's father. During the pregnancy and the first year of Clara's life they had had almost weekly arguments about the girl's provenance, Maria contending that the only person who could possibly have squired her was the beautiful, muted film star. While Dora was willing to concede, certainly, that Maria had entertained this man, the sad fact of the matter was that she had become pregnant a full three months after his death.

It was cruel, Dora realized, but she had never been able to suppress a smile when comparing the men who might have sired Clara to the one Maria had originally plumped for. Where the Russian's profile was strong and definite, jutting out at hard, attractive angles, the other men had barely a chin between them. Where he had been polite and chivalrous (stripping off his trench coat and diving into that swimming pool) the other men were coarse, hard-bitten and outspoken. Where he was a fêted star of the screen, with an estate the size of a small principality, they were crew members on fair to middling salaries, who might afford a two-bedroom bungalow in Long Beach, but nothing too showy or sybaritic. Dora could understand, she really could, why Maria had plumped for the Silent Russian when she first learnt she was pregnant. She'd just never understood how she could overlook the vagaries of rigor mortis.

'Maria, honey,' Dora tried to sound upbeat, no arguments today, 'you know I just want you to be happy.'

'I know.'

'But,' Dora paused, 'I'm not sure that having Clara on the lot is going to work out.' She reached for Maria's hand. 'I know you won't want to hear this, but Clara saw me with a client today. She saw me going down on Max.'

'No.' Maria's hand clapped to her mouth. 'You're lying.'

'I'm sorry.' Dora's voice was gentle. 'I don't know how long she was in the room for, but it was long enough to see something. It's no good, is it?'

Maria shook her head.

'When we agreed you could stay here, Maria, we talked about this, didn't we? About keeping Clara away from the house?'

'I know. I'll be more careful, Dora.' She held up her hand. 'Promise.' Maria scrambled to her feet. She couldn't hear more. 'I'll make sure that she stays away from the house, that she stays back here. She'll be in school soon anyway, away most mornings. It'll be OK.'

Dora stood up. 'You really think it can work?'

Maria nodded. 'Of course, of course. No doubting, Dora. We'll be fine.'

Looking at her watch, Dora smiled. 'Well, OK then, we'll see how it goes. I'm sorry, I can't stay for lunch actually, there's a drink delivery around back this afternoon and I'd better be ready. They've busted a few of our suppliers recently. I can't afford to lose another.'

'That's OK.' Maria was smiling now too, arms flung wide, keen to end the conversation. 'It'll all be fine again, Dora. Delicious. Don't worry.' And, with that, she ran inside the bungalow.

Maybe it could work, thought Dora, still sceptical, as she walked back to the brothel. Even though it had been her suggestion, she had never been entirely convinced by this arrangement: Maria working as the brothel's laundry mistress, living with her child in a converted dressing room. Back when Clara was a baby, slung around her mother's back in a cotton papoose, it had seemed fairly reasonable. Since Clara had found her legs, though, it was proving more tenuous.

Dora climbed the stairs to her office, located in the brothel's roof. She needed the paperwork for her drink order, stashed somewhere on her desk beneath a mess of books and invoices. Thinking about the situation, she was still glad that she'd convinced Maria to stay all those years ago, if only because it had allowed her to watch over the Caesar girls. They both needed care and attention, she thought, a sense of permanence and place. Last month she had visited schools in the district, posing as Clara's mother, armed with headed paper from the Pantheon Studios office that termed her 'a leading scenarist'. With this, she had ensured Clara's attendance at one of the very best schools – not the third-rate holding pen where most Mexican kids were relegated. It would be a good start for Clara, she thought. A real chance.

Chapter Eleven

Downtown Los Angeles, summer 1936

'Buenos dias.' Consuela leaned towards the dark, sinewy man wiping his bloody hands across his apron. 'That over there.' She gestured to a slight, scrawny chicken. 'I'd like the legs and breasts, hey.' She watched as he took his knife to the bird, cleaving it into pieces with great satisfying thwacks. Wrapping the flesh in brown paper, he held it out. 'Gracias. That's perfect. Gracias.'

Turning, Consuela faced a cluster of people, all clamouring for other cheap cuts, and was forced to shoulder roughly through the crowd. Grand Central Market seemed particularly packed today – thousands cramming into the place, perched at the lunch counters, sipping bowls of coffee or bartering beside the big burlap sacks of grain. Consuela had wanted to get her shopping done quickly, but the sheer weight of people looked bound to hold her up. Just reaching a street entrance would take strength.

Arriving at her favourite produce stall, she checked through a large bag of limes, searching for breaks or bruises, before brandishing it at the holder and tossing him a few coins. 'Gracias, mi querida!' he called, as she continued through the stalls. She smiled to herself. He had always been mischievous.

Glancing down at her bags now, caught up in the rush, Consuela ran through her ingredients. She planned to make hot tamale pie for her niece, a proper welcome home dinner, and that would require corn meal, chicken, peppers, tomatoes, mushrooms, olives, a large squeeze of lime and a handful of chillies. Check, check, check, check. All done. Putting her head down now, splaying her shoulders, she pushed through to the nearest exit.

Emerging into the morning's sunshine, Consuela couldn't suppress a laugh. There was something crazy about the market, so vital and crushing, the people so tight that they became part of the organism, ebbing and flowing through the place's main arteries, no obvious chance to change direction, unless stepping away so fast (it was a tough manoeuvre) that you had to catch your breath at a coffee stop. Every time she went there she resolved that next time (that fabled 'next time') she would haul herself out of bed earlier and visit the place at dawn, before the throng had descended. Somehow, though, Consuela knew that the crowds were part of the attraction. She might dislike the elbows, the shoulders, the bruise of a knee in the back of her thigh, but there was still something strangely exhilarating about it.

Pacing up the street now, she passed a long queue of people, pencils thrust out, then apples, oranges, a small fraying kitten. The hustlers seemed to multiply daily, but she guessed, like the market, that she had simply chosen the wrong time to visit. It was midday now, an hour until Clifton's Brookdale Cafeteria opened, and so the line of beggars stretched on, block after block. They often began queuing at that place, with its five-cent bowls of rice and soup, three or four hours before the doors swung open, most staring dourly at their feet, while others took the opportunity to preach, extolling the virtues of Jesus and Mary, the Precious Virgin of Guadeloupe and occasionally, confusingly, Judas Iscariot. She felt sorry for these men, brought so low by the Depression that they had to scavenge for food. She wondered, too, where all the women were.

There was still an optimism about this place, though, thought Consuela, a vibrancy that defied the city talk of deficits and overdrafts, bankruptcies and falling stocks, all the tough, loaded terms of recession. Crossing the street, Consuela passed one of the bigger teatros, a collection of men milling furtively around the entrance (they must be showing one of their seamier productions), and then the Repertorio Musical Mexicana, the lilting chords of a favourite corrido passing through its walls and taking her right back to the fields of Jalisco. Whatever the situation for the national banks, she thought, people were obviously still saving money for entertainment. There seemed no better sign than that.

Turning on to a residential side street, Consuela put down her bags, took out the sheaf of paper, and checked the address. Not far to go. Striding along, she realized how excited she was to see Maria again, after all this time apart. Without children of her own, Consuela had always loved her niece, the one relative who could really make her laugh, with her long flailing arms and constant stories, tales that always tended to showcase her clumsiness or stupidity or some forgivable stretch of moral torpor. In all the years she'd been gone – more than a decade now – Consuela must have thought about the girl daily. She had always remembered the thin silhouette of that red skirt, clinging to Maria's haunches, barrelling out of the door and receding into the distance.

It had been just last month that Consuela had heard from her again, a note wending its way from Culver City, passing from one relative to the next, fourth cousin to third, each time inching that little bit closer, until it had arrived at her door and confirmed that her niece was now a legitimate woman, and that she and her young daughter, Clara, were ready to move off the Pantheon Pictures lot and back downtown, where she planned to earn a living as a dressmaker, just like her aunt. Consuela understood that she already had some commissions underway, some work set up. Maria was a wilful girl, she thought hopefully. There was every chance she might succeed.

Consuela had never liked to dwell on the circumstances of Maria's former employment, but sometimes, late at night, lying on her mattress and staring up at that worrying wet sag in the ceiling, she had found it hard not to brood, picking over the events that had led to her niece's choice, spinning her into the vicinity of such stench and corruption. Gazing into the dark she had always found it hard to square the ugly life she imagined in a brothel with the girl she had known, the pretty niece who would ruffle her nose at the neighbourhood boys, calling them ruffians and beasts and slobs, before heckling out a hyena-laugh and running away. Maria had never shown any particular interest in men, had always been dismissive, in fact, of her few boy-crazy peers, with their constant preening and that hip-cocked pose. It was as if she was above it all. Chasing boys was such an earthbound pursuit.

Maria had always been loftier than that, thought Consuela, not snobbish, just unimpressed by the predictability of the life set out for her, the daily grind that was supposed to follow the expected early marriage. Consuela remembered her niece's frustration, on arriving back from school each day, having yawned her way loudly through a string of 'homemaker' classes: the cooking, cleaning and sewing tuition that the authorities felt essential for young Mexican women. While the boys were taught to read and write, do joined-up letters and arithmetic, the only science that the girls were taught was of the domestic variety. Maria had been given a few reading lessons by both Toribio and Consuela, struggling to pick their way through simple English books, but it was obvious she would have liked more detailed instruction. She loved stories, thought Consuela, would have loved the chance to lose herself in another world, if just for an hour. But, it seemed, that option was closed.

She wasn't alone in her frustration, of course. There were hundreds of girls in the LA barrios, perhaps thousands, who held that same fear of the humdrum days ahead, that same wish to flee the demands of housework, those incessant deadening chores, the cooking, cleaning and sewing tasks that somehow always replicated themselves, a new one announcing itself as soon as the last was finished. The men of the barrio, her brother-in-law included, must have recognized this desire, so keen they seemed to keep their women tied to the home, confined by cries for burritos and bandages, far from the flirtations of the outside world, with its lights and electricity, its whispered promise of sex and adventure tickling against their ears. Toribio hadn't been as bad as some, she supposed: he had encouraged Maria's English at first and allowed her to attend school for a time. But still, the life he had envisaged for his daughter was completely at odds with the life she imagined for herself. While Maria clung to thoughts of transcendence, the sly shock of brilliance that would transform it all in an instant, Toribio saw a future for her based firmly within the barrio borders. She would, he thought, be just the same as her peers.

Consuela knew what that life involved, the unending drudge of food preparation and laundry. On the death of her husband, Marquez, fifteen years before, she had been surprised and a little disgusted to find that beneath her red eyes and grief there pulsed a tiny glimmer of joy, a glancing knowledge that she had been unbound. She had loved Marquez, had nursed him anxiously through those brief months of consumption, but still: there was that nag of relief. A week after his death she had wanted to mark her freedom in some way – something subtle, but significant, that only close family might notice. Standing before her small square of mirror, she had carefully untied her rebozo, the colourful shawl that she'd always worn to cover her head when out in public. Striding through the streets then, shorn of her modesty, her face had formed a split-pea grin.

It was a relief, thought Consuela (veering on to Maria's street), that her niece had finally decided to leave the brothel, had summoned the energy to start anew. On hearing of this a few weeks ago, Consuela had written to Toribio to tell him. This very morning she had received his reply, reticent as usual but not especially terse, asking her to send his regards to Maria. Since being deported (a direct result of his union activities) Toribio had returned to Jalisco and was happily remarried, settled with Emilia, a young widow with three children. Consuela knew that Maria would be excited to hear news of her father, and particularly his tacit forgiveness. Somehow the message seemed to solder the situation, signalling a firm end to that messy period of Maria's life.

Arriving at a rather shabby brownstone, Consuela checked the address. This was it. Knocking loudly on the door, heart racing, she stood back and waited. She felt slightly sick, she realized, and light-headed, as though she'd fasted for days. Waiting a minute, there came no answer, so she knocked again, louder this time. Maria's letter had said that she'd be around all this week, finishing up a big order. It had promised that she'd only leave the house for supplies in the morning and evening, but would be available any other time Consuela might like to visit. Surely she hadn't forgotten.

Leaning forward to knock again, Consuela was stopped by the swing of the door opening on to a dusty hall. Lurking just inside she spotted a girl, who must be Clara (though she didn't look as old as eight), clad in a greying undershirt. Beneath the garment her legs stuck out, stork-like and gawky, covered in scratches, as though she'd been pulled painfully through a blackberry bush. Hanging from her hand (she seemed to find it comforting) was the brownest of banana skins. Edging into the hall, Consuela tried not to scare the girl. There was something wrong here, that much was sure, and she would need to be careful.

Falling to her knees, she gently touched the girl's elbows, entreating her to speak. 'You're Clara, aren't you?' she said. The little girl nodded warily, mouth waspish and skewed. 'Well, that's good,' said Consuela, 'because I'm your aunt.' She wanted to keep the tone fairly light. 'I'm your Aunt Consuela, Clara. I've come to see your mama.'

'Oh.' Clara still looked suspicious, but, clearly listless, she seemed accepting. Taking Consuela's hand, she led the woman down a long dark corridor and some stairs into a suffocating basement apartment.

Having steeled herself for the worst, Consuela still couldn't control her repulsion, coughing back her gag mechanism, hand slapping to her mouth. She had lived in some dives herself – the barrio circa 1915 had been nothing to boast about – but they had always been clean at least, as tidy as she and her cousins could make them, given a water hydrant between thirty. This place though. She had never seen the like.

They were standing in a space that housed the kitchen and a few chairs, the floor covered not in sawdust but vegetable peelings, undulating creepily as the cockroaches ran through, the bugs appearing everywhere now: through cracks in the wall, a broken light fitting, the hairy, thickening strait of a plughole. Consuela's skin felt suddenly baggy and borrowed, as if, in an ideal world, she could peel it right off. She wanted to leave. Glancing down at Clara, though, she knew it was impossible.

'Where's your mama?' she said, almost afraid to open her mouth, lest one of the roaches fly in. Led into the adjacent room now, Consuela felt the bile rise higher in her throat. Collapsed on the floor, insects swarming about her, Maria lay naked and sore-ridden, a fleshly column, the very opposite of the movie stars and fairy tale princesses she'd chattered about as a child. Going to wake her, unsure of her bearings, Consuela found Maria in some kind of trance. She had a pulse, certainly, and her dead-fish eyes were wide open, but there was no response, nothing to suggest that she could see or hear.

Crouching again, ignoring the roaches, Consuela grasped at Clara. 'Mi hijita, mi hijita, how long has she been like this?'

Clara shrugged. 'A few days I guess.' She looked scared. 'I don't know.'

'And you haven't been to any of the neighbours? You didn't call on anyone to help?'

'I don't know the neighbours.'

'So you've just been down here all alone, with your mother like this?'

'Yep.'

'You haven't seen anyone else?'

'It's not my fault!' Clara stamped a foot. 'It's not my fault! I can't help that she's like this, I don't know why it happens. She was right the other day and I was fetching some vegetables and when I came in here, she was like this. I didn't do anything, though. Nothing. I didn't make her like this. You can't blame me.' She began to cry.

'Oh.' Consuela was surprised. 'That's not what I meant, Clara. It's just that we need to get you both out of here. This isn't a very nice place to live, is it? And your mama.' She looked back at Maria. 'She doesn't look well.'

'She's been like this before. She's always been OK.'

'She has?'

'Yep.' Clara swallowed a sob and clasped the banana skin hard against her chest, skids of mucus smearing her shirt. She resolved to stop crying now. It was no use. 'She's like this a lot. Usually Dora stays with us until she's better, but Dora's back at the big house. She hasn't been here at all.'

'So your mama's been exactly like this? It's nothing different?'

'You just gotta stay with her, and after a while she wakes up.'

'And she's OK then?'

'Yep. She's OK.'

Casting around for help (divine, practical, miscellaneous), Consuela considered their options. There could be no arguing that this was a good place to convalesce. No one could rally here.

'Will you pack your things,' she said softly. 'You're coming to stay with me.'

Chapter Twelve

'Hydrogen, helium, lithium, beryllium,' Rita Mae paused. 'Then it's,' she paused again, nose scrunching, 'I don't know actually, I hadn't got much further than that.' Johnny looked up at her expectantly. 'What?' He was always pressuring her. 'What do you want? I told you, I don't know. It's not as though this stuff has any reason to lodge in my brain. Not as though it's vaguely interesting.' He was still looking. Still expectant. 'Oh,' she was angry now. 'Gaaah, I don't know. Sodium? That's one of them, right?'

'Nope. I mean, it *is* one of them, but sodium doesn't even come close.'

'I said to you, I told you, I don't *know*.' She lowered her hands to her hips and gave an irritated pout. 'Could it possibly be,' she sighed, laughing slightly to herself, 'tedium?'

Johnny narrowed his eyes. 'Well, since you mention it,' he smiled, 'there is a link.'

'Oh, will ya just get over yourself and tell me,' Rita Mae sat down beside him, her recitation of the periodic table clearly over. A particularly short performance. 'It's not as if I'm gonna guess. I'll bet you either know this stuff or you don't. And I have a sneaking suspicion,' she wagged an accusatory finger, 'that you do. Which makes you both quite clever and very—'

'Boron.'

'You shouldn't be so hard on yourself. But yep.'

Johnny rolled his eyes. 'You heard what I said. At number five on the periodic table is boron.'

'Oh. Huh. Well I guess I might remember that now.' Rita Mae tilted her head. 'Doubt I'll get beyond it, though. When's the test?'

'Tomorrow.'

'Ah.' Rita Mae shrugged. 'I'm screwed.' Reaching over to Johnny, she took the book from his hands, closed it decisively and laid it down. 'No more. It would be so much easier,' she said, 'if the elements were named after traits, wouldn't it?'

'What do you mean?'

'Well, like the seven dwarves.'

'Huh.' Johnny seemed uncertain. 'I, well,' he didn't want to offend her, 'it's a very good point.'

They were silent for a second then, gazing out from the wooden chamber where they sat, the dusty, disused shooting range that had been their hidey-hole for a long few years now. It was a Saturday afternoon and most of the island kids were gathered at the parade ground, playing organized sports: basketball, baseball or tennis. As usual, Johnny and Rita Mae had opted out. Chemistry homework had somehow seemed more inviting.

'When do I get to give up chemistry? Remind me?'

'Well, it's timetabled until you're sixteen. Unless you prove completely remedial, I guess.'

'Johnny,' Rita Mae was imperious, 'I think we both know who's remedial.'

He smiled. 'You're absolutely right. It's so good of you to admit it.'

'Oh,' she slapped him on the arm, 'you're so rude. I find it very hurtful when you say things like that. Very hurtful indeed.'

'You don't really?'

She smiled. 'No, I don't really. So,' she paused, 'if I stay here on the island it's gonna be a good few years until I can ditch chemistry, that's what you're telling me.'

'And you are staying on the island.'

'How do you know?'

'Well, unless your father's planning to get another job or something,' Johnny felt a jolt of sickness, 'which he's not, right?'

'Why does it depend on my father moving?'

'Oh. Well,' Johnny shrugged, 'because you're officially classed as a child, Rita Mae, aren't you? I mean,' he cast his hand back and forth between them, 'you and I both know you're terribly mature, but, well, you're still not really meant to leave home until you're sixteen.'

'Those are the rules.'

'Yes.'

'But who said anything about abiding by them?'

'Really?' Johnny had never considered this idea.

'Look, Johnny,' Rita Mae jumped to her feet again, pacing before him, 'if we're not careful we could end up stuck on this island for literally,' she paused, 'well, literally months! It's a terrible scenario. Don't tell me you haven't thought about it.'

'Well, I suppose it had occurred to me. I mean,' he coughed, 'I-I obviously want to get off here as soon as possible, but there aren't many options are there? I just thought that, well, uh, once I turned sixteen I'd, kind of, make arrangements for the mainland, lay down some plans. I'd, I'd never really thought there was any chance of leaving before then.'

'That's it though,' said Rita Mae, pointing at her head, 'you just don't think, Johnny. You're being entirely closed-minded about this. I mean, realistically, if you have the will to do something, if you really want it, then there has to be a way, doesn't there? It just has to be a case of thinking these things through and coming up with a plan.'

'So,' he wanted to get this straight, set his mind at rest, 'you don't actually have a plan then? It's just, sort of, a dream at the moment?'

'No. It is not just a dream. What I'm saying, Johnny, is that we should come up with something between us. I'm saying that, with a little thought, we could devise an escape plan.'

'Oh.' Right. 'So did you have anything particular in mind?'

'Well,' Rita Mae sat down and clasped her hands in her lap, 'the obvious way to get off the island is to board the boat right?'

'Right.' That was, in fact, the only way, thought Johnny.

'So, I figured that we could stow away on the *Warden Wright* next time it docks. I mean, I know it's not huge, but it's big enough, and there must be some nooks in that thing, some place we could hide. I bet we could find somewhere below deck.'

'Have you ever been on that boat?'

'Only when I was a kid.'

'Oh.' Johnny looked down. 'I went on it last year, do you remember, when I had to go to my grandfather's funeral?'

'Sure.'

'And I'm not sure it would be possible to stow away. Before that thing sets sail one of the officers checks through every inch of it—'

'Oh.'

'Twice.'

'When you say every inch?'

'I mean it.'

Rita Mae was silent for a second. 'Oh. That's a pity. I really thought that might work. Huh.' She paused. 'I did have another idea.'

'What's that?'

'I-I suppose it's a little more ambitious. I guess you might think it's fanciful.'

'You want to hitch a ride on a dolphin's back?'

'Not that fanciful.' Rita Mae looked a little embarrassed. 'Well, almost. I wondered whether – if I trained really hard – I might have a chance of swimming to the mainland.'

Johnny snorted. 'You're joking?'

'No, I'm not!' Rita Mae sighed. 'It's just that we need something radical if we can't board the boat. I'm quite a strong swimmer, or I probably could be, and, apparently, if you smear yourself with animal fat you can carry on through really cold straits and survive just fine.'

'You're not really thinking of swimming across? It must be miles further than anyone's ever swum before. Ever.'

'Oh.' She looked down at her feet. 'I didn't know that. Geography's not my strong suit, is it?' Rita Mae sighed. 'It's just that I look out over that water sometimes and I almost think I can see California, all those lights. I know it's not possible, not really, but sometimes it seems to be blinking back at me.'

'I know.'

'I'll come up with something, Johnny. You know I will.'

'I don't doubt that.'

Rita Mae shrugged sadly. 'No doubting at all.'

Chapter Thirteen

Downtown Los Angeles, 7 June 1943

Mouth stuffed hedgehog-full of pins, Maria Caesar leaned over the machine, needle tapping frantically to the end of the hem. Unsure where her scissors might be (she knew they were on the floor somewhere, hidden beneath the waxy layers of pattern paper) she leaned in still further, spitting pins across the desk, before clenching her teeth and pulling the thread clean. Holding the pants away from her, she appraised the afternoon's work. Fashioned in bright blue cotton, they certainly weren't subtle, but she was sure that the boy who had ordered them – a pachuco whose hair defied both gravity and taste – would be pleased. He'd asked for the pegging to be particularly pronounced, and this was most certainly the case. Now she was just left to tackle his jacket. An outlandish design, it would require some serious constructive genius to ensure the wide shoulders didn't droop.

Pushing her chair out, standing up and stretching, Maria called into the next room. 'Consuela, are you back there? I need to find the fabric for that jacket. I'm not sure we have any left.'

Her aunt shuffled through the door, back hunched but

smiling. Consuela was inching close to sixty now, and her brown skin seemed to have shrunk so that she vaguely resembled one of those shrivelled heads that lurk darkly in museums of anthropology. Passing Maria, she crossed to a chair in the corner, stacked high with coloured fabrics. Leafing through, she shook her head. 'I think the blue was one of the lengths that Clara was due to collect,' she sighed, 'so I guess we'll have to wait. Still,' she came over and held up the pants, 'it looks as though you've done a good job with these, mi hijita. They're crazy! The boy's going to look like he has thighs as big as this,' she held her hands out wide and puffed her cheeks until the skin was deceptively smooth. 'He's not coming for that order until tomorrow, is he?'

Maria nodded. 'He said he'd come in the afternoon, after work, I think.'

'Ah well then,' Consuela shrugged and laughed, 'we should take the opportunity to relax. Clara will be home soon, but there's nothing we can do till she arrives.'

Maria smiled. 'Ah, Consuela, you're work-shy, I tell you.' Her aunt's nose wrinkled mischievously. 'I guess you're right, though.' She folded the pants and placed them carefully alongside the sewing machine. 'There isn't so much else we can do.'

Pattern paper crunching beneath her feet, Maria headed to the kitchen area – a small gas fire and collection of dirty pans in the corner of the room. 'You want a coffee, Auntie? I'm making one for myself.'

'Of course, of course.' Consuela sat heavily on the couch, noticing yet another spot that needed to be patched, wiry stuffing spilling through. Not right now, she thought, settling back comfortably. Hand splayed, she counted the orders they had lined up. It was going to take all their work and concentration to fill those, she decided, and meanwhile they would need to snatch whatever rest they could. If business continued like this they'd have to start sleeping in three-hour shifts.

'Clara's been gone a long time,' Maria was saying, the kettle whistling. 'Was she gonna eat in Hollywood too?'

Consuela shrugged. 'She didn't say anything, I don't think so. She was just going to pick up the fabric. It's a big order, though, and you know what Ernst's like—'

'Never prepared.'

'That's right, so she's probably waiting for him to measure up.'

'Oh yeah.' Maria brought over a cup of coffee and sank down beside Consuela. 'It's not that I'm upset with her taking too long over her chores, you know, Auntie.' A smile played lightly across her lips. 'It's just I wondered whether Clara was maybe sneaking around a bit and using this as an excuse to—'

'What?'

'Well,' Maria laughed shyly. 'I wondered whether she'd been seeing anyone, Consuela, whether she'd been meeting up with a boy.' Maria poked her aunt softly in the stomach, prompting a spluttered gasp. 'Come on, Consuela, she speaks to you much more than she does me. What is it?'

Consuela smacked both hands to her mouth, eyes wide and teasing.

'She's met someone, hasn't she? She's met someone and you know all about it!' Maria sprang to her feet, her aunt still silent. 'Oh, you can't do this to me, Consuela.' Her voice was pleading, hands falling pointedly to her hips. 'If you know something like this then you gotta tell me. What's he like? Have you seen him? Is it serious?'

Her aunt toppled over on the couch, convulsed with laughter, face growing red.

'What is it?' said Maria. 'If you don't tell me right now, Auntie, then I'll,' she paused, thinking fast, 'I'll,' Consuela was giggling, clearly not threatened, 'I'll throw your coffee right out this window.' Maria grabbed Consuela's mug and held it at arm's length over the street. 'I'm quite happy to do it, you know.' She pouted before tipping out a single drop. 'And it's really hot coffee, Consuela. It's boiling, steaming.' She dipped a finger in the liquid and held it up. 'Yow! That's how hot it is. Who knows, though? I could pour it right now and there might just be someone below, some pretty cholita off to see her beloved, who would get horribly burned. Her beloved would break with her, the wedding would be off, and eventually she'd have to join a convent, no other choice, just because of this one moment. Oh,' Maria paused, free hand rising to her throat, 'it would be terrible, just terrible. It would be like one of those movies, except without the happy ending where the ugly girl lets down her hair and gets all pretty. And that,' she held up her hand, a pantomime swoon, 'would be on your conscience for ever, Aunt Consuela. You'd be trying to sleep at night, and you'd just see those burns, the scars on that poor girl's face. It would be my fault, too, I know that, but I'm easy, aren't I, Auntie? I don't have so much conscience as you. You're a woman of God, Consuela. You wear a rosary. You'd never be able to live with yourself.'

Consuela stood up now, still laughing, and walked over to Maria. 'Are you finished now, mi hijita, finished? You're right, I wouldn't be able to live with it.' She took Maria's empty hand. 'You've gotta come away from that window, before there really is an accident.'

'OK.' Maria smiled and handed back the coffee cup. 'But you have to tell me everything, Consuela. Everything. You have to give me the whole story.'

Consuela sat down, sighing. 'I was only joking with you, Maria, there isn't any special boy really.'

'Oh.' Maria perched on the edge of the couch. 'Well you don't sound very convincing, Auntie.' She narrowed her eyes. 'I'm not sure I believe you.'

'Well . . .' Consuela fingered her rosary, thinking suddenly of Jesus and the commandments and the many moral conflicts of truth.

'Well?'

'Well,' she paused, gulping, 'perhaps there have been a few boys.'

'A few?' Maria stood up again. 'A few?'

'Yes.' Consuela smiled at her. 'Just a few, but none of them have been serious, no proposals or formals. And also,' she lowered her voice, 'they've all been American boys, Maria, not a pachuco among them. It seems our Clara has quite a liking for the pale skin. She doesn't like the view on this side of town. She says the boys are vulgar.'

Maria's eyes had widened until her brows encroached on her hairline. 'She's been out with American boys? You're sure?'

Consuela nodded.

'Well.' Maria was quiet now as she sat back at her sewing machine. 'I had no idea. I can't believe it. When did she tell you all this, Consuela, how long have you known?'

'Ah, Maria,' Consuela could see her niece's disappointment, 'did you hear what I said? None of these boys has been serious, none worth commenting on really. I only know about them because I happened to be out at the store one day, buying lemons, and I saw Clara talking to an American boy. That's the only reason.'

'But she's spoken to you about it?'

'Well,' Consuela shifted slightly, suddenly much more irritated by the stuffing poking up through the couch, 'perhaps just a little. But only because she knew I'd seen her. She only told me because it would have been awkward not to. Not because there was anything important to say.'

'Oh, OK.' Maria snatched up the pants again, staring intently at one of the hems, obscuring her face. 'I suppose she doesn't feel so comfortable talking to me now.'

'That's not it. Not at all.'

They were both silent then, Consuela sipping at her coffee, Maria making a great show of inspecting the pegged pants. However she played it, thought Consuela, annoyed with herself now, these conversations were always awkward, they always ended uncomfortably. She understood, of course, why Maria would want to plug her for information – Clara hardly spoke to her mother these days – but she wished that there were some way to avoid the fallout when her niece uncovered some new, hidden snippet.

It had become much more tricky, of course, since Clara began working with them. In the last few years, the business Consuela shared with Maria had burgeoned massively, largely as a result of the War Preparedness Board's ban on pleats, cuffs and long jackets, a decision which had forced all legitimate traders to stop stocking that barrio favourite: the draped suit. Since this decree had been passed, Consuela and Maria had found themselves at the forefront of a successful underground trade in the suits, their reputation spreading quickly across the neighbourhood, word passing from pachuco to pachuco. It was said amongst these brilliant, bequiffed boys that the women could make any-thing, however screwball or extreme. They were unshock-able. Each day, then, new customers would arrive at the apartment, designs sketched deftly on paper napkins, the proportions always that little bit more radical.

With the orders rocketing up, their hands blurred and blistering, Consuela and Maria had conceded that they must employ a third seamstress. The best candidate – Clara – had been obvious to them both, but Maria had been worried about asking her, nervous that her daughter might laugh derisively and dance away. Recognizing this concern, Consuela had started a gentle bout of diplomacy, aimed squarely at reassuring Maria. In the two years since Clara had left school, she reminded her, she had worked just a string of temporary shop jobs, never really settling into anything, so there was every chance she might agree. Finally, after some effective persuasion (and a crippling night of hemming), Maria had told Consuela to go ahead and ask. Clara's answer was affirmative.

Both women had been wary of working together, Consuela knew that, but she had hoped, fervently, that the move might elicit some connection, override the broken promises and bitterness. As it was, though, Clara's hostility seemed to increase daily. It was there in her sarcasm, her ironic laughter, the belligerent insistence on making coffee just for herself and her great-aunt, whether her mother called for a cup or not. It was there in her constant references to 'certain crazy people', twinned with a sly nod in Maria's direction. Caught between the two women, Consuela was in a particularly hazardous position. An acrobat balanced atop widening stilts.

'Consuela?'

'What is it, mi hijita?'

'You would let me know if Clara was really involved with someone, wouldn't you? You wouldn't keep something as important as that from me?'

Consuela laughed. 'Of course not. You shouldn't worry so much, Maria. If Clara was seeing someone serious, I'm sure she'd come and tell you herself, you wouldn't have to wait for me to say something. It's only because these other boys have just been friends that she hasn't told you. No other reason.'

'Right.' Maria didn't sound convinced.

Consuela didn't blame her.

There was a banging at the door then, a flurry of fists, echoing loudly through the apartment.

'Did Clara have a key?' Maria ran to peek through the peephole. Seeing her daughter, face bulging distortedly in the magnifying lens, she unlocked the door. Holding Clara still, she saw that something was terribly wrong.

'What is it, Clara? Tell me what's happened.' Maria's daughter, usually so flawless, looked oddly dishevelled. Her hair, which had earlier been set in a broad, high pompadour and lacquered hard, was slumping heavily against her forehead; her sweater was ripped at the shoulder, falling open to expose her collarbone; her black stockings were ripped and laddered, sagging now around her ankles; and her black skirt was wet and stained. Everything, Maria noticed, was in descent.

'What's happened, what's happened? You've been attacked? Tell me who did this? Who's hurt you?'

Clara looked uncomfortable as she shrugged off her mother's grip. Gazing at Maria, seeing her mother's concern, she said nothing.

Standing a short distance away now, Consuela pushed for an answer. 'Come on, Clara. Tell us.' She hurried forward, gasping suddenly. 'Are you bleeding? Is that blood on your skirt?'

Maria cried, stretching towards Clara, but her daughter pushed right past her. Reaching down, Clara squeezed her skirt, blood dripping to the floor. Seeing Consuela's look of astonishment and fear, she rushed to explain. 'It's not my blood, Auntie, don't worry, there's nothing to be done.'

Consuela held out a hand and led Clara slowly to the couch. 'Come now, mi hijita, tell me clearly. What's happened? Maria,' she called over to her niece, who was still staring blankly at the blood on the floor, 'why don't you make some more coffee and I'll find out what's going on here.' She put an arm around Clara, who was shaking now. 'Where were you, sweetheart? Was there another riot?'

Clara rested her head against her aunt's sunken chest and began to breathe deeply. 'It was awful, Consuela, I didn't know what to do. There was so much blood.'

'I know, it's all right, all right. We'll work this out, won't we? If you tell us what happened, though, then we can help you, Clara, we can make it better.'

Clara sincerely doubted that. Some things were irretrievable. 'I was on the street car, Auntie, coming back from Hollywood with the material, five bags of it.'

'Right.'

'And everything seemed fine. I'd been on there awhile, and I was only a few blocks away, when this group of cars, jalopies, gathered all round the trolley, till the driver was forced to stop. I didn't know what was happening, everyone looked so scared, and then there was this man in uniform forcing the doors open, fighting his way into the carriage –

he had a crowbar I think – with a whole crowd of men behind him. They were sailors, most of them, all military. Anyway,' Clara took a deep breath and placed her hands rather formally in her lap, 'they were able to get through the doors eventually, and they just started pulling out any of the boys who looked Mexican and beating them in the street. They took this boy – he can't have been more than twelve – and they were ripping all his clothes off him, while his mother,' she paused, 'she tried to stop them. She was pleading with them, on her knees at one point, and they just smacked her in the face with a blackjack. It was awful. And then they were hurting other people, really beating them – they had these handkerchiefs filled with coins that they were using to hit people – and there just seemed to be more and more sailors arriving all the time.'

Maria handed Clara a coffee and sat down at her feet. 'Where did the blood come from, darling? How did you get so ripped up?'

'Oh.' Clara pursed her lips. She tended not to speak to her mother about anything other than work, but the question seemed fair really, she could see why the woman would be worried. 'I was out on the sidewalk, trying to decide whether to run or help someone, when I saw this man, this really young man, and,' she paused, gulping now, 'it's too horrible.'

'What?'

'Well,' she paused again, 'there was a group of sailors around him, you couldn't really make it out, but then I realized that, well, they were gouging his eyes out with a spoon.'

Maria and Consuela were silent.

'I tried to help him when they left. I gave him some of our

cloth for bandages – there was a woman on the streetcar who was a nurse – but there was nothing else anyone could do really. There were policemen who could have taken him to hospital, I s'pose, but they were just waiting around. They didn't do anything. When the sailors started to move down the street, they were arresting the Mexican kids who had just been beaten, charging them with vagrancy—'

'No!'

'They were, they were charging them with vagrancy and breaches of the peace. One of the sailors tried to grope at me, but I got away.' She paused, turning to Consuela. 'I lost the fabric, Auntie, I'm sorry.'

Consuela flapped her hands dismissively. 'It's fine, mi hijita, don't even think of it.' She pulled Clara close again. 'Me and your mama are just worried about you, and whether you're OK. We don't care about the cloth. You say this man tried to touch you? You got away, yes?'

'Of course.' Clara was crying now. 'He tried to put his hand down my sweater, Consuela, he was tearing at it, but I managed to run. It was only a few blocks from here, and he didn't follow me.'

'Good.' Consuela paused. 'Thank goodness you got away.'

They sat in silence for a minute then, sipping their coffee, until Clara stood up. 'I have to go and change, thank you, thank you,' she said, stepping over her mother, making her way to the bedroom. Her skirt, she realized now, was still sopping with blood, streaking down her legs, as if she'd been stabbed. Stripping off her clothes, she threw them in a pile in the corner – something she'd never done before, normally so careful – and stretched out on the bed. She was determined to put aside all those scenes (the benevolent squelch of the eyeball against the spoon, so much like jello at a party) but she couldn't quite do it. She had heard people talk of the riots around here in the last few days, but she had thought the stories exaggerated.

Could it be that those sailors really hated Mexicans so much? As they set to work in the streetcar, she had overheard snatches of conversation, comments that these young boys were traitors, that they should be in uniform, prepared to go overseas. 'If they want to live in this country, if they want to use our stuff, our women, they gotta be fighting our fucking wars.' The truth was, though – and Clara couldn't believe they didn't see it – some of those boys were as young as ten. Those kids, patriotic or not, couldn't have gone to war. And now, with some of their injuries, they probably never would. Even if this war stretched out endlessly, ticking past 1950, 1960, 1970, Clara still couldn't imagine how the army might use a blind man.

She thought of that man now, how the blood had welled so suddenly in his sockets, congregating in thick, sticky pools before streaming down his face. The irony, she realized, her last two thoughts colliding and connecting, was that he had quite clearly been wearing (she could see it now, so obvious) his defence-plant identification badge. He was a defence worker, out for the night, probably off to see a movie or to meet his woman at a dance hall. And then that had happened.

He had been stumbling after the attack, screaming and hitting out at anyone who tried to help. This included Clara, who, approaching him with some muslin, had taken a sharp blow to the ear. It didn't hurt that much, she thought now, rubbing it gently, perhaps slightly bruised. She wondered vaguely whether that man would survive.

There had been so much blood pouring out of him, his head seeming to empty, and he wouldn't let anyone close enough to help. She would be surprised, on balance, if he did make it. The least a blind man needed was trust.

Hauling herself on to her elbows, Clara reached for the mirror that sat beside her bed. Staring into it, she tried to figure whether she looked clearly Mexican, whether those sailors would have picked her from the crowd. It was difficult to tell. Whenever her eyes strayed to her strongest features – wide brown eyes, full lips – she was reminded of her mother, and that brought another, quite different, vulnerability to her face. People had always remarked on how alike she and Maria looked, suggesting they came from the same pod, that they could really be sisters. It was frustrating.

Perhaps, Clara thought now, she was destined to turn out just like her mother. Perhaps she would inherit all that stupidity, neglect, the inability to take care of herself, the sheer, blinding conviction that she could fly. And then there was the untidiness; that might afflict her too, and she would find herself copying Maria's habits, piling possessions high around each room, idle columns swaying each time she walked past, arrayed tightly, like a model of New York by a failing architect. Perhaps all that madness was just latent in her, biding its time, the lowliest parasite. Her mother hadn't always been crazy. Consuela said she'd been just fine as a kid.

And who knew what she might inherit from her father, what secret affliction was his to pass down, as hidden and obscure as his name? There was a whole half to her background, thought Clara, which stood blank and hollow, nothing to fill it, no information that might alert her to her future self, suggest how she would pan out. Ever since she'd recognized this void, understood that Maria had no idea who he was or might be, she had hated her mother for the blankness, for bringing her into the world a bastard. Not just illegitimate, but the child of a whore.

Now, though, as she lay there, Clara suddenly saw that empty half as something else: an opportunity or a solace, a space to step into. There was another world out there, just past the barrio, where she could become someone different – not a Mexican girl, a cholita, but a thing without labels. She could start anew, no traits at all, and make herself up gradually. She would not become her mother, she thought, thankful. It simply would not happen.

Standing up suddenly, head slightly dizzy, Clara clasped her hands tight and held them to the ceiling. She didn't know what she was doing – wasn't religious, didn't believe in the spirits – but she felt good standing there, body stretched out, poised. Closing her eyes, she considered her options. Decision made, she flopped back to the bed and burrowed beneath the covers. The next day, it was official, she would start a new life. Across town, someplace safe, she would be another person. A new Clara Caesar.

Chapter Fourteen

'It's crazy,' said Larry Jones, prodding at the meatloaf. 'Just crazy. I can't believe they're cutting the tower guard back again. So soon as well.' He shook his head dumbly, as Rita Mae sat mute and watchful beside him. 'Crazy.'

Placing a bowl of black beans on the latticed table mat, Clara smiled tightly. She pulled her chair up and out, anxious not to scrape the floor, and sat down, back straight. 'It's obviously not a problem,' she said firmly, 'or Warden Wright would never have proposed it, would he?' She began cutting the meatloaf into thick slices. 'He's a clever man, you know, Larry. A careful,' she tripped over the next word, 'strategist. He wouldn't have suggested this if it was putting his staff at risk.' She stirred the gravy. 'You're just worried that they'll shake up the department and transfer you to another job. Something a little more taxing.'

'No I'm not, don't say that.' Larry's voice took on the tenor of a teenage whine. 'I genuinely think this is a bad idea, Clara. They've cut back the tower guard from six men to three in the space of, what? Two years? They've halved the number of officers watching over the island. Halved them. That just can't be good.'

As Clara gave a shrug, Larry began tapping his knife

against the table. It was true, he thought, lips forming a pious pout, he really was concerned about the Warden's decision to cut back the tower guard. If this move proved wrong it could jeopardize every inhabitant of Las Focas: man, woman or child. All that was needed was a well thought out escape plan – and the inmates seemed to get cleverer on this count by the hour – and the loss of those tower officers could be fatal. Without enough outdoor security it was just possible that an inmate could escape the cell house and run amok across the island. If he wasn't caught quickly or shot by one of the remaining tower guards then he might just be able to take hostages.

Also (and Larry lowered his head now, only barely allowing himself this thought at the table), the changes meant that it was going to be even harder to get close to an inmate. Although the transfer of guards into the cell house would be small, its effect would no doubt be significant. It would become almost impossible to develop a relationship, however discreet, with a prisoner. If he did decide to act on his current plan, if he did take it all to the next level (Larry's knife-tap built to a crescendo), he would have to exercise extreme caution.

'Will you stop that, Larry. Now,' Clara snarled. She snatched up his knife. 'I can't stand that any longer.'

Clara began serving the food, the layout of each plate following a carefully preconceived pattern. First a slice of meatloaf was placed on the right-hand side, before a hill of beans was balanced precariously on this mound, a handful cascading off and into the centre. To the left Clara poured a half-moon arc of gravy, which neatly cupped the other contents.

If this pattern hadn't been so precise it might have

suggested some kind of flair or flamboyance. As it was, thought Rita Mae, her mother's movements were more those of an automaton than an artist. She watched as Clara seasoned the plates now with a dusting of pepper. Her right arm was exposed below the elbow and Rita Mae could just see her mother's tendons bucking up through the skin, tense with control and limitation.

As Clara handed the heaviest plate to Larry, Rita Mae noticed a change in her father's posture. His sprawling form – legs splayed wide, elbows perched clumsily on the table – sprang suddenly shut, like a clam, and he leaned in hard and protective above his food. His fervour reminded Rita Mae of the time he'd told her about the art exhibitions his mother had dragged him to as a kid, the only thing he recalled being the steak sandwiches they'd chow afterwards in Musso and Frank's. Larry Jones had a restlessness about him when he ate, which only subsided as the last traces were wiped from his plate. Until then he was desperate and hoggish, snuffling up the meatloaf as if it were the finest of white truffles.

Rita Mae's gaze moved back and forth between her parents as they set about their food. She had liked watching them ever since she was a small kid, shoring up evidence for her vague, hopeful theory that she might have been adopted. This time, though, there was a new reason for scrutiny.

Over the past few years the movie magazines that her grandmother had sent had made regular references to an acting technique called 'The Method', which was practised by all of Rita Mae's favourite stars – Monty Clift, Marlon Brando, the late, great Jimmy Dean. From what she could gather (the magazines were a little vague, not much given to intellectual detail), the key to the technique was that actors should use their own memories to inform the characters they played. By picking carefully over their reactions and responses to past events they could learn to apply these during a performance, bringing an edge of reality to their acting.

Reading about this process, Rita Mae had felt a little cheated. How was she supposed to build a useful body of experience out here on Las Focas, a tiny island where nothing ever happened? Sure, there were the cell-house riots, the regular, bestial murders (most involving some form of biting), but the repercussions of these events only ribboned their way out to the staff quarters on rare occasions. Rita Mae was jealous of the actors that she admired, all of whom had cultivated some great inoperable grief (even if based only on the death of a goldfish) to be spirited forth whenever necessary. They had a welter of experience, she thought, deep wells to draw. She, on the other hand, had nothing. Well, almost nothing. All she could cling to was the small smudge of trauma that she felt whenever she saw Jenna's feet hoofing past in her dreams. That feeling was definitely real, a sharp, undirected spasm, but she had no idea quite what it related to. It was useless, thought Rita Mae, useless.

Still, flicking through a magazine recently, she had come to an article by a 'world-famed' acting instructor named Eugene Hoffenmeyer III, which had made her feel slightly better. 'Although some actors draw material from difficult memories of their past, many work equally well with more subtle experiences,' wrote Hoffenmeyer. 'Sense memory can be developed simply by observing your friends and family at play and making a precise mental note of their speech and movements.'

Rita Mae wasn't sure whether eating a hunk of meatloaf constituted a family 'at play', but dinner time seemed her best opportunity for observation. Watching her parents, she pushed her own spoon carelessly through the puddle of gravy, before lifting it to her mouth. Just missing her lips, it splashed messily across her front.

'Rita Mae!' cried Clara, leaning over the table and patting violently at her daughter's chest with a napkin. 'I wish you'd concentrate when you eat. You've ruined that blouse. You're disgusting.' She turned back to Larry. 'I just don't think you have anything like the Warden's expertise when it comes to decision-making. He knows what he's doing.'

'You don't understand,' said Larry, masticated beans catapulting from his tongue. 'This could really damage island security, Clara, it could put you and Rita Mae at real risk.' He sat upright for a second, gesticulating with his fork now. 'It could be a disaster for all of us and you just have no idea.' He bent back over his plate then, shoulders set low, cutting the rest of his meal into chunks. 'You'll realize if there's an escape. I tell you that much.'

Clara tilted her head, chewing slowly. 'You're exaggerating, and you know it. There hasn't been an escape from that building since – when was it?'

'Nineteen twenty-eight.'

'That's right. Nineteen twenty-eight. And the cell house had only just been set up then, hadn't it? There was nothing like the number of security systems they have in place now. There have been all those attempts, and just one escape. It's a waste of time having officers on those outdoor guard posts all the time, watching for something that's not going to happen. It's a waste of resources. Surely it's much better to move those guards inside, ready to help stop any of the riots. That's where the danger lies.' Clara held her fork an inch above her plate, before plunging it down and spearing a bean expertly on to each prong. Her smile was reptilian. 'With all the problems you've had in the cellblock, Laurence, I'd have thought you'd have realized that by now.'

They both fell quiet for a second then, Clara preening slightly at Larry's silence, her hands creeping upwards and patting her pristine wave of hair. In that moment, it was suddenly obvious to Rita Mae how hollow her mother really was. Clara was just a cipher, an empty space waiting to be filled with received ideas and opinions: in this case, the Warden's thoughts on island security. She had probably never responded intuitively to anything, mused Rita Mae, had never been taken aback by a painting or a piece of music, had never formed her own argument about some issue of national importance. Instead, she fed right off others.

Her father – he of the twinkling Scott Fitzgerald childhood – was sitting even more awkwardly now, as though he hadn't quite grown into his body. Rita Mae had read an article recently that suggested an individual's personality stayed suspended at the age at which they'd been happiest. If this was true, thought Rita Mae, then it seemed that her father's heyday had come at the age of about eighteen. His body language was that of a boy concerned with basketball rather than business, sailing rather than the stock market: an uncontrollable sprawl of limbs. At times like this, when he'd been roundly criticized, his posture was at its most pubertal. His long back hunched like armour, face crumpled in a guileless sneer.

Watching her parents, it occurred to Rita Mae – for the

gadzillionth time – how utterly unsuited they were. It wasn't just that they were so different, but that none of their differences were complementary. If Clara had been maternal as well as strict then perhaps she could have mothered Larry through his protracted adolescence. As it was, though, Clara was about as yielding as the plastic imitation fruit that sat in ceremony on the Wright family's coffee table.

'I think you know you're wrong,' said Clara, enjoying the argument. 'If you were capable of making this kind of decision they would have promoted you to management by now, Laurence.' She watched as her husband's sneer intensified. 'You'd be much further up the ladder.'

Finishing his meal, Larry scraped back his chair. 'I guess you're right,' he said quietly, 'but I still think it's a bad idea.' Glancing at Clara's plate he shrugged. 'There's no more meatloaf?'

Clara shook her head.

'Well, I might go and do some reading then.' Throwing his napkin into the last traces of gravy, Larry lurched into the bedroom. He couldn't stand these mealtime disputes, he thought, as he searched for his new magazine, couldn't stand Clara's endless carping. It was bad enough when she was simply pulling him up about his manners (something that she had done, without fail, at every meal since their marriage), but his annoyance started to bubble over when she addressed issues she knew nothing about. It bothered him especially that she tried to claim some insider knowledge on the subject of prison management. The fact was, thought Larry, that she knew fuck all about what went on in the cell house. She was clueless. She had no idea about the hierarchies and handshakes, the secret layers of power.

Her strategy was simply to side with the Warden, whatever the problem at hand. Clara loved authority, thought Larry. That was it, plain and simple.

With her plate half empty, Clara sucked at her cheeks. She wished her husband would observe some basic rules of etiquette, like staying at the table until his fellow diners had finished. It was so uncouth to just get up and leave. And he'd thrown his napkin into the gravy! The final insult. There was no use in calling him back and asking for an apology, though. She would just find herself repeating the words incessantly, blaring them out like one of those public service announcements that no one ever seemed to heed.

Rita Mae was eating quickly now, shovelling up her food. 'Calm down,' snapped Clara. 'Just calm down, Rita. Let's sit here, eat slowly and enjoy our meal.' Her mouth pinched a smile. 'That would be good, wouldn't it?'

Rita Mae shrugged. 'Right.' Closing her eyes, she began scooping the food towards her mouth in slow motion, trying desperately to mimic her mother's movements, to capture the forced daintiness. Clara looked on, confused. She pushed her own plate to one side, the meatloaf seeming shrivelled now. She'd lost her appetite.

Rolling the cool, rounded edge of her glass against her lips, Clara thought back to that morning, and her fleeting encounter with the Warden. She had been on her way up the hill when it happened, striding to an appointment with Mitzi Earl, the doctor's wife. Dr Earl's house was just a little way up from the Warden's and was counted by everyone who mattered as the second-nicest residence on Las Focas. It was a couple of metres short of this destination that Clara had caught sight of them: first the

Warden, and then the tall, tanned man beside him in a ten-gallon cowboy hat.

They seemed to be on their way from the cellblock, talking quietly as they walked. It would be inappropriate to stop and speak to them, Clara had thought initially, and so she had simply tilted her pillbox hat gently and bobbed as she came near. There had come no acknowledgement, though, and so, suddenly afraid that this mish-mash greeting was insufficient, she had blurted out, 'Good morning,' and as an afterthought, 'Warden Wright.' Drawing level, it was the men who had stopped.

'Why, Mrs Jones, hello,' drawled the Warden, his voice just retaining the lilt of his Louisiana upbringing. 'How are you?' She had nodded nervously. 'I'd like you to meet Commissioner Albertson. He's over from Washington to inspect the prison today.'

The man in the cowboy hat had held out his hand, which hung there expectantly as Clara bowed her head for a curtsey-cum-misstep. 'It's good to meet you, Commissioner,' she said, as he withdrew his untouched palm. 'I sure hope you enjoy your visit.'

'Absolutely,' said the Commissioner, 'it's been very interesting so far.' He turned to the Warden, laughing slightly. 'And just who is this lovely lady?'

'Ah,' said the Warden, 'this is Mrs Jones. She's one of the main dressmakers on the island, definitely amongst the best. She's married to one of our officers here. They've put in – how many years of service is it?'

'Uh, ten I think, almost eleven.'

'Eleven years.' The Warden smiled beneficently. 'One of our biggest success stories.'

That was what he had said, thought Clara. 'One of our

biggest success stories.' What could he have meant? Looking up, she saw Rita Mae staring pointedly at her now, her plate scraped clean.

'Can I leave the table too? I'll clear up the plates.'

Clara nodded, waving her hands distractedly. 'Whatever you want,' she said. 'Whatever you want.' He had stopped her, hadn't he, quite voluntarily, while in the middle of official business. He had stopped her and introduced her to the Commissioner, one of the most important officials ever to visit the island. She felt, just then, a small pang of hunger sickness, of hope. It might still happen, she thought, gulping at her water. There might still be a way.

Larry came bustling back into the kitchen. 'Either of you seen my *Sports Illustrated*? I was hoping to read it in the bath but it seems to have gone missing.'

Clara stood up and pointed to her left. 'Living room, beside the couch,' she said, stacking up the glasses on the table. Rita Mae was standing at the sink, running water for the washing-up, but Clara pushed her gently away. 'Go to your room and do your homework, Rita Mae.'

'I can do the washing-up,' she protested.

'No you can't.' Clara was adamant. 'You always make a mess, don't you? You're better off with your schoolwork, Rita. I'll do this.'

As Rita Mae slumped off to her room, Clara leaned over the sink. She could just hear Larry in the distance, stepping sloppily into the bath. He had obviously found his magazine. She grimaced as he began whistling a high-pitched, fast-paced rendition of 'Come Fly With Me', changing key each time he faced a note up out of his range.

The whistling would never stop, thought Clara, the flat,

uncertain soundtrack to their married life. Larry had been whistling since the day they'd met, on that basketball court in Beverly Hills, his lips puckered then, too, tuneless.

Her sigh just loud enough to be heard, Clara began scrubbing her hands.

Chapter Fifteen

A Beverly Hills basketball court, 16 July 1945

Nervous laughter pitched in with the odd muffled sob, a group of bespectacled scientists, high in the mountains of northern New Mexico, surveyed the results of their experiment. They had been planning this day for months now in the Los Alamos ranch school where they worked and bunked, stealthily developing means of nuclear fission. None of them had really been sure – not even Robert Oppenheimer, their preternaturally confident boss – that 'the gadget', as they called it, would work. Now, though, as they looked out over the burned grass, carpeted with glowing green glass, they knew that they'd been successful. All those months in isolation, poring over lab results and test proposals, had paid off.

That morning's explosion (a flash of red light that had risen 30,000 feet before mushrooming into a dirty brown cloud) had been so big and bright that more than a hundred miles away a blind girl would claim to have seen it. These University of California scientists – men who floundered in social settings, outfoxed by the demands of girlfriends or passable personal hygiene – had harnessed the most devastating power yet known.

Descending the bleachers of a Beverly Hills basketball court, blissfully unaware of all this, Clara Caesar scouted around for somewhere to sit. It shouldn't have been difficult – the bleachers were empty – but she wanted to choose the perfect position, someplace prominent yet unassuming, where she could observe, and be observed, from a distance. Edging into a middle row, she arranged her bag carefully by her side. In black pencil skirt, tight blouse and short lace gloves, she was obviously dressed for attention, but, for now, she was content with watching. Hands clasped knuckle-white, she thought about her own experiment – a rather more organic one in this case, involving simple chemical fusion. As a scheme its consequences could naturally never come close to the fallout of Oppenheimer's Project Y: even Clara Caesar wasn't that ambitious. On a personal level, though, there was every potential for destruction.

Clara had travelled here this afternoon all the way from Culver City, and, in particular, the Pantheon Pictures dormitory where she lived with other junior workers. She had been employed at the studio for the past two years, ensconced in its grounds ever since the downtown riots that had destroyed both her favourite outfit and limited sense of humour.

The morning after those ructions – she could still picture the eye sockets of that defence worker, pooling so effort-lessly with blood – Clara had headed for the nearest public telephone and dialled up Dora. Words stringing fast together, she had asked her makeshift aunt if there might be a job at the studios, anything that could help her flee downtown. She needed to leave immediately, she'd cried, couldn't cope with her mother any more, or the violence of this place. She'd do anything, she said, no matter how menial. (Even as this plea fell out, Clara had been cursing her imprecision. Don't let it be a cleaning job, she had thought. The 'menial' claim simply wasn't true. Please never a cleaning job.)

Recognizing the desperation in her goddaughter's voice – a tone she'd heard from so many girls before – Dora had marched off across the lot, storming the set and costume-making sheds, thrusting past the massed ranks of Civil War outfits and corsetry, leaving miniature models of Alabama in her wake, ignoring the flat painted boards of Broadway, Venice, Antigua and the Palace of Versailles. Deep inside, she had found a group of costume girls pausing for coffee, and, quickly colonizing their conversation, she had been as dominant as ever. 'I've got a girl who wants work,' she'd said, 'right now, today. You won't find anyone more determined, I tell ya. This one's a hardhead. She won't ask for a proper salary, I'm sure of that – you could probably cut the usual pay in half.' She laughed. 'Which, let's face it, is hardly gonna be a living wage. But she needs a job right now, girls, and a place to stay. She really fucking needs it.'

If this girl was so desperate, they'd all asked, why couldn't they make use of her at the brothel? At this, Dora had snorted derisively, swiped aside the suggestion and reformulated her question. 'Are there any jobs, girls? Are you wasting my time?' As her aggression grew (Dora's temper was legendary at Pantheon), one of the lowliest seamstresses had nervously stepped forward. She had just been promoted to pattern cutter, she explained, and so, she assumed – she hoped that she wasn't speaking out of turn, didn't want to upset anyone, wasn't looking for trouble – her job was now empty. Dora had nodded triumphantly then and swept back to the brothel. By July 1943, Clara had been firmly embedded in the costume shed, bent, grim faced, over a sewing machine.

Clara had felt sure, even on her first day at the studio, that this was only the germ of what her life would be, that what awaited her was much more than this: the calloused existence of a junior machinist. It wasn't possible, she reasoned, that she'd managed to escape downtown only to toil away her days in Culver City. That just couldn't make sense. With this certainty uppermost in her mind, then, she had begun to plan the project that had brought her out here today, on her afternoon off.

The project was, in essence, a hunt, her prey being that rarely spotted species, the rich but malleable male. Early on in this search (in the first of just two occasions that Clara would ever get drunk) she had sat in Dora's top-floor office, the two of them sinking red wine from a flagon, and told her of the plan, explaining that she needed someone in equal parts wealthy and compliant. 'I figure he needs to be flush, definitely, but dumb, you know? Not quite in control of his finances. He needs to be someone I could take on and organize. Arrange his life to my liking.'

With this, Dora had thrown her head back, laughing so hard that girls across the house stopped, mid-gulp, and peered anxiously at the ceiling. 'Why, that's what we're all looking for!' screamed Dora, clapping her hands together. 'That's what every girl in this place came here for. It's what we all want.' Seeing how serious Clara was, though, she had stopped laughing, stood up and backed away. Tilting her head, she stared critically at her young charge.

Clara had changed her looks dramatically in the few months she'd been living on the lot, starting by bleaching her hair baby-white, and continuing with a beauty regime in which she covered her face with panstick and a thick layer of powder. It was a deeply unnatural look, thought Dora, and not really very flattering. It made her skin look dusty and cold, like a badly prepared cadaver.

Even with such a caking of cosmetics, though, it would have been obvious to anyone that Clara was an attractive girl: lithe, full-lipped, straight-nosed. 'You might just do it, you know,' said Dora, before sitting back down. The older woman had then begun to sketch out the details of Clara's search – the places she should visit, the type of men to trace. It was best, suggested Dora, to focus specifically on young heirs, men who would prove both idle and profligate. Someone who had made his own money, Dora explained, scraping determinedly from the slums to high society, was much more likely to protect himself and his earnings, to be aware of noisome predators, sniffing them out and burrowing long before they could pounce. It was the next generation that Clara needed to target. The shiftless sons of fortune, who weren't like you or I, who had lazed their way through school as they would later do through life. The Tribe of Indolents, she'd called them. And the place to find these men, of course, was Beverly Hills.

It was hard to believe, thought Clara, cross-legged in the bleachers, that just a few hundred metres from here lay the seething chaos and paranoia of Los Angeles. In the years since the war broke out the city authorities had lost all semblance of control, she thought primly now; all order had been ceded to the crush of people, the influx of immigrants. Not that the authorities hadn't tried to combat this, thought Clara. After all, they'd taken the unusual step of imprisoning the city's entire Japanese community, coming for them in the confusion of night and barracking them, nose-to-nose, in concentration camps. That should have made a difference, she thought, but it hadn't seemed to. There were still people sleeping on each street corner, queues for the last tomato at grocery stores, Red Cars stopped in their tracks by the sheer weight of travellers.

Beverly Hills was quite different, though. This area, annexed away, a city within a city, was tree lined and tranquil, utterly benign. Here, it seemed, gas rationing had never really caught on, and the widest cars Clara had ever seen rolled quiet and smug down the centre of the street. There was none of that populous disorder to be found, either – the well-manned police force made sure of that. Instead, Beverly Hills remained as it had been since Douglas Fairbanks and Mary Pickford decided to colonize its lima bean fields in 1910. Exclusive, quiet and strangely sterile. It reminded Clara of one of those brightly coloured snow domes you could pick up from street vendors. Beverly Hills existed like the scenes inside – a pretty place, too pretty to be real, suspended inside a giant glass bubble.

She liked it here, thought Clara; she liked the cleanliness and sense of order, the containment. Beverly Hills was a place where boundaries were respected and good manners prevailed. She would like to stay here, she decided. Uncrossing her legs, leaning back on the bench, Clara struck her most alluring pose.

The man she was trying to impress was down on the court now, pounding the concrete with four of his friends. They were knocking the ball around aimlessly – as they did each afternoon – whooping when one of them scored, back-slapping and laughing. To Clara (at heart a puritan) it was impossible to understand why anyone would want to spend hours just trolling up and down the court, not even scoring a game properly. These boys, though, clearly loved the back and forth.

'Here, here,' the tallest one – the boy Clara had targeted – was motioning to the freckled redhead, his constant companion. Passed the ball, he began dribbling frantically down the court, pursued by them all, before jumping three feet in the air and slamming it hard through the hoop. It was an impressive dunk – even Clara could see that – and as the boy's fellow players crowded around him, clapping and hollering, she stood and joined in the applause.

As the game started up again, Clara sank back. From the first day of this project, she had approached her task both professionally and technically, buying a hardcover notepad and ensuring that she carried this and a sharpened pencil at all times. Her scribbled notes began with Dora's advice and then ran through page after page of lists, evidence and counter-evidence, ideas and arguments. The rate at which she scribbled had increased in the past six months, ever since she had decided upon her prey and started gathering information. Now, though, the preliminary period was over.

Pursing her lips, Clara ran through the details she'd uncovered so far. She had not yet spoken to Laurence Jones himself, but, talking to his friends and acquaintances, she had gathered that he was twenty years old, a sophomore at Los Angeles City University, who was yet to decide conclusively on a major. Feckless, she thought, smiling. His brother, Grady, four years older than Laurence, had sailed through his time at Harvard, regularly regaled with prizes and honours, before tackling a postgrad year at Columbia. He was now a high flier at the Pentagon – apparently they'd never been close. Bitter, thought Clara. In truth, Laurence wasn't a hugely social or clubby type – his daily game of basketball being the exception – and instead he enjoyed just the loyal companionship of his friend Virgil Messing, the short, freckled boy with whom he'd attended school. Lonely, thought Clara.

These details were all quite important, but the single most significant fact was that Laurence's father, Joseph Jones, was one of the city's most successful insurance brokers. Since the birth of his two sons, Joseph had built up his company from a small-time, one-man operation, to a multi-million-dollar concern. In the space of just two decades, his firm had become one of the most trusted and popular brokerages in the state (renowned for its reasonable rates and relatively quick payouts), and was intent on claiming this mantle nationwide. Joseph now presided over fifty offices, scattered right across the country, which he spent most of his time visiting, a constant tour of duty. It had been all his own work, as he liked to explain, and it had made him one of the richest men in Los Angeles.

While Clara pondered Joseph Jones's wealth, Larry was horsing around on the basketball court, holding the ball high in the air and refusing to give it to any of the other boys. If every day could be like this, he decided, crouching suddenly, breaking into a run and dribbling expertly up the court, life would be a breeze. Planting the ball through the hoop, Larry imagined the years stretching out in a vaporous haze, each day hot and leisurely as this one, free from any outside pressures: the nag of his mother; the jibes of his father.

It could all have been so different, he realized now, passing the ball to Virgil, watching as his friend scooted up the court, ducking and weaving, threading the ball through his legs, providing quite a display. On leaving Beverly Hills High two years before, both he and Virgil had spent the summer stretched out on sun loungers, relaxing in the Joneses' backyard and discussing their plan to join the army.

For some reason he couldn't fathom now, the two of them had been determined to serve, talking about it incessantly, lying in those eight verdant acres of yard, sipping cocktails and smoking cigarettes. Where would they be posted, they wondered: Europe, or Japan? And would they be sent straight to the front line, training their guns on the enemy?

Larry's parents hadn't been thrilled by this plan – his mother had gasped when he told her, clutched a handkerchief to her mouth and muttered darkly about the officer class – but they had gradually come to realize that, with his stark lack of drive or focus, the army was perhaps the best place for him. 'It'll teach him responsibility,' Joseph Jones had said to his wife that night, filling his whiskey glass for the fifth time. 'He'll become regimented, I suppose, much more tidy and organized. He'll have respect beaten into him, good manners.' It was only on taking a sip of his drink that Joseph Jones grimaced, realizing how much he hated all the qualities he'd just listed.

Arriving at the offices of the armed forces, though, it had become clear that signing up was less simple than Larry and Virgil had supposed. With their fit bodies and obvious enthusiasm (not to mention the small issue of an ongoing war) they had expected nothing less than yelps of excitement from the recruiting officer and an almost immediate dispatch to some war zone or another, having been kitted out with the requisite camouflage and guns. (Guns!)

War or no war, though, they were apprised by the desk clerk, potential enlistees were still required to complete a full physical and psychological exam, no shirking or excuses. Slightly surprised, nonetheless this hadn't fazed them. Sitting in the waiting room, discussing the oncoming tests, they had laughed and joked, poking each other in the ribs, fingers bending hard against the muscled wall beneath their shirts, confident that they would make it through.

First on the schedule was the fitness test. Bounding into the gymnasium, they had crashed perfectly through a round of pull-ups, push-ups and bends, barely breaking a sweat. It had been so effortless, they agreed afterwards, that they had been surprised when it ended, sure that the instructor must have forgotten some of the tasks, let them off easy. As they shook the man's hand, he had wished them well for the future.

Next up, though, came a more invasive physical. One at a time, Larry and Virgil were called into the military doctor's poky office.

Larry had gone in first, nonchalant, at ease, his shoulders loose, smiling. He remained relaxed while his pulse and temperature were checked, but, as the physical progressed, he noticed a change in the doctor's demeanour. This seemed to happen about halfway through the exam, when Larry was asked to open his mouth and stick out his tongue. On doing this, the doctor had thrust a wide wooden stick inside, pushing until it stretched just a short way into Larry's throat. Having had no warning of this, but desperately wanting to pass, Larry had closed his eyes, held his breath and stifled his gag reflex. The worst thing he could do, he reasoned, was to splutter uncontrollably in the doctor's face.

Larry's concentration had worked, but, to his surprise, this didn't seem to impress the man. Removing the wooden stick after a few minutes, the doctor had screwed up his face, uttered a loud and suspicious 'hmmm' and begun writing a series of frantic comments on notepaper divided into columns. As he scribbled he shook his head, sighing intermittently, his jowls wobbling. It seemed he would have preferred the prospect of air-bound saliva.

Not sure what this meant, Larry decided to stay confident. The next part appeared to go no better, though. Bending over, trousers around his ankles, Larry was treated, unexpectedly, to a full rectal inspection. This unpleasant business was punctuated by a variety of noises from the doctor, none of them positive. On asking Larry to get dressed, the doctor's head had retracted deep into his neck, nestling there in the folds of fat, censorious and disgusted.

It was Virgil's turn next and (to Larry's thinly disguised happiness) the doctor was no more encouraging. They were told then, without delay, that a psychological examination would be unnecessary. Unfortunately, it seemed they simply weren't appropriate army material. It would be best if they sought alternative employment.

To this day, Larry had no idea why the army had so summarily dismissed them, but now, as he bounded about the court, he felt relieved. They had been deluded, that summer before applying (it was the cocktails, perhaps), into thinking that life in the forces would be one long, noble adventure. He remembered the two of them now, lying back on those sun loungers, toasting half-naked to the sun, honestly believing that the privilege and ease of their lives would continue in any setting. They had been arrogant, Larry realized, and supremely adolescent.

For some reason Joseph Jones hadn't seemed surprised at the result of Larry's application, almost seemed to have been expecting it. Throughout that long hot summer, Joseph had been making regular entreaties to the staff at LACU (coupled, of course, with large donations) asking them to accept his younger son. It had taken some concerted effort on his part – Larry's high school scores were exceptionally low – but eventually Joseph had found a professor in need of a new research lab. With the Joseph Jones Chemistry Center well on its way to fruition, Joseph had apprised Larry that his next four years were to be spent at college.

LACU wasn't bad, thought Larry now. With a careful choice of courses the hours could be kept fairly low, and this, combined with the fact that Virgil had joined him there, meant that there was almost daily opportunity for basketball. Naturally, if he didn't raise his grade point average at some point, there was the risk of trouble, maybe even expulsion. But hopefully it wouldn't come to that. Smiling, he watched Virgil shoot an expert hoop. If their other plans panned out then perhaps they could leave college early of their own accord. They could pack up with a clean slate.

The other boys were dispersing now, slapping at Larry as they passed and shouting over their shoulders. 'Tomorrow? Four?' Larry nodded, jogging over to the lowest rung of the bleachers, where he'd stashed his bag. Sitting down, motioning for Virgil to join him, he rooted amongst his belongings before pulling out a large metal tube, about two feet long. Prising off the lid, he pulled out some sheets of paper and unfurled them carefully on his lap.

Craning her neck as subtly as she could, Clara tried to

make out what Larry and his friend were looking at, what it was that had caused the two of them to slump so intently over those swathes of paper. Suspended halfway up the bleachers, though, it didn't matter how much she narrowed her eyes. She just couldn't see.

Larry slung an arm around Virgil's shoulders and leaned even closer to the page. 'So,' he was saying, 'I checked out all the plans and it's at least eight hundred acres they're saying now, maybe a little more, just outside Santa Barbara. They couldn't tell me so much about the land, but from what they were saying it's got good grazing potential, a lot of space for livestock. It's not being run as much of a business at the moment, but they reckon it could be.'

He pulled out the next map, staring so closely that the notes and measurements glazed before him. To live someplace like that – a huge, isolated ranch – would be incredible. Him and Virgil, a basketball court out back. Total isolation.

'And you really think your father might put up the money?' Virgil snaked an arm around Larry's waist. 'You honestly think he might do it?'

Larry sighed. 'Well, there's a chance. I've been sounding him out for the last few weeks, and he doesn't seem against the idea, that's for sure. What we need to do, we need to sit down and work out a plan, a way of presenting it as a really good business venture. Profits,' Larry laughed, 'that's what we gotta concentrate on, Virg. If we can come up with some kind of projected profit graph – and we make those profits look huge – then he'll definitely go for it. He can't resist a business proposal.'

'Well, that's what we have to do then. It's gonna be brilliant, isn't it?' Virgil stood up, slinging his bag over his shoulder. 'I could talk to my brother about it, he knows numbers, and he's back here on vacation next week.'

'Of course.' Larry rolled up the maps and pushed them slowly back into the tube. 'That would be great.'

'Anyway, I've gotta go now.' Virgil squeezed Larry's knee, before heading up the stairs. 'I'll see you tonight, yeah, you're still coming for dinner?'

Larry nodded. 'Sure, sure. Absolutely. I'll just head home now and get changed. About seven?'

'Sounds good.'

Larry watched as Virgil ran up the stairs, taking them two at a time. The ranch idea could really work out, he thought, it had real potential. Out there, all the hassles of city life – the midterms, the parents, the pressing reports of war – would be pushed permanently aside. He and Virgil would be lost to the wilderness.

Picking up his bag, checking through the contents, Larry began to whistle. He heard a noise behind him, the tapping of heels on wood, and turned to see a girl descending the stairs. He recognized her – she had been watching their basketball games regularly over the past few weeks – and she was striking anyway, with her radioactive hair and ghostly complexion, a person caught in negative. Noticing that she seemed to be smiling at him, Larry smiled tentatively back. She was coming closer now, inching along the final row of benches towards him. Lowering his bag, a hand above his eyes to block out the sun, Larry wondered what on earth she wanted to talk about.

Chapter Sixteen

A Beverly Hills dining room, late 1945

'So,' Mercy Jones prodded at her fillet steak, blood seeping languorously around her knife, 'tell me, Clara, where do your parents come from? East Coast, West Coast?' She paused briefly, head held so high that her sightline included the slope of her cheekbones. 'My family,' Joseph Jones sighed as Mercy fed him a look, 'hail all the way from Boston. That's where I grew up, where I was raised. Our line's been traced to the founding fathers.'

Clara stared down at her plate, noting the thin filmy skin that was growing on her cheese sauce. She had known this question would arise (it was, after all, quite fundamental) and she had planned to prepare an answer, she really had. She had even thought about it earlier today, ticking through the options, aiming for something plausible, perhaps even a touch impressive. Now, though, here she sat, with no response. Mercy Jones's fork clattered pointedly against her plate, and Clara knew that an answer was necessary right away. Stalling would be futile.

'California,' she said softly, modulating her voice, trying to match Mercy's accent. 'We've always come from this area so far as I know. My parents were raised in Los Angeles, I think. That's where they met.'

'Los Angeles, *really*?' Mercy patted at her perfectly clean mouth with a napkin. 'How unusual. It's so rare to meet someone whose parents actually, I don't know,' she paused, '*derive* from this area. What business is your family in? Farming? Ranching?'

'Oh, well, as you know . . .' Clara took a mouthful of steak now, aware that this was rude, but hoping that the necessary chewing might buy time to craft an answer, something that could compensate for the slight. 'My father, unfortunately, he died when I was a small child. And my mother, well, she's very ill at the moment, she can't go out at all. But, some years ago, a long time really, the two of them owned a ranch.' She paused, aware that lies always profited from a pinch of detail. 'An orange grove.'

'They did?' Larry had hardly spoken up to this point, already on his second serving, having shovelled down the first. This revelation, though, had clearly caught his attention. He had known, Larry thought triumphantly, that this situation could turn out for the best, that he and this new wife, almost a stranger really, could somehow prosper together. He leaned across the table towards Clara. 'They had a ranch? Do they still have a stake in it? Maybe we could take it on.'

'No, no.' Clara almost spat out her mouthful in her hurry to clear this up. Seeing Mercy Jones's horror, though, she chewed quickly before taking a gigantic gulp. 'This really is lovely food,' she gasped, as the steak edged slowly, painfully, down her throat. 'No, no, Larry, I'm afraid not. They sold the ranch when I was very young, I don't even remember living there. We don't have any money in that now.'

He should have guessed, thought Larry, disappointed, hunching back over his food, the dinner table silent except for the scraping of silver knives on porcelain.

On finishing his steak, Joseph Jones, wordless until now, looked up and raised his glass. His eyes were slightly rheumy, trickles of moisture flowing through the great porous crevices of his face, and his voice, when it sounded, was blunt. 'This is meant to be a celebratory dinner, isn't it? Surely that's the point?' Mercy, Clara and Larry stared blankly back at him, not sure where this was headed. 'We're meant to be celebrating the wedding of my youngest son,' Joseph kicked Larry beneath the table, 'who we never expected to get married, did we, Mercy?' His wife said nothing, tossing her hair before looking down. 'It's a happy occasion, a wonderful occasion.' Some whiskey slopped over the rim of his glass. 'Let's all have a drink.'

Standing up abruptly, Joseph began filling every wine glass on the table, even those set mistakenly by the maid (who, naturally, had been expecting a much bigger wedding party). As he poured, Joseph was vaguely aware of the stares being directed at him, and particularly that of his wife, which was as reproachful as they came. And she was a critical kind of gal, he thought wryly, allowing himself his first smile of the evening. It was true, though, what he'd said. This was supposed to be a celebration. Raising his glass again, he couldn't contain a laugh. He didn't care how Mercy reacted – she really should loosen up – he, Joseph Jones, was going to toast to this, his son's brilliant, rapturous, shotgun wedding.

Joseph began laughing more, suddenly almost doubled over, his glass still held high, sloshing happily, as he thought again about this union. His son Larry had never been particularly daring or unconventional up till now and, in truth, if Joseph had been asked to lend him a sobriquet it would have been 'Mama's Boy'. Not that Larry was especially close to Mercy in some sweet, warm, baked-goods-from-the-oven kind of way. With Mercy that simply wasn't possible. It was more that Larry had always seemed in awe of his mother – abiding by her choices, warnings and decisions. The one time that Larry had broken ranks before had been his plan to join the army, and that had been doomed from the start.

But this most recent act, Joseph had to admit, was truly audacious. It wasn't just that Larry had run off one weekend, completely unannounced, and got married in Las Vegas. That was only the pinnacle. Joseph grinned as he stared back at his wife and son, both stonefaced opposite him. Here was Larry, perched beside his mother (known, throughout Los Angeles, as the city's most highly strung hostess), with a seventeen-year-old wife across from him, three months pregnant and showing, who was quite obviously of Mexican descent. For all they knew, the girl had probably started out as a hooker or a thief, some kind of hustler. Larry had scored a full house, thought Joseph. If this were a game of cards the boy would have swept the table.

'Right.' Joseph held a finger to his lips, trying to think of an appropriate comment. 'Right. Well, I guess we should just be toasting to Larry and Clara, shouldn't we, Mercy?' His wife gave a tiny shrug, not hiding her scowl. Joseph clapped a hand to his mouth, then cocked his glass, motioning towards Clara's stomach. 'Of course, how embarrassing! I know why you're angry with me, Mercy, it's because I've left out the most important person, haven't I?

The baby! We can't forget him, can we?' He threw a smile between his three companions. 'Right, so that's it. To Larry, Clara and Baby Jones. A completely unexpected family!'

He sat down heavily and glanced around as the others gingerly raised their glasses. For all the mischief-making potential of this evening, thought Joseph, tapping his foot absently on the floor, this dinner was proving interminably dull. Despite his best efforts to entertain the crowd, nothing seemed to be working.

Grasping the table's edge, Joseph rose to his feet. There was dessert on its way, of course, but maybe the best thing to do was to twin that with some warm liquor. This tactic wasn't guaranteed to succeed, Joseph knew that, but it seemed his best chance of relaxing them all, of bringing a touch of levity to the occasion. And, besides: he really liked warm liquor.

As her husband ambled off to the kitchen, Mercy Jones went to follow him. 'I just have to help Cook with our dessert,' she said. 'She sometimes needs a little direction.'

Keen to preserve her poise, Mercy was determined to ignore Joseph's behaviour. Maybe this new addition to the family, Clara Jones, wouldn't notice her father-in-law's performance, thought Mercy, wouldn't recognize the laughter and drunkenness. And actually, she decided, face contracting as she marched down the stone corridor to the kitchen, who cared if she did? On the evidence available so far, Mercy wouldn't have been surprised if Clara's family were all drunks and wastrels. And not drunks like Joseph, who could function on many levels – expertly running a business that spanned all America – but real gutter-hungry types. People whose pasts bulged with stories, but who lacked any real sense of heritage.

It wasn't that the girl's manners or accent were terribly bad, conceded Mercy (her most charitable thought of the evening), although they could certainly use some refinement. It was more that her account of herself seemed so patchy. That story, for instance, about her parents having been ranchers in California, in the early part of the century? If that were true, thought Mercy, her family would be people of some wealth and community standing, people whose daughter would never have found herself unmarried and pregnant. And, more than that, illness or no, the girl's mother would have made contact with the Jones family, a missive apologizing for the situation, perhaps, or at least offering some words of hope and consolation. As it was, they had heard nothing from Clara's family. Mercy wondered now whether even this surviving parent was a figment of the girl's imagination.

As Joseph lined up a long row of shot glasses – three for each person – Mercy grabbed at her husband, keen to stop him wasting the liquor. 'We don't need that now, Joseph. I think you've had quite enough.'

Prising his wife's hand from his wrist, Joseph leaned forward and began filling the glasses haphazardly, overshooting on each one. 'On the contrary, Mercy,' he slurred, 'it's just what we need. A little bit of a pick me up. This hasn't been much of a party so far, has it?'

Mercy walked over to the wooden work surface, where Cook had left the four chocolate mousses. 'Much as I appreciate your joie de vivre, Joseph,' she drawled, 'not all of us are feeling quite so celebratory. I know you're finding all this very amusing, but the fact is, our son's life has probably been ruined.' She peered at the mousses, checking vaguely for stray hairs. 'Larry may never have been the most,' she paused, '*ambitious* of people, but given the right match – well.' She stared pityingly at her husband. 'We all know what the right match can achieve.'

Slumping into one of the kitchen chairs, Joseph Jones wagged a finger at his wife. 'I just think you're looking at this in the wrong way, darling, completely the wrong way. Let's face it,' he picked up one of the liquor glasses and poured it fulsomely down his throat, 'if this hadn't happened then our boy might never have married.' He winked at Mercy now. 'Things certainly seemed to be heading that way, didn't they?' Joseph started laughing again. 'So, this girl has probably done us a favour, Mercy darling. A big ole favour. And anyway,' he picked up another liquor glass, 'I think she's sort of sweet. Very pretty.' He threw more of the liquid into his mouth, before gargling it down. 'She's a hot tamale, Mercy. A sexy cholita.'

She had been about to lunge for the table, keen to stop her husband downing more alcohol, but this last comment made Mercy Jones freeze. 'What did you say?'

'Aaaah.' Joseph Jones stood up, hands encircling his wife's waist, before he suddenly raised them above his head, twitching his fingers as if playing the castanets. 'She's a gorgeous little chiquita, isn't she? Quite a beauty.' He couldn't control his laughter now. 'They're going to have lovely babies.'

Mercy pushed at her husband then and sat down. 'You think she's Mexican?' Her mind started sifting through the connotations of this, the possibilities.

'Sure she is.' Joseph went to sit on the chair again. 'At least in part. I think it's great, Mercy, very good. She's a very pretty girl.'

As Mercy contemplated this last revelation (the ignominy

of it all, the shame!) and Joseph conveniently forgot that he had intended the liquor for his guests, Larry and Clara sat silently at the table. They had been married just a week now, most of that holed up in a Hollywood motel, but already each knew that the ensuing years would be full of these ellipses, the growing silences that could never be filled.

Stretching across the table, Larry took his bride's hand. She was a pretty girl, a sweet thing really, and he didn't want her to feel uncomfortable. 'My mother's slightly,' he paused, 'difficult, when you first meet her, but,' he wasn't sure how thoroughgoing this lie should be, but realized there was no point stinting, 'I can tell she really likes you.'

Her head lowered, Clara's throat constricted. 'That's kind of you to say, Larry.' She knew, of course, that he was fibbing, but appreciated his attempt to buoy her up, to smooth over the situation. Somehow (and it seemed ridiculous now that she was sat here at the dinner table, skin so prickly and red) she had had no idea that this evening would pan out so badly. She hadn't anticipated the anger, or, indeed, the awkwardness.

Up until this week she had been concentrating exclusively on the game. Looking at Larry now ('It'll be all right,' he breathed softly) she remembered the months spent trying to ensnare him, the thrill of the chase, of hunting her prey and then using all her skills to trap him. There had been the elocution lessons with Dora, wiping almost every trace of Spanish from her accent. There were the afternoons alone in the public library, poring over dusty books on manners (Emily Post's *Etiquette*, Nelson Doubleday's *Book of Etiquette*), making long and detailed notes. There was that subtle but pressing interrogation, her probing of Larry's thoughts and feelings, the happy breakthrough when she suddenly felt sure that he would stand by her should she fall pregnant, that she could go ahead with her plan in full. Clara had enjoyed her project more than anything before, those sudden jolts of power and excitement. With her charts and graphs and bulging notepad, she had, for once, felt in control. There was nothing that could come between her and her goal: not even, it seemed, the freak force of circumstance.

'I wonder what Ma and Pa are doing in the kitchen?' Larry gave a tentative smile. His wife seemed so distant. 'I'm looking forward to my chocolate mousse. Cookie makes the best ever. It's like silk.'

Clara remembered those dark sheets in the brothel now, the ones she had coveted so badly. She supposed, thinking more clearly, that she had never really considered what would happen after she'd won the game and married Larry. She had imagined, somehow, that everything would fall into place, that, despite the circumstances, his family would quickly accept her, give them a generous expense account, and, of course, the expected house in Beverly Hills. A beautiful house, defined by large windows, the rooms dressed entirely in dark silks.

She should have thought about this earlier, Clara realized. The clues had all been there, the obvious signs that Larry himself was far from wealthy, that he was yet to cash his trust fund if one truly existed.

Their first date had held hints enough: a ride around town in Joseph's oldest Cadillac, before stopping at a roadside diner. And not a classy joint. Contrived in the shape of an owl (complete with eyes fashioned from blinking headlights), the diner was a dive that served the worst hamburgers either of them had ever tasted. Thin, concave meat patties, filled with a deep pool of grease, Clara had been able to stomach only a few small bites of hers, fearful, otherwise, that she would gag. It wasn't treatment you'd expect from a wealthy man. In fact, considering it now, primed clear through perspective, it wasn't treatment you'd expect from a hobo.

'What are you thinking about?' Larry had edged his chair back, stretching his legs. Clara shook her head, but he insisted. 'Come on, tell me. What have you been thinking about?'

Clara felt on the verge of tears. 'Nothing,' she muttered. 'Honestly, nothing.'

'Oh well.' He didn't want to push her. His new wife really was inscrutable, though, thought Larry. A mystery. He cocked his head, staring curiously at that face, its eyes lowered to the tablecloth.

There was something unreal about her, thought Larry, supremely detached, as if she'd sprung into life suddenly and from nowhere, a character without anchorage: no past or hometown, no relatives or regrets. In the few months they'd been together they seemed to have spent all their time talking about him, a gabble of questions, questions, questions. When Larry had occasionally countered this, asking Clara about her childhood or family, she was instantly less talkative. That story that Mercy had just prompted, the one about the orange grove, was the most detailed information he'd yet heard. Everything else was fragments. She had lived somewhere in the spaghetti scrum of downtown, before moving on to Culver City. Her father was dead, her mother ill. Aside from those snippets of information, here she was. The least explicable person he'd ever met.

Given that she never seemed to visit her mother, and certainly barely mentioned her, he gathered that they didn't get on, were quite seriously estranged. Larry hadn't wanted to dig for those details. Naturally, he thought, if Clara's mother ever needed funding for healthcare or living costs, then he was happy to ask his father for help. Beyond that, though, he was almost glad they didn't have to meet. He had enough of a mother to cope with.

If Larry was honest, it wasn't only his wife he found inexplicable. Another mystery, he thought now, was how, within the scant space of a few months, he'd gone from committed bachelor to married man, with a child well on the way. It had all happened so swiftly and seamlessly, he thought, that he had hardly noticed the process, the silent machinations.

Staring at the ceiling, Larry tried to trace the stages that had brought him here, to this crushingly uneasy wedding dinner. The beginning was obviously that first day on the basketball court, when Clara had approached him in a tight outfit, the flanks of her legs showing through, blouse unbuttoned as low as possible. He hadn't really been interested in her then – fixated as he was on the ranch plan – but she had been incredibly persistent, brushing dust from his shirt, laughing sunnily at his comments, insisting she was headed in his direction. Once she'd walked all the way home with him (a good mile, and she was clad in heels) he had realized how rude it would be not to ask her on a date. She was pretty, after all, even he could see that, and she had clearly taken a shine to him. 'Friday?' he had said. 'Eight o' clock?'

That evening had been strange, too. Larry had never risked such a cheap date before – he knew how those LACU types could snipe – but in this case the girl was a studio hand, and he had been anxious not to encourage her. Still, despite having planned carefully, scheduling a night of plain mediocrity, Larry actually felt he'd gone a touch too far on delivery of their food at the roadside diner. The meal looked hideous. Disgusting. Larry was naturally used to classier joints, even when ordering a burger, and on sampling the food (realizing that it tasted still worse than it appeared) he had been both faintly embarrassed and absolutely certain that his plan would work. Clara must lose interest now. No girl could accept this. It was so clearly disrespectful.

Oddly, though, if anything, the grease seemed to act as an aphrodisiac. After eating, Larry had driven them up into the Hollywood Hills, planning to catch the view and then head home. Before he'd even had a chance to park, though, Clara had lunged. As he adjusted the gear stick, she leaned over suddenly, missing his cheek and pecking clumsily at his ear.

Larry had never met a girl like Clara before, someone so voracious and uninhibited, and after that first date he had decided that actually he might be wrong to pass her up, that he should take advantage of her willingness, her obvious interest. Joseph Jones had been teasing Larry for years now about his apparent lack of libido, the taunts increasing wildly since his sixteenth birthday, when Joseph had spirited him to a high-class brothel, ordered the most beautiful hooker in town (there was no denying it: she *was* peachy) and the boy had run out of the room, terrified and flaccid. He would prove to both his father and himself, thought Larry (making out with Clara in the back of the Cadillac), that he could be a proper man. He would cancel out all those times Joseph had crept into his room, drunk and laughing, waking his son with whispered jibes of 'eunuch', 'fruitcake' and 'pretty boy'.

What had made it even more perfect, he'd thought, was the fact that she obviously hailed from a different world to theirs, that, despite her accent and slight air of gentility, she evidently came from across the tracks, somewhere far removed from Beverly Hills. Beneath that panstick he had noticed the more interesting darkness of her skin, and suspected that she had some other heritage: Mexican, Indian, Puerto Rican. He would show his father, Larry had thought, that he was no longer a Mama's Boy, bounded by Mercy's obsession with class and propriety. He would date whomever he wanted, and perhaps sleep with them too.

Clara's eyes seemed unnaturally wet. 'They'll come around,' said Larry, his smile strained. 'They just need to get used to the idea of you and I being together, Clara.' He laughed, determined to lighten the mood. 'Let's be fair, sweetheart – *we* need to get used to the two of us being together.'

Clara smiled weakly, dabbing at her eyes with a napkin. Everything else had been planned out thoroughly, she thought, so why hadn't she envisaged what would happen after the wedding? How could she have been so short sighted? She thought now of the table that she had pinned to her wall at the Pantheon Pictures lot. Given to her by Dora, it mapped out her most fertile times of the month, clearly marking the ten-day period in which she was most likely to get pregnant. Telling Larry that these dates marked the opposite – the times she was barren – they had happily had sex through those periods without a sheath. It had taken just weeks then. With just good health and a little planning it had all been that easy.

And now it was growing in there, this baby, the reality of which she had never really wanted or planned for, a means but never an end, which would keep burgeoning and arrive regardless. This thing had taken root in her body, thought Clara anxiously, parasitic, hungry, leeching off her blood and food supplies, sapping all her energy. She had never felt maternal, had never shared that girlish desire for a cluster of children. But it was in there now. And it was growing.

She remembered a conversation with Consuela a few years before, in which her great-aunt had suggested that marriages in Mexico were sometimes arranged between two compatible families from the time that the bride and groom were just tiny children. These unions, she had said, often worked out as well, or even better, than those based on passion. They might not have that initial spark, the six-month moment of lust, but that worked in their favour really – it gave them greater staying power.

That was what she had created, thought Clara, an arranged marriage, but then she supposed the mechanics, the balance, were slightly different when just one partner had been aware of it. Perhaps that was why the situation seemed so awkward right now, so uneven. Perhaps it was just a case of waiting awhile. They would settle into it soon.

Larry stared at his new bride. He had to make this work, he thought, had to prove to his family that he had made the right decision and could survive alone. It had been just a few weeks now since Clara had apprised him of her pregnancy – she was two months along by then – and the shock of the news was still very much alive. He had been unsure of his response at first (there was the ranch to consider, and his studies, and Virgil), but it had taken just a few hours for him to decide that he must do the right thing and marry her. This had all been unexpected, of course, a mystifying twist, but he had realized that in some way the situation could prove a blessing. All this time he had imagined that his only option for a happy life was to escape his peers, flee to the wilderness and opt out. But now, he thought, he had a real chance for a conventional life. Despite all previous doubts, he might really fit in.

Mercy and Joseph Jones were approaching the table now, the former maintaining a wince, the latter smiling widely. They set a chocolate mousse on each of the four place mats, before sitting down.

'Eat up,' said Joseph, nudging his daughter-in-law. 'You'll need all that strength. How've you been feeling anyway? Any sickness at all?'

Mercy's wince deepened. 'Really, Joseph, I don't think that we need to be talking about that sort of thing over dessert. That's the last thing we all need.' She tilted her head slightly towards her son. 'What we want to know, Joseph, don't we, is exactly what Laurence's plans are.' She turned to Larry. 'What do you intend to do, Laurence, now that you've got a wife and child to care for?'

'Right.' Larry sucked on his spoon, before remembering how much his mother hated that. He needed to protect any positive ground. 'I haven't thought about it in depth, to be honest, but I'm sure with a little time I can come up with something suitable.'

'What?' Mercy Jones had known that this would be the answer – that was, indeed, why she'd asked the question – but, in true parental fashion, she contrived to seem both bemused and disgusted. 'You haven't thought this through? You're telling myself and your father that you just cha-chaed off to Las Vegas, got married, and hadn't a thought for the consequences? Well,' she exhaled loudly, 'I find that utterly irresponsible. Truly shocking. You can't stay at college now, you know.'

'I can't?'

'No, of course you can't. You're going to have a child to provide for, Laurence, you're going to need money to spend. Surely you must have considered this?'

'Well, I thought—'

'What?'

Larry knew it would be suicide to admit he'd been expecting money from his father. 'I thought that maybe I could come up with some kind of business plan, a new venture.'

'Oh no.' Mercy's voice was adamant. 'You're not going to have time for that. No. Your father and I have spoken about the matter and we've decided that you should join his company.'

Larry's shoulders plummeted. 'I should?'

'Yes, as a Junior Executive. Isn't that right, Joseph?'

Joseph Jones was staring at his daughter-in-law, fascinated, as she ate her chocolate mousse. 'Absolutely, dear, sounds wonderful.'

'But what if—'

'What?'

'Suppose I had other plans to support Clara and the baby?'

'And they are?'

Larry shrugged. 'I don't know right now.'

'As I suspected. Look,' Mercy's voice softened unexpectedly, 'this is going to be hard for all of us, that's guaranteed, but if you join your father's company, Laurence, then we'll happily buy you a house. Something modest, of course.'

Mercy paused. 'A two-bedroom bungalow, something like that.' She looked over at her daughter-in-law. 'How does that sound?'

Clara nodded silently.

'It wouldn't be in Beverly Hills, of course, somewhere less expensive, but we'd set you up until you'd worked your way through the business and could afford to pay us back. What do you say? That's the deal.'

And, with that, Larry Jones knew that his fleeting moment of rebellion was over. From now on it was all to be done by the book, and that tome had clearly been written by his mother. Mustering a stiff smile, he reached for Clara's hand. 'Thank you,' he said, 'from both of us.'

Chapter Seventeen

'What in hell are you doing?'

Clara Jones barrelled suddenly across the room, a speeding blur of limbs and cotton, grasped the metal clip in her daughter's hair, and yanked it with such velocity that a clump of curls dislodged.

'Youch!'

Glanced at quickly now, the hairclip resembled nothing so much as a rat-trap, a baby rodent stuck in its jaws.

'I told you not to wear this.' Clara brandished it in her daughter's face, Rita Mae stumbling backwards. 'Didn't I, didn't I? We're going to a formal screening, aren't we? There are going to be other people in attendance. Don't you see? There's supposed to be a certain standard of dress. That clip's a disgrace: it doesn't match your skirt, it makes your hair seem thin, your face look pointy. It's ridiculous.'

Rita Mae said nothing, scowling and rubbing at the bald patch of scalp just exposed. She watched as her mother crossed the kitchen and threw the clip in the garbage, her arm movement so windmilling and hyperbolic that it was almost a piece of physical comedy, aping the deliberate, clumsy humour of the Keystone Cops or Buster Keaton. (Except, of course, that it wasn't meant to be funny. That would be the crucial difference.)

'All I'm trying to do is make you look presentable,' Clara screamed, pacing around the table. 'It's not like I have great raw material to work with, is it? Not like you'd win prizes for elegance. Why won't you listen to me, Rita Mae, why do you ignore what I say? I don't give out these instructions for fun, you know. It's for your own good.'

Not wanting to provoke her mother, Rita Mae remained mute. It seemed, at last, after years of false promises, the empty threats uttered shockingly in the slow dip of a Sunday ('I'll go mad if you don't stop doing that. I will. I will. You'll see. Are you trying to make me crazy, Larry? Are you trying to push me, Rita Mae?'), her mother was finally lurching into a full nervous breakdown. All the signs were there: the volatile ambush, the nonsensical speech, the pointed lack of proportion. And the anger had come on so quickly too. That must be a sign.

Rita Mae would concede, if ever pushed on the matter, that she had known her mother disliked the hairclip. That much was true. The accessory had been sent by Granmaria about six months before, and Clara had swiftly pronounced it cheap and tacky, deriding it over dinner, declaring it unacceptable, unfit for public display. Still, despite this prior knowledge, Rita Mae hadn't realized the sheer violence of Clara's aversion. Personally, she had thought the clip looked quite pretty, taming her unruly tresses. It seemed, though, and not for the first time, that she had been wrong. When it came to hair, there was evidently a whole world of social etiquette that she just didn't understand.

'We've got to go out now,' Clara was saying, still pacing, her cheeks pink, brow wet. 'I'd wanted everything to be perfect today, Rita Mae, for us to look the best, but you've gone and ruined that, haven't you?' She darted into the bathroom, stared at the mirror and let out a tiny gasp. 'You've ruined me, Rita Mae, ruined me.'

Clara Jones slapped at her face with a large white powder puff and tried to compose herself, concentrating on her breaths, which had multiplied rapidly. She should have known, she thought, that Rita Mae would pull some trick like this, some gross act of disobedience, but somehow she had ignored it. Clara had warned Rita Mae, as soon as she received that hairclip, that it was both cheap and unsightly and should therefore stay well hidden. It wasn't as though she had been unreasonable or banned her from wearing it altogether – she was quite happy, despite her aesthetic reservations, for her daughter to wear the clip indoors. But still, Rita Mae had disobeyed her. She simply hadn't listened.

Just this afternoon Clara had spent an hour styling her daughter's hair, ensuring it was bleached to perfection, not the tiniest speck of brown peeping through. And this was her reward? Utter defiance? She had given birth to a monster, she decided now. A monster. Over the years, through supreme acts of will and coercion, she had managed to exert some control over Rita Mae, but, thinking about the future, picturing it clearly, Clara could see that her daughter was set to become increasingly ill-mannered, messy-haired, clumsy, gangling and rude. And it wasn't as though Clara could rely on her husband to stem the spiralling chaos. Larry was just too placid. He couldn't see the enormity of things. He wouldn't accept that behaviour like this – a wilful act of rebellion – was a portent of things to come.

Face hidden beneath a blanket of powder, Clara decided that her appearance would have to suffice. She had wanted to look perfect today, as radiant as possible, but her daughter had gone and upset all that. Once again, she sighed, she had been stymied by her family, her plans undermined, outlook blackened.

'Right.' Clara strode back into the kitchen and snatched up her purse. 'We're going right now, Rita Mae, I won't have you making us late.' Looking over at her daughter, she saw that the girl was still rubbing plaintively at her head. A sound, somewhere between a cough and a snort, fell from Clara's mouth. 'Oh, I see. This is how you're going to play it now, is it, Rita Mae? This is your strategy? I'm sorry, but I simply won't have you pretend that I hurt you just then. It's ridiculous. Honestly, Rita. If it's not enough that you completely let me down, hold us up and upset me, you're then intent on manipulating the situation? You're intent on some kind of sympathy?' She laughed. 'I don't think so.'

Clara opened the door, holding it as Rita Mae passed meekly through, and then slamming it hard behind them. Running ahead of her daughter, she made sweeping hand movements, urging her to hurry.

'We're not going to be late, Rita Mae, did you hear what I said?' Clara held up her watch. 'We should have left ten minutes ago if we wanted one of the best seats. It's all your fault. Everyone else will be there already, and they'll stare at us as we walk in, all those beady little eyes, all blinking, boring into us.' Her heels were clacking angrily. 'I have to call at the shop, too, so that's going to slow us down. It would have been fine if you hadn't played your dirty tricks. There would have been more than enough time.' She was panting. 'It's a disaster.'

Rita Mae could see her mother's point. She, herself, had been looking forward to this screening for a month now, and she would agree that the events of the past ten minutes had somewhat tainted the experience. The two of them were on their way up the hill, heading for the officers' rec hall, occupied this evening by a 'ladies only' showing of *Marjorie Morningstar*. The movie's title role was being played by Natalie Wood and Rita Mae was eager to see how the eighteen-year-old actress handled the responsibility. She knew, after all, that on reaching Hollywood such up and coming starlets would prove her main rivals. Success relied at least partly on research. If you needed to make it as badly as she, thought Rita Mae, then it was important to analyse the enemy.

They were arriving at the island store, where Clara had to pick up some milk. Passing through the door, Rita Mae repressed a laugh as she noticed the change in her mother's gait. Striding up the hill, nostrils flaring, piston-limbed, it would have been clear to even a distant onlooker that Clara was consumed with rage, furious and flustered. Somehow, though, it seemed that the store entrance (an ordinary wooden door, its paint peeling desultorily) was a mystic portal, a passport to another personality. As she walked through, Clara Jones effected a complete transformation. In that single second, her shoulders dropped, pace slowed and grimace fell into an insipid smile. Approaching Vera Ellis with the necessary pint of milk, she verily sashayed through the aisles, before placing the carton carefully on the counter. When it came to speaking ('Just this milk please') her voice – in comparison with her previous subhuman screech – was unrecognizable. Low and gentle, it could best be described as mellifluous.

That a whole life could be arranged around impressing the neighbours seemed strange to Rita Mae, and perhaps a little sad. With her strangulating approach to appearance and manners, Clara Jones had probably never had the chance to relax properly, her pulse regulating, a calm descending. Instead, Rita Mae supposed, her mother's tension was exorcized in those out-of-the-blue screaming fits, the excoriating cries emanating deep from her body, insults whipping together, she and her father lambasted for a torrent of crimes: their smudgy disorder, piggish stupidity, tiptoed steps away from her orbit. Thinking about it, Rita Mae guessed that a lot of people were like her mother, that perhaps this rigidity was almost the norm. Somehow, though, this stopped the laugh in her throat.

On a positive note, her mother's need to impress Vera Ellis seemed to have improved her mood. As they hurried out of the store and up the hill, Clara even waited a second for Rita Mae. 'Come on,' she said, voice quiet, 'we need to walk quickly.'

Her tone raised Rita Mae's hopes that the outburst was over, and, wanting to confirm this, she tried to think of a question she could ask her mother, something cheerful that couldn't cause offence. Nothing jumped to mind (Clara clearly found the most innocuous things insulting) and so, after a few seconds, Rita Mae piped up, 'Did' (her mother shot her a look), 'did' (she was truly nervous now) 'did we happen to have any post today?'

Clara shook her head firmly. 'No.'

It was difficult to determine much from this mono-syllable, and so, keen for some clarity, Rita Mae pushed on. 'Oh, we didn't?' She paused, tentative. 'We haven't had anything for a while now, have we?'

Clara stared back. 'What are you talking about, Rita Mae? It's hardly as though we get letters that often.'

Shaking her head and trying to keep up, Rita Mae continued. 'No, I know. That's true.' She paused, aware of how provocative her next comment might be, but keen to broach it anyway. 'I usually get a letter from Granmaria each month, though, and I haven't had anything since my birthday parcel.' She watched, stuttering, as Clara's shoulders rose. 'And, and, and that was four months ago now.'

Clara turned to Rita Mae, her mouth pursed. 'You think that everyone revolves around you, Rita Mae? You think that everyone's time should be spent on you?' She reached out to slap her daughter, before realizing she might have an audience. Leaning in closer, her voice thinned to a whine. 'It disgusts me, honestly, that I've raised someone so selfish.'

With that, she stalked ahead, as tears gathered in Rita Mae's eyes. She hadn't meant to sound selfish, she thought, she really hadn't. Maybe she just hadn't explained herself properly. It wasn't the fact of her empty mailbox that worried her, but that Granmaria might be hurt or taken ill. She would never even have mentioned it if it hadn't been so unusual for Granmaria to miss her monthly letter. She would have kept quiet.

It was irritating, thought Clara, that her daughter was so inquisitive, so nosy, that she could never refrain from questioning every detail of their lives, every tiny anomaly. She would have told Rita Mae about her grandmother eventually, but for now she had hoped for a stay of execution, some time for the reality to sink in, for decisions to be made and carried out. It was, after all, a very tough situation, and it would take a while to assimilate, to make a firm judgment. As her last comment had proved, though,

Rita Mae was pushy. She couldn't let things pass. She had to ask all these questions, picking a thing apart and reassembling it, often so chaotically that it was bound to malfunction.

The fact was that Clara had indeed received a letter recently, not from Maria Caesar, but, rather, about her. On being handed this missive by Vera Ellis, she had been slightly bemused, struck first by the store manager's smirk and then by the large government stamp that adorned the envelope. Clara knew, at that moment, that Mrs Ellis suspected trouble. She had therefore thrown out the most dazzling smile and cast the envelope nonchalantly into her bag. 'Thank goodness that's arrived,' she said, 'I'm so relieved. Thank you again for your help, Mrs Ellis.'

Arriving back in her kitchen, though, it had taken some laps around the table, a glass of water and several very deep breaths before Clara had been able to slice the envelope open. As she had guessed (half expecting this for two years now, ever since Consuela's death) the letter concerned her mother's pressing need for psychological care. Apparently – and the letter wasn't specific – Maria Caesar had begun causing problems in her neighbourhood, low-level but regular disruption. In addition, the official stated, the hygiene standards of her bungalow had degenerated until it had been deemed uninhabitable.

The upshot was that Maria Caesar – with no immediate family on the mainland – had been committed to an institution. The letter confirmed that she was not considered a danger to herself or the community, and so she could, of course, be released into the care of a family member, if anyone chose to step forward. Should no one volunteer, though – and the faceless letter writer sincerely hoped that this was not the case – she would be incarcerated indefinitely in a secure unit.

Clara hadn't known quite how to deal with this situation, and so, with powers of avoidance developed since childhood, she had simply filed the letter in the large locked box she kept for all her private papers, laced the key back on to her necklace and thus ensured the document's safety from her family's prying eyes (Larry often badgered her about the box's contents, so she was always especially careful). She supposed that she would have to reply at some point soon, but for now, she decided, her mother might benefit from a short stay in an institution. If nothing else, thought Clara, she might recognize the error of her ways and set about some self-refinement.

This outcome had been inevitable, of course, thought Clara. Since the loss of Consuela – an emotional mainstay if ever there was one – she had been expecting her mother's behaviour to deteriorate, but nonetheless, despite this prior knowledge, she was still disgusted that her mother had sunk so quickly. The letter hadn't given details of her mother's squalor, but Clara could imagine the scene. There would be foodstuffs rotting everywhere, a carpet of dust and peelings, a variety of infestations: insects, vermin, noxious germs. All this mess breeding, of course, a seething hive of hormones, amoebas and disease, with Maria replete in the stink of it.

They were arriving at the rec hall, Mrs Wright waiting at the door to greet them. As they approached, she peered pointedly at her watch, before holding it up to her ear. 'Mrs Jones,' she drawled sardonically, 'it may just be that my watch has stopped, but,' she paused, 'if I'm not very much mistaken, you and your daughter are,' she held the timepiece close to her face, 'five minutes late.'

Clara Jones dredged up a smile. 'I'm so sorry, Mrs Wright, we were just seeing to some chores at home, and we must have let ourselves get carried away.' Turning to Rita Mae, she squinted. 'As my daughter always says, cleanliness is next to godliness, don't you agree?'

Casting an eye over Clara and Rita Mae, Mrs Wright laughed. 'Perhaps.' She paused. 'Oh well, the two of you have been very lucky today anyway. We decided, you see, not to start the film until you arrived. I told the women, just a few moments ago, that you were responsible for holding us all up, and we voted on whether to wait. There was a touch of resentment, I think, but,' she smiled, 'you won by a vote.'

Rita Mae saw that her mother's hands had balled into tight, vein-studded fists. 'Why, thank you, Mrs Wright,' she was saying, her voice taut as a violin string. 'Thank you so much. That's really very kind.'

Chapter Eighteen

A Santa Monica backyard, summer 1948

Hanging clothes out in the backyard, squinting, Clara Jones heard a scream start to build indoors. The sound rose quickly and she recognized its distinctive tremor, the cry of a spirit not easily broken. Still crushable, though, she thought. The noise now loud and apparently heartfelt, Clara ignored it and carried on.

It was one of those leaden days, she realized, the air hot and heavy, when you just knew that your cottons would be baked cardboard stiff. She had read quite recently (in a magazine, at the doctor's) of people who envied Californians the heat. Taking one of Larry's shirts and smoothing it as best she could, Clara pegged it carefully to the line. If she envied anyone, she thought, it was the Finnish folks featured in the same article, who enjoyed whole seasons of darkness. Not for them the lag of the day, the recognition that arrived come this hour (she glanced at her watch), 11.30 a.m., that it wasn't yet afternoon, that there were still at least ten hours to fill before it started all over again. Not for them the tyrannical daylight.

Pegging up a couple more shirts, starting in on Rita Mae's underwear, Clara heard the scream intensify. It seemed incredible, she thought, that a small child (unable to make the briefest speck of conversation, her lungs just the size of cheap pork chops) could make such a horrific noise. Were all children like this? she wondered. Could they all reach such eviscerating pitch?

Still, she carried on. Clara had half a basket of clothes left to hang and she was determined to get it done. She would not stop. Just as she was hanging the last sock, Clara heard a knock at the gate, and a timid voice.

'Mrs Jones. Mrs Jones?'

Peering around the side of the bungalow, Clara saw her neighbour, Dotty Spitz, balanced shakily on her tiptoes, brow just visible above the wrought-iron gate.

'Can I help you, Mrs Spitz?' Coming closer, Clara realized that the woman was still wearing her curlers – outside, in daylight – the big pink cylinders clipped haphazardly to her head. Typical, she thought. Faced with the drudge of housework, the least a woman could do was maintain some finesse. Dotty so rarely looked washed.

'I'm sorry, Mrs Jones, I wasn't sure if something had happened to you. It sounded,' the woman paused, aware of her neighbour's temperament, 'as though Rita Mae was home on her own. I thought she might have hurt herself.'

The scream still throbbing through the wall, Clara shrugged, laughing sunnily. 'Oh, you mean that noise, Mrs Spitz?' Her neighbour nodded, saucer-eyed and silent. 'No, that's just Rita Mae having her hair done. She does make the most awful fuss, but, as I'm sure you've noticed,' Clara's gaze lifted a little, fixing pointedly on the curlers, 'we all look much better for a good coiffure.'

'Right.' As always when speaking to her neighbour, Dotty felt summarily chastized. 'Well, I was just worried she might be hurt. I'm sorry to bother you.'

'No need to apologize,' Clara called cheerfully as her neighbour disappeared. Hearing the bang of Dotty's door, though, Clara grimaced. Truth be told, Dotty had every need to apologize. Coming over to her house in the middle of the day, not yet dressed, and daring to criticize Clara's child-rearing skills? It was disgusting. After all, it was hardly as though Dorothy Spitz knew anything about children herself. The woman was barren, or so Clara assumed, since she and her husband, Buck, were well into their thirties with not a hint of a child to show for it. Dried up, thought Clara. Probably a result of those godawful meals she could sometimes smell, the errant casserole fumes wafting in through an upstairs window.

Heading through the back door now, she marched to the bathroom to find Rita Mae. The girl, two years old, was sitting on the stool that Clara had assigned her, and on seeing her mother her mouth snapped firmly shut. Not that the burning of Rita Mae's scalp had receded (still sizzling softly, it bore the sound, if not the allure, of bacon on a grill), but she knew better than to scream in her mother's presence.

'Well, thank heavens for that.' Clara directed Rita Mae's head to the sink and began washing away the peroxide mix. Her daughter's skin did seem a little fiery beneath the bleach, but there was no excuse for such a show of anger. Rita Mae was just going to have to grow up a little, Clara decided now; she was going to have to control these childish emotions, keep them properly in check. Someone like Clara Jones (her busy hands marking time as surely as a conductor) simply couldn't stand for this nonsense.

Arranging a towel around her daughter's shoulders (the

last thing she needed was a wet floor) Clara heard a key in the lock. Rita Mae was on her feet then, 'Papa, Papa!' and Clara had to watch the usual sickly greeting – the hugs and kisses, the baby voices. She had told Laurence often enough that this would lead to trouble, that a child needed to be disciplined first, loved second, but her warnings were clearly being ignored. Having tickled his daughter into a frenzy (she was lying on a corner of the couch now, doubled over, laughing), Larry walked across to Clara. There followed the usual kiss, Larry's lips pursed slightly and hovering for just a second, an inch from his wife's cheek.

'So,' he affected a smile, 'how are you, Clara? Did you have fun while I was away? Out on the town with the boys, my sweet? Out dancing?'

Clara scowled. She couldn't bear his false bonhomie. 'As you know, Larry, I happen to be very busy here, I certainly haven't been relaxing. Your daughter has been making herself quite difficult actually, upsetting me, upsetting the neighbours.' She retrieved a cloth from the kitchen and made a great show of dusting the living-room mantelpiece, its painted surface already so polished that glimpses of wood blinked through. 'How about you, though?' she said wearily. 'How was your trip?'

'Oh, you know.' Larry shrugged off his jacket, as images of the past week flickered unbidden through his mind. 'Pretty dull, really, pretty dull. The New York boys had nothing much to say. Everything in their office seems fine. I sometimes wonder why they send me out there. They all seem so,' he paused, 'capable.'

'And did you go out much? Did you have fun?'

'No, no. The boys over there are very serious. They seemed very concerned about figures actually, everything adding up. Wanted to spend hours going through the finances, cross-referencing everything.' Larry sighed. 'Not my field really. I spent most of the time in my hotel room.'

Greetings accounted for, all present and correct, Clara concentrated more closely on her dusting. 'I'm just going to take a shower,' said Larry. 'Is that OK?'

'Just don't make a mess. I cleaned before breakfast. I don't want to do it again.'

Loosening his tie as he entered the bathroom, closing the door behind him, Larry began to strip off, smoothing his suit carefully over the towel rail. Balanced on the side of the sink he noticed the small white dish that held Clara's bleach mix, which had evidently just been used. So that was why Rita Mae smelled so antiseptic, he thought. Larry had put the glow of his daughter's head down to the sun, but now he realized the true culprit. He was going to have to say something to Clara again, he thought. It just wasn't right.

Even as Larry formed this idea, though, he knew he wouldn't challenge Clara on the subject, that a comment just wasn't worth the ructions. His wife was so obsessive about her and Rita Mae's hair, frantic when a mere pinch of black bled through, that it was dangerous even to mention the words 'bleach' or 'roots'. From Larry's perspective this seemed strange – he was sure they would both look much better with natural hair. That was women, though. When it came to their appearances all bets were off. Nothing you could say would persuade them.

Stepping beneath the shower, he tried (not for the first time) to pinpoint when Clara had morphed into a less wrinkled version of his mother. The girl had been so sweet when he'd first met her, so accommodating, but after just a few months of marriage she had suddenly seemed an entirely different person. Where she had first been happy to eat burgers at a roadside diner, sucking the grease eagerly from her fingers, she was now almost fanatical about manners. Larry had lost count of the times he'd been rapped on the back of his knuckles, his wife barking 'no', as he scraped his fork around the plate. And where, in those early months, she had been almost comically coquettish (he seemed to remember her winking on one occasion) she had soon become stern. Many of her outfits had remained the same, that was true, but the tight fitting that had once spoken of sex now denoted discipline.

It was in her attitude to other people, though, that Clara had become most like Mercy. For someone who had started out as a seamstress on a studio lot, Clara was incredibly dismissive of her peers, thought Larry, always keen to deliver some verbal jab that would fell their reputation stone dead. Not that she would do this to their faces, of course. No, in public she was icily polite. It was at the dinner table with Larry, after they had met someone new, that she would really start picking them apart. A monologue would begin, completely unannounced, and she would spend five or ten minutes deriding all details of said person's speech, appearance and manners. Considering it now, Larry realized that he had never heard his wife say a positive word about anyone.

The transformation had begun, he thought, during her pregnancy, becoming most obvious after Rita Mae was born. Larry remembered a conversation with one of his colleagues recently, who had said that his wife was suffering the most awful post-natal interlude, moping around the house half-dressed, hair ragged, ignoring her baby and breaking things. Maybe Clara had some version of that malady, thought Larry. Maybe her behaviour and outlook were coloured by some long-extended bout of the baby blues. If so, he wondered, was it possible that Clara might some day emerge from the anger the girl he'd first met? Could she revert to that old persona? Excitable but soothing? Conciliatory?

Lathering his armpits, Larry fervently hoped so. He closed his eyes now, rubbing soap through his hair, thoughts turning to New York and the man he had met in a basement bar that week. Devlin, he had called himself, a good name, thought Larry, although he guessed it wasn't real. As a local you'd probably be careful. Still, he'd known him as Devlin, and he was perhaps the most attractive man he'd ever been with, excepting Virgil of course. He wouldn't see him again, Larry guessed, that was the nature of these things. None of these men was ever really available. Just creeping shadows, lost in the half-light. You would never actually catch one.

Still dusting assiduously as Rita Mae bounced on the couch, Clara was irritated to hear the phone ring. It was never for her, she thought, was bound to be some chump from Larry's office, asking for annual figures or an expense claim, some banal request. Or it would be Virgil again (she nodded, tight-lipped, crossing over to the phone), asking in that runty little voice if Larry could come out and play basketball. Virgil had had the sense not to call so much recently, ever since Clara had made it politely but definitively clear that her husband was too busy for boys' games. Still, she wouldn't be surprised if he tried his hand again. The man knew no shame.

Picking up the receiver, 'Hello, the Jones' residence,' Clara heard Mercy's voice on the end of the line.

'Could I speak to Laurence please? I need to speak to my son.'

Mercy sounded odd today, thought Clara, composed as usual but tense, as though her refined shell was about to break, sending forth a sticky yolk. She had never heard Mercy like this and knew, in that moment, that she had won a small victory. There was ammunition here. 'I'm so sorry, Mrs Jones,' there was a palpable smile in Clara's voice, 'but Larry's just stepped into the shower. Can I take a message?'

'No, Clara, no.' Mercy Jones paused. 'I really need to speak to him,' she said slowly. 'There's something I need to discuss.'

'He's only just got in.'

'I know that,' Mercy's voice gave an ugly squeak, 'but it's important. If you'd just go and fetch him for me I'd be very grateful.'

Clara sighed. 'All right. Of course. It might take a while.'

Banging both fists on the bathroom door, she eventually received a 'What?'

'Your mother's on the phone.' Clara heard the shower being turned off. 'She says she needs to speak to you.'

'Can't I call back when I'm dry?'

'Well, I'd prefer that,' Clara thought of all the mopping she would have to do, the possibility of mould on the living-room carpet, 'but it sounds quite urgent.' Larry was poking his head around the door as Clara whispered, 'She seems a little upset.'

'OK, OK.' Larry, still wet, padded to the phone, a towel draped loosely about his hips. ('Don't drip,' implored Clara.) Lifting the receiver, he adopted a note of concern. 'Hello, Mama, are you all right? What is it?'

Sending Rita Mae to her room, Clara took up a position just a few feet from Larry, allowing for both dusting and eavesdropping. She knew that something critical had happened, and she was keen to hear details.

Mercy Jones was sobbing loudly now, forcing Larry to hold the receiver a few inches from his ear. Whatever had happened, he realized, it was serious. He had never known his mother to shed so much as a tear of frustration before. 'What is it, Mama? What's happened?'

'It's your father.'

'Is he ill?'

'No he's not,' Mercy snapped. 'He's not ill, Laurence. He's . . .'

'What?'

'Your father's been found dead. He was found dead yesterday, in Las Vegas.'

'What?'

Mercy went to repeat herself, but Larry cut in. 'It can't be, Mama, stop crying. It can't be. Pops was in Chicago this week. He was at the office. They must have got the wrong guy.'

'No.' A great convulsive sob wracked down the line. 'They've got it right, Larry, they've checked it out. He hasn't been to Chicago,' she paused, a deep breath. 'He hasn't been to the Chicago office for years now, years. Bill Eastleigh's been covering for him, saying that he's there, when he's been miles away.'

'Bill Eastleigh? I don't—'

'It's true, Laurence. I had a call yesterday morning, and they said that he was found in a hotel room.' Another sob shuddered down the line. 'I shall never live this down, never live this down—'

'What?'

'With a girl.'

'A girl?'

Clara moved closer to the phone, mind sifting through this information as she strained to hear. If Joseph was dead – and it seemed he was – then an inheritance was sure to follow. Much of the money would still be tied up with Mercy, of course, but, from what she'd picked up over the years, a substantial chunk was set to be passed direct to the boys.

On pursuing Larry, Clara had been misled by his friends, given the impression that he possessed a hefty trust fund. This had clearly been either a lie or a misconception. But an inheritance could solve their problems. Even with just a quarter of Joseph's wealth, a fifth, they would have more than enough money to move to Beverly Hills. Clara could invest in couture, lunch with the philanthropy set and send Rita Mae away to an expensive academy. Setting aside the tragedy of it all – which really couldn't be helped now – this might be the most fortuitous of events.

'Who was this girl? One of the hotel staff?' Even as he said this, Larry realized his naivety.

'Of course not, Laurence, it was a, a—'

'Don't tell me.'

'It was a prostitute.'

Callous as it was, Larry found himself smiling. 'That's terrible,' he said. 'I don't believe it.'

'But that's not it.' Mercy was crying so hard now that even Rita Mae, shut inside her bedroom, could hear her. 'It's worse than that, much worse.'

Clara moved closer to the phone. What, she wondered, could be worse than your husband being found dead with a prostitute?

'Joseph was found yesterday—'

'You said.'

'That's right, I didn't want to contact you in New York, and today they went through his files, they went through his office.' She paused.

'And what?' Larry sighed. 'Are they worried about his filing system? It's a mess, that office, I guess he's lost a few papers along the way.'

'He hasn't lost any papers, Laurence.'

'So, what is it?'

'The company's going to have to go bankrupt, no profits, nothing.'

'What?'

Clara sat down on the edge of the couch, aware that this wasn't such good news.

'Your father has been stealing money from the company accounts for years, they're saying, all the evidence was there in that office. Almost every other week he's been gambling in Vegas. Gambling it all away. The day before he was found, they say that he lost a hundred thousand dollars.' She paused. 'A hundred thousand!'

The old dog, thought Larry. Since starting his company, Joseph had narrated a series of self-penned radio ads, in which he'd cast himself as 'your best insurance friend' and preached enthusiastically about good business practice, diligence and the importance of financial security. And all that time he'd been filching money from the coffers. People had invested millions to feel secure, and now some inveterate gambler had swept their safety net right away.

'Surely it's something we can smooth out? There must be some way around this.'

'Don't you see!' Mercy screeched. 'It's all gone. Everything. They're saying it'll be in all the papers tomorrow, East Coast and West. I'm going to have to sell up the house, everything here, we're going to have to sell your bungalow too, the cars. There's no way we'll be allowed to get away with anything, there's nothing we can do. I'm going back to the East Coast, Laurence. I don't know how I'll cope with it all – I'll probably be snubbed, that's probably what'll happen – but I want to be with my sisters. I'm leaving next week.'

'But . . .' Needing to sit down, Larry slumped to the floor. 'What about my job? I need a job.' He looked around to see Clara, face held in her hands. 'How will I support my family, where will we live?'

'Well, Larry,' his mother paused, 'that, I don't know.'

Chapter Nineteen

'**S**hit.'

As the first uncertain notes of the riot alarm rose through the cell house (the noise designed to wake and panic every living thing on Las Focas – even the grass outside seemed to blanch), Larry pulled Chuck Fletcher up off the cold, tiled floor of the hospital toilets where he'd been kneeling.

'Quick,' said Larry, 'quick,' a sweat breaking over his chest.

'Shit.' Chuck was buttoning his shirt.

'You need to get back to your bed, quick.' Larry straightened his uniform as best he could. 'Shit.'

Chuck right behind him, Larry rushed out of the hospital toilets, barrelling into Ogden Barker, the Medical Assistant in charge of the ward. The weight of this impact saw Ogden's hands, packed full as they were of small glass prescription bottles, splay out in spasm, the tiny receptacles flying high in the air, arcing up around him like an icon's glow. As they fell, the majority shattering, a flood of brightly coloured pills spread out across the floor. In that same moment, the sick inmates, writhing pathetically in their beds until now, seemed suddenly redeemed, and there came a desperate scrabbling and swallowing, as a crowd of hands danced over the ground.

If it hadn't been for the alarm, Ogden would still have been safely out of the way for the next hour or so, sat behind a desk in front of the hospital ward, his back to the inpatients, doling out the daily quota of drugs. The first lunch shift had just ended and the usual snake of inmates had lined up to collect whichever cocktail of uppers and downers it was that kept them docile. The sounding of the alarm, though (which seemed to have come from the dining hall, a riot breaking up the second lunch shift), meant that all convicts had to be returned to their cells immediately. The drugs would wait.

Five minutes before, Ogden had nodded happily when Larry asked to enter the ward. He needed to see Chuck Fletcher, he had said, one of the work duty inmates he supervised on the island farm. Fletcher had been admitted to the hospital that day with stomach cramps, having vomited a bowlful of leaf-green bile.

'I need to talk to him about the crop rotation he's setting up. It's kind of important.'

'Sure,' Ogden had laughed, waving Larry in. 'You guys and your vegetables. He's in the third bed on the left – don't think he's really so ill, but you can judge for yourself.'

Now, as his patients scavenged on the floor around him, Ogden stared at Larry and Chuck, brow tight with suspicion. 'What the fuck are you . . .?'

Larry steadied himself, pushed past Ogden, and broke into a run. 'I can't stop – can't stop. I'm on gate duty, gotta get down there.'

He heard no response as he broke out of the ward, careful not to slip, and began running down the adjacent stairs, feet pounding quickly into rhythm with the alarm. Luckily, his path to the prison entrance ran through A-Block, which housed the lowest security inmates. He could imagine the scene in the other blocks, particularly the Treatment Unit, where the most disturbed convicts were held. The corridors would be alive with missiles by now, huge, fragrant pats of faeces being catapulted gleefully at any officers unfortunate enough to be assigned there. The prisoners in those blocks somehow always found a place to hide their bodily emissions, saving them up proudly for just this occasion.

How could he have been so stupid, thought Larry, as he ran down the walkway, why hadn't he second-guessed this episode? Hatching the plan to meet Chuck in the hospital toilets – the only secluded spot in the cell house – he had tried to account for every one of life's inconsistencies, every behavioural tic and permutation. He had watched Ogden Barker from afar for weeks now, confirming for himself that Barker never used the ward toilets, always the staff facilities at the opposite end of the cell house. He had consulted the employee timetable, making sure that there were no other Medical Advisers on shift on a Wednesday afternoon, no staff members, therefore, who might have cause to enter the hospital toilets. And, scanning the ward list this morning, he had checked that there were no potential stool pigeons amongst the patients, anyone who might have a 'special relationship' with the officers.

He thought he'd been thorough, had felt quite confident, arrogant even, but he had failed to account for such an obvious problem. Larry could hear his wife's voice now, in a whisper that crept up and above the alarm, chastising him through clenched teeth. 'Larry,' she kept repeating, 'stupid, stupid Larry.' He couldn't help agreeing with her. 'You never were a clever man.'

Around him the noise was swelling as prisoners pulled

their metal cups hard across the bars and kicked or head-butted the walls. Some were bleeding, thick gashes opening up on their foreheads that they would no doubt pick at over the coming weeks, keen to keep their wounds open, blood fresh. The alarm always brought a touch of the asylum to the men, even those in A-Block. It was as though the sheer, trembling noise of the thing had woken the part of each inmate that lacked language and civilization, the part that festered deep down and had allowed them to mutilate children or torture their wives, that felt no compunction on slicing through their lover's eye as she stared out at them in terror. Its sound was a prompt to this unleashing, this wild banshee meltdown.

'Officer Jones, Officer Jones, what's behind you?' screamed Bobby O'Brien, a young, schizophrenic inmate, whose main hobby was self-mutilation.

Larry turned. Nothing. A scream passed between the inmates, shot right through with laughter. They all took up the chant then, determined to unnerve him.

'What's behind you, Officer Jones, what's behind you?'

Larry kept running.

'I'd like to have you, Jones,' said a voice to Larry's right, and he glanced briefly at Allen Agnelli, whose genitals were poking through the cell bars. Agnelli gave a shy smile and raised his eyebrows. 'I'd like to have you, Officer Jones, and then I'd cut out your veins with a blunt knife until you bled to death and could be stuffed.'

Larry kept running. What was it in him, he thought, that made him so reckless, so ready to jeopardize everything for that one lost moment? He was no better than these prisoners, he reasoned, as the screams climbed somehow louder, each chiming in at a slightly different pitch. All the inmates had an animal streak, and he was no different. It was the same taint, thought Larry, that they all shared.

Would Ogden tip off the authorities? Would he notify the Warden, call for a disciplinary? Perhaps he would be too confused by the noise, the chaos, his patients gobbling those spilled pills all around him, to really ponder the incident. That could happen, thought Larry, slowing as he came to the administrative offices at the front of the cell house. Maybe there was a chance that Ogden would forget it. Consign the incident to a moment's confusion.

'I need to get out. I'm on gate duty.'

Tommy Irvine checked his clipboard and nodded, before levering open the three consecutive doors to the prison.

It was only when Larry had passed through the final door, the alarm still pumping across the island, that he felt relaxed enough to breathe. His panic didn't derive simply from the fact that he'd been caught, in questionable circumstances, with an inmate. Although that had added to the stains beneath his armpits, the riot alarm alone had the capacity to terrify him.

Most officers, despite their denials, loved the alarm, with its open invitation to a fight. If they were honest, it was these situations that had convinced them to enter the prison service, these times when they would have free rein to threaten, beat and subdue the inmates. Just as the riot alarm freed the prisoners from their usual constraints so, too, the officers. In the context of a riot rules were forgotten in favour of a huge survivalist frenzy. Both officers and inmates could vent their anger, all railing against the claustrophobia of island life.

Larry didn't have that safety valve, though. He didn't enjoy violence, could never quite grasp its appeal. He imagined the scene in the dining hall now, the flailing soup of limbs, the thwack of flesh against flesh, the small puddles of blood that would start muddying up the floor, and the occasional slapstick slip as men skidded in them. When a riot started no inmate could ever afford to watch from the sidelines. Even those who would have liked to creep away and find a safe haven (the child molesters were usually keen) ended up being forced to fight. Abstention meant being branded a pussy or a fag and ensured a much more violent beating later. Terrified prisoners simply showboated – circling their arms as menacingly as possible, foot flying into another man's stomach – and hoped that one of the officers would act quickly to drag them from the mêlée.

Lighting a cigarette, Larry began swallowing great hungry drags. The siren always had the same effect on him: a suffocating flood of nerves, followed by choking relief as he stepped out of the gates. From the very first note he would have difficulty breathing, the memories seeping over his lungs, the shadows of that night ten years ago, at the start of his career, that he had spent hunched behind a concrete pillar, listening to the screams of a fellow officer compete with the alarm.

That had been the only time that Larry had seen active riot duty on Las Focas. Following his rank cowardice on that one occasion he'd been permanently assigned to gate duty in the event of an alarm, a demotion he'd gratefully accepted.

As the prison entrance creaked behind him, Larry turned to see Edwin O'Hare emerge into the sunlight, blinking like a furless rabbit.

'I'm assigned gate duty too,' shouted Edwin. 'I guess we're gate buddies, huh?'

Larry stared back. There were always supposed to be two officers on gate duty, but he had been hoping that his opposite number might be off sick, or caught up in the midst of the riot. Larry could have used some time alone. But, no, he was stuck with O'Hare. Larry peered at the young officer, whose face, grown accustomed to the light, was so wide eyed and eager that he resembled a puppet on a hook, strings pulling his expression permanently northwards. The thought of another hour or two with such an eager man was draining, but there was nothing to be done. Larry nodded balefully.

'So,' O'Hare was determined to speak, despite the noise, 'I guess this is the first time this has happened since I've been here, huh. It's exciting, isn't it?'

Larry sucked on his cigarette and stared straight ahead.

'I was expecting it to be a lot nastier, not so thrilling, but it really gets the heart racing, doesn't it?' O'Hare put a hand contemplatively to his chest. 'Feels like it's going to break right through, if I'm honest. Is that the same for you?'

Larry coughed. 'You want a cigarette?'

'Oh no, no. Apparently they're bad for you.' O'Hare banged his fist against his chest. 'They think that's one of the reasons there's such a high mortality rate amongst inmates, you know, because we give them so much free tobacco. They reckon it's bad for the heart.'

'Right.' Larry lit another. Despite the fact that O'Hare was his upstairs neighbour (he and his wife having moved on to the island in early spring), Larry had tried to avoid the young officer as much as possible. He was wary of the other man's fledgling enthusiasm, his excitement at arriving on Las Focas. It was an attitude that tended to tire him.

Now Larry knew that his instincts had been correct.

O'Hare's ability to babble over and above the alarm was truly incredible.

'I mean, how much danger are we actually in at the moment? Do you think that it can be quantified? Has anyone ever calculated it in percentage terms maybe? That would be interesting, wouldn't it, working out the relative danger levels of any one riot? You'd just have to study other incidents, I guess, and average it all out. Wouldn't be hard.' He licked his lips. 'That might be a good project if they keep reports of these riots on file. Might be a useful job.'

Larry shrugged.

'I mean, really, as correctional officers, that's what we're here to do, isn't it?'

'What?'

'Well,' O'Hare's hands were curving through the air now, making vague, diagrammatic gestures – boxes, hexagons, vertical stripes, 'well, it's our job to look at a situation, weigh it up carefully, bring all the information to bear on it and then address it. By doing that, we can find new ways to improve the behaviour of the inmates and,' he paused, 'thus,' he paused again, 'their living conditions. By studying situations scientifically we can find out why they happen and create safe ways to combat them.'

'Right.' This had been exactly the kind of conversation that Larry was anxious to avoid. O'Hare was a college boy who had studied psychology at the University of California, taking a penal reform class as one of his modules. The course had been taught by a Dr Benedict Dale, a leading adviser to the Bureau of Prisons, and a figure of much derision amongst correctional officers. A few years earlier, Dale had visited Las Focas, keen to check out the conditions at America's number one supermaximum security prison.

He had quickly ended up fleeing the island, however, after witnessing a vicious fight between inmates that contradicted his central theory that most men – convicts or otherwise – were essentially altruistic.

Nevertheless, when O'Hare had approached his tutor and asked him about the reality of prison work ('Do you think I'd find it rewarding?'), Dale had been effusive in recommending the island. There was real work to be done there, he said, real progress that could be facilitated by someone as committed as O'Hare. And, as luck would have it, they were desperate for new recruits. Dale had handed O'Hare an application form, which was filled in then and there.

The college boys had started coming in the mid-fifties – with their charts and theories and empathy – and had superseded even Larry as objects of contempt. The older officers all loved to mimic their young counterparts, picking at their arguments like monkeys trapping fleas. These impersonations had soon become one of the staple entertainments in the officers' games room, always guaranteeing an outbreak of spittle-heavy laughter.

Not that O'Hare seemed to have noticed the ridicule. There was something almost repulsive about a person so insensitive to their surroundings, thought Larry. Something subhuman.

'I mean, rehabilitation has to be the key,' O'Hare shouted, as the alarm finally sputtered out. 'Oh,' he smiled widely, his voice still pitched frighteningly loud, 'it's stopped. That's better.' His volume dropped slightly. 'How long do we have to stay out here now? It's an hour, isn't it?'

Larry nodded.

'So, Officer Jones, you've been here much longer than

me. What are your thoughts on reformation? How would you go about reforming one of these men?'

'I don't think you can.'

O'Hare sighed. 'It upsets me so much when people say that. It's so cynical, isn't it? I mean, Officer Jones, don't you believe that everybody has a right to change? Don't you think we should encourage that possibility?'

'People don't change.'

'Of course they can, Officer Jones, of course they can.' O'Hare's hand had flown to his throat. 'I don't know if you've heard of Dr Dale, but he's done numerous studies – just numerous – that show that friendship and care can change a person. I'd love to show you the figures sometime. They're very compelling.'

Larry grimaced. 'People don't change.'

'But what about the projects that we run here, the work duty projects – the laundry, the kitchen responsibilities? Surely those are meant to be ways of building on an inmate's confidence, setting them up for life outside?'

'People don't change.'

'But what about the men on your work duty team then? The ones that you supervise on the farm? Surely you've seen a change in them since they started?'

Larry thought of Chuck Fletcher and the way his smile curled crookedly at the corners.

'Building a man's esteem can make a difference, can't it? It can affect him. Surely you've seen that?'

Larry turned to O'Hare, suddenly determined to end the conversation.

'Look,' he said, stepping towards him, 'we run work duty programmes on this island because we need the products they provide, the food they generate, the costs they save on labour. Las Focas is the most expensive prison in the world, and it couldn't stay open without the inmates working. We don't run those programmes, then, for altruistic reasons, we're not interested in whether an inmate feels confident or not, whether he's happy or entertained or bored out of his fucking mind. The fact is that most of these prisoners – the vast majority – are in for life, and that's because society recognizes that they can't change. Whatever it is that's in them,' he paused, 'whatever that thing is that makes them rape or murder or torture, is never going to go away. Got that? Never. It'll always be down there in their belly, just waiting to escape. We house them, we clean them, we feed them, and that's as humanitarian as we get. People don't change.'

'Oh.' Officer O'Hare was shaking.

He began to blink again, a defensive tic. 'I see.'

Chapter Twenty

Las Focas, summer 1952

Staring in the mirror, face edging closer and closer to the glass, Clara Jones pulled roughly at the skin that cornered her eye. Bucketing out, it exposed the gory red rim of her eyeball, a stark reminder of the veined mass that pulsed beneath. Clara wasn't interested in this, though. Her gaze focused instead on the skin she was fingering, a half-inch square on which she had located her first ever wrinkle. Peering even more closely, she jerked her finger hard, and was relieved to see the line suddenly fall away, fluttering into the white enamel sink. It had been an eyelash. That's all.

Hugely reassured (she was just twenty-four), Clara began dousing her face with water, before quickly applying her make-up. Usually this process was long, drawn out and intricate, a careful application of layer upon layer, until her skin was completely hidden. On this occasion, though, time was the only essential. Glancing at the clock, Clara counted the minutes. If she was lucky, she thought (and was it ever thus?), she might have up to two hours with him, two full hours. But it was a question of moving quickly, getting up there soon.

Standing outside the bathroom door, staring at the ground, Rita Mae heard her mother sing that song, the one about the paper moon, which she'd never really understood. It was unusual to hear Clara sing – she wasn't really the lullaby type – and so Rita Mae gathered that she was especially happy and that this almost certainly meant a visit to the Warden's house. Rita Mae had no idea why happiness should be connected with that place (it was too big to be welcoming) but she had seen her mother in this mood only a few times before, and it was always followed by an appointment with her father's boss.

'Right.' Clara strode into the kitchen, crouching suddenly to hold Rita Mae at arm's length. Her daughter, six years old, was clad in a white confection of cotton and lace, an outfit fashioned primarily for her Sunday school visits. Standing there, arms thrust out, Rita Mae seemed almost as starchy as her dress. Neglecting the familiar drill of hair, nails and pantie inspection, Clara simply looked her daughter up and down, before pulling lightly at her hem. 'There we go. All straight.' It was then she saw that Rita Mae was holding something in her right hand, slightly behind her back, and went to grab it from her clutches. 'You know you're not taking this with you, don't you, Rita?' She held the greying toy rabbit in the girl's face. 'It's dirty, disgusting. Put it in your bedroom.'

'But, Mama.' The rabbit was Rita Mae's favourite toy (her choice, albeit, limited) sent by Granmaria when they had first arrived on the island and a source of comfort ever since. Rita Mae wasn't a hugely confident child (on the rare occasions her parents had had visitors she had hidden beneath the bed) but the rabbit acted as a kind of shield. In the few years she'd had it, Rita Mae had managed to wear the cloth ears down to just the right consistency, perfect now for stroking through her fingers as she drifted off to sleep.

'You can't take it with you, Rita Mae. You just can't. What will Jenna think? She'll think you're a big baby, won't she? That you haven't grown up properly. That animal's a disgrace. I've been thinking of getting rid of it actually, you're lucky I haven't thrown it out while you've been at school. Look,' she held the toy away from her, dangling it by the ears, 'it's probably riddled with disease.'

Seeing the tears pool in her daughter's eyes, Clara chided herself. If the child cried – and that seemed almost inevitable – then, even at a conservative estimate, it would take at least ten minutes to dry her eyes, wash away the redness and make her presentable. Considering this, Clara decided that a few soothing words were for the best. Dropping to her knees, she took Rita Mae's hands. 'Don't cry, Rita, come on, we don't have time for that.' She passed the bunny back. 'Look, just this once, you can take the rabbit with you. How's that?'

'You won't throw him away?'

'Well,' Clara paused, 'no.' She rose to her feet. At least not today, she thought.

They were out of the door then, clattering down the apartment steps and starting the trudge up the hill. Clara was way out in front, eager to get there, still humming that inscrutable tune. Trotting along behind, rabbit dragged headfirst along the ground, Rita Mae was soon out of breath. She wasn't a sporty child, was really more given to reading than running. 'Come on,' said Clara, shouting over her shoulder. 'The Warden will be cross if we don't hurry.'

A few minutes later, record time, they reached the

Warden's house. It had just that very week been repainted, and standing back now, the sunlight hitting it at a perfect angle, Clara realized what it reminded her of: a picture she'd once seen of angels gathering at the gates of heaven. Walking slowly, reverently, up the garden path, she paused before ringing the bell.

As the heavy wooden door swung open, Clara was surprised to be greeted by Wally Wright, the Warden's teenage son. A lonely kid, it was unusual for him to be at the house during the day. Most of his free time seemed to be spent at the shooting range, firing off incessant rounds of ammo.

'Oh, Walter.' She was flustered now, not sure what to say. The boy was looking at her and Rita Mae curiously, his expression both smug and sullen. 'I'm so sorry to bother you, I'm sure you must be busy with homework, mustn't you?' Clara gave what she hoped was a sunny laugh. Wally was silent. 'Your father and I had an appointment, you see, a fitting for his new ceremonial suit. Rita Mae was going to play with Jenna.'

'Oh.' Wally made no move to let them in, and Clara was suddenly aware of her empty hands, the stark lack of a tape measure, scissors or notebook.

'I mean to say,' she thought quickly, 'the fitting has already been done. I have your father's measurements on file, but we just need to discuss the style.'

As Wally nodded, Clara was relieved to see the Warden cross the hallway.

'That's all for now, Wally,' he said, slapping his son convivially on the back. Then, to Clara, 'Walter will be quite happy to look after Jenna and,' he stared hard at Rita Mae, 'it's Reba Jane, isn't it?' Neither Clara nor Rita Mae answered, so he continued, pleased with his memory, 'Just while we're discussing the suit, of course.' He gave a subtle wink.

They dispersed then – Wally's heavy hand on Rita Mae's back, leading her to the playroom, the Warden waiting a few seconds before he pecked Clara on the cheek and beckoned her upstairs.

Over on the other side of the island, Mrs Wright was complaining of a headache. 'It's so close today, isn't it?' she said, the members of her quilting circle nodding obediently. They had been working a half-hour now, deftly stitching the large, multi-coloured quilt that would soon adorn the Wrights' bed. 'I know that it's terribly lame of me,' said Mrs Wright, 'but I think I might have to head home for a lie down.' She pressed her hands contemplatively to her temples. 'This pain in my head,' she paused. 'It's very worrying.'

'What do you mean?' said Vera Ellis, looking up from the bright four-leaf clover she was embroidering.

'Oh, it's nothing.' Daphne Wright batted the question away. 'You know how it is, though,' she smiled, 'you get a little older and every headache's a worry, a warning. You think everything's going to kill you. I'm fine. I just need some time in bed.'

'Well, you look after yourself,' said Mitzi Earl, as tongues around the table clucked agreement.

Emerging into the white light of mid-morning, Daphne Wright tried to decide when this headache had started. Had she woken up with it? Had it been pulsing there before the meeting, or had it started as she leaned in to concentrate on the heart motif she was stitching? Perhaps it derived from eye strain? An offshoot of the close work she'd been doing.

That was one explanation, she thought, but she didn't really believe it. Daphne had recently suffered a series of these headaches – a hard dry thump in the pit of her brow – and somehow she was sure that they stemmed from anxiety. She had been worrying a lot lately, strange scenarios arising in her mind, rubbing against each other, like rock formations shifting and settling, more friction on the way. Whatever was causing this concern was quite intangible, she couldn't put her finger on it, but Daphne knew, she was certain, that something in her world was awry. She would never have shared this suspicion with the other women, of course – wasn't given to public concessions to frailty – but it was the truth.

Nearing the house now, she felt slightly better, sure that the thud would subside once she entered those thick walls, arrived at her bedroom. It was the maid's morning off, and so, scrabbling in her bag, she searched for her keys. Finally locating them, feeling calmer, she opened the door. Stepping through on to the welcome mat, though, she was assailed by a loud shriek, quickly muffled.

Hurrying through the house, Daphne Wright tried to place the noise. It had sounded like a child (hadn't it?), a child being hurt perhaps, certainly frightened. She had thought, at first, that it must be Jenna, but, as she ran towards the back of the building, she could hear her daughter's voice building, chanting something, louder and louder. 'Do it, do it.' She could hear a stamping on the floorboards, too, in time with the chant, and some kind of groaning. What could it be? Was this the source of it all? The headache's root?

Bursting through the playroom door, Daphne gasped, screaming, hollering. She was going to vomit, she thought, but held it in, the stomp of Jenna's feet stopping as the girl stared shocked at her mother, amazed to see her home. On the floor, unconscious, lay a little girl, the Jones child, thought Daphne, blood spreading across the white dress that had wrinkled around her waist, Wally Wright on top of her, pants around his ankles, grunting desperately. Flying across the room now, Daphne grasped at her son's neck (he wasn't her son, how could he be?), pulling him off the girl, throwing him forcibly over the floor, screaming at him, she wasn't sure what at first. 'Pull up your pants,' she shouted then, crying as she saw the blood, the girl's blood, that spread right across his thighs up and beyond his stomach. 'And get out of here, both of you.' The door was open, the exit to the garden, and she swung her hand towards it. 'Stay outside, I don't want to see you.'

The little girl was unconscious, thought Daphne, a safe distance from the body, too frightened to move closer. She was lying there, perfectly still. There was every chance she was dead. What should she do? What could she do? She remembered then that her husband was home, he must be upstairs somewhere, too high up to hear the noise. Running for the stairs now, her voice rising, Daphne screamed for her husband, 'James, James.' She was sure he could do something. Sure he could help.

Arriving at the top of the stairs then, she saw her husband and Clara Jones, stumbling from the bedroom, faces red, clothes dishevelled. No, thought Daphne, legs wanting to collapse, knowing that she could do nothing about this now, that it was somehow, at this very second, irrelevant. 'It's your daughter,' she yelled at Clara, tears coursing down her face. 'Your daughter's been hurt.'

Chapter Twenty-one

Las Focas, summer 1952 (a few hours after the attack)

Larry Jones, his nose smudged up against the glass, gazed intently into the ward where his daughter lay, watching as the doctor questioned her, anxiously trying to lip-read the answers. Beside Rita Mae stood five empty beds, stripped down to their horsehair blankets, vacated quickly this morning after word from the Warden that this young patient required utmost privacy. The ward's inhabitants – three poisoned teenagers, an officer bitten on duty and a young pregnant woman – had all been shunted off to the third floor of Dr Earl's house, where they'd crowded, bad-tempered, into the spare bedroom. The staff infirmary was thus an even lonelier place than usual. Painted chemical green, it reeked of chalk and bleach.

Having only ever seen Dr Earl deal with inmates – mocking their suicide bids, refusing them painkillers – Larry had been worried about how he would cope with Rita Mae, whether he would treat the young girl gently enough. Watching him now, though, he was relieved to see the big man stroke Rita's hair back and chatter away quietly. All the pressing physical work, it seemed, had been done. On arriving at the ward, Rita Mae had been swabbed and stitched, cleaned of the browning blood, administered with morphine and tested for concussion. With these tasks out of the way, it was time to gauge her mental state, what psychological trauma – if any – she had sustained.

Making no headway with the lip-reading, Larry still couldn't prise himself away from the glass. It had been four hours since the attack – two since someone had thought to tell him – and he was becoming increasingly frantic about the repercussions. The doctor had said that Rita Mae would make a full physical recovery – he had seemed fairly positive about that – but what of the other effects? How much would this unsettle her? What madness might ensue?

Speaking to Clara (sat beside him in the corridor now, staring at her feet), she too had suggested that the prognosis was good, that, as far as they could tell, Rita Mae remembered almost nothing of the attack. It had been the Warden, apparently, who had brought Rita Mae round (Daphne Wright and Clara huddling, terrified, a few feet from the girl), and on waking her he had asked, almost immediately, what she recalled. Rita Mae's answer had, unsurprisingly, been confused, comprising just a few disordered images: Jenna's feet stomping through her sightline, a hand looming towards her head, the opening words of a chant. Nothing joined up or fluid. Nothing at all after her head had slammed, crack, against the floorboards.

But who knew what would emerge later, thought Larry. Could anyone really tell if these moments would stay abstract, whether the stark, deathly stills would one day fall together? She was on morphine now, that would make her fuggy, and memory, anyway, as everyone knew, was unpredictable, thousands of scraps mixed together, tangled and twisted as a child's puppet, springing alive as the last knot pulled free. Sometimes you could tell what had triggered a memory – the glimpse of an ankle, the jolt of a smell (the olfactory sense always the best reminder of forgotten places, forgotten people), but sometimes even these sensory factors were unnecessary. A memory could just ricochet forward, suddenly untethered, bouncing from the jumbled mass. An unexpected and, often, unwanted guest.

Mitzi Earl arrived on the ward then, bearing a tray of milk and cookies for Rita Mae, and Larry finally fell back from the window, sinking down on the corridor bench beside his wife. Hands clenched tight in his lap, he tried to calm himself, taking long, deep breaths, biting hard on his lip. He had known before, of course, what it meant to be a father, had always felt some silent connection with his daughter, an invisible thread spun strong through genetics and experience. Larry had always liked having Rita Mae around, too, this confusing, funny, mercurial child who couldn't help but lighten his mood. Still, it wasn't until today, he thought, that he'd really felt that primal pull, the ancient doomy sickness of wanting to protect your child and realizing, too late, that you couldn't. It wasn't ever possible. Not really.

He had been on shift at the time of the attack, Dr Earl eventually sent out back to the farm to find him, and at first he had thought the words of the good doctor a joke. A dare, perhaps, a tale put together for a bet. Some things, after all, just couldn't happen. Looking at Dr Earl's face more closely, though (the man wasn't given to humour), Larry had known it was true, running off behind the rows of runner beans to vomit. His body had felt spent then, entirely hollow, as weak and empty as that story would have been, if anything but true.

'So,' Larry turned to his wife, her face blank and composed as ever. 'So,' he started again, 'they think Rita Mae will be all right?'

Clara sighed. 'Absolutely. You've got to quit worrying and be strong, Larry – you'll make yourself ill otherwise. Everyone who's seen Rita Mae says that the outlook is positive as can be. I spoke to Dr Earl just before he came to find you and he said that the blood loss was minimal, actually. He said it always looks much worse than it is.'

'Right.' Larry's head fell into his hands. 'Right. Did he say how long she'll have to stay in here?' He glanced around at the sterilized walls, the pile of bedpans in the corner. 'It's not exactly homely, is it?'

'No. That's true enough. I didn't speak to Dr Earl about that, but I doubt it'll be long – just a day or two probably, nothing major. She'll have to come back to get the stitches seen to, but aside from that—'

'I'd like to kill that boy,' said Larry quietly.

Clara touched his shoulder. 'I know, I know.'

They were silent for a while then, Larry devising murder defences, Clara thinking vaguely of the Warden's hair.

'So,' Larry's voice was briskly efficient, 'what's the situation with the charges against Wally? Do you know who we need to talk to about that? We should get on to it as soon as possible really, as soon as Reet's gone off to sleep. Do we need to speak to an officer on the mainland? Will we need to get someone across?'

Clara looked down, her foot tapping. 'You mean you want to press charges?'

'You're kidding, aren't you? I want that boy locked up right now. Why?' he paused, a bitter laugh. 'What were you planning? Lynch mob? Contract killing?'

'I'm just not sure.' Clara assembled her words carefully. 'I just don't necessarily think that pressing charges would be the best thing. I mean, it might be quite disruptive, don't you think?'

'For whom?'

'For Rita Mae, of course. If we brought a case against Wally I think it might really upset her. It might,' she paused, 'prolong things. It would probably affect her recovery. It could slow it down.'

'You are kidding? Surely?' Larry stood up and began pacing, 'I hope you are, Clara, because otherwise, well.' He paused. 'I don't know what to say. I mean, come on. We have a watertight case against this boy, lots of witnesses, people like the Earls who would give statements, who would support our version of events. I know,' he sighed, 'that he'll just get thrown into some kinda kids' jail, not a proper prison, but that's better than nothing, isn't it? I'd obviously like him to be put in here.' Larry jerked his head towards the cellblock. 'That would give him a taste of his own.'

'Larry, stop.' Clara laid a hand on her husband's arm and beckoned him to sit down. Tired, he concurred. 'Look, I know you're very angry and so am I, so am I.' Her husband raised an eyebrow. 'But I think that we need to approach this carefully. We need to really consider what we're going to do.'

'What do you mean?'

'Well,' Clara's voice was at its most measured and dangerous, 'think about it now, just for a second. I know that we have a few witnesses, people who could testify for us, people who could maybe be,' she paused, 'what do they call it – subpoenaed?'

Larry nodded.

'But, let's face it, that would be asking a lot of Dr Earl. It would really be putting him on the spot. Look at him in there.' She gestured at the window. 'He's done such a good job on Rita Mae, he's really put her back together, and how would we repay him? By asking him to testify against his boss's son. Does that seem fair? I mean, it's quite a big ask, isn't it?'

'He raped our daughter, Clara. He didn't, I don't know,' he paused, 'steal a bag of apples. He raped our fucking daughter.'

'I know.' Clara's tone was balanced. She needed to maintain some calm. 'What he did is terrible, unforgivable, of course, I'm not arguing with that. But,' Larry's face was incredulous, 'think of all the problems it would cause if we took this case to court.'

'She's six years old, Clara. They've had to stitch her back together.'

'Yes. Yes. Larry, let's face it, you've never got along with the Warden, have you?'

'What's that got to do with it?'

'Well, you admit that, don't you?'

'Yes.'

'Exactly then. You've never really got along well with him and it's pretty obvious that helping put his son away would make it worse. It could make living on the island,' she paused, 'completely untenable.'

Larry's voice arched in frustration. 'Then we'll move off the fucking island, Clara, can't you see? I'm not letting that bastard get away with this. He's evil, isn't that clear? How could someone do this to a little girl – knock her out and do this? He deserves much worse than we'll give him. He'll get off lightly anyway.'

Clara decided it was time for a different approach. 'I agree, Larry, I completely agree. You're right, of course, you're always right in these situations, but,' Larry sighed, 'our best chance of giving Rita Mae the comfort and stability she's gonna need is if we stay on the island, if you keep your job. That makes sense, doesn't it?'

'I guess, in a way.' Larry was grudging. 'But I can't see that kid get off. It would kill me, Clara, and I can't believe you'd take it either, I can't believe you could bear seeing him around. And think of Rita Mae. If anything's gonna stall her recovery, it's that little fucker walking around the place, totally free. Who knows what memories that would prompt? He'd be so smug, too, can you imagine, knowing that he'd been allowed to get away with something like this, just because of his father.' Larry paused. 'And how do we know that he wouldn't try it again, hey, what about that? We're assuming that this attack was,' he thought for a second, 'opportunistic, but he could have been targeting Rita Mae for months. We just don't know. Soon as our backs are turned – and they're bound to be some day – then he could be on to her again.'

'That's all true.' Clara nodded her sympathy. 'You're right, Larry, but I think there might be another solution, something that could work for all of us.'

'What?' What could it possibly be?

'Well,' Clara knew she had to tread carefully now, 'I was speaking to the Warden.'

'You spoke to him about this?' Clara nodded. 'Before you spoke to me?' Larry was stricken. 'I-I don't know what to say. Oh. Right. How could you discuss this with him, before you'd spoken to me? Can't you see how wrong that is?'

Clara worked quickly to rectify this. 'It wasn't so much *me* talking to *him*, Larry, it was more,' she paused, 'that *he* was talking *at* me. He'd been good to Rita Mae, he'd brought her round and sent for the doctor right away. I had a few hours with him before they could find you—'

'Everyone fucking knew where I was. You knew where I was. You could have told them.'

'Well, I did, of course I did, but they had some difficulty, it took a while, and in that time the Warden told me about this plan he'd come up with, something he felt might work for us.'

Larry tensed self-consciously, trying to control the shaking of his shoulders. 'So. You'd better tell me about this,' he spat the word, '*fantastic* plan that he's come up with. I can't wait to hear it.'

'Right.' Clara knew Larry was still angry, but she could sense she was on the right ground, edging ahead slowly. 'Well, I know it's not prison, Larry, it's not quite what we'd want ideally, but the Warden has agreed to send Wally away to boarding school, a tough boarding school that he's heard about on the coast. He'd be miles away from all of us.'

'That's it? That's his punishment?'

'Well, obviously it's not very harsh, but, honestly,' Clara moderated her voice, 'the person we really need to be considering is Rita Mae. The main thing is that he shouldn't have any contact with her at all, and that's what this plan could achieve. James,' Larry glanced at her strangely, 'I mean, the Warden, says that Wally could spend his vacations with his grandparents, Mrs Wright's parents, out in Vacaville. He wouldn't be back at all.'

'And he wouldn't be punished? He'd be free to do this again?'

'Look, Larry,' Clara was firm now, keen to conclude her

argument, to tie all the elements down, 'there's every likelihood that this was just a one-off, boyish curiosity, a strange kind of anomalous thing that just got a little out of hand.'

'You think?' Larry sneered.

Clara ignored him. 'What we've got to consider – our only real responsibility – is Rita Mae's happiness. I've thought about this, and I think that the best thing would be for her to stay with my mom awhile, a few weeks maybe—'

'But you don't speak to your mom. I thought she was crazy.'

'No.' Clara paused, her voice tightening. 'She seems to have been in very good health actually, Consuela's been looking out for her and they both seem fine. Her letters have been quite lucid really. What I thought was that Rita Mae could go for a stay on the mainland – Mitzi Earl's due a trip there, I'm sure she'd agree to chaperone her on the way across – and that would free up some time for the Wrights to get rid of Wally. That way, Rita Mae's in a different environment for a while, somewhere that'll keep her mind off the attack, and we ensure that there's no chance of her bumping into him. By the time she comes back, everything'll be worked out and we can all just relax.'

As usual, Larry realized, he was being worn down by his wife's pragmatism, her ability to take each and every situation and apply some flawed logic. 'I don't know,' he said, shaking his head. 'I don't know. Maybe you're right. I'm not happy about this, but if you think it's for the best . . .'

With Larry lurching back towards the glass, Clara allowed herself a small smile. Despite the tenderness of the situation she had assured the Warden that she could talk her husband round, and so it was. After the day she'd had, this came as a huge relief. Clara knew that she'd have to put her affair with the Warden on hold for now (Daphne had seen them together, she had obviously guessed), but perhaps the favour she'd done for him in this corridor would convince him she still had potential. Perhaps the door would remain open.

Peering beyond the greasy smudges of sweat on the glass, Larry started to speak, his tone low and morose. He commented now, to no one in particular, 'I can't believe she's so small.'

Chapter Twenty-two

'Mitzi! Mitzi!'

Seeing Mrs Earl just a little way ahead, bent over with grocery shopping, Clara rushed to catch up, legs scissoring snippily beneath her tailored skirt. It was a fine, lustrous morning, the petals wide open, stamens erect, birds winging low and weeping their cries, the buzz of the insects somehow endearing, the ocean glinting a hypnotic blue. It was, in short, a perfect day, the colours as defined and graphic as the brightest of orchids, a radiance that even Clara Jones (her eyes so often blinkered to beauty) could appreciate. She had been walking to the Earls' house anyway, due for an appointment with Mitzi, a final fitting for a mother-of-the-bride outfit, and she was pleased to be able to help.

'How funny to bump into you, so soon before our appointment! Can I take some of those bags? I don't mind.'

As Clara proffered an arm, Mitzi Earl stared back, mouth tensing into a pout, years of cigarette use written inside her prunish wrinkles. 'No, no, don't worry. There's really no need, Mrs Jones. I'm fine.' Stopping for a second then, she shifted a large string bag into the crook of her elbow, the muscles of her upper arm flexing and flattening.

'Oh look, but honestly, I don't mind.' Clara smiled widely. 'Come on.'

'I'm fine.'

'It'll be easier.'

'No.' Mitzi spat the word, and then lowered her voice. 'I don't need your help, Mrs Jones. Is that clear? Let's just get up to the house and get through with this fitting. All right?'

'All right.' Clara scuffed along a few paces behind then, chastened. She had the definite sense, a bitten-lipped worry, that something was askew, something had upset her client, put her on edge. There was a climate between them right now which she'd never experienced with Mitzi before: the sharp bite of dry ice. Clara had been the Earls' dressmaker for years, and she and Mitzi had been on first-name terms for almost all of that time, had thrown out the formality of 'Mrs Jones' within the first few months. Why was she being so terse today? thought Clara. What could have caused this? Perhaps, she thought hopefully, Mitzi Earl had just had some bad news, some personal word that had prompted this mood. Or maybe she was suffering from women's pains. It was unlikely that this hostility was directed at her. Paranoid to assume so.

They were arriving at the Earls' house, the maid answering the door and relieving Mitzi of her shopping. 'You really should let me collect the groceries for you, Mrs Earl, there's no need for you to put your back out.'

Clara watched curiously as Mitzi threw her maid a huge smile, patting her lightly on the shoulder. 'That's really very sweet of you, Darva, very sweet, but you know how I like to do some of these things myself.'

'Would you and Mrs Jones like a jug of lemonade?'

Mitzi shook her head firmly. 'No. Thank you, Darva, but this won't take long, we won't be needing refreshments.

We've done all the preliminary fittings, so this can just be a short session, can't it, Mrs Jones?'

Clara nodded, slightly bemused. 'Sure,' she said quietly. 'Sure.' They were due to discuss beading today, an important topic, and she was worried by Mitzi's apparent rush. 'Well, that is,' she paused, 'we can make it short if you'd like.'

'I certainly would.' Mitzi began climbing the stairs, and Clara assumed she should follow. 'I have a lot to do today, Mrs Jones' (there it was again) 'and I don't have much time to spend with you. I'm sorry.'

'OK.' They were entering the hobby room, a huge space reserved mainly for Mitzi Earl's paintings, large abstract canvases daubed in the colours of the flag. Clara had never really liked them. 'OK, well, what we need to talk about,' Clara rooted in her bag for a pattern book, 'is the kind of embroidery you want on the dress. I have some samples here,' she held them out, smiling hesitantly, 'and a few photographs of outfits I've made before, but it's up to you, naturally, to choose.'

Silhouetted against the bright light of the window, her back to Clara, Mitzi held up her hand in a cautionary gesture. 'Mrs Jones,' she said, 'you're a very accomplished dressmaker. If you could just make these decisions yourself, I'd be grateful. Just do what you think is best.' She turned, sighing. 'Whatever's best.'

'Right.' Clara withdrew the pattern book and eased it into her bag. Whatever was wrong with Mitzi Earl (and she really couldn't guess), Clara's paranoia was growing. She had obviously done something to affront her, she thought, even if she couldn't remember. Something had obviously triggered this. 'Well,' she said breezily, 'I just have to take a few more measurements for the bolero. Is that all right?'

'Of course. Let's get it done.'

Clara inched towards the doctor's wife then, like an errant child edging past a sleeping parent. Whatever it was that had irked Mitzi Earl, she didn't want to exacerbate it, couldn't bear to see this mood drift into shouting, or worse. 'Could you hold your arms out?' she said softly, Mitzi complying with a sigh. 'That's great.' Empty praise was clearly in order. 'Here we go.' Unravelling the tape measure, Clara held it just a slight distance from the woman's arm, concerned that any unexpected contact might set something off.

'So.' Clara's voice was still pitched low, but she decided to risk some small talk. It might help calm her client. 'It's been great weather lately, hasn't it? Nowhere near as humid as usual. It's been so fresh, actually, that last night Laurence and I put a blanket on the bed, first time in months.'

Mitzi Earl flinched visibly. 'Yes.'

Clara persisted. 'Do you like the weather here? I sometimes find the heat,' she paused, noticing her client's face, 'uh, I, uh, sometimes I find it quite oppressive. It can be tiring, can't it?'

'Yes.'

'And I-I know Rita Mae struggles with it too. I can't imagine what it must be like for those men up in the cellblock. I mean,' she laughed, 'they deserve it, of course, but it must be like a chuck roast up there.'

'Look, Mrs Jones,' Mitzi Earl flung down her arms, trapping Clara's tape measure, 'I told you before, I just don't have time for this. I don't have time for talk. What with all the preparations for the wedding, I have a lot to think about. Could you cease the chat,' she paused, a twinge of regret as she caught Clara's eyes, 'and, well,' she threw up a hand, 'just take my measurements.'

'Oh. Of course.' Clara sucked her cheeks between her teeth. She could play this game too. 'I'll just get on with it then.'

The next five minutes were silent, Clara padding deftly around Mitzi Earl, scratching down measurements and making small, unconscious supping sounds with her mouth. She just wanted to leave.

Rolling up her tape measure, Clara gave a whistling sigh. 'Well, Mrs Earl, that's done. You need the dress, when? Two weeks' time, yes?'

The woman nodded.

'That shouldn't be a problem. I'll have to make a decision on the beading, I guess, like you said – I just hope it's what you have in mind.'

'I'm sure it'll be fine.'

'Good.' Clara checked through her bag and headed towards the stairs. 'I'll let myself out, shall I?'

'If you could.'

Passing into the Earls' front garden, where a hummingbird was worrying the bougainvillea, Clara exhaled hard. Starting down the hill, her mind entertained a crowd of thoughts, each clamouring for her attention. What, she wondered, could possibly have caused Mitzi Earl to behave like that – so pleasant and well-mannered with the maid, but unbearably testy towards her? What unconscious slight had she committed, and when the hell had it been?

Clara felt angry and irritated now, but also slightly worried. Of all the women on the island, it was Mitzi Earl (a strong individual, with unshakeable beliefs) who had generally been most civil to her, ignoring the petty rivalry and point scoring of the others. It wasn't that they were especially close (they had never shared confidences or childcare, for instance), but ever since the day of Rita Mae's attack, when Dr Earl had patched up the girl and tended her so gently, Clara had felt an even pulse of sympathy from his wife, a recognition of their hurt.

One of the reasons they'd never become proper friends, thought Clara, was probably Mitzi's relationship with her neighbour, Daphne Wright. However much Mitzi might sympathize with Clara and Rita Mae, her loyalties lay firmly with her best friend. Those two had been tight as far back as people could remember, hosting regular clambakes together and collaborating on quilts and choir trips. Clara would often catch them walking around the island, arm in arm, unselfconscious, heads bent together like the conjoined twins she'd once seen pictured in the *National Geographic*. They had the unanimity of sisters, those two, she thought. A deathless bond.

She wondered then, feet tripping suddenly together, whether Daphne had seen fit to tell her best friend about James Wright's affair. Clara had always assumed, somehow, that this would be kept private, that Mrs Wright would be loathe to even hint at this chink in her marriage. Now, though, she had her doubts. Perhaps, she thought, Daphne had told Mitzi recently, explaining the source of her aversion to Clara. They might have got tipsy together, that could have been the prompt, uncommonly candid over a jug of red wine. Clara could imagine how Mitzi would react to such news: shrieks of horror, followed by a retraction of her head into her shoulders, that withering and shrinkage, until she looked at least three inches shorter. Mitzi Earl tended to keep her evangelical beliefs quite private (for one of those types anyway, thought Clara), but she would react with horror at even a sly rumour of adultery. Extramarital sex wouldn't play well with her.

Veering towards the island store, Clara remembered the bag of onions she needed and ducked inside. Picking up a few other items – baking soda, white flour, corn cobs – she was suddenly aware of Vera Ellis's presence, an unmissable grin floating a few feet above the counter. Crouching behind the trays of eggs stacked neatly on the floor, Clara pretended to inspect the top row for damage. She couldn't be sure that Vera's smirk was aimed at her (there was a magazine open on the counter, perhaps it was a comic title?) but she had a sneaking suspicion it was. Peeking around the eggs, she caught sight of the woman again, staring back, even more amused.

'You hiding down there, Mrs Jones?'

Clara rose quickly, dusting her skirt. 'Of course not, Mrs Ellis, of course not.' Clara didn't need any eggs, but felt obliged to buy a large tray. Approaching the counter, she coughed out a laugh. 'You can never have too many eggs.'

'Absolutely.' Keying Clara's purchases into the till, Vera Ellis's grin showed no sign of subsiding.

Watching Clara stride into the store, Vera had warned herself not to say anything, that to mention the situation (she thought of that word in inverted commas) would amount to sheer nastiness. Unbridled spite. Now, though, with Clara standing before her, coiffed and smug as usual, Vera just couldn't resist. As the woman began packing her groceries into a paper bag, Mrs Ellis placed a hand heavily on her arm.

'Oh,' said Clara, glancing up, startled.

'I just wanted to say,' Vera couldn't contain herself, 'I'm so sorry for what's happened with Larry. I know it must all seem pretty desperate right now, quite bleak, but, you never can tell.' She paused. 'Perhaps it will blow over.

These things don't always end badly. You might even be allowed to stay.'

Smiling weakly, Clara cocked her head in what she hoped was a sprightly fashion. 'Oh,' she said, nodding. 'Definitely. Of course.'

Chapter Twenty-three

She should have known, thought Clara, should have guessed that all this morning's problems stemmed from Larry, that at the root of Mitzi Earl's snub she would dig out her husband, cowering, incompetent, obscured by dirt, causing trouble for her yet again. Stumbling downhill from the island store, Clara's eyes began to sting, she felt a swell inside her head and her nails pierced the skin of her palms. Larry had been nothing but a millstone throughout their marriage, she thought, social halitosis. Had she come to this island alone all those years ago, a young, single dress-maker, then she was sure she would have built friendships more easily, fielding invites to the quilting circle and the weekly keep fit classes. As it stood, though, she had taken his weight like a mule hefting carrion. They had been pariahs from day one, and after all this time she felt well and truly spent. If this continued much longer, she thought, she would be good for nothing but the glue factory.

Whatever he had done (and Vera Ellis's comment had been, at best, oblique) she would find a way to make him pay. He would have to amend for it somehow. Hanging her head, anxious to avoid eye contact with anyone who might pass, Clara considered the possibilities, trying to guess the offence. It wasn't as though this was unprecedented. Larry had been in trouble before.

His worst transgression had been his lousy behaviour during that first riot, but, since then, there had been many more incidents that had brought him (and, by extension, his family) into disrepute. Two years into their tenure, for instance, he had forgotten to count the farm tools after a work duty session (apparently he'd been chatting to one of the inmates) and a half-yard of hacksaw had gone missing, only to turn up a week later embedded in the neck of a prisoner. The man had died quickly. Then there was the time that he'd recommended an inmate for parole – on the basis, he said, that he was clearly rehabilitated – and, on release, the man had set about the San Francisco docks, stabbing and decapitating six sailors in succession.

Alongside these infractions there was his fat record of misdemeanours: warnings for poor dress, tardiness, a stark failure to discipline inmates. Perhaps the problem Vera Ellis had referred to stemmed from cumulative misconduct, thought Clara, rather than anything new. Perhaps the Warden had just tired of Larry's ineptitude and decided to punish him for years of poor service. She wouldn't blame him. Just wished she could do the same.

Taking the stairs of the apartment block two at a time, Clara arrived breathless at her floor. Going to unlock the door she found, to her surprise, that it was open. Inside she saw Rita Mae, perched at the kitchen table, reading a magazine.

Crossing to the sink, Clara threw down her bags and began dousing her hands with disinfectant. She wasn't sure why. Scrubbing them under the tap now, her voice rose above the running water, thin and suspicious. 'Why aren't you at the canteen, Rita Mae? I didn't expect you to be home. You know you're meant to eat in the school building. I don't have anything for you back here.'

Turning off the tap, she shook her hands, drops of disinfectant spraying against her daughter's face.

'I didn't like what they were giving us today, the food looked bad, so I decided to come home.' Rita Mae shrugged. 'It was that meat and vegetable stew again, the one they make from leftovers. We found toenails in it once. I heard it made lots of kids sick last time.' She smiled hopefully. 'You wouldn't want me to be sick.'

'So you've been sitting here?'

Rita Mae nodded.

'Doing nothing?'

'I'm reading.'

Clara frowned. 'So that's what you call it.' She wasn't sure she had the energy to upbraid Rita Mae right now – she would usually have punished her immediately for missing lunch – but, flipping to the cover of her daughter's magazine, she caught her breath. It was a copy of *Confidential*, one of those sent by Maria all those months ago, in the last package she'd been fit to mail. Despite careful treatment, it was thoroughly dogeared. 'Disgusting,' said Clara. 'You know I don't like you reading these.' Her voice grew more severe. 'They're tawdry. Dirty.'

'Have you ever read one?' Rita Mae lamented the words, even as she uttered them.

'No I have not! But just looking over your shoulder gives me all the information I need.' Clara swept up the magazine and began scanning the article that Rita Mae was reading – a profile of the starlets who peopled the hippest joints. 'Hotties at the Hotspots,' spat Clara. 'Meet the gorgeous young glamourpusses who make Hollywood purr!' She paused. 'I'm horrified, Rita Mae, I really am, that you can find this material interesting. It's revolting. How do you expect to build a happy home life, some kind of moral family structure, when you have trash like this,' she paused, hands aloft, 'wafting around your head.' Holding the magazine at arm's length (as she might a maggot-infested apple core) she carried it to the garbage can, ripped it in half and tipped the pages in.

'Don't, oh.' Rita Mae watched as the can clanged shut and knew all argument was pointless.

'Now, go to your room. I know there are some books in that bedside drawer of yours – surely you could read one of those? Or homework. You should be doing homework. It may be lunch time, Rita Mae, but these are still designated school hours. I won't have you slacking. Get to your room, and I don't want to see you until you're due back at school. That can't be long.' She glanced at the clock. 'Ten minutes. I can't have you in this kitchen – I've had a very busy morning and there's a lot to sort out.'

As Clara barked these last words, Rita Mae was already in her room, scrabbling beneath her bed for her stash of magazines. Pulling out a few, she started leafing through, eyes blurring before the page. Her mother made her so angry, she thought, she was so nasty and unreasonable. 'Vindictive'. That was a word they had learned in class yesterday, and she had an inkling it would be useful.

Maybe, thought Rita Mae (nodding to herself), if she had been brought up somewhere exciting, with more weekend options than out-of-date movies and other girls' parties, then the lives of those magazine people, Technicolor as they were, wouldn't seem so interesting. Had she ever actually been to a restaurant – even a drive-through, for

Chrissakes – then she probably wouldn't have been so fascinated by the goings-on at Romanoff's, Perino's and Chasen's. But, the fact was, she hadn't. She hadn't been anywhere. Instead she was interred on this island, surrounded by criminals, completely against her will. There should be a law against it, thought Rita Mae. Parents really shouldn't be allowed to bring a child to such an isolated place, especially when said child was too young to make a case against the plan. Aged three, she had had no say in their decision at all. It was false imprisonment. It really was.

Eyes focusing more clearly now, she saw teardrops strewing the page, ink pooling in places. Reaching for a handkerchief she patted firmly at her cheeks. If she looked at the situation more positively, Rita Mae consoled herself, then really it wasn't so long until she could leave, not much longer at all. Holding up her fingers she counted the months to her sixteenth birthday. Two and a half years.

It didn't sound like much, but considering this more carefully Rita Mae suddenly realized the slog she was in for. Two and a half years! That was the exact length of time since she'd turned eleven, a period so far back in the dusty annals of history that she could hardly remember a thing – what teacher she'd had, the clothes she'd worn, her favourite of the then-current MGM stars. There was every chance, thought Rita Mae, that she would fail to make it through such a stretch – certainly not unscathed. After all, even if the time went smoothly, uneventfully, then there was still the prospect that she would succumb to boredom, drifting from her current state (lively, impulsive, fiercely intellectual, she thought) to some virtual catatonia, a fish-eyed, stumbling, zombie-ish condition, much like that of the townsfolk in *Invasion of the Bodysnatchers*.

Was it possible to die of boredom? Could a person simply disintegrate under the weight of ennui? And, if so, how long would it take? Rita Mae wondered whether any of the inmates had been found dead in solitary, their brains shutting down after a prolonged stint, clean forgetting to send the signals that reminded their lungs to breathe.

So, two and a half years, in reality, was an age. Couldn't have seemed longer if her timetable had comprised nothing but chemistry classes. And, thought Rita Mae, it wasn't as though boredom was the only thing that made Las Focas unbearable. She would have to put up with two and a half years of the people, too.

Rita Mae was used to the jibes by now, of course, the catcalls hurled her way each day before class, but that morning the taunts had been even more virulent than usual, spreading quickly through the room as she sat silently at a middle desk, head down. As always they concerned her father, who, it seemed, had committed some ripe indiscretion, details of which had passed around the island yesterday evening. Sitting there, reading a math problem over and over again, she had struggled to decipher the words being yelled around her. It was only once the situation had escalated, Jake Hardwick standing before her desk, pelvis thrusting repeatedly into her sightline, that she had pieced them together. Mr Curtis had arrived then and shouted at Hardwick to sit down. It had been too late, though, thought Rita Mae.

Outside in the kitchen, Clara was cleaning, frantically polishing the dull metal taps, the ones that always refused to shine. With Rita Mae banished to her bedroom, Clara was able to think more clearly, but still she hadn't reached a conclusion on the events of that morning. Checking Larry's calendar she saw that it was seven hours before he was due back from shift. Seven hours! She couldn't wait that long. She needed decisive evidence of what was at stake. From Vera Ellis's look of moral rectitude, she knew that it must be something awful, devastating even. But who could she ask? If the news was as humiliating as she expected then Clara chose not to hear it from an acquaintance. She had spent all her years on Las Focas cultivating a mask of disaffection and she wasn't about to let that slip.

But she had to know, she thought, moving on to the sink now. If this were something that jeopardized their stay on the island, then she would need all available time to make plans for the mainland. If he'd done something truly ruinous – and that seemed more and more likely – then she would take the first boat off Las Focas, no arguments or goodbyes. She had stuck around, thought Clara, through all the failures of their marriage, hidden by the embarrassments just as surely as her family inside that chicken shit. She wouldn't feel guilty about leaving them both. Sometimes you could only save yourself.

Catching sight of the bleaching bowl, upturned beside the sink, it occurred to her, just then, that Rita Mae might know something. It was unlikely, of course: if the girl had heard rumours then surely she would have brought them straight to her mother. But then again, thought Clara, Rita Mae's bad behaviour had made their last few exchanges faintly abrupt. Perhaps she knew something that she hadn't had a chance to say. Children talked a lot between themselves, after all, chattering away, a constant cacophony, and whatever Larry's offence was she supposed it had become quite widespread knowledge.

She would ask Rita Mae.

Marching into her daughter's bedroom, Clara indicated she should lower the magazine (Rita Mae was surprised she hadn't snatched it), and sank on to the bed. She wasn't sure how best to approach this, but knew there was little time for subtlety. Leaning back on one arm, hoping to appear both nonchalant and confiding, Clara smiled. Staring back, wary, Rita Mae had never seen her mother look so alien.

'Well, Rita Mae,' there must be at least a short preamble, 'did you have a good morning in class today?'

Rita nodded, apprehensive.

'And you learned lots of interesting things?'

'Yep.'

'It's "yes", Rita Mae, "yes".'

'Yes I did. I learned many wonderful things.'

'Don't be facetious. Now,' Clara paused, 'I wondered,' she leaned forward slightly to adjust Rita Mae's dress, a small crease having formed on the collar, 'and you probably haven't, I realize that, but I wondered whether any of your friends had said anything—'

'About what?'

'Well,' Clara gulped, 'about your father. I thought you might have something to tell me. I seem to have heard his name bandied about the island a lot this morning.'

'Oh.' Rita Mae was slightly startled by this. What did her mother have in mind? Could it be that everything the boys had said was true? Was the situation really that bad? Looking at her mother, reclining there, so falsely benign, she knew that Clara hadn't heard the worst of the allegations, if any had reached her at all. She was going to blow up when she found out. Truly explode.

Face blithe, Rita Mae finally answered. 'What do you mean?'

'Well, I picked up on a few conversations people were having and I thought perhaps there was some new gossip flying around. If that's true, Rita Mae, then I want to get it stopped immediately. We can't have people spreading lies about your father. It's just not fair.'

Fair to whom, thought Rita Mae. She had never heard her mother defend Larry, not once in her thirteen and a half years. Now, though, she was faced with a dilemma. If she told her mother what she knew then there might be repercussions, one of them a beating, a chance for Clara to vent her anger. It was never wise to pass on bad news and then stand directly in the firing line. Seriously flawed tactics. On the other hand, there was the delicious prospect of apprising her mother that the small shred of social standing she'd constructed had finally been knocked out from under her. It was tempting. Clara had made a lifestyle of belittling people, thought Rita Mae, criticizing their looks, taste and intelligence. It would be interesting to see her dissolve.

'Well,' said Rita Mae, voice low and conspiratorial, 'I have heard something.'

Chapter Twenty-four

So that was it. Clara stumbled into the bathroom, lowered the toilet seat and sat down. Head slumping between her legs, she tried to think clearly, but all logic had vanished, replaced by this dizziness, her thoughts pulsing, undefined, populous and seething as a bucketful of maggots. Clasping her neck, she concentrated as hard as she could, but still she couldn't work it out. It was as if she'd been asked the ultimate trick question.

Her head jerked up as the front door slammed – Rita Mae off on her way back to school. She had seemed so calm about it all, Clara realized now (a thought plucked finally from the wormy mass), as though she'd known about Larry all along, her response pitched somewhere between a sigh and a shrug. It was as if she could stand apart from all this, not revolted or tainted by her father at all. There had been no hint of nausea. Nothing.

Sitting upright, her thoughts became less jumbled, the streams and tributaries flowing in one direction, gathering quickly to form a stagnant pool. Larry was queer. That was it. Her husband was sick-minded, diseased, a man who had foregone all morality for some scattered moments of relief. Clara couldn't fathom it. Gulping down the bile, she leaned back her head.

More focused now, she started to sleuth, piecing together the signs and clues she had missed, the once simple exchanges that glared suddenly, violently, too obvious to miss. There was the conversation that they'd had, a few months after their wedding, when Clara had made it clear that sex would be an occasional treat, weekends and holidays, nothing more. She had expected an argument, some resistance at least (Larry had been enthusiastic until then, despite her pregnancy), but he had just nodded, agreeing that they should avoid having more children unless their finances improved.

After that, she remembered now, he had begun spending all his spare time with Virgil again, the small, skinny boy he spoke of with such affection. Clara had been struck, even back then, by how close they were, the gossamer tenderness between them that had seemed, somehow, so unmanly. Brought up around women, though, she had not been sure that such behaviour was strange.

Still, instinct had told her to curtail Larry's time with Virgil, and she had achieved this quickly, applying the pressure, not stinting until he agreed to limit their meetings to one night a week. He had kept to that, too. It was then, Clara remembered, that he had begun jetting off on business trips, twice-monthly sojourns that he always described in the vaguest terms, skirting the details with questions about dinner or Rita Mae's dental health: any diversionary sleight of hand.

He had been equally slippery, she realized now, in explaining the bruises he'd often arrive home with, including suspicious-looking crops on his neck. They reminded Clara of the bite he had landed on her that first time they'd been together, parked up in the Hollywood

Hills. Confronting him about these, though, Larry would always laugh and cite clumsiness, suggesting that he had walked into a shelf set precariously at neck height.

She had never believed him, of course, wasn't that mutely naive, but had found it easy to cope with the idea that he was seeing someone else: another woman, or, indeed, women. In some ways she was grateful for the reprieve it provided, the acquittal from niggling sexual demands, any intimation that she was failing him. It should have occurred to her, she thought now, that the explanation was more complex, that within the illicit catacombs she'd imagined lay grubbier enclaves, places too sordid for her to conjure. She, who had been born in a brothel, had been too green for all this. She, who prided herself on her capacity for suspicion, had had not the tiniest inkling.

And now Larry had been caught, finally, in the grimiest circumstances, accepting sexual favours in a toilet block, surrendering himself to an urge that he really should have been able to ignore. He had been having sex with a convict, thought Clara, the tears arriving with a dry heave that left her throat sore. There was to be a disciplinary next week, a formality really, and then it would all be over. Their lives here kaput.

There was no recovery from this, she realized, no way of fixing the situation. Larry had made mistakes before, had jeopardized their position on Las Focas time and again, but this was so much worse than those other infractions, lapses of judgment that now seemed glancing blows. He had let her down completely, she who had spent their whole married life grafting for them, trying to claw out some status, respectability, from the disastrous actions of he and his father. Her task had always been difficult, a constant game of catch-up, like the fat girl in gym class who had perfected her back flip but would still never quite make the team. She had done everything she could, but her task was impossible.

Clara thought of all her work, those hours before she even approached Larry, when she had planned out their lives so perfectly. It hadn't been easy, entering such a white-bred world (and there was truly no place whiter than Beverly Hills), but she had put in the time: modulating her accent, learning vocabulary, studying dusty books on etiquette and correctness. Then there were the changes she'd made to her appearance: the bleaching of her hair, the application of all that pale panstick. She knew that there were still people who suspected her of being Mexican (it had been difficult to ignore Joseph Jones, muttering in Spanish, his breath hot on her neck) but somehow that hadn't mattered. The fact was that, as she saw it, she had managed to leave the Mexican part of herself – the part that was poor and hurt and vilified – behind completely, secluded in that downtown apartment with her crazy mother. And she was glad to escape it. People might mutter about her, cast aspersions amongst themselves, but they could never risk a public comment. She had slipped into that white world and she knew that she could have made a success of her time there, could have gained a foothold. There had been the potential at first for she and Larry to be proper, highly regarded, society folk.

But, like his father, he just couldn't control his appetites. Looking in the mirror now, Clara saw her eyes, albino-pink, staring piteously back at her. Perched on the side of the sink was the pair of scissors she used to trim Rita Mae's bangs, and now, absent-mindedly, she took these to her own hair, hacking at it with all the finesse of a child. Larry had given in to every urge, she thought, however wrong and lascivious; he had completely disregarded what was right, what could reasonably be accepted. She wouldn't have minded so much, were it not for the fact that she had given up every one of her appetites on marrying him. Clara's adult life had been a triumph of self-control: logic over emotion, planning over impulsiveness. She had thought that if she lived like that – trading her feelings for rules – she would be safe. She would exist inside a life as orderly as her mother's was chaotic.

But the problem, she realized now, the scissors accidentally scratching her brow, was that, try as you might, you couldn't control the people around you. While she had been striving to create the image of a perfect family, Larry had been dwelling on other things, making decisions based on urges unimaginable to a moral being. All her attention to detail, her care that Rita Mae was appropriately dressed, their language expletive-free, their apartment polished to a blameless shine, all this had been for nothing. Every inroad she had made, each social contact extended, had been undermined by her husband. She could never have won.

Opening the bathroom cupboard now, scrabbling amongst the contents (soap, magnesium milk and cough mixture all toppling out), she uncovered two bottles at the back: one large, one small. Larry had brought them home a few months ago, having confiscated them from a pair of work duty inmates who were intent on starting a bootleg scam. Clara had told him to get rid of them immediately but (and it was hardly a surprise) he had clearly decided to keep them.

Unscrewing the large bottle full of liquid, she took a long

swig, the claggy sour drink burning her reddened throat. Almost retching, she managed to hold it down. The smaller bottle was full of pills: goofballs, Larry had called them. Tipping out a handful, Clara stared at them intently, as if they might speak, offer up an answer. Her gaze moving back to the mirror, she saw her face for the last time, bleached blonde hair sticking up in tufts and clumps, steady trickles of blood pouring down her brow.

'Fuck,' she said quietly, there being no other words, as her hand rose decisively to her mouth.

Chapter Twenty-five

She didn't fly any more. There was no space at all. There was a window in this room, but it was too small to squeeze through, no chance of escaping out into the city. She had had time to muse on this (a long stretch, to be fair), but even if she lost weight, fasting for months, it wasn't just size that was an issue. The window presented other obstacles.

It was too high up to provide a view, so she had no sense of her surroundings, where this place was, what the adjacent streets held, the shape of the buildings, the lie of the parks, all the detail she must know before launching up into the ether. Before any flight a route must be plotted, however sketchy. To journey blind was impossible.

She was bed-bound then, just the ceiling for company, and the sheet (a loose weave, cheap) that she pulled over her head occasionally, before a nurse passed by and scolded her. They needed to see her face, they said. She'd never asked why. It was easier to think with her eyes covered, but even with them bare and open the pictures never failed to come, always cluttered, a constant, marching parade.

She remembered her mother, Perita, laughing and dancing, as she led Maria miles from the lean-tos (Toribio still asleep and snoring) to trespass the hacendado's land in the perilous search for peaches. Perita would stoop a little as they reached the grounds (as though a lapse in height might make her invisible), holding a finger to her lips and smiling so hard that her face changed structure, the lines of her forehead curving up as surely as her mouth.

'We're going in, mi hijita,' she'd whisper, lifting Maria atop her shoulders to pick the extra fruit. Then, once done, they'd run from the land, baskets bulging, until, safe at last, Perita would drop to the ground and heave out some laughter, stretching her legs and rolling through the grass, enjoining her daughter to do the same. 'You mustn't tell Papa,' she'd say, hands held in prayer, 'he'd be very angry.' And Maria would simply flex her eyes and nod: a look that swore silence.

She thought of the Hollywood Athletic Club, that capsule of sweat, a space defined not so much by its walls as the stench of male bonding that spread past those limits, attracting the men in. She had been sent there to meet a client, one of her very first call-outs, and was excited to see Valentino, earnestly lifting weights, clad in just a chest-baring leotard, the smell of men all around him, coursing through the place (or was it 'coarsing'?), all those just-freed droplets sporing and cloning, a mist that hung heavy as Errol Flynn's, well (she laughed to herself), reputation.

And other smells, here they came, she sensed them now, nose ruffling. The meat-packing plants that had set up beside the barrio, the rot of flesh grinding hard through the streets, embedding itself on their drying clothes, until everything smelled, just a touch, of chorizo. The chilli sauce at Tommy's, North Broadway – that sweet, spicy tang that tempted the crowds in. She recalled standing in line, sometime in the thirties, and there was Mae West, just a few yards ahead, ordering the Chilli Size Burger and drawling suggestively: 'It's just gotta be hot, baby.'

She thought of the cornhusk she'd used to bathe herself in Jalisco, scraping it across her skin while the smell of cinnamon coffee wafted to the river. And then the queues in the barrio for the outdoor hydrants, people crowding and jostling, old washcloths in hand, just praying the water would last.

She remembered the lights of the city, that blistering shock as she'd looked up to the hills and seen it for the first time, the Hollywoodland sign, blinking its four thousand bulbs, with their promise that this place would dazzle you, until, hysterical with happiness or tears, you were brought, either way, to your knees. And the Babylon set on the corner of Sunset, ornamental elephants standing their guard, so majestic that it kidded you there were other worlds beyond, mythic places on clouds or far-off planets, sequestered beneath the ocean, places that might be found and con-quered, with you as their queen. She remembered sneaking on to that set with her cousins as kids and climbing the towers, stealthy as ants, not worried at the talk of toppling scenery, knowing that just to be present at Babylon's fall might be worth the dying.

And beside that structure all those other crazy buildings, each more literal than the last: Dutch restaurants that were windmills; hot dog stands that were dachshunds; juice sellers cowering inside their giant, swollen oranges. And then there were the barrio houses built from refuse (discarded cartons, hammered-out oilcans) with newspaper insulation and mud-strengthened walls. No less amazing.

The brothel, those years she only half recalled, erasing each encounter firmly from her mind, leaving just the colourful grace notes of in-between times, the memory of scenes like devilish jokes, as delicious and instant as a popsicle. She remembered posing for George Hurrell, leaning across furniture or a soon-to-be star, her cigarette holder a carefully broached weapon. There was one shoot she recalled, early on, Hollywood's handsomest actor arriving at the house, face bandaged from chin to brow (every bit the invisible man) after a recent visit to 'Dr Bob the Butcher'. The house had been abuzz with stories of surgery, but none of these experiments in nose-shortening or cheekbone-raising had ever seemed to turn out well. Once those bandages were off the man had been forced to leave the business, side-stepping into interior design.

There was the afternoon Clara Bow had arrived at the house, not famous then, but trying, brandishing pairs of roller-skates, all the girls taking turns, whisking around the brothel drive, cackling out laughter as they stumbled and fell and skidded to their feet again. Nights at the Coconut Grove, tangoing between palm trees, watching, wonder-struck, as Marion Davies and William Randolph Hearst rode into the place on a thoroughbred, the poor horse sagging slightly beneath their weight. She was always afraid that she'd be caught out there, that someone would point a shaky finger, blow her cover and embarrass her client.

And then that man who'd died, the silent boy who might have been perfect, who knew or could tell? She thought of those days in the cemetery, sometimes joined by other women, always marvelling at how small his tomb was, just a narrow drawer amongst many others, a tiny marble encasement. Maria remembered lying on the ground once and measuring her girth against the lowest tomb. It seemed impossible that he'd fit in there. Too claustrophobic.

Shifting in bed, feeling her stomach, there arrived that night in the brothel, so heavy and aching, when she had taken her chances and pushed Clara out. All the girls had been gathered, Dora whispering encouragement, while the sounds of Duke Ellington scratched their support. It had been a short labour, a few hours, Submarine Daisy (her voice like an angel) soaring through 'Ah, Sweet Mystery of Life' at the very moment Clara appeared. She had wondered then, as the child was pulled clean, whether it was possible for her to be born as well, whether, in that moment, she too was perfectible.

She supposed not. For all her promises – to herself and Clara – the moments of that childhood had never quite meshed together, riven by sudden lapses, the days she would come to to find her daughter poised above her, arms crossed, eyes unreadable, clothes shabby. She remembered the last time that she had looked for Clara, convinced that she would see her, sweeping through the crowd at the end of the war, the people dancing and singing all the way down Hollywood Boulevard, waving their flags and banners. She had pushed through that crowd, calling for her daughter, lashing out as they restrained her, until Consuela caught up, dispersing apologies and pulling her gently home.

They had talked about loneliness that night, Consuela looking at her with confusion, not quite understanding the English word or how it translated. There was nothing like it in Spanish, she declared finally, only 'soledad', solitude, which wasn't so bad at all. They had never had need of such a word in Mexico.

And there was another conversation, years later, a discussion of the barrio, the troubles of those early years, the ramshackle housing and marauding pigs that would arrive in a front room, plainly vengeful. Consuela had laughed as they spoke and voiced an old Mexican expression that they'd used back then. Communing with the ceiling, Maria remembered it suddenly. 'I thought I'd died and gone to heaven,' she breathed softly, 'until I realized I was in prison.'

Chapter Twenty-six

Through the thick lace veil of her mourning hat (a gift passed down by Granmaria, years before), Rita Mae watched as Reverend Wilcox, the island's holy man, started in on the eulogy. Eyes raised to the wood beams, voice booming to the heavens, he certainly seemed sincere. With each word that tripped out, though, it became clear that he'd had only the flimsiest of acquaintance with Clara (she had once fitted him for a pair of thermal pants) and was, in fact, adhering to an ancient script, a cast of adjectives saved for just this emergency. On hearing her mother described as 'warm', 'sentimental' and 'loving', Rita Mae felt her concentration wane. Casting around for distraction, she found nothing.

It wasn't as though there were many people to exchange looks with – just Larry, sat beside her in the front pew, head bent, and a small scattering behind them in the cheap seats. Her mother's suicide had prompted an unexpected religious revival on Las Focas, people who had never expressed the slightest Christian belief suddenly adamant that it was wrong, immoral even, for Clara to have a church funeral. Countless residents had seized on this argument, their chosen excuse for staying away.

It was Rita Mae who had found her mother's body, a week

ago now. Arriving home from school that day, she had gulped down a cup of lemonade, leafed through a few magazines and then padded to the bathroom. It had been difficult to open the door at first (her mother's body slumped hard against it) but after some serious pushing, Rita Mae had catapulted into the room, Clara toppling forward, head falling heavily into the toilet. Edging past her mother, she had felt shocked for a second, but somehow pragmatic. Lifting Clara's head, she had laid her out awkwardly on the floor and checked for signs of life. Nothing. Rita Mae had washed her hands then, gone into the living room, sat on the couch, and waited.

It was four hours later that her father had come home, and, after an initial look of shock, he, too, had seemed faintly unsurprised by events, picking up the internal telephone that linked every apartment and office space on Las Focas, and calling Dr Earl. They would need someone to collect the body. The two of them had sat there for an hour in silence, staring at the opposite wall. Rita Mae really wanted the toilet – she had drunk half a bottle of lemonade by now – but she couldn't face going in front of her mother. Clara didn't look like the dead people she'd seen in films: composed, serene, arranged carefully beneath velvet sheets. Instead, her body lay twisted on the bathroom floor, legs in one direction, arms the other, foam drying slowly around her mouth.

Rita Mae hadn't cried since her mother's death, had found, in fact, that she felt calm about the situation, almost prosaic. In some ways she knew that this was strange, particularly given her tendency to cry over other deaths: characters in films, victims in the news, stars who'd wrapped themselves decisively around trees, all these prompting a great triumph of tears, a display that often lasted for days. The grief she felt for those people, though, thought Rita Mae, was more of a selfish thing. She wasn't shedding those tears for the death of the person in question, not really, but for the inevitability of her own. In people you hadn't known, death was always noble and tragic, the loss of a truly terrific person, those skewed eulogies all you had to go on. You couldn't help but cry at the wrongness of it all.

In Clara's case, though, Rita Mae had, of course, been fully aware of her mother's character. Not that this made it entirely straightforward, but it allowed for the thought, at least, that the woman couldn't possibly be less happy in death than she had been in life. To be truthful, it wasn't her mother's death that had surprised her, but the fact that Clara had actually survived to adulthood: thirty-two, no less. This was somehow completely amazing.

During her years on Las Focas, Rita Mae had come to marvel that anyone escaped childhood alive, this long grey stretch of Sundays, super-elastic, the end as unreachable as a mythic lost city. The human body was, after all, very vulnerable, and death had a trillion ways to ambush a person, each moment offering up some new opportunity, a chance to snatch it all away like a conjuror with a table-cloth. There were the long flights of stairs, all ready for a tumble; the pieces of chicken, breeding disease; the vehicles on the mainland, speeding precariously; the lazy hot baths you could slip under with ease. Death had all the best tricks.

Of course, it wasn't just the human body that was fragile, thought Rita Mae, but the mind too. Even if you went out of your way to avoid charging hippopotami, poisoned berries, falling machinery and vicious murderers, there was still the chance that your psyche would give out and you'd let down your guard, willingly invite him in, that unhappiest of house guests. She was surprised, on balance, that more people didn't take this option. The equation for suicide was, after all, just a moment of despair mixed with the conviction that life, from this point, would get no better. All it took was a quick series of events – the loss of your job, your lover and your nerve – and surely most people would succumb. But, it seemed, most times, they didn't. Human beings were obviously more resilient than she gave them credit for.

Sitting stiffly beside Rita Mae, Larry had also stopped listening to the eulogy, switching off when Reverend Wilcox described Clara as 'superbly affectionate'. He *was* thinking about his wife, though, a timely analysis, picking carefully over the events and revelations of the past week. On reflection it had been a confusing time, and he wanted to straighten it out in his mind.

Seeing Clara's body that day, splayed on the bathroom floor, Larry had felt: what was it? Not grief exactly, but a sharp pang of guilt. He had known something like this would happen, had been dreading her hearing of his upcoming disciplinary, just praying that she possessed that last sliver of optimism she would need to start anew. They had never really been close, that much was true, but, despite this, Larry had always held a sneaking admiration for his wife, this woman who had shown so much stoicism in the face of social exile. He knew that he had disappointed her, that their life together hadn't been as she'd hoped, but he had always been impressed by her nobility, the weary heroism that she wore so heavily. Ever since he'd known her, Larry had never seen Clara appear in public without perfect make-up, a well-considered image and her mouth set in that unnerving line that could be a smile, perhaps a snarl. She had been determined, all their time together, not to reveal a hint of frailty, and, regardless of the obstacles, she had achieved this. Preternaturally aware of his own weaknesses, Larry couldn't contain a sense of awe.

Were it not for the revelatory wiles of death, this respect would likely have grown. It was so much easier to admire the dead, garlanding them with generosity. However well a person concealed themselves in life, though, Larry realized now, death had a nasty habit of unravelling those efforts, offering everything up for perusal: the porn beneath the mattress; the stains upon it. Larry had known, of course, that his wife had an inner life, some unseen hinterland (nobody could consist so entirely of appearance), but, up until this week, he had never suspected its extent. He had missed the frantic beat of it, so far beneath the surface.

Throughout their marriage, Clara had kept her private correspondence and papers in a large wooden box, its key swinging lazily around her neck. On enquiring about the box's contents, Larry had always been denied, each rebuttal piquing his interest just that little bit more. Finding Clara's body, then, he had made sure to retrieve the key, placing it carefully in his pocket until such time as he could use it.

He hadn't had long to wait. The day after Clara's death, Rita Mae having swept off to school (Larry wanted her to keep to routine), he had rushed to the box and opened it. Turning the key, he was unsure what he'd find: some invoices perhaps, old letters, photographs. It was possible, he thought, that Clara had had a lover before they'd met, some long ago Romeo, all dark hair and blue eyes, quiet passion and gifts, who made up for the emotional dearth in their marriage. Somehow that idea appealed to him.

Sifting through the contents, though, Larry had gradually become dismayed. First arrived news of Maria Caesar's nervous breakdown, the official letter having apparently gone unanswered. Larry had known that his mother-in-law was ill, certainly, but he'd had no idea that she'd come so completely adrift. He could imagine the kind of place she'd be interred, a tiny room, much like those in the cell house. The only difference, he supposed, was that there'd be even more screaming.

This disclosure was followed (no pause for breath) by Clara's affair with the Warden, unfolding through a long series of love notes, the box containing both his and hers. The letters had a sweetness about them, a slow tenderness that Larry would never have suspected from his wife, a woman who'd long since seemed to lose all stomach for romance. Reading them carefully ('I wish we could have more time together, an extra hour, to lean against you') he'd realized that this was, in fact, the Romeo in question. James Wright. His boss.

Larry had been bewildered by this revelation, wondering at the pair's duplicity, the pillow talk they must have had, some of it, no doubt, about his incompetence. Checking the dates, he realized that the affair had occupied the months leading up to Rita Mae's attack, all those years ago. Coming to the last missive – a letter of thanks from James Wright – it was suddenly obvious why Clara had argued so persistently for Wally to escape charge. She had colluded with the Warden, chosen the welfare of her lover's son over that of her daughter.

Musing on this, a sly pressure building in his head, pressing nastily against his inner temple, Larry had finally arrived at the bottom of the box, its last item staring up at him. Reaching in, he had pulled out the hardcover notepad, the date '1945' scrawled deliberately on the front.

That had been the year they met, thought Larry, his anger briefly trumped by curiosity. He wondered whether this was a diary, something that revealed the Clara inside that finely manicured shell. Opening the first page, beginning to flick through, he was surprised to find a host of lists, graphs and diagrams alongside carefully inscribed notes. If it hadn't been for the date he would have suspected this was just an old exercise book, packed full of classwork. Going back to the beginning though, he had started to read.

On just the third page (headed '5 January 1945') Larry found a mention of his name, along with details of his father's career and company progress. This led to a series of graphs, charting Larry's supposed trust fund and the interest that could be expected to accrue. Clara actually seemed to have spoken to specific analysts about this, her graphs reflecting the growth patterns suggested by each one.

He came to the rhythm-method chart then, Clara's menstrual cycle picked out meticulously, the days of her greatest fertility marked with large red dots. Beneath the chart were scribbled notes, pinpointing and numbering their first times together, calculating her fecundity. The book had none of the normal diary elements, Larry realized, no record of feelings, events and people. Instead, it was completely factual, focusing entirely on figures and pro-jections. As he read on, horrified and intrigued, the true meaning of all this dawned on Larry, the fact that his marriage had been built on a seismic and sustained manipulation. Their relationship had never been based on anything but business. He had just been an acquisition, ill-starred as it turned out, his performance never quite matching his potential.

All the flirting of those first months, the coquettish flicks of the head, the eager sucking of grease-laden fingers, all that had been choreography, a lead dancer manoeuvring her partner. He had known Clara was a strategist, her days planned according to the strictest data, but, still, he had thought that those early months, at least, had turned on some whim of chance and attraction. He had imagined a connection there, however fleeting.

Sitting in that front pew, the Reverend's voice a rhythmic backdrop, Larry tried, once again, to make sense of these revelations. Clara's decision to target him had affected everything in his life, he thought, most of it badly. Had she chosen someone else (someone with a real trust fund, perhaps), he could have been free, living on that Santa Barbara ranch right now, working in the fields with Virgil, playing basketball on their floodlit court well into the night. That idea of theirs had been full of possibility, a proposition that might really have worked.

Instead, of course, his merger with Clara had seen him forced into a lifestyle and job he detested. The Junior Executive position at his father's firm had been bad enough – he had never fitted in there, try as he might to wear the right brogues – but his time on Las Focas had been truly terrible. He had been an outcast here from day one, his status plummeting with each new mistake, his condition more and more afflicted. The island's social scene was so tied up with work that any mistakes in the cell house immediately ended tentative friendships. He had made some glaring mistakes, he would admit that, and it had led quickly to his isolation. It was one thing to be lonely on the mainland, thought Larry, but to be lonely here, on an island in the midst of the Pacific, was devastating.

If he had to analyse it (and he really didn't like to), it was this feeling that had led him into relationships with prisoners, including this latest one, which looked set to finish it all. Larry's disciplinary hearing had been set to unfold that morning, but due to Clara's death and funeral it had been pushed back by a month. At least, thought Larry now, his friendships with inmates had been built on a base level of genuine interest and attraction. Emotions sinful in the eyes of most people, but real nonetheless. He knew that, on a social basis, his relationship with Chuck Fletcher would be considered utterly wrong, but there was a truth to it that beat his marriage hands down. Nothing conniving or manipulative. Prefabricated. Just two people who understood each other, drawn tight through affection, something nameless that fed them both. It was that simple.

Reverend Wilcox was winding up the eulogy now, and, without further ado (they'd kept hymns to a minimum) he announced that the body was to be wheeled on to the pyre. Larry bowed his head again then, but Rita Mae watched intently as her mother's coffin vanished into the waiting gulch of the cremation chamber. The doors were pulled closed, leaving just an inch-wide gap through which the congregation could glimpse the rising flames. Sitting there, the minutes ticking by without a lick, Rita Mae sensed that there was some kind of problem. As Reverend Wilcox glanced at his watch, one of the crematorium workers, clad in overalls, ventured to the altar and began whispering intently. Could it be, thought Rita Mae, that her mother (so inflammatory in life) was now proving flame-retardant?

Chapter Twenty-seven

'He should be here in just a minute, you shouldn't have to wait long. He's just upstairs talking to Jenna, I think. They're so close.' Daphne Wright glanced curiously at Larry as she led him to her husband's study. The man seemed nervous, she thought, distracted, his belongings clutched close to his chest, almost as one would imagine a first-time assassin, gun secreted in his pants. Looking Larry up and down she satisfied herself that there was no firearm. Of course, she supposed, a man in his position had every reason to be preoccupied, what with the death of his wife, and the upcoming disciplinary. She assumed that last was why he had come here today – a Sunday – for a prearranged meeting with her husband. He probably planned to plead his innocence.

Opening the door to the study, she swung her arm in the direction of James Wright's desk, and nodded. Acknowledging the gesture, Larry padded over to the waiting seat, bag still held tight against his body. Keen to get back to her embroidery, Daphne Wright nonetheless hesitated in the doorway. The man did look so terribly uncomfortable. 'Would you like a drink?' she said.

'Oh, really, I don't want any trouble.'

Daphne laughed. 'It wouldn't be any trouble. Coffee? Lemonade?'

'No, really.'

'I can get the maid to do it. It wouldn't be a nuisance.'

'I'm fine.'

'I see.' Mrs Wright shrugged. Marching through the house now, she tried to imagine the conversation about to pass between Larry and her husband, but found it impossible. She hoped, whatever the case, that James wouldn't be too harsh. She knew that the charges against Laurence Jones were supposed to be very serious (she had not wanted to hear the specifics) but still the thought of the man being brought down upset her. Ever since the business, all that time ago, with Clara and the Warden, Daphne Wright had felt a little sorry for Larry. He hadn't known about the affair, she was sure of that, and the fact that he had been betrayed along with her struck a note of empathy.

Laurence Jones had a very distinctive air, thought Daphne. In the years since he'd arrived on the island he had gradually taken on the mantle of the undesired, the eternal outcast. He was, naturally, not someone she would ever wish to spend time with, but she couldn't help pitying him. He had that unavoidable expression, cowed but hopeful, like the last puppy left in the pet store.

Sat perfectly still, back straight, Larry stared around at the Warden's study, a large white room, modelled on the Oval Office, dominated entirely by its desk. He had been dreading this meeting ever since setting it up a week ago, the day after the funeral. Reaching into his bag, checking its contents for the final time, he told himself firmly, in a voice reminiscent of his late wife, to stay calm. If he were to win this point he would need to focus.

There was a small noise behind him then, and, turning slightly, Larry saw James Wright veer into the room.

'Good to see you, good to see you.' The Warden bubbled with false jollity. Sitting opposite Larry, he shuffled some papers on his desk and then laid a pen securely on top. 'Now Mr Jones, Laurence, what can I do for you?'

Larry shifted in his seat, arms encircling the baggy leather bag, leaning slightly forward. 'Well.' He paused, not used to this kind of behaviour. He'd never been pushy. 'Well.'

'Yes?'

'It's just that,' Larry cleared his throat, 'what I need . . .'

The Warden glanced at his watch. 'You've only got a half-hour.' He laughed. 'Better spit it out.'

Larry hugged the bag closer. 'What it is,' he said, knowing he must speak now, 'well,' he looked down at the box, just visible, 'I want you to drop the charges.'

'What charges?'

'All the charges against me. I want you to cancel the disciplinary.'

James Wright's eyes narrowed, his mouth slightly open. Then, leaning back in his large leather chair, he released one of his trademark laughs, a resonant creation that undulated around the room, bouncing up towards the ceiling, until Larry felt that he was actually inside the sound, inhabiting it as certainly as his own body.

Watching the Warden's eyes close with mirth, Larry felt profoundly irritated. This wasn't how their meeting was supposed to start. 'I'm serious,' he said quietly.

'I'm sorry?' James Wright's reddened face loomed forward. 'What was that?'

Larry's voice grew smaller. 'I'm serious.'

The Warden sat up then, adjusting his waistcoat. 'You're telling me,' he retrieved the pen and held it precisely between the tips of his index fingers, 'you're honestly suggesting that I commute all charges against you?' He sighed. 'I know that you've had a difficult time, Mr Jones, and for that,' he paused, 'I'm very sorry. The death of your wife, and the way that it happened, must have been,' he looked down, searching for the right word, 'hard. She used to make some of our clothes, I believe, when you first came to the island, and I understand she was very accomplished. It must be tough to face things without her.'

'That's not what this is about.'

'But,' the Warden ignored this last comment, 'the important thing is that you carry on, that you accept your responsibilities and make a stable home life for your daughter. What's her name?' He struggled. 'Rita Maud, is it? Matilda?'

'It's Rita Mae.' Larry felt his fists clench. He didn't even remember her name. 'Look, you might want to hear what I have to say, before you dismiss me. It might be worth your while.'

The Warden was briefly convivial. 'Look, Laurence, if you're going to try and bribe me then we've obviously been paying you far too much.' He stared at Larry's lap. 'Is that bag full of dollar bills?' Rubbing his hands together, he laughed again. 'If so, then you might just be in luck.'

'I don't want to joke about this. Obviously I'm not going to bribe you.' Larry reached into the bag and pulled out the wooden box. 'I just think we could probably make some kind of deal. An arrangement.' He paused, slightly more confident of his bearings. 'If you promised to drop the charges then I could help you.'

James Wright squinted and sighed. 'Laurence,' he said briskly, 'goddamit, it's a Sunday. If you have something to say, then let's hear it, but otherwise I'd like to go play with my daughter. Would that be all right with you? Or do you intend to treat me to these cryptic little,' he held his hands aloft and waggled his fingers in frustration, 'conundrums all afternoon? Because I don't have time for that. Let's have some plain speech.'

'Right.' It was his decision. Taking the key from his pocket, Larry flipped open the box and handed James Wright one of the letters. As he accepted it curiously, Larry watched his expression shift first to recognition, then anger.

'Why are you giving me this?'

'Why do you think?'

'These aren't what they seem, I can assure you. They're not what they seem at all.'

Larry snorted. 'Oh, really,' he said. 'It's hardly as though they're,' he paused, 'what did you say? Cryptic?'

'Right.' The Warden's smile had faded completely now. 'Well, I expect you've read them all then, and you know what they say. I'm sorry. Nothing more I can give you than an apology. It was a long time ago and your wife was lonely.'

'That's not the point,' snapped Larry. 'I don't want explanations. Now,' he cradled the box, 'if you were, say, to drop all charges against me, then I might refrain from showing these to your wife. What do you think of that?'

'I'm not dropping the charges.'

Larry delved into the box. 'I'm sure Mrs Wright would be interested in this one,' he said, brandishing it in the air. 'Let's see.' He brought it close to his face, better to decipher the Warden's scrawl. 'You say here that, were it possible, you'd like to leave Daphne and marry my wife.' He peered even closer. 'Of course, that's followed by the caveat that you simply can't do this because Mrs Wright is a Catholic. How romantic.'

'You're taking them out of context. I just wrote them because she asked me to.'

'Who?'

'Your wife.'

'Look.' Larry paused. 'I can hand these letters over to Mrs Wright, or not. It's up to you.'

The Warden went to rise before sitting heavily back down in his seat. The fumbling of his arguments was replaced with a more precise tone. 'I won't be dropping the charges against you, Mr Jones, not now or in the future. I believe very strongly in the disciplinary procedures that we run at this prison, and,' he grimaced, teeth showing, 'let's be honest here, the charges against you are extremely serious. If you want the truth, Daphne knows of the affair that I had with your wife, and, while I would obviously prefer her not to see those letters, I doubt that they would have any bearing on our life together. Some men, you see,' he couldn't resist, 'offer their wives more than fidelity. For a man of a certain stature women tend to forgive,' he paused, 'the occasional indiscretion.'

Larry's eyes rolled up to the ceiling, where he noticed a huge crack running the length of the room. 'I see.' He'd had an inkling that Daphne Wright knew of the affair (she had taken to treating Clara so icily) but hadn't been certain. He would have to change his approach, move on to his next strand of attack. 'Well,' he said, 'then I guess these letters aren't of much use.'

The Warden sighed. 'Good man. Probably best that you destroy those, Laurence. You don't want them littering up your apartment.'

'Maybe.' Larry shut the box and placed it by his side. 'Not all the letters were in there, though.' He withdrew a sheet of paper from his pocket. 'There's one I've sent to a friend on the mainland for safekeeping, but I've got a photostat here. You might remember it.' Looking down, Larry began to read. 'I'm starting a little way in, of course, but here we go: "Thank you so much for what you've done for Wally. It's certainly appreciated. I know how much trouble he could have been in, and if it weren't for all your efforts things might have been worse. Although our friendship has changed, I just want you to know how indebted I am for that act of kindness. And I'm sure, though she might not acknowledge it, Daphne is too."'

James Wright went to snatch the paper then, but Larry held it away from him. He knew that the Warden would follow this up with some bravado or posturing, some new Swiss cheese argument, but, realistically, Larry was sure he had seized control. He watched contentedly as a single bead of sweat broke on James Wright's brow.

'There's nothing explicit in that letter, nothing concrete. I could have been referring to anything in those lines, anything at all. If you think you can use that to blackmail me, then I'm afraid you're sorely mistaken.'

Larry sucked at his lips. 'You certainly are oblique in the letter. That's true. But combined with all the other evidence, I don't think that it would be difficult to show the truth. And how are people going to feel when they find out you hid something so significant? I mean, an affair might be forgiven, but it would be very difficult for you to take a high moral ground on issues of law and order if people knew about the attack. And it happened in your house, too. Something like that happened under this roof.'

Larry paused. 'And, of course, although it would look bad for you, the person hit hardest would be Wally. I mean, once word got around and' (he offered this as an aside) 'with you being one of the most accomplished men in the country, it would get around fast – Wally might start finding life very difficult.' Larry looked down, suddenly a little ashamed at using his daughter's past like this. 'It was a horrific attack, Warden Wright, even you must realize that. Rita Mae could have been killed.'

James Wright was leaning so far back in his chair that there was a chance he would topple over. Eyes closed, he nodded. 'Tell me again. What was it you wanted?' He opened one eye. 'There are a lot of people involved in these charges now, a number of staff who have come forward to give evidence. It's going to be very difficult for me to explain this away.'

'I can see that, and I've thought it through. Now,' Larry paused, 'I know I've never been a particularly strong officer,' the Warden restrained a laugh, 'and so I don't intend to stay here much longer. All I'd like, and I don't think this is asking too much, is the chance to stay here for the next four months while I make plans for the mainland. I'll need that time to work out the logistics of it all, and at least sound out some other jobs.'

'Right.' The Warden nodded.

'So perhaps the best plan is if you could simply push back the disciplinary date to mid-summer, something like that. By the time the date comes up I will have left.'

'People will ask, though. They'll want to know why it's been moved again.'

'So you just say that you need to collect more evidence. I want to keep on working, of course. I can't afford to be suspended—'

'Well,' the Warden muttered darkly, 'we always need the staff.'

'And then I'll just carry on through to June. If you push back the disciplinary, I assure you I'll be gone by the end of June. No later.'

'I see.' The Warden held his fingertips together. He would never have expected all this from Larry, a man so doltish that even the word 'plan' had previously seemed beyond him. Thinking about it, though, he had to concede it was a fair trade-off. The headaches that could be caused by those letters were of migraine proportions. Stretching his arms above his head, he coughed lightly. 'Right,' he said, proffering his hand. 'June it is.'

Chapter Twenty-eight

'So how's school at the moment? Have you been working hard?'

'Sure.'

'Good, good.' Larry paused, gazing contemplatively at the parting in his daughter's hair. A couple of inches of black had emerged from beneath the blonde, the old regime growing out quickly. 'And what about plays? Are any coming up this summer? Have you landed any more starring roles?'

Rita Mae shrugged. 'Don't know. They'd probably all go to Jenna anyway.'

'Right.' Larry had asked Rita Mae to come for a walk with him this afternoon and had so far led her all the way up the concrete path to the cell house. Now he veered past the block's entrance on to the thin patch of grass that bordered the prison complex, snaking around beside the barbed wire fence that housed the farm. Holding out his hand, he helped his daughter up.

'Why are we going off here?'

Larry smiled. 'If we walk a little way around, then you'll be able to see the farm. I can show you the orange grove we're planning, and the vegetable patch. You can see where we grow your dinners. I thought you'd like that. And, anyway,' he paused, 'it would be nice to be somewhere quiet where we can talk. No one ever comes around here.'

'OK.' Rita Mae stared closely at her feet then, picking hesitantly over the bumpy earth. There was a reason no one came around here, she thought, and that was that the narrow path was potentially fatal. To her right the ground sloped dead away, straight down to the water. For someone as clumsy as her, it was especially precarious.

After about a hundred metres Larry stopped suddenly, clutching at the fence, pressing his nose right through. There was no one on the farm at the moment, all the work duty inmates currently at a late lunch, having toiled through a shift with Larry that morning. 'Look,' he said excitedly, as Rita Mae caught up with him, 'that's where we've been planting all the vegetables for this summer. We've rotated the crops this year, should be an even better harvest than usual.'

'Oh.'

'Yep. We'll be growing corn and tomatoes, cucumbers, mushrooms. They should do really well.'

'That's good.'

Larry started moving again, gesturing Rita Mae to follow him. 'It's better than good,' he called over his shoulder, 'it's brilliant. Actually, I can't really take the credit myself, it's mainly because I've let one of the inmates take charge on a few projects, and he's really very talented. I should have let him do a lot more of the planning before, but I just hadn't noticed him.'

They were arriving at a larger verge now, just wide enough for them to stretch out safely, and Larry sat down, entreating Rita Mae to do the same. Staring out to sea, Larry pulled up a long strand of grass and began to chew on it rather absently. Watching the grind of his teeth, Rita Mae struggled to think what it reminded her of, and was blindsided by the image of a mountain goat she had once petted through the barbed wire fence. That had masticated in much the same way.

'I wish you could meet this man actually.'

'Who?'

'The convict, I mean inmate, who's been helping me on the farm. He's a remarkable man, Rita Mae. Extremely astute when it comes to the land and how it should be used. And his drawings. Well. If you could see those I think you'd be really blown away. He's one heck of a talent.'

'Oh.' Rita Mae guessed that this must be the man her classmates had referred to. The one Larry had been caught with. 'What's he in for?'

'Well, that's the tragedy really.' Larry threw the chewed stem towards the sea. 'He's been in for five years now, for the murder of his wife and son—'

'Oh. That's pretty serious.'

'But he didn't do it. I think it was one of those situations where the police had no real leads, and they just fingered the man who was closest. It must have been terrible for him – he really seems to miss the two of them. I can't imagine what it would be like to be framed up for something like that. You'd think you'd lose all trust in people, but he seems to keep as upbeat as possible. He definitely tries to stay optimistic.'

They were silent a second then, but Rita Mae had to ask. 'Don't all the prisoners say they're innocent?'

Larry sighed. 'A lot of them do. That's true. But the fact is, Rita Mae, that when you've worked with someone as long as I've worked with Chuck – that's his name, by the way – you come to know whether they're genuine or not. This is someone who's been on my team for a few years now, and it's given me the chance to really look in his eyes when he's saying these things and judge whether they're true. And they are, I know it. The problem, of course, is that there's no way for him to prove it. He'll be stuck in here for ever.'

'Oh.' Rita Mae inspected the grass beside her. 'That's sad.'

'It is, isn't it?' Larry seemed to seize on this comment. 'That's exactly it, Rita Mae, it's incredibly sad. Can you imagine how you'd feel if you were put away for the killing of the two people you'd been closest to? It would be torture. I mean, he's tried to plead his innocence – at the trial, of course, and plenty of times since – but he's never been given a fair hearing. Can you imagine?'

Rita Mae sensed that her father had been planning this speech – it was slightly too formal – and that it was about to swerve somewhere unpredictable, even reckless. Steeling herself for the fall, she smiled. 'I can't imagine. No. It would be awful.'

'Worse than awful. You know, I'm glad you understand that, Rita Mae. I'm glad,' Larry paused, 'that you can empathize with Chuck's situation. I think empathy's a really important quality.'

'Right.'

'The thing is,' Larry began combing his fingers through the grass, afraid to look at his daughter, 'I've been trying to come up with ways for Chuck to get off the island, some way of righting the injustice. It's taken a few weeks now, but I think I have a plan which could get him to the mainland.'

'Is he able to go back to court then? Is there new evidence?'

'No.' Larry turned to his daughter, fingers covered with mud. 'I think we'll have to be more ambitious than that, I'm afraid. A bit more, what's the word? Audacious. The plan I have in mind involves an escape. It's a little risky, of course, but I think it could work.'

Rita Mae closed her eyes, knowing that if she opened them she would betray her conviction that Larry had gone mad. 'Oh,' she said softly, scared she might laugh. 'Oh.'

'I know it probably seems crazy, but I've thought it all through, and I think if Chuck and I escape together then we've got a good chance of making it to the mainland.'

Rita Mae's eyes sprang open. 'But you're a prison officer, you don't need to hatch an escape plan. I know there are, well, things you have to go through—'

'Procedures.'

'That's right, procedures that you have to go through, but that wouldn't be a problem. I bet if you wanted to give up your job they'd let you go in an instant.' Rita Mae realized how this sounded. 'Not that they wouldn't want to keep you, but because,' she paused, then began to speak slowly, wondering why she had to clarify this, 'you're not actually a prisoner.'

'Right, yes, well that's true, but the fact is, Rita Mae, Chuck'll need a companion to help him steer the boat across to the mainland. It's possible for a person to steer one of those things alone, I guess, but you'd have to be one heck of a sailor, and Chuck just isn't. Also,' Larry had obviously thought this through, 'if Chuck were to escape successfully while I was still on the island, then our friendship means I'd immediately be implicated. The Warden would call me in, I'd be charged on the spot, and,' he jerked his head backwards, 'I could end up inside that cellblock. The only way we can both escape is to go together.'

'And you're definitely going to do it?'

Larry swallowed, 'I think so.'

'When?'

'Right.' Larry shifted around to face her then, leaning in for emphasis. 'Well, I've checked the rotas, and the night of May fourth seems particularly understaffed – they've put the least experienced men on duty that night. Now, there's a roll call in the cell house at two thirty a.m., but after that there's nothing through until six a.m., so the best time to escape, I think, would be three in the morning. Does that make sense?'

Rita Mae tried to unpick this in her head, but was stymied by the numbers. 'I guess so.'

Larry smiled excitedly. 'Good. I've worked out everything that's going to happen in the cell house, of course, you don't need to know the details, but I was wondering,' he paused, knowing he had to convince her, 'whether you might help me with something outside.'

Rita Mae's eyebrows jumped. 'You want me to help you? Oh.' She looked down. 'Do I have to?'

Her father's eyes raced nervously over her face, searching for a hint of willingness, some way he might persuade her. 'You, you don't have to,' he stuttered, wondering if this was the moment it would all fall apart. 'I'd be so grateful if you would, though, Rita Mae. I mean, it wouldn't cause any problems for you, I'm sure of that. They wouldn't prosecute you for this, you could just say that it was an innocent mistake. A very coincidental one, of course, but a mistake nonetheless.'

'So what was it that you wanted me to do?'

'Well,' Larry smiled, relieved, 'it's quite simple really. You know there was that reduction in tower guards earlier this year?'

Rita Mae shook her head. 'I don't remember.'

'Oh, well, basically the guards stationed around the island, the ones in the watch towers, they've been reduced down to three.'

'OK.'

'And this means that were a guard to leave their post, for even a few minutes, one end of the cellblock roof would be completely without cover. It would be quite possible to descend the outside wall without anyone seeing.'

'What does this have to do with me?'

'Well, as I said, I've checked the rota, and Edwin O'Hare is due to be stationed in that tower outside the apartment block – you know the one,' Rita Mae nodded, 'all night on May fourth. What I thought you could do was distract him, get him down from the tower for a while.'

'How?'

'The easiest way, I thought, would be to climb up there and tell him that you'd heard crashing in his apartment and that you thought there was an intruder, that someone had broken in on his wife.'

'You think that that would get him down?'

'Probably not for long, and I guess he'd hesitate a bit, but I think it might. I mean, you wouldn't even have to get him back to the apartment block, that wouldn't be necessary. It would just be a case of distracting him sufficiently for five, ideally ten, minutes. If you stood a little way down the stairs of the tower, then he'd be forced to come towards you – and away from his post – to hear what you were saying. It wouldn't be hard.'

'So,' Rita Mae decided to test her father now, 'you're planning to escape Las Focas on the morning of May fifth with one of the convicts in tow?'

'That's right.'

'And you're sure that May fifth is the right date?'

'Absolutely.'

'I see.' He had clearly forgotten her birthday. 'And what would happen to me once you were off the island? Who would look after me?'

'Well.' Larry had been hoping to avoid this question. If he was perfectly honest, he couldn't think of any way he might contact Rita Mae after the escape, and that upset him, obviously, but, having weighed the situation, talked it through carefully with Chuck, he was sure this plan was for the best. As Chuck had pointed out, it was all a matter of relative freedom. Rita Mae, much as she might hate Las Focas, would be able to leave of her own accord within the next few years, pursue her life wherever she saw fit. Chuck had no such option. He needed Larry. 'I'd obviously find a way to send for you.'

'How?'

'I haven't worked that out yet, but it's only a matter of time.'

'Could I go and live with Granmaria?'

Larry paused, thinking of the letter about Maria Caesar, which he had thrown in the garbage a few weeks before. He had enough to contend with without a sick mother-in-law. 'I don't think that would be such a good idea really. No, you could stay here for a while and then I'm sure I could find a way to contact you. You could come live with me and Chuck.'

Aside from her key role as a distraction, her father clearly hadn't factored her into this plan at all, thought Rita Mae. It was plain – though not enunciated – that if Larry and Chuck were to escape successfully, Rita Mae would then for ever be followed by prison staff, police chiefs, perhaps even the FBI, in the attempts to trace him. Realistically there was no way that her father could contact her. To do so would mean prison.

Rita Mae would have expected this kind of behaviour from Clara, but Larry had always seemed more caring, concerned – even warm. Nonetheless, she thought, he was happy to leave her here, stranded amongst the low-lifes, a sacrificial offering to the clearly unhappy gods of this island. He wasn't worried that she would be left alone, her future shakily uncertain. Rita Mae felt a sob working its way through her throat but was determined not to voice it. Gulping quickly, she looked up.

'I'll do it.'

'You will?' Larry's eyes grew wide as he leaned forward to hug her. 'Thank you so much, Rita Mae, you can't know what this means.'

'It's OK,' she said, voice muffled. 'I'm sure you'll make it up to me.'

Larry clambered to his feet then, dusted himself down, and held out a hand for his daughter. They began walking again, edging around the farm, steps falling in silence. Out in front, Larry was thinking about how well the conversation had gone, how quickly Rita Mae had agreed. She was a good girl, he thought, steadfastly loyal. He hoped, ideally, that some twist of fate and circumstance might bring them together a few years hence. If he had known where he and Chuck were headed then the situation would have been easier, but that was a decision that they'd planned to make later, on reaching the mainland.

Watching the waves as they lapped hungrily at the shore, Rita Mae was also thinking about the escape plan. She knew that she had agreed to help her father, had actually given her word, but, really, as his plan stood now it offered an object lesson in selfishness. There was no place for her, aside from that role as an accomplice. Why should he and his lover be allowed to leave, while she was stuck here, island-bound and alone? It just didn't seem fair.

'This is where we're going to plant the orange grove,' said Larry, pointing animatedly at a large patch of ground, newly aerated. 'In a few years' time this space'll be covered in trees. It'll be wonderful.'

'Pity you won't get the chance to see it.'

'Oh well,' Larry shrugged, 'there'll be orange groves on the mainland too. Chuck and I want to find a large tract of land somewhere, far from everything, where we can work together in peace. We don't really care how overgrown or barren it is at the moment. We're up to a challenge.'

'Good.'

The grass reach widened now and swerved around a corner. Following the bend, Larry and Rita Mae were surprised to find a couple lying on the ground, blocking their way. Entangled together, half naked, they didn't seem to notice their company at first, the person on top still thrusting, unembarrassed. Holding a finger to his lips, Larry indicated that they should turn around, but the couple were suddenly distracted, staring up at their audience.

'What the—?'

It was Jake Hardwick, face twisted, looking as irritated as Rita Mae had ever seen him. As he pulled back, grabbing his shirt, she caught sight of Jenna Wright, and uttered an involuntary gasp. Stumbling around, Rita Mae began marching in the opposite direction, eyes pricking with tears, hand held tightly to her mouth.

She had been lying there once too, she thought – except it had been a floor in her case, a floor somewhere on this island, boarded with varnished wood. She had been lying there that day, she remembered, immobile on the floor-boards, wanting to scream but somehow silent, as Jenna stomped past, back and forth, back and forth. There had been a man on top of her, no, a boy, must have been about the same age as Jake Hardwick, parting her legs, she wanted to scream, and she couldn't do a thing. Her head had hurt, it had been banged on the boards when he threw her down, and then she felt her dress being pushed up, panties pulled down and that pain suddenly stabbing between her legs, excruciating. There was blood, she thought, blood on the boy's hands as he brought them back up to her face, blood seeping through her white-blonde hair as he clutched at clumps of it, crashing her head against the boards again. And then, nothing, until the low voice of Warden Wright had broken through, asking what she remembered.

Running to catch up with his daughter, Larry took her shoulder and forced her to stand still. Drawing Rita Mae to face him, he noticed her wet eyes and felt sorry.

'You mustn't worry about what you saw, Rita Mae. Just two kids messing around. They're not much older than you, are they?' He tried to lighten the tone. 'I'm glad I've never caught you in that position. It's really something a girl should wait for.'

Pulling away, Rita Mae began to walk faster, feet tripping carelessly over the stubbled ground. Her cheeks striped with tears, she tried to decipher it all, the images suddenly flashing through her mind, that day, seven years ago, at the Wrights' house. She remembered everything now, realized the true significance of Jenna's hoofs as they'd stomped past her eyes.

Nothing had been done about it, she thought. No one had been punished. There had been no recriminations, no day in court, no case for the Wrights to answer. Oh well. Her pace slowed a little and she found herself, despite it all, laughing out loud. Her parents weren't the only ones who could do nothing, she thought.

Chapter Twenty-nine

Chewing on her pencil, staring absently at the dirty plates piled up in the sink, Rita Mae considered her next move. The start of the letter had been relatively straightforward (it didn't get much simpler than 'Dear Granmaria'), but now she was faced with a quandary. There was an obvious subject to address and she wasn't quite sure how to broach it, or even, indeed, if she should.

There was always the option of skirting the topic, she thought, focusing instead on recent school and community highlights, thus evading it. Unfortunately, though, thinking carefully, she realized that there were no school and community highlights, so prevarication was going to be that much harder. There were lowlights, certainly, she thought, anxious to grasp at something, but perhaps it would seem strange to include those ('Our class rabbit's sick. We think Jake's fed him rat poison'). To do so might have the opposite effect to that intended, actually emphasizing the subject under avoidance. It was no use, she thought, she would just have to address it all as honestly as possible.

'I guess you've heard about Mama by now,' she wrote slowly. 'Well, I guess someone will have told you anyway, and I hope that you're not too upset. That is, you shouldn't be.' No, that last line was wrong, thought Rita Mae, taking her eraser to the page. She started up again. 'That is, you mustn't be, because there was nothing that anyone could have done. I think it was probably a mistake really, not suicide' (some lies were utterly moral, thought Rita Mae), 'and she wouldn't have been in any pain at all.' She looked at this line and realized that, for all their morality, some lies were also transparent. She decided to backtrack. 'At least, she might have been in pain, that's true, but if so, then it was only for a very short time. We think she went quickly,' she chewed zealously at the pencil for a second, 'or certainly within, you know, four or five hours.'

'So!' An exclamation point was clearly in order. 'You mustn't worry too much. Me and Papa are getting along just fine at the moment.' (Looking at these last three words she decided to erase them and then scrawl them out again, this time in capitals.)

'If I'm honest, though,' (should she say this?) 'I don't know how much longer we'll be on the island. Papa seems keen to move away, but I'm not sure where. I was thinking, and it's only an idea, that maybe if he did move off the island, I could come and live with you. I know your apartment's pretty small, and that I'd have to sleep on a couch and all, but that would be OK by me. With your help, anyway, Granmaria, I'd be a huge star within months (!) and then we could buy a big old mansion somewhere nice. You wouldn't have to worry about anything – not cooking or cleaning. It would be great!'

Surveying her handiwork, Rita Mae felt satisfied. The letter was the perfect mixture of sensitivity and directness, she thought. 'Lots of love,' she wrote at the bottom, before signing off her name with the panache she'd been prac- tising for autographs. Holding the page away from her, she admired the heart on top of the 'i' of 'Rita Mae'. The letter communicated exactly what she wanted to say.

Folding the paper and placing it carefully in an envelope, she paused again as she came to write the address. Given the recent lack of correspondence from Granmaria, she wondered what might be best. The obvious move, of course, would be to trot to the island store and post it straight to her Orange County apartment. Perhaps more creative ideas were in order, though. She might have better luck, thought Rita Mae wryly, simply strolling to the beach, rolling up the letter, inserting it into a watertight bottle and sending it on its way.

Chapter Thirty

'Look, you can see everything. All its insides. Its guts. Its heart.'

'Do shrimp have hearts?'

Rita Mae threw her spare hand carelessly into the air and laughed. 'I dunno, Johnny. I thought every creature had a heart, but maybe not.' She picked the shrimp up out of her fishing net and inspected it more closely. 'Can you imagine what we'd look like if we were like this? Completely see-through? You'd be able to see all those veins they show in our biology books. Great big arteries and all those spindly little ones branching off. Gross. It would be like a horror movie.' She growled. 'Revenge of the Bloody People. And just beyond the veins there'd be all the organs, wouldn't there?' She laughed, crouching down to throw the shrimp into their bucket of water. 'Instead of looking at someone and thinking they had nice hair or good skin, you'd probably think, wow, he's got really fine-looking lungs.'

'Yep.' Johnny laughed. 'Or you'd be really impressed by the size of their liver.'

'And you'd be able to see their brain. You'd be able to see whether there was much going on up there or not. Do you reckon the brain tenses when you're really thinking hard?'

'Maybe,' shrugged Johnny. 'It sometimes feels like it.'

Rita Mae was off then, bare feet tripping through the rock pools that lined this stretch of shore. Johnny watched silently, as transfixed as ever. On other occasions when they'd ventured to the beach Rita Mae had become bored very quickly, slumping on to the sand after five or ten minutes, stretching out and declaring herself sick to the gills of fish (she always found this joke very funny). 'They don't talk or perform tricks, do they?' she had often argued, persuasively as it happened. 'And we never catch anything worth eating. So what exactly is the point? Why did you drag me out here, Johnny? I know you like being outside, but people like me,' she would lower her voice, 'cultural people, we have more of an appreciation for the cerebral. Books and the theatre, those are our things. We're not given to this outdoorsy, fishing, rubber boots and waterproofs sort of life. It's diminishing.'

Today, though, thought Johnny, smiling broadly, Rita Mae's interest in fish seemed to be burgeoning. He watched as she jumped to another rock pool, misjudging the depth, screaming suddenly and finding herself thigh-deep in water. This would usually have upset Rita Mae, sending her stalking back to the beach with the verdict 'rock pools are stupid', but this time she simply tilted back her head and bellowed out a laugh, like a mother bear calling her cubs.

Johnny had thought, these past months, that his attraction to Rita Mae had reached its apotheosis, that he couldn't possibly find her more beguiling. Staring at her now, though, skirt clinging to her legs as she gambolled (yes, gambolled) across the rocks, he knew that it had reached a new high. Closing his eyes for a second, he started to pray, but, remembering Rita Mae's comment that God was a bearded myth, he sent his invocation to the wind instead.

He would exchange anything, he thought, anything, for just a single kiss. It could be his health or the health of his mother, his life, the life of his father, the chance of ever enjoying a moment's happiness again. All this, he was quite willing to barter.

'What are you doing, you dill?' Rita Mae's voice broke through the reverie. 'Open your eyes and come help me fish. This isn't a one-gal job, you know. Even Mae West would be having trouble out here. If we catch some more shrimp like that last one – big enough to see their gut and everything they've eaten today – then we could make a shrimp,' she paused, 'what is it? Gumbo? Isn't that what they make with shrimp down South? Is it like jambalaya?'

Johnny jogged towards her and stopped, squinting at the sun, head cocked. 'We don't know how to make gumbo.'

'Yeah, but my dad's not back at the apartment until tonight. He's pulling a double shift. We could just see what's in the house, put ingredients in a pan and hope for the best. Oh yes,' she yelped, clapping her hands together, 'and we could make toffee. Apparently all you have to do is mix butter and sugar until it goes all sticky and then wait for it to dry. It would be fun.'

'Sounds good.' Johnny rolled up his trousers just a little more and waded out to join Rita Mae. 'Don't know how many shrimp we're likely to catch, though. We've pretty much dredged this area.'

'Oh, Johnny.' Rita Mae shuddered the words, her best Gloria Swanson, finishing with a disparaging sigh. 'Don't be such a pessimist, you fruit. There's every chance that there are thousands of shrimp still bobbing around these pools. It's just a question of looking hard enough.'

They were both quiet then, staring down into the sandy

water, pulling their nets determinedly through and gazing at the contents. After five minutes of this, still singularly aware of his companion and her unexplained levity, Johnny just had to ask. 'What's made you so happy today?'

Rita Mae stared up from the mossy rock she'd been examining, quizzical. 'I'm allowed to be happy, aren't I?' She clambered over to a dry patch and sat down. 'For Chrissakes, I mean, isn't a girl allowed to smile? What are you? The laughter police?'

'Don't be silly.' Johnny rushed over to her, sinking on to a supremely damp patch of rock, grimacing as the water seeped up through his pants. 'I didn't mean anything bad by that, anything wrong. It's just that you're not normally quite so chipper as this. I wondered whether something particularly good had happened, something that you were excited about. I love to see you happy. It's great.'

'Oh. Well.' Rita Mae went to speak candidly, but stopped herself. 'It just happens to be a beautiful day, doesn't it? Look.' She turned to face the sea, hand sweeping across the horizon. 'The water's clear, the sun's hot, there's no one else around. It's a perfect day. Normally there'd be something wrong, wouldn't there?' Johnny shrugged. 'Like Jenna or Jake or one of those bastards coming down to ruin it all. But,' she held up her hand, fingers crossed, 'they should all be at Jake's party this afternoon. We shouldn't catch a lick of them.'

'So, it's mainly just that it's good weather?' Johnny found this a little confusing. The weather on Las Focas was *always* good. Maybe, though, he thought hopefully, the focus of her argument was actually that second detail she'd mentioned: the fact that they were alone here, together. Maybe what she was trying to say, somewhat inadvertently of course, was that she thrilled to the radiance of his company. Maybe she felt the same way as he did, and was just expressing it obliquely. 'You like the sun that much?'

'Well, in a way.' Rita Mae watched as Johnny's eyes grew beseeching, his body leaning towards her. 'The weather's certainly very good.' She stood up and peeled her skirt away from her thighs. She didn't want clammy skin. She'd read about trench foot. 'Come on, Johnny, we need to get on.'

He wasn't about to let up, though. 'So there's nothing else about today that's making you so,' he paused, 'jaunty?' As soon as he'd said this he regretted it. 'Jaunty'? What had he been thinking? It was such a dumb word. Rita Mae would hate it.

'Well . . .' Rita Mae fell quiet for a few seconds, scouting through a neighbouring pool, before looking up abruptly. Gazing at Johnny, so perfectly young and unformed, blinking back at her with all the consciousness of a single-cell organism, she knew that she could trust him. Whispering now, she stepped a little closer. 'There is something else.'

'There is?' Johnny could feel the pulse sprint through his ears. 'There is?'

'Yes,' said Rita Mae. She stretched out now, feet on the bottom of one pool, back curving across a large rock, head tipping right over the other side and hands reaching for the bottom of the adjacent dip. As her head filled up with blood, she let out a tinny laugh. 'I didn't want to tell anyone,' she said, still whispering, 'but I'm not going to be on the island much longer.'

Johnny descended with a thwack, the water luckily no deeper than a puddle. 'You aren't?'

Rita Mae sat up, enjoying the head rush. ''Fraid not.' She

wiped her sandy hand on the rock. 'I'm going to live with my Granmaria, you see, my grandmother, in LA.'

'But,' it couldn't be true, thought Johnny, it just wasn't possible, 'what about your father? Surely he's your guardian now, he's the one who should look after you.'

'Well, he's looking after me at the moment, I guess, but,' she paused, 'you know men. They're not the best homemakers. Who even knows if he'll be around much longer?'

'What do you mean?' Johnny's voice broke on the final word, a stress fracture. 'Surely you know whether your dad's gonna be around or not?'

Rita Mae frowned. She didn't want the boy to get overwrought. 'Well, not for certain. Anyway, it doesn't really matter what my father decides, it's sort of irrelevant now. Whatever the case, I'm definitely going to live with my grandmother in Orange County within the next month. It's fated basically. It's written in the stars.'

'But,' there must be some alternative, 'didn't you say that you hadn't heard from your grandmother for a while? You were worried about her a few months back, you thought she might be ill.'

'Oh, that's all been cleared up,' Rita Mae lied. 'I mean, if anything really serious had happened to her I'd know about it by now, wouldn't I?' She would, she told herself, absolutely. 'Obviously what's been happening is that there's been some trouble with the post in that part of California, and Granmaria's letters just haven't been getting through. I know she's always wanted to look after me, though, so I'm just gonna get off the island as soon as possible and go visit her apartment.'

'What if she's not there? What if something,' Johnny

paused, 'I don't want to worry you, but what if something really bad has happened to her?'

Rita Mae was firm now. She had tired of Johnny's attempts to pick holes in her plan. 'She'll be there. Where else would she be? And if she's moved – which I suppose is an outside possibility – then one of her neighbours will know where she is. All I've got to do is get to that apartment, and then I can track her down from there. Even if she has moved,' Rita Mae sighed, 'it won't be far.'

'Oh,' Johnny looked down. Then, pointedly, 'But won't you miss the island? Don't you think there are things about being here you'll miss?'

Rita Mae's voice was scornful. 'What?' she snorted. 'The people? The bullying? The boredom? No.' She was sure. 'Apart from you, of course, Johnny,' he brightened slightly, 'there's nothing I'll miss about being here. I mean, think about it,' she gave a tiny squeak of euphoria, 'I'll be hanging around Hollywood, making my way, really getting some- where for a change. At some point,' Rita Mae gave a sharp intake of breath, wanting the next statement to sound truly portentous, 'a girl has to announce herself. There's only so long you can spend in the wings. It's important to make the right entrance. And if you haven't done that by the age of fifteen, then you've really missed your mark. There's no point after that.'

'Huh.' Johnny was thinking. 'But isn't Orange County quite a way from Hollywood? It's not as though it's walking distance.'

'No,' Rita Mae slapped her hand flat on the surface of the water, sending it spraying up into Johnny's eyes, 'I know that, stupid, but it's a lot nearer than I am at the moment, isn't it? Granmaria loves Hollywood, anyway, she used to work for one of the film studios and she knows the area really well, so she's bound to get the bus with me and show me around. The first thing I have to do,' Rita Mae's voice was serious now, as she reminded herself of this, made a strict mental note, 'is catch up with whoever's making that film version of *Breakfast at Tiffany's*.'

'What's that?'

'It's the book by Truman Capote. You know the one. Mr Curtis lent it to me. Anyway, apparently they've cast Audrey Hepburn in the lead, so I've got to get out there and meet the producers as soon as possible.'

'Why?'

'Because,' he was so naïve, 'I'm perfect for the role!' Rita Mae stood up now and began dancing around Johnny, soaking him even more thoroughly. 'They'll know as soon as they meet me that they've made a mistake and cast the wrong girl. It'll be like one of those flash of a light bulb moments. Completely. I'm perfect for Holly Golightly, just perfect. The film'll never work without me.' She paused, leaning down until her face was a few inches from Johnny's. 'It's like if they were to make a film of *Welcome to Berlin* with anyone but me in the role of Sally Bowles.' She laughed wildly. 'I was born to play those parts!'

Rita Mae ran on to the sand now and began doing the Charleston, hands whirly-gigging through the air, feet moving in a blur. After a few minutes she was out of breath, collapsing on the sand, laughing. Lying down beside her, Johnny decided it was best just to humour the girl.

'So, where's the first place you're gonna go in Hollywood? What are you gonna do?'

'Well, after meeting with the *Breakfast at Tiffany's* producer,' she paused, 'hmm, I'll probably go to Musso and

Frank's for some brunch.' She turned to him. 'I will have got up early that morning, you see, way before breakfast, to apply my mascara and those inch-long false eyelashes you can get through the mail. Anyway, I'll be sitting in Musso and Frank's, eating my huevos rancheros—'

'Extra spicy?'

'That's right, extra spicy, and then I'll order a gin and tonic and sit back in my booth to enjoy it.'

'Are you on your own in the booth?'

'Yep,' she nodded, 'that's right, I'm on my own, all mysterious, and I'm wearing the most astounding green pillbox hat pinned full of peacock feathers. There are people who say that peacock feathers are unlucky, but in this case,' Rita Mae laughed, 'that proves completely untrue.'

'Why? What happens? Does some producer spot you and offer you a lead?'

Rita Mae turned on to her front, elbows bent, fists balled up and held close to her cheeks. 'Better than that, much better. I'm sitting there, minding my own, thinking about philosophy and wrong turns and the price of stockings, expensive, expensive, when this man walks over from the other side of the restaurant.'

'A man, huh?'

'Yep, that's right. I put my sunglasses on, naturally, because I'm just so bored—'

'So bored.'

'Right, bored of people bothering me. Every time I walk through Hollywood I have people approaching me, asking which agency I'm with, which films they've seen me in, whether I'm free for a dinner date at Trader Vics, three courses and cocktails, to which I always say, "I don't need your dinners, darling. I can buy my own."'

'Naturally.'

'But, as the guy comes nearer, he gradually seems familiar.'

'He does?'

'And once he's right up against the table, reaching for my hand and kissing it, I realize that it's none other than—'

'Who?'

Rita Mae sprang to her feet now, and began twirling on the spot. 'It's Paul Newman,' she shouted. 'Paul Newman! He's looking absolutely gorgeous as usual, those blue eyes unbelievably dazzling, despite the low lighting, and as he comes up from kissing my hand, I say, "Oh, Paul, what brought you over here?" And he says, "Your beauty!" and I say, "Really?" and he says—'

'What?'

Rita Mae stopped abruptly, staggering a little and laughing. 'He says, "Marry me and I'll make you the most famous girl in the world!"'

She sat on the ground again, panting.

'But isn't Paul Newman married to Joanne Woodward? I read something in one of your magazines about it. They got married last year.'

Wrinkling her nose, Rita Mae batted at the question. 'Flash in the pan,' she said. 'There's always divorce.'

'And, anyway, isn't he a little old for you? You should be going for someone younger.'

'Like who?'

'Tab Hunter?'

'Tab Hunter! Is he younger than Paul Newman?'

'I don't know. He looks really young. I thought all the girls liked him.'

'Maybe all the *other* girls.' Rita Mae lay on her back, legs bent, and stared up at the sun. 'The thing is, Johnny, I could never be attracted to an actor who wasn't really talented: bona fide, gilt-edged wonderful. It would be impossible for me. It would be ridiculous. You saw *Cat on a Hot Tin Roof* when it showed in the rec hall, didn't you?'

'Sure.' He was slightly affronted. 'We snuck in together, remember? We crouched at the back.'

'That's right, and Paul Newman was so wonderful, wasn't he? He's like the perfect combination of James Dean and Marlon Brando. Gorgeous, gorgeous. So talented.'

'Well, if you're looking for talent,' said Johnny, 'then that throws the field wide open.'

'It does? Surprise me.'

'Well, it's obvious really, who you should be with.'

'It is?'

'Yep. Think about it. The guy I have in mind is talented, sensitive, he won an Oscar a few years back.' Johnny struggled to suppress a smile at the thought of the roughshod, buck-toothed, porcine features of the man in question.

'He did?' Rita Mae's eyes widened, trying to think.

'He sure did.'

'So, come on. Who is he?'

Johnny jumped to his feet, ready to start running. 'You'd be a perfect couple, no doubt about it.'

'Who is it?'

'You'd have babies and dogs and a mansion in the hills.'

'Tell me!'

'Ernest Borgnine!'

They were both up then, Johnny pounding down the beach, Rita Mae in pursuit, not a chance of catching him. Realizing this, Johnny doubled back, tackling her on a particularly powdery stretch of sand. As she eventually stopped screaming, heartbeat ebbing from its ultimate high, Rita Mae was suddenly reminded of one of her favourite scenes: Burt Lancaster and Deborah Kerr frolicking in the waves in *From Here to Eternity*. She certainly didn't want to reprise the scene, wasn't quite that bewitched, but, still, in that second she couldn't entirely help herself either. Leaning forward, eyes closed, she pecked Johnny softly on the cheek.

Chapter Thirty-one

Crouched in the cell-house cleaning cupboard, wedged beneath the worktop, the dirty slop buckets closing in around him, crowding and jostling, Larry Jones breathed heavily and wiped his hands along his thighs. Pulling them back and forth, he was surprised by the slip of his palms against the canvas. It felt so odd. Incongruous. In the last few minutes he had been shoring himself up with the mantra 'It'll work, it'll work', but wiping his brow he was aware that the general wetness of his skin undermined this statement, slapping against it like a breaking wave, tamping it down, flattening it. He felt sicker than he had all day, Larry realized, cocking his head. This somehow seemed impossible.

To think in definite statements now, he supposed, to think, especially, in the affirmative, was just a wishful sleight of hand, a confidence trick that could never quite convince. The task ahead was just too risky, had too much potential for pitfalls and paralysis. The only things he could cling to were more tenuous: hope, of course, and an essential righteousness. If what he was about to do really possessed all the justice he had assigned it, thought Larry, then the cosmos should smile on them, and he and Chuck should have a tangible chance. If they were successful, he nodded, it would prove their rectitude.

Eyes closing, breaths regulating, Larry saw himself in his Beverly Hills backyard, his fifteenth summer, lying in the tall grass that hemmed the land, just out of sight of the house. Beside him was Virgil, laid out, naked save the baggy white shorts that swathed his hips. Larry had been staring at his friend a while, losing himself to the rhythm of those ribs, with their calm rise and fall, pushing up through the boy's skin before bidding their retreat. He was wondering, as he stared, what judgment might pertain to touching Virgil, when there it was, an opening in the sky, a cloud parting slightly and a rogue shaft diving through, planing determinedly to the earth. Larry watched as that beam sought its subject, alighting, finally, on Virgil's chest.

He recalled his friend's face as he'd awoken then – blinking, disorientated, lips parting subtly as that cloud, before he broke into a smile of such slow-burning goodness that it seemed to promise everything: happiness, solitude, companionship, peace. It was a smile so simple and accepting, thought Larry, that the sense of it could never be misconstrued. There could be nothing remotely sordid about it at all.

It was in that fleet moment, he realized now, that he had been truly happy, all the doubts of his childhood ebbing away, the fear of derision, of not fitting in. There was no one but them in the world, Larry had thought, and with that came the certainty, the easy knowledge, that this was right, and he was sure. That feeling had arrived and then, just as suddenly, it had disappeared. He had had it, he had felt it, and, ever since, there had been nothing. Just the ache of its absence. A dull cavity.

Head falling to his knees, Larry was jolted, right on cue, by a shriek, the carnival ripple of cups against bars, followed by self-conscious laughter, screaming. The bribery had worked. Vomiting into one of the buckets, Larry's mind went blank. He heard Agnelli's voice then, rising above the din, gleeful and carping, 'Cannibal, cannibal. Flesh, flesh.' Stumbling out from beneath the worktop, Larry stood slowly and tried to focus on his counting. Stay calm. Stay calm. It would take no more than thirty seconds for the duty officers to rush from their posts, snake around A-Block, and arrive at this outbreak. He must maximize the timing. He must choose the best moment.

Lying in bed, tucked in tight, Rita Mae dug a finger violently into her navel and shuddered. Was she doing the right thing? she thought. Could there ever be a simple *right thing*? There had been a time, only days ago, when she had been sure of her decision, when it had seemed as definite as daybreak, say, or extinction, but now . . . She didn't know. All that biblical, Old Testament surety had gone, snatched right away. And in its place: just sickness.

The pull of the sheets reminded Rita Mae of her father's arms, the circle of those gangly limbs, roping her in with their promise of complete and happy exile. She had sensed, way back, even as young as two, that he couldn't protect her from Clara, but still she had accepted the haven of those arms. No one could be everything, thought Rita Mae. No one could save you. The best they could do was to be around. And that, if all were lucky, was enough.

Rita Mae wanted to do it then, wanted to help him, but she couldn't bring herself to move, even to look at the clock, sure as she was that that vital twisting moment had passed. Weeping drily, she felt subhuman, as if her body had been siphoned of fluids, veins emptied out, nothing left to pump or twitch or react. Perhaps it would be all right, she thought.

Perhaps he would get away. And, if not, then at least it might be painless. Pistol quick.

Sitting on the cold hard floor of his cell, bed stuffed with blankets, Chuck Fletcher watched as Larry Jones approached, the officer's legs pounding forth in a blur. They were really going to do this, thought Fletcher, and, looking up at Larry, face looming between the bars, he saw something in the man's expression, a mixture of love and hope and memory, that almost touched him. In that glancing second – everything suspended – Fletcher felt himself tempted, for the first time in years, by a human emotion, some mélange of friendship, gratitude, a twinge of concern, sparring its way towards him, teasing him and daring him to accept. Here it came, and then, gone. Oh well, thought Fletcher, as Larry worked the key. That was that.

The fire escape was only three cells along, and, as they ran across, Larry broke into a grin. He had spent the past month in a state of nervous tension, Chuck's name revolving round and round in his head, not letting up for a second, always that question of whether he was planning the right course, of whether his bond with Chuck justified this act. Now, though, as he spun the combination lock and they pitched straight up the stairs, all those testing uncertainties seemed suddenly allayed. There was something about the scale of this, thought Larry, the intensity that had brought him here, which prevailed over logic or rationale, and held its own essential credence. For him, a basically cowardly man, to be risking his life for a fellow human being, suggested that, whether Larry could fathom it or not, there *must* be a bond between him and Chuck, something that went deeper and was more vital than the sum of those cell-house encounters. That was what this meant, thought Larry, ecstatic. It must be. The answer to all his questions was Chuck Fletcher, a sign as much as a person, a man who held a truth that, Larry felt sure, would refract right through him, make this life, so hopeless up until now, entirely worthwhile.

Arriving at the roof exit, panting loudly, Larry raised the hatch, pulled himself through and extended a hand to his companion. Crouching as low as possible, he ran to the west end of the cell house, feeling for the rope he had secreted a week before. He pulled it out delightedly. Showing it to Chuck, he saw the other man smile and couldn't help but grasp his hand. 'Yes,' he said: a second perfect moment of clarity. Jumping lightly on the spot, he breathed the word again.

Standing in the guard tower, poker-backed as usual, Edwin O'Hare was unsure at first, but, yes, there it was – a movement on the cell-house roof. Jerking forward, squinting, he wondered if it could be birds, a small flock gathered up there, circling in a strange vertical formation. It seemed unlikely, of course, but on Las Focas assumptions were generally unwise. The place, its environment, its flowers and fauna, all had a flavour of their own, a Technicolor quality that suggested anything might happen, and that, given every precedent, it was most likely to be bad. Reaching for his binoculars, O'Hare realized his mistake – they weren't birds at all – and, lowering these, he replaced them with his gun. Training it on the moving figures, he waited patiently.

It happened then, the world slowing down, two unreasonably expert shots, ringing and winging their way through the night, hitting those men in the chest, Larry first, then Chuck, the blood fanning lacily from their wounds, as pretty as uncorked champagne. They toppled forward, one by one, Edwin O'Hare dropping the gun to his side, watching with interest, wondering whether they were dead as they fell or if it was the ground that had finished them. And, finally, there they lay, on the grass verge of the cellblock, just a few yards apart, bodies broken and pulped. The consistency of peach flesh.

Hearing the shots, Rita Mae hunkered, resolving not to look from the window. She couldn't see. Didn't want to see. So that was it, she thought, her father was gone. Shivering into the weft of her sheets, she started to cry, the sound echoing from sobs to weeping and back again. She was boiling, Rita Mae realized, as though a bomb had exploded in her stomach, mushrooming out, hot waves undulating into every crevice, the tips of her fingers, the tips of her toes, each nerve stormed in turn and deftly obliterated. It had all gone, she thought, it had all died inside her. Somehow she had managed to kill her surroundings and absorb all the debris.

She would feel like this for ever, thought Rita Mae, the guilt and sadness: all this would not leave her. In years to come she imagined herself, still cloistered in this bed, the sheets having mouldered and stiffened, softened occasionally by the flooding tears, but otherwise intractable, holding her here in this moment of grief, like a fully grown moth, dead in the chrysalis.

She felt sure there was no recovery, it was so definite, so crushing, but then, as she crept into the third subsequent hour, the fourth, Rita Mae found, to her surprise, that the tears were subsiding. With the sun starting to rise, Las Focas bathed once again in its strange, unholy yellow light, the world seemed to flip around and she found that her feelings were reversing too, everything emerging new and replaced. It was shocking, thought Rita Mae, but she actually felt much better than before, cleansed, as though every ounce of her was a transfusion, a wild new injection of blood.

All that fever, then, was superseded by happiness. Stretching and shaking herself down violently, Rita Mae padded to her parents' bedroom, sat naked at her mother's dressing-table and tried to place this sensation. She had felt like this a few times before, she realized, and it was a euphoria that usually came with music, a song heard suddenly that chimed right within her (perhaps she had always loved it, or had never even noticed it before), sounding not in her ears but her gut, playing her more surely than she could ever have played it, forcing her, compelling her, to dance.

There was something about being the last one standing, thought Rita Mae, something that made her special. She was chosen. Picking through the dusty cosmetic jars, she thought about this, about the coming thrill of success, her chance to reap the rewards that her parents had missed. What if – thought Rita Mae excitedly – what if a person's happiness and achievements stood in direct inverse proportion to their family's failure, to the misery of all those around them? What if that was how the universe meted out justice – rewarding an unlucky bloodline with a freak burst of triumph, a surfeit of brilliance for one unusual individual? If that were the case then she would be guaranteed the most startling life imaginable!

She was alone now, thought Rita Mae, and there was a gift in that, a freedom. She could become whomever she wanted. Reaching for the bone-handled tweezers, she held them cautiously to her face, steadying her right hand and plucking deftly at her eyebrows until they veered up starkly, like articles of French punctuation. On reaching the mainland she would need to be perfect, thought Rita Mae, brushing assiduously at her bob. She couldn't rely on her orphan glamour to get ahead, but would need a genuine, self-possessed beauty. Grooming would be essential.

Surveying the dressing-table, Rita Mae carefully chose the cosmetics that she would take to Granmaria's, bouncing back to her bedroom and zipping them into her suitcase pocket. She was going to get there, she thought, would finally reach Orange County, that place she had imagined daily through the past few years, a paradise of fertile citrus groves. She would go to live with Granmaria, wherever it was that that woman had got to, and they would thrive together, planning their strategy and then preparing Rita Mae for stardom.

Glancing at the clock, she noticed, with surprise, that it was already 10.30 a.m. Rita Mae would have expected the island welfare officer to have arrived by now, to tell her of her father's death and start arranging travel plans, her passage to the mainland. She knew that he liked to leave the news until morning – Bessie Smyth's father had died on night duty recently and she and her ma had been told over breakfast – but he didn't usually wait this long. Crossing into the living room and over to the record player, Rita Mae slipped a 78" from its sleeve and positioned the needle in its outermost groove.

An hour later, when the welfare officer finally arrived, he would find Rita Mae clad in her prettiest dress and a pair of pink socks, shuffling rhythmically across the carpet. With 'Don't Be Cruel' whirring on the stereo, he would ask, with a flustered frown, why she was dancing. Throwing back her head with carefully construed abandon (part Raquel Welch, she hoped, part Elizabeth Taylor) Rita Mae chuckled loudly. 'I have to dance,' she purred. 'It's my fourteenth birthday.'

Acknowledgements

Thanks to my editor, Kate Lyall Grant, for all her excellent advice and patience.

Thanks to my agent, Darley Anderson, and his brilliant staff, especially Lucie Whitehouse and Julia Churchill.

Thanks to Tessa Cochrane for being at the end of the telephone line.

Thanks to Oliver Ridley and Laura Paterson for the constant entertainment.

Thanks to Jethro Armstrong for promising to read it.

Thanks to Debs and Sam Edden for keeping the drinks cold through the summer.

Thanks to Mark Atkins for the flowers and support.

Thanks to Louise Byrne and Gareth Bushell for Australia.

And finally, thanks to Alex Brewer, for everything.

POCKET
BOOKS

Also by Kira Cochrane

The Naked Season

Growing up isn't easy when your mother is a figurehead for
feminism and the most famous lesbian in the world. All her
life, Molly Flynn has been intrigued and exasperated by
her mother Augusta's increasingly bizarre claims about
who she is and where she came from.

Now, as Molly sets off down America's west coast to confront
her estranged husband and serve him divorce papers, she
looks back on her strange and unconventional childhood
with a mixture of nostalgia, irritation and a wry
sense of humour.

But Molly will be waylaid on her journey from Seattle to
California, and sidetracked – with dramatic, hilarious and
very unexpected results.

ISBN 0 7434-9248 X

PRICE £6.99

POCKET
BOOKS

Good in Bed
Jennifer Weiner

Cannie Shapiro never wanted to be famous. The smart,
sharp, plus-sized reporter was perfectly happy writing
about other people's lives for her local newspaper. And
for the past twenty-eight years, things have been tripping
along nicely for Cannie. Sure, her mother has come
charging out of the closet, and her father has long since
dropped out of her world. But she loves her job, her
friends, her dog and her life. She loves her apartment
and her commodious, quilt-lined bed. She has
made a tenuous peace with her body and she
even felt okay about ending her relationship
with her boyfriend Bruce. But now this . . .

'Loving a larger woman is an act of courage in our world,'
Bruce has written in a national woman's magazine.
And Cannie – who never knew that Bruce saw her
as a larger woman, or thought that loving her
was an act of courage – is plunged into misery,
and the most amazing year of her life.

'Wildly funny and surprisingly tender'
COSMOPOLITAN

PRICE £6.99
ISBN 0 7434 1528 0

POCKET
BOOKS

In Her Shoes
Jennifer Weiner

Rose Feller is thirty; a successful lawyer with high
hopes of a relationship with Jim, Mr Not-Quite-Right,
a senior partner in her firm. The last thing she needs is
her messed-up, only occasionally employed sister Maggie
moving in: drinking, smoking, stealing her money – and
her shoes – and spoiling her chance of romance. If only
Maggie would grow up and settle down with
a nice guy and a steady job.

Maggie is drop dead gorgeous and irresistible to
men. She's going to make it big as a TV presenter,
or a singer . . . or an actress. All she needs is a lucky
break. What she doesn't need is her uptight sister
Rose interfering in her life. If only Rose would
lighten-up, have some fun – and learn how
to use a pair of tweezers.

Rose and Maggie think they have nothing in
common but a childhood tragedy, shared DNA and
the same size feet, but they are about to find out that
they're more alike than they'd ever believe.

'A seriously smart and classy read' HEAT

PRICE £6.99
ISBN 0 7434 1566 3

POCKET
BOOKS

These book and other Pocket Book titles are available from your book shop or can be ordered direct from the publisher.

0 7434 9248 x	**The Naked Season**	**Kira Cochrane**	£6.99
0 7434 1528 0	**Good in Bed**	**Jennifer Weiner**	£6.99
0 7434 1566 3	**In Her Shoes**	**Jennifer Weiner**	£6.99

Please send cheque or postal order for the value of the book, free postage and packing within the UK; OVERSEAS including Republic of Ireland £2 per book.

OR: Please debit this amount from my VISA/ACCESS/MASTERCARD:

CARD NO: . . . .

EXPIRY DATE: . . . .

AMOUNT: £ . . . .

NAME: . . . .

ADDRESS: . . . .

. . . .

SIGNATURE: . . . .

Send orders to SIMON & SCHUSTER CASH SALES
PO Box 29, Douglas Isle of Man, IM99 1BQ
Tel: 01624 677237, Fax: 01624 670923
Email: bookshop@enterprise.net
www.bookpost.co.uk
Please allow 14 days for delivery. Prices and availability subject to change without notice

Read a preview of Kira Cochrane's novel
The Naked Season,
available in Pocket paperback
June 2005

1

Me and the Showgirl

'She was a showgirl, your real mother, all sequins and blue eyes. A fading beauty' – my mother pauses – 'fading fast. She had slightly hunched shoulders, a stooped back and she seemed somehow – I don't know – collapsible. She had the look of someone who's waiting for the wrecking ball, just staring at the clock, about to be demolished, like one of those tower blocks you see on TV. Wired up, detonated and crashing to the ground – boom.' She claps her hands together happily and smiles. 'Crashing to the ground and then bouncing in her own dust, almost imperceptibly, like a shrug.'

My mother takes a long drag of her cigarette, licks her finger and smooths it across my right eyebrow. She stretches out on the bed.

'That's better. Anyway, your mother was unhappy. Depressed. Not unhappy like you or I might be, Molly. Not unhappy like the other day.'

I look at her, confused.

She continues, 'The other day when I sent you to school with that ice-skating sprain—'

'Fracture,' I say.

'OK, that ice-skating sprain that turned out to be a fracture – but properly unhappy. Reno, Nevada unhappy. It's not like being an unhappy kid here, you know, Molly. Not unhappy like a Sunday in London when you can still see a film or go to the library. There's no place quite like Reno if you want to be depressed. I think it's the dust.'

My mother runs a hand through her hair and lights another cigarette. Her voice is dry and nicotine-brittle. I've been asleep for a couple of hours and my eyes adjust slowly to the light from the hall. I yawn pointedly. She ignores me.

'It was the summer of seventy-five when I found you, and me and Ellie had been on the road for almost a year, driving across America on a lecture tour. We had packed up our place in Oakland the August before, the apartment we had lived in while I taught at Berkeley. It was a great little place,' she sighs, exhaling a dragon-puff of smoke. 'White-slatted on the outside and a bit dilapidated, but not too near the industrial part of town. There was a good community, tinderbox politics – it was exciting. We had two bedrooms, one we used as my study, and a shared garden where all the residents grew tomatoes and industrial-strength pot brought down from Humboldt.' She smiles. 'Such great pot. There was an iron fire escape that ran down the back of the house and sometimes Ellie and I would perch on the steps after dinner smoking or sharing some wine and the neighbours would come out and join us.'

My mother sits up, stretching over to rearrange the Minnie Mouse doll that's sitting on my pillow. She crosses her legs, head tilted. 'We had a huge party just before we left,' she says, 'huge. We'd got the whole place stored away that day, all my books boxed up ready for shipping to London. I'd tied an old offcut of curtain around my head like a pirate while we packed' – she leers at me and laughs, doing her best to look piratical – 'and before the party Ellie and I had gone to bed, hoping to rest for an hour or two.

'Anyway, having drunk a couple of bottles of wine in between

4   kira cochrane

the stacking and lifting, we fell asleep, curled up together, the humidity creating a kind of' – she waves her hands vaguely – 'metallic fug in the room. Hours later we woke up, legs flailing in the air, to find one of my women's studies students, Jen, tickling our feet with a peacock feather. We had given her the key to the apartment – she was going to live there until the lease expired – and she had let herself and a bunch of friends in. I'll never forget it. Me and Ellie huddled together, laughing hysterically, kicking each other as we pulled our feet away, surrounded by Berkeley students. Grateful Dead T-shirts and denim everywhere.' She pauses. 'There was a lot of hair in that room.'

She takes a long slug from a glass of water that's sitting beside my bed, rocks her head back and gargles. 'Mmmm. Anyway, the party was great. Memorable. There was a wooden table out back which was laden with barbecue food – kebabs, salad, burgers – and Jen and I had sex beneath it, great sex, while the other guests helped themselves to sweet pepper couscous.'

My mother smiles and strokes my head. 'The next morning Ellie and I set off along Highway Eighty, straight to Salt Lake City and right on through the Midwest, with packed halls at every stop. All these students nodding lazily in the theatres, as if they were at a rock concert, as I spoke about motherhood and paternalism and sex roles. We went through Cleveland to New York, past Philadelphia and the Carolinas, sloping around through Texas. There were seductions all along the way of course, a string of affairs – the physics professor who fucked me in a turban' – my mother grins – 'she kept quoting de Beauvoir in bed. There was the dean's wife at a private college in New York, all mahogany skin and blonde hair.' She sucks contemplatively on her cigarette. 'I should have snaffled her for good. There was the eighteen-year-old literature student, away from home for the first time, who said I was old – old! – at thirty, and that she couldn't believe she had gone to bed with someone famous. She made me autograph her pillow.

'And always, at the back of the hall, Ellie, knitting the longest scarf in the world, the striped one that's on the top shelf of your wardrobe. It's faded now. She was drifting along as usual, playing the guitar and writing poetry on envelopes and drawing. Stars, she kept drawing, and tiny portraits of me in profile. They drove me mad, littering up the car. She'd bought *Blood on the Tracks*, that album about Bob Dylan's divorce, and I swear she played it a zillion times. It was like water torture. God. It was like that time in the bath when you wouldn't stop singing "Yellow Submarine" and I had to gag you with your flannel.' She laughs. 'Bob Dylan's whine coupled with the fact that the songs were all about relationships ending, nothing upbeat. There was this vocal tic on one of the songs that just drove me mad' – she bangs her foot against the bed – 'a stress on the final word of each line, a complete over-emphasis, and after a while I began to believe that he was doing it just to torment me, Augusta Flynn. I started having delusions, nightmares, that Bob Dylan was torturing me. Rock and roll schizophrenia. Anyway, it wasn't music for the road and it only stopped when I snapped the tape in half and slung it out the window in a potato field.'

My mother's stomach gives an alcoholic gurgle and she pauses to swallow.

'So,' she nudges me, 'when the tour ended, we stopped in New Mexico for a while, in Taos, and rented a house for the winter and spring whilst I wrote a thesis on Georgia O'Keeffe. *From stamen to semen*, it was called I think,' she laughs, 'very subtle. Come May, when the heat really kicked back in, we decided to carry on through to San Francisco, see a few friends and head home. Back to London after nine years.'

6   kira cochrane

She pushes a strand of hair off my face, hooking my fringe behind my ears. She kisses me gently on the forehead.

'Hey there, beautiful, you still listening?' I nod sleepily. 'Good. So as we were getting close to Reno we decided to make a stop. We had been talking about seeing some showgirls for a while and we figured that it would be cheaper than Vegas, more accessible. We decided that we'd find a gambling den, hunker down for the night and watch some high-kicking women.' She sighs softly. 'It would be just like the Folies Bergère.

'We were just outside Reno when we found a revue in a tiny shack by the roadside. You could see the Sierra Nevada, all snow-peaked in the distance, but apart from that the place was completely barren. Just dust bolls and dry grass. Desert. A metal sign was propped against a wall – "God Bless America" – and there were some disused petrol pumps out the front too, still showing nineteen-sixties prices. The old man on the door was cleaning his fingernails with a penknife and there was blood just pouring from his hands. It reminded me of the first meeting between Picasso and Dora Maar,' says my mother, 'when she skewered her hand to the table with a kitchen knife.

'Anyway,' she continues, 'the blackboard beside the entrance said "Nude girls tonight, eight pm" and so we decided that we might as well stop. We paid the old man a dollar each and then went right in.'

My mother shifts on the bed, pulling the covers away from my chin. She turns her face to me. 'The place was like something out of a Western inside – silent, with sawdust on the floor and men playing cards. It could probably have been in *The Dukes of Hazzard*' – she prods me – 'that dumb TV show you like, it could probably have been in that. Anyway, it was really dark, foggy with smoke, and the women were at the back of the room, performing behind chicken wire to stop the men molesting them.' She takes a drag on her cigarette. 'All the men there were disgusting, just pigs, with this wet, fatty quality about them, like the residue left in a frying pan. They were just meat really, those men, flesh and gristle. Me and Ellie were getting drunk and laughing behind our beers as they watched the girls dance, digging their hands into their crotches. It was horrible really, their erections so obvious, but we found it funny after a few drinks. You could tell that the girls were bored, because their kicks were always a little behind the music, lethargic, and their heads rolled back, like this—' My mother's head lolls onto her shoulder, just the whites of her eyes visible beneath the lids.

She goes to stub out her cigarette and spills ash over my blankets.

'Mum,' I say, whining, and brush it onto the floor.

'Shhhh,' she says, putting a finger to her lips. 'I'm telling you a story, Molly,' and she lies across the bed and winks at me.

'So there was this one girl in the revue, this one girl who both me and Ellie liked. She wasn't the most beautiful – her skin was lined, leathery, even though she couldn't have been more than about twenty – but she had a dusky quality, a darkness.' My mother pauses, thinking. 'Like the cadences in a blues song, the clusters of minor chords. She was wearing an incredible outfit – the Southern Cross picked out in sequins on a tiny leotard – and her hair, which was blonde, was piled right up on her head, all ready to topple over.' She smiles. 'She reminded me of Dolly Parton.

'Anyway, I caught her eye and nodded at her, holding up my beer. And when she smiled back it all fell away. The sleaziness, sawdust, the men and their hard-ons, Ellie. It was just me and her.' She starts singing throatily, 'You're just too good to be true,' before coughing. 'Her smile was full of light and happiness and,' my mother sighs, 'and sex, I guess. But not the seedy kind.

No. Carefree sex. Timeless.' She pauses and rolls onto her back. 'I'll always remember it.'

She's crushing my legs and I push at her from under the covers until she props herself up on her right elbow.

'So after the show me and Ellie went out to the back of the bar and found the girl sitting there, head bowed, on a step beside the bins. There was a chicken, scrawny and almost featherless, pecking at a rubbish bag, the contents spilling out around it. Broken beer bottles, Oreo wrappers, an old, used porn mag. "I was waiting for you," she said, and she took both our hands and started marching us across the wasteland. It was really late by then and once we were away from the bar, far from the lights, it was pitch-black and unknown in the way that only the early morning hours are.

'We slowed down after a while and started talking, and when she found out that we were British the girl was ecstatic. She kept cupping her face and squealing, "It's perfect!" before grabbing our hands again and hugging them to her stomach. Ellie and I were laughing obliviously, giggling all the way back to her home, which turned out to be a trailer propped on a few pieces of wood. The wheels had been stolen years ago. Inside, the place was decorated with cross-stitched homilies and when I asked her about them she pointed at one that said "Love thy neighbour" and screwed up her nose. "My mom made them but I ignore that one. My neighbour is a fat fuck called Wayne who tried to pimp me when I first came to town." Then she lowered her voice and whispered, "He also has crabs, which is not a sign of godliness."'

I find this interesting, since I don't know anyone who keeps crabs as pets and I can't see why God would mind. I'd spent the whole of the last summer holidays catching crabs on Frinton beach – sometimes as many as fourteen a day – letting them swim around in a water-filled bucket and then freeing them out into the sea. I almost ask my mother about this, but I'm tired and want her to finish.

'So we were looking around her trailer which, let's face it, didn't take very long, when she went to an open drawer in the corner and brought out what looked like a rolled-up towel. Holding it to her breast she edged towards us, looking sort of worried and excited. "This is Molly," she said, "my daughter," and we saw that nestled in the towel was a tiny child, days old, with tendrils of hair splaying out like a halo and huge limpid eyes. They were like fish eyes,' she says, laughing, 'wide and goggly. The girl sat on the edge of the bed and held the baby on her lap and Ellie and I just glanced at each other, nervous. We were concerned about the situation but we were also drunk and we ended up sitting on either side of the girl, taking turns holding the baby, stroking her hair and making her smile by pulling faces.' My mother lunges at me, gurning, her fingers holding her eyes up at the corners, her mouth open, tongue out. I can't help laughing.

She smiles widely, her eyebrows rising, and strokes my hair. 'There you go. And so we all ended up going to sleep that night, fully dressed, the four of us on the double bed, with you between me and the showgirl. It should have been one of those nights when you hardly sleep and find yourself dreaming a lot, conscious here and there. But it wasn't. We were all completely comfortable. And in the morning, when we were still groggy, the girl asked me to take you to London. "I've heard about England," she said. "I've heard that you still wear sackcloth and that you don't have electricity, but that you're good to each other, real civilised. The other day I was reading about your royal family too, and they seem great."' She pauses. 'And so me and Ellie brought you home.'

My mother stretches out again and after a few seconds I

realise that she's asleep. I kick her, gently at first, and then violently, she comes to and I get out of bed and pull her, stumbling, into the next room. I start to undress her and, unable to reach the shirt buttons, I sit her down on the bed.

'Molly,' she mumbles, 'are you glad I adopted you? You are, aren't you?'

I smile. 'Yes, Mum.' I undo her bra, take it off and put her pyjama T-shirt on. In big black letters on the front it says, 'Choose life, lose Thatcher.'

'Ellie'll take you to school tomorrow, Moll, OK? She should be back from work at about eight in the morning, so she can walk you. Don't wake me up or anything, because I haven't got lectures until the afternoon.' I lift her legs and pull the duvet across before kissing her on the cheek. 'I love you, Molly Flynn,' she calls after me, 'even if you're not my girl.'

I reach up and turn off the landing light then climb into bed, tucking my blankets in on either side. As I'm drifting off to sleep I wonder whether I am really adopted. It seems unlikely since everyone says how much I look like my mother – same olive skin, strong jaw, dark eyes – but maybe it's true. Maybe my mother's not really my mother at all. For years now she's been telling me these stories. That I'm the daughter of Mormon missionaries, students at Brigham Young University, who were posted to Africa, had a love affair and concealed my birth. That I'd been born to a Vietnamese woman, the product of a forced relationship with an American soldier. That I was the bastard child of a Protestant woman and a Catholic man in Northern Ireland, both of them later kneecapped.

She's made even more outrageous claims about my provenance – that I'm the child of Elvis and Jane Fonda, of the Pope. There was the story about me being the daughter of Fidel Castro, a love child, who'd been born in Cuba and smuggled out in a fishing boat, only for my mother to find me abandoned on a beach in Key West. When I was very young she'd told me that I'd been found in a seashell and that as I grew up I would notice scales on my arms and would start finding it hard to breathe. My toes and fingers would grow webbed and my legs would meld together. Eventually I'd be unable to survive outside water and I would discover the secret of my birth – that I'd been the product of a mermaid mating with a human. Lost in the ocean, I would find my way back to Neptune.

My real parents are revolutionaries and saints, rock stars and visionaries. 'You were never mine,' my mother always says after a few drinks. 'I know I'll never keep you,' and after this she tends to pass out.